BEOWULF'S
CHILDREN

BEOWULF'S
CHILDREN

LARRY NIVEN,
JERRY POURNELLE &
STEVEN BARNES

TOR®

A TOM DOHERTY ASSOCIATES BOOK
NEW YORK

BEOWULF'S CHILDREN

Copyright © 1995 by Larry Niven, Jerry Pournelle, and Steven Barnes

This book is printed on acid-free paper.

A Tor Book
Published by Tom Doherty Associates, Inc.
175 Fifth Avenue
New York, N.Y. 10010

Tor Books on the World-Wide Web:
http://www.tor.com

Tor® is a registered trademark of Tom Doherty Associates, Inc.

Design by Basha Durand

For information regarding reproductions of works by Michael Whelan, please contact Grass Onion Graphics, P.O. Box 88, Brookfield, CT 06804.

Library of Congress Cataloging-in-Publication Data

Niven, Larry.
     Beowulf's children / Larry Niven, Jerry Pournelle, Steven Barnes.
          p.   cm.
     "A Tom Doherty Associates book."
     ISBN 0-312-85522-2
     I. Pournelle, Jerry.   II. Barnes, Steven.   III. Title.
   PS3564.I9B46   1995
813'.54—dc20   95-23537
                                                                   CIP

First edition: November 1995

Printed in the United States of America

0 9 8 7 6 5 4 3 2 1

For Marilyn, Roberta, and Toni

*

The authors gratefully acknowledge the invaluable assistance of Dr. Jack Cohen of the University of Warwick in the creation of the biology and ecology of Avalon.

✳

And there was war in heaven: Michael and his angels fought
    against the dragon; and the dragon fought and his angels,
And prevailed not; neither was their place found any more in
    heaven.
And the great dragon was cast out . . .

✳

DRAMATIS PERSONAE

EARTH BORN

CADMANN WEYLAND: Onetime Colonel of UN Forces; Avalon Security Chief.
MARY ANN (EISENHOWER) WEYLAND: Botanist and Chief Wife of Cadmann Weyland.
SYLVIA (FAULKNER) WEYLAND: Biologist, Cadmann's Second Wife.

ZACK MOSKOWITZ: Governor of the Avalon Colony.
RACHAEL MOSKOWITZ: Colony Psychologist and Zack's only wife.

CARLOS MARTINEZ: Remittance man. Historian, sculptor, and a hero of the Grendel Wars.

JOE SIKES: Engineer: Onetime lover to Mary Ann Eisenhower, and a hero of the Grendel Wars.

HENDRIK SILLS: Pilot. Hero of the Grendel Wars.

CHAKA MUBUTU ("BIG CHAKA"): Biologist.

CAROLYN MCANDREWS: Onetime Administrator and Agronomist. Heroine of the Grendel Wars.

JULIA CHANG HORTHA: Agronomist, nurse, and Minister of the Unitarian-Universalist Fellowship.

STAR BORN

MICKEY WEYLAND: Mine Engineer and Forester; oldest son of Cadmann and Mary Ann Weyland.
LINDA WEYLAND-SIKES: Daughter of Cadmann and Mary Ann Weyland, mother of Cadzie Weyland. Lives with and is engaged to Joe Sikes.
RUTH MOSKOWITZ: Daughter of Zack and Rachael Moskowitz.

Grendel Scouts

JESSICA WEYLAND: First child of Cadmann and Mary Ann Weyland.
JUSTIN FAULKNER: Only surviving child of Sylvia Faulkner and her first husband. Adopted by Cadmann Weyland.

COLEEN McANDREWS: Older daughter of Carolyn McAndrews.
KATYA MARTINEZ: Acknowledged child of Carlos Martinez.
EVAN CASTENADA: Skeeter pilot.
EDGAR SIKES: Computer specialist; son of Joe Sikes and Sikes's first wife.

Bottle Babies

AARON TRAGON: Unofficial leader of the Star Born.
STU ELLINGTON: Mathematician, skeeter pilot.
CHAKA MUBUTU ("LITTLE CHAKA"): Biologist; adopted son of Big Chaka.
TRISH CHANCE: Bodybuilder.
DERIK CRISP: Hunter, Grendel Scout Supervisor.
TOSHIRO TANAKA: Sensei to the Star Born; karate and yoga instructor.

Grendel Biters

CAREY LOU DAVIDSON
HEATHER McKENNIE
SHARON McANDREWS

OTHERS

CASSANDRA: An artificial intelligence.
OLD GRENDEL
LONG MAMA: Not precisely an eel.
TARZAN, ZWEIBACK, and others: Chamels.
COLD ONE: A snow grendel.
THE QUEEN: A lake grendel.
ASIA: A Scribe.

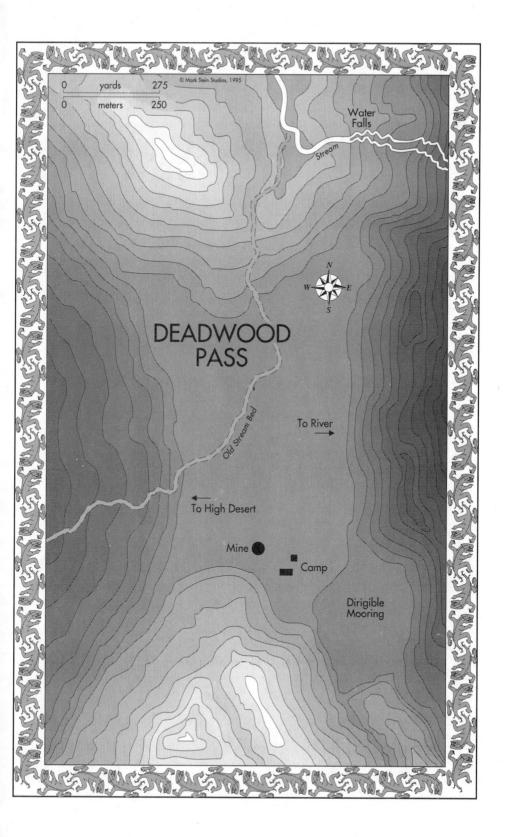

© Mark Stein Studios, 1995

Water
Falls

Stream

DEADWOOD
PASS

N
W E
S

To River

Old Stream Bed

To High Desert

Mine

Camp

Dirigible
Mooring

0   yards   275
0   meters   250

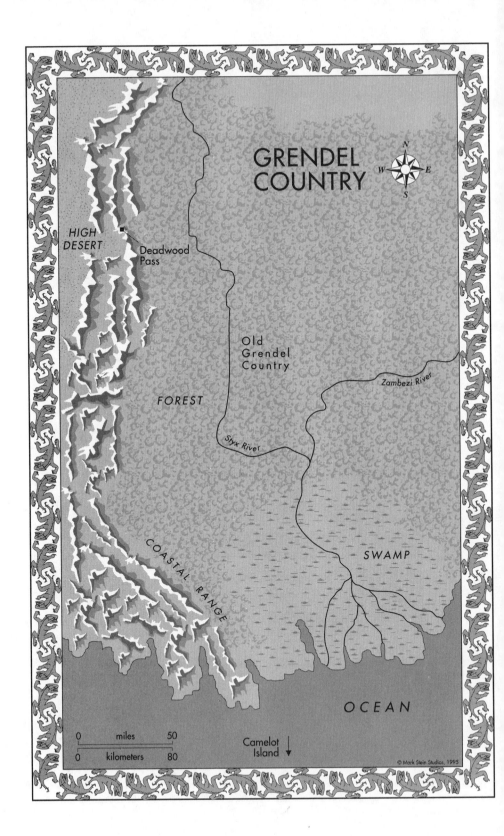

GRENDEL
COUNTRY

HIGH
DESERT
Deadwood
Pass

Old
Grendel
Country

Zambezi River

FOREST

Styx River

COASTAL RANGE

SWAMP

OCEAN

0   miles   50
0   kilometers   80

Camelot
Island

© Mark Stein Studios, 1995

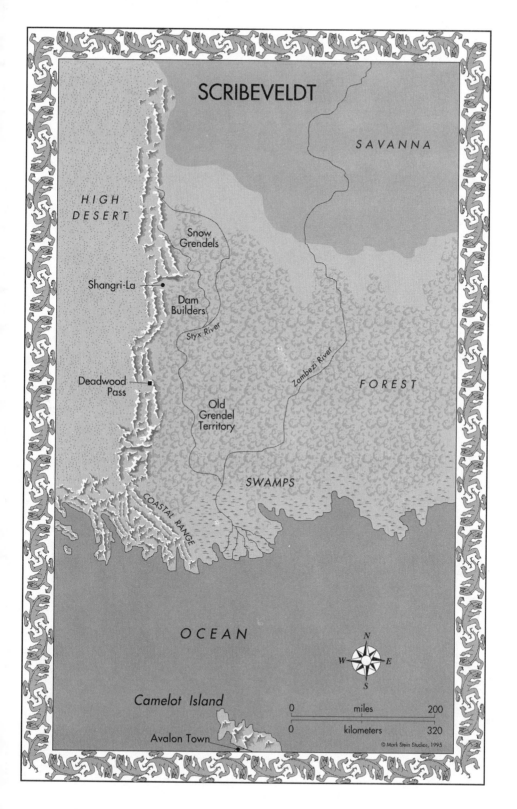

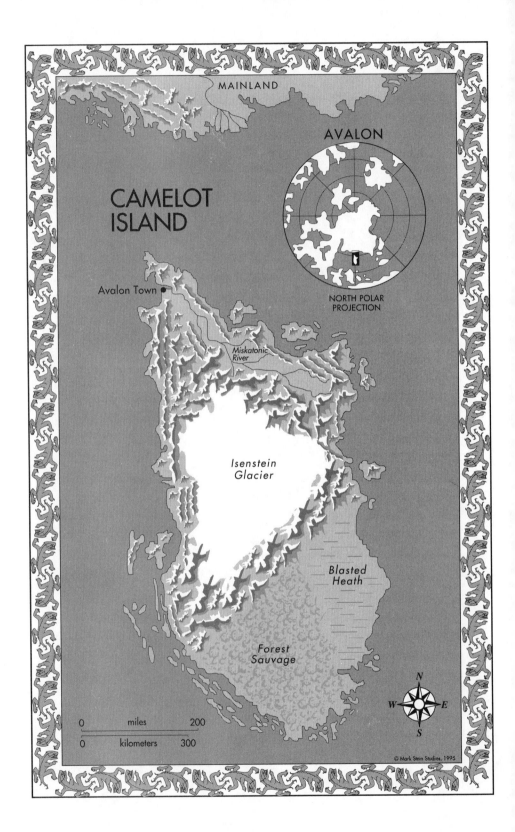

MAINLAND

AVALON

CAMELOT
ISLAND

NORTH POLAR
PROJECTION

Avalon Town

Miskatonic
River

Isenstein
Glacier

Blasted
Heath

Forest
Sauvage

0   miles   200
0   kilometers   300

N
W   E
S

© Mark Stein Studios, 1995

PROLOGUE
CAMPFIRE

"Once upon a long, long time ago, our parents and grandparents left a place called Earth. They traveled across the stars in a ship called *Geographic* to find paradise. But their paradise turned into a living hell . . ."

The campfire jetted white flame as it reached a gum pocket in the horsemane log. The flame held for almost a minute, then died back to glowing coals. A cast-iron skillet balanced on firestones sizzled in the embers. A sudden gust momentarily sent sparks toward the misty night sky and the stars frozen overhead.

A dozen wide-eyed youngsters were packed shoulder-tight on makeshift seats of logs and stones, huddled expectantly in the dying firelight. They had waited all their lives for this night.

Justin Faulkner's voice growled, caressed, leapt, burned hotter than the ebbing flames. "From the stars they came," he stage-whispered. "Seeking to build homes where no human had ever walked. Avalon was a land untamed, stretching beneath a sky strange to human eyes. A paradise for the taking. These men and women were the best, the smartest and the bravest Earth could offer, two hundred chosen from eight billion people. Our parents. They are the Earth Born. But they didn't know the truth about their new world, a truth that *you*—" His long sensitive fingers, sculptor's fingers, bunched and stabbed as if each and every child were guilty of unspeakable crimes. "—you Star Born, have never been told . . . until now. Until this week. Until tonight."

Justin's voice carried the authority and infinite wisdom of all his nineteen years. None of the children was older than thirteen. Now they were youngsters, Grendel Biters. Tonight would be their first step toward becoming Grendel Scouts. At dawn they had left the human settlement called Camelot and hiked across the plain, along the Miskatonic River, then up Mucking Great Mountain along the minor tributary called the Amazon. Lunch and dinner were little more than stream water.

Their curious and eager shining eyes were black and brown and blue and jade, carrying genetic gifts from every people of Earth. Their limber young bodies were as perfect as the night stars, their minds filled with dreams more incandescent still. These were the exhausted young inheritors of a world new to Man.

". . . the rivers were filled with a fish they called samlon. And they caught the fish, and ate the fish . . ." Justin slipped a knife from his belt sheath. He poked its point about in the smoking pan, skewing a morsel of sizzling meat. He held it up, worrying the ragged, black-burnt chunk of flesh with his teeth. Then he passed both pan and knife to his right, to a ten-year-old girl with blond, shoulder-length hair.

She bit gingerly at first, then harder to tear a piece loose. The texture resembled tough beef, not at all like fish. She chewed—and the meat bit back. She clawed at her throat, gasping, but managed to pass both pan and knife to her right. A boy dark-skinned as the surrounding night made a choking sound, and whispered "Water. . . ."

Their eyes misted. Some struggled with wretched coughs, but no one moved. The pan circled the campfire until there was nothing left but smoking iron.

"But one night the river which gave life to the colony, brought death. Even now, even here, high up on Mucking Great, if the wind is very quiet, on a night like tonight, you can hear old Misk calling. . . ."

Justin trailed off. With superbly theatrical timing, the wind dwindled to a murmur. There in the distance roared the mighty Miskatonic, rushing past the foot of Mucking Great . . . or was that only the Amazon?

"The samlon developed legs, and teeth, and a taste for human blood. They became . . . grendels. They clawed their way from the river, gasped air, and found it good. They moved so fast that other animals looked like statues to them. They slaughtered everything they saw. Our parents fought back, but it was no use. The camp was lost. Cadmann Weyland led the survivors here to his stronghold on Mucking Great, where they made their last stand.

"And there—" Justin's thin finger cast an unsteady shadow toward the irregular chunk of stone called Snailhead Rock. "That was where my father died, torn to pieces by the ravening horde. And there on the verandah is where Phyllis McAndrews was killed, still screaming reports to the orbiting crew of *Geographic*. And there . . ." Justin was lost in the story now, beginning to hyperventilate. ". . . others were caught, torn apart and devoured by frenzied grendels moving faster than eyes can see. Down there by the cliff edge—" The dark hid it. "—two men waited in a wrecked skeeter while grendels battered the walls in with their heads. And *there* was where Joe Sikes sent a river of fire flowing down, finally killing the grendels, saving every human life—"

Pause. The wind had picked up. When it lulled there remained no sound save the rushing waters.

"That was a long, long time ago. But sometimes on a night like tonight, if you press your ear to the ground, you can still hear the screams of the dying, as teeth tear their flesh open and devour their vitals. And you can thank the spirits of the dead that there is no longer anything to fear.

"No more monsters, no more grendels . . ." Justin paused for effect. "But if there are spirits of men, who can say that there are not spirits of monsters as well?"

His audience's young eyes were wide, and still. Their chests hardly moved as they struggled to keep control. The dogs were tethered well away from the campsite, and now, sensing the children's fear, they began to growl and strain at their leashes.

"Some say that the spirits of the dead war nightly, up here on Mucking Great Mountain. Our dead parents and grandparents pit rifle and spear and knife against fang and claw and *speed*, night after bloody night. They don't want to—but they must. Because if they lose, just once . . . just once . . ."

He narrowed his eyes fiercely. "The grendels will claw through the portal that separates life from death, and return to ravage Avalon again. And not just Avalon. They'll go across the stars as we crossed between stars, back to Earth. . . ."

A light dew of sweat dampened his forehead. His voice dropped to a hoarse whisper. "What was that? Was that a scream? It sounded almost like a scream, a human scream. The scream of a soul already dead, but dying yet again. A soul now cast into some deeper, more terrible pit. And is that another? And another . . . ?"

The boys and girls strove to still their breathing and quiet their heartbeats, attempting to capture every word.

"But if the ghosts of the humans are dying once again then—"

There was a terrible shriek, and from beyond the ring of firelight lurched a woman soaked in blood. She staggered, one hand held piteously to her cheek. One eye was clotted with gore and the other was insanely wide, as if witness to all the terrors of hell.

After her, in a blur, came something inhuman.

Ten feet of hissing reptile bounded into the firelight: splay-clawed, barb-tailed, eyes dead to gentleness or love, merciless as glass.

It smashed her to the ground, perched atop her and *howled*—!

The children scrambled in all directions, screaming, crying—

Then silence, save for the crackle of the fire. The girl's bloody body lay still upon the ground, grendel perched above, triumphant—

And then she sat up, sputtering with mirth. "Justin Faulkner, you are an utter bastard!"

"It's the company I keep, Jessie." He grinned like a shark. "All right, round 'em up!"

The "grendel" sat up, and a stocky, muscular Japanese boy of about seventeen Earth years climbed out of its hollow belly. His face was darkened with charcoal, and he laughed so hard he could barely breathe. Jessica slapped him on the back. "You should make some little tiny buildings, some miniature artillery, and do a giant monster movie, Toshiro."

"Godzilla versus a four-hundred-foot grendel?" He shrugged out of the grendel skin. "You know, if we hadn't had to rebuild Tokyo every six months, Japan would have ruled all of Earth."

From all around them, just beyond the reach of the firelight, larger human figures returned, shepherding their younger siblings back to the firelight.

"Come on back!" they roared. "Sissies!"

Shy, embarrassed, the stragglers returned by ones and twos. They protested loudly but hid grins behind small heads, and wrung crocodile tears from laughing eyes.

Tentatively, then with growing enthusiasm, they examined the hollow grendel carcass, its thick forelegs and wide jaws, its stubby spiked tail. They ran their small fingers along its scales, each imagining that it was *his* father, *her* grandmother who slew the dragon.

Justin took his place at the center by the fire, and this time spoke in a normal voice. "All right, it was a joke. Not a pointless one. We want you scared. Grendels are dangerous. The Earth Born killed all the grendels here on this island. As children you've been safe here all your lives. Now it's time to learn about your world, *all* of it, not just this island. We are the Star Born. This world is ours.

"You've seen a dead grendel. Now you're growing up, and pretty soon you'll go to the mainland and see live grendels. And more. It's time to learn what happened to those two hundred, Earth's best and brightest, each of those Earth Born chosen from among more people than there are stars in these skies.

"Up to now you've lived by Earth Born rules. Now it's time for you to learn why they make rules, and why we live by them.

"Time to go to the mainland, time to learn why the Earth Born act so strange, and—it's time to learn what eats grendels. Now, off to sleep."

The children reluctantly headed toward sleeping bags and bedrolls. A few of the candidates tried to ask questions, but the Grendel Scouts wouldn't answer. "Bedtime. You'll learn, but not tonight."

"Why not tonight?"

"You'll learn it all. Now scoot!"

"Can Rascal sleep in my bed tonight?"

"Sure, your dog can sleep with you."

The children tumbled off to bed, pleasantly tired, utterly ready for sleep.

Jessica winced as Justin wiped the slaughterhouse blood from her face. "Yerch. Tomato juice would have been just as good."

"Such a thought offends my creative soul."

"I did like the wasabi in the beef heart, Toshiro. Nice little touch. You didn't do that last year."

"Musashi said to 'pay attention even to little things.'" Toshiro stretched until his back crackled, and poked his bare feet close to the embers.

"I thought it went well," Jessica said. "Just the right balance. Justin, you brought Sharon McAndrews. She's not twelve yet."

"She's bright, she's curious, and she's been asking questions about her mother," Justin said. "We have to tell her."

"Zack isn't going to like it."

"Freeze 'im."

"We have agreed to the rules," Toshiro said. "We don't interfere until the Grendel Biters are twelve—"

"Wouldn't work," Justin said. "Either we tell Sharon now, or in a year she'll tease the whole damn story out of Cassandra, and then she'll tell the rest of the Grendel Biters. No preparation, just *bang!*, they know. This isn't the last time this is going to come up, either. Sharon won't be the only one to ask the right questions." He grinned. "And what's Zack going to do to me?"

"The Earth Born aren't always wrong," Toshiro said. His forefinger traced the scar on Jessica's neck. It was years old, almost faded, and most of it was hidden under her hair; but it trailed down her neck to her left shoulder. She snatched his hand, and kept it.

"I'd be more interested in what Dad thinks," Jessica said. "How does Coleen feel about this?"

"She thinks she can't go on fooling her little sister much longer," Justin said. "And I agree. You know their mother."

Toshiro nodded gravely. "Oh, well. Here, I brought some real food."

They moved closer to the fire to roast chunks of turkey breast over the dying coals, and they sat talking of and laughing over small or important things: the season's fish yield; skiing on the southern peaks; a review of the previous week's hysterical debate between Aaron Tragon and Hendrick Sills. (Postulated: Adam Smith's *The Wealth of Nations* was actually a misinterpreted satirical essay.) Modifications in the huge dirigible, *Robor*. The odds on next month's surf-off. The conversation went on for hours, until the laughter finally died down, and yawning took its place.

They were the Star Born. Their electronic servants could bring them all of Mankind's knowledge: history, science, drama, the great literature of a dozen cultures, and a hundred soap operas; but they lived in a primitive paradise, utterly safe, inoculated against every disease. There was more than enough to eat, meaningful work to do, and few dangers. They were a strong, clean-limbed clan. Their parents had been chosen after tests that made the old astronaut selection procedures look like child's play. Physically perfect and bright-eyed, they radiated the kind of relaxed familiarity that only those raised in an insular community can ever really know.

There were a few minutes of intense quiet, during which eyes met across the ember light, and nods preceded gentle touches of offer and acceptance. Two at a time they linked arms and drifted off into the shadows.

And then at last there were only four left: Jessica, Justin, Toshiro, and a young redhead named Gloria.

"Success?" Jessica yawned, a question that was not a question.

"Success," Justin agreed. Another round of chuckles.

"Now it's time for the chicken run," Jessica said.

Toshiro yawned. "Ruth still wants to try it."

Justin and Jessica locked gazes, and both laughed simultaneously. "Ruth?" Justin said incredulously. Then both said at the same time, in the same little-girl singsong: *"But what will Daddy say?"*

They broke up again, the laughter subsiding to hiccups. "'Pon my word," Justin said finally. "Zack *ruined* that child."

"She's asked to become a Grendel Scout," Gloria said. "And asking why we won't let her in."

The others shook their heads in unison. "No mainland for Camelot's eldest virgin," Jessica agreed. "Not until she breaks the leash."

Justin stirred lazily. "You have to admit she's a hell of a chamel trainer, though."

She nodded. "Chamels are fun. Justin, the Earth Born used to explore! I remember when they brought the first chamels back from the mainland."

"And lost Josef Smeds to a grendel catching them," Toshiro said carefully.

"Yes, but—" Her eyes were locked on the northern horizon. "I won't say it was worth that, but you can't explore without risks. And every trip teaches us more. Teaches me more about myself."

"I just wish . . ."

"I know," she said quietly. Jessica intertwined fingers with Toshiro, and gave his hand a squeeze. She affected a huge yawn. "I think . . . that it's time to turn in."

They rose, and retreated from the firelight. From out in the darkness there came a gasp, followed by a prolonged and girlish giggle.

Justin watched her go, and then, belatedly, became aware of the weight of a feminine head on his shoulder. "Behind us," Gloria said. "*Geographic*, just rising."

He turned; Gloria turned with him. *Geographic* was a silver line with a dot at one end. No details showed, but it looked huge, just above the line of the ocean.

Twenty-four years ago . . . God. "Ten times the mass, back when it went into orbit. Interstellar brakes! I wish we had photos. Can you imagine how *bright* that drive flame must have been?"

"No humans to see it from down here. Maybe it blinded a few grendels." Gloria was almost behind him, her hands toying with his hair. "Is that really your wish?"

To see it myself! "I wish . . . that tonight was Fantasy Night," he lied.

"It's any night you want," she whispered. She reached up, turned his face with her fingertips, and kissed him blisteringly.

His hands found the warm, soft places on her body, and they sank down together by the firelight. There was no fumbling; latches and straps unbuckled as if by magic.

If anyone saw them there, no one commented. There were no gawkers as their bodies, gilded by the light of embers and twin moons, entwined for almost an hour before release finally calmed them both.

They cuddled for a time, whispering, then, suddenly freezing, scrambled for a thermal sleeping bag.

Then there was silence, save for the distant sound of water, and the call of some far-off night creature. No one heard. The fire consumed its last morsels of fuel, and began to fade. No one saw.

The only eyes that remained open were grendel eyes. Open, staring, glass eyes.

Dead eyes.

Eyes that saw everything, and felt nothing at all.

✳

TWENTY-FOUR YEARS BEFORE....

It should have been dead of night. Her body knew that, even though the whole world glared silver-blue in the light overhead. The grendel had tried looking near it, and had been blind for most of a day. Blind with the agony in her head, eyes that saw only at the edges; blind long enough to die, but the lake monster hadn't killed her.

Since then she had not looked up, though she would wonder about that spear of fire in the sky for the rest of her life.

For a long, long time there had been nothing but the hideous pain in her head. Now the agony in her head was receding. Now she could remember that she was hungry. Feeble with hunger. How could she feed herself if she was too feeble to fight?

And how was it that she had never had such a notion until now? She had never fought the lake monster, but hunger would never have stopped her. Only fear.

At the southern end of a vast lake, where the water emptied out into a sluggish muddy river, there the grendel had lived as a swimmer. There she had first drawn breath, and killed a sibling for food. She began to remember, now, how hungry she had always been. She and her sibs had fought for room to swim and room to run, for space to hold their own swimmers, and had eaten what they killed, until only three or four remained. She remembered the sister who had challenged the monster of the lake, and died almost before the grendel could turn to see.

The lake monster lurked along the west side of the lake, where pebbly mud-flat gave way to horsemane trees. Farther south the forest was different, a tangled mass of vines and hives and trees that grew like puzzles and snares. The lake monster lurked sometimes in the horsemanes, but never in the tangle forest. And south of the tangle forest was where the grendel and her sisters lived, and a myriad of their spawn.

Her sisters died, and there were only the grendel and her own spawn. And still it was not enough. She'd grown too large. Eating her own spawn felt wrong, repulsive, and that wasn't the worst of it. She and they didn't have the room. If they tried to spread out, the lake monster took them. No room to feed, not enough moss and insects for the spawn, meant that they never grew large enough to feed their mother. She had to move.

Here the muddy river flowed into the lake. By the silver-blue light of a thing in the sky that fit no pattern at all, she looked south. The patterns linking in her mind now showed her how strange it was that she had ever come here alive. She hadn't had the sight, then. Wherever she looked, then, was only fear, no patterns at all.

She'd seen how fast the lake monster was in the water.

And on land . . . but not the southwest shore. Something so peculiar had happened there that the images remained even now. . . .

It had only been a little time since the change, for her and for the sister she must drive away. Her sister, beaten, had retreated to land. She had crossed that patch of pebbly mud and into the tangled forest beyond. No web of plants could stop the juggernaut that was a grendel. Her sister might find new turf.

The grendel watched her from the southern shore. Food was scarce, and there was the lake monster too.

Her sister was in the tangled trees, and into some kind of dust or mist. She screamed once, and burst out of the trees in a spray of wood and vines. Even the lake monster had never moved that fast. The grendel watched her streak down the pebbly mudflat at the head of a dust-cloud comet.

The lake monster lifted her terrible head—and let her pass.

She was nearly out of sight when she tumbled to a stop. She seemed little more than a heap of bones. The grendel had never dared go for a closer look.

And beyond that place was the lake monster's favorite lurk.

No, the west shore was impossible even to the senseless being that the grendel had once been. The route around the east shore was twice as far, twice the distance in which the lake monster could find her. . . .

She must have had just a trace of pattern-making ability, even then.

She had waited for a hard rain, then gone wide around the east shore. Prey was fast and wary. On *speed* it could be caught. When the rain stopped she must enter the lake to shed the heat, and out of the water before the lake monster could come—

And so she had lived until she reached the river inlet.

The river was what she sought. She had arrived starving, but bottom feeders had fed her for many days. Then came a sickness in her guts, that moved into her head and inflated. For days she had known nothing but the pain in her head.

And now she felt cold and weird, and her bones were stretching her skin taut, and her mind was making patterns.

Way down there in silver-blue light: her own patch of water and land, with too little food for herself or her spawn. Probably the lake monster had already cleaned them out. Only one thing had been desirable about that place. There she could taste the lake monster in the water, and gain some sense of where she was.

Closer: the lake to her left, and on her right the pebbly mud, and the tangled wood where her sister had turned to fog at a *speed*-enhanced run.

Closer yet: more pebbly mud and horsemanes behind, and one huge old horsemane very near the water. The lake monster spent most of her time in the water offshore, but when the woods were wet they could shield her too. Grendel spawn could turn to grendels anywhere in the lake, and their surprise could be brief and intense when the lake monster burst from the trees.

Here: she could see muddy river and know the food beneath. The river would bring bottom feeders. She could eat now . . . and the lake monster would taste her anywhere in the lake, and know she was here. If she had seen patterns then, she would not have come here.

But she saw another pattern now.

The grendel bore her hunger. She watched the woods and the water. Of prey she saw no sign, and no sign of the lake monster. The silver spear of light failed to rise, but the strangeness of her world did not go away.

And so a day passed, and a night.

At midmorning of the following day, the grendel began to walk toward one great horsemane isolated on the mud.

No sign of the lake monster.

At a moment that was nothing but guesswork, the grendel began to run.

This was the first puzzle she had ever solved, and she had no faith in it at all. She ran, but she was not on *speed*. When a wave moved where no wave should be, terror and vindication surged and *then* she was on *speed*. She was skating on slick mud, her legs a blur, homing on the one isolated tree in a plume of mud and gravel.

The lake monster came out of the water, screamed challenge, and was on *speed*.

The grendel veered right and dug in. She'd pass the tree on the right. If the lake monster came straight at her, hit her broadside, she would be torn, smashed, dead. She could see, *feel* her own death in the pattern! But a notch more speed changed that, pulled her ahead, and now the lake monster would hit the *tree*.

The lake monster saw it. Veered left. She'd strike the grendel after she passed the tree.

Hah! The grendel veered left. She missed the tree by a toenail's width, just behind the lake monster's spiked tail. The lake monster was turning in a spew of gravel and dust, but falling behind for all that.

It slowed her for only a moment. She had been eating while sickness melted the flesh from her daughter.

There was dust blowing out of the tangle forest as the grendel swept past them, burning inside, her enemy far too close behind her. But the lake monster swept through the dust, and the dust followed her like a comet tail.

Enough! The grendel veered out over the water. She could run on water if she ran fast enough, but the *speed* was broiling her from inside. She looked back once, and saw what she had hoped for. She ducked, and smashed into the water, and sank, cooling.

She lifted her snorkel. Then, cautiously, her eyes.

The lake monster was a comet of dust running straight at her across the water.

If the lake monster dived now she'd be free of the fog and the heat within, but the grendel would have her. The lake monster didn't dive. Probably she never thought of it. When she stopped, she was invisible in a restless dark cloud.

The cloud drifted away. Red bones sank through water. The grendel gnawed at them, and was still hungry. Hungry and triumphant. Now she would hunt the shoreline where the lake monster no longer ruled.

PART I

ICE ON THEIR MINDS

Youth holds no society with grief.
—EURIPIDES

1

THE RETURN

The optimist proclaims that we live in the best of all possible worlds; and the pessimist fears this is true.

—JAMES BRANCH CABELL, *The Silver Stallion*

"What in the hell is *that?*"

Jessica Weyland heard the words without recognizing the voice. It originated just outside the stone walls of the Hold's guest bathroom, where she was scrubbing her cheeks with ice-cold water piped from the Amazon Creek.

The bath was part of the Hold's guest suite, attached to a guest bedroom that had been hers before she built her own place at Surf's Up. Toshiro Tanaka, her previous evening's entertainment, still sprawled unconscious across the bed. Sleep-cycle incompatibility prevented them from having anything but an occasional fling. Too bad. Like many a musician, he had *such* good hands. . . .

"Frozen bat turds! Will you *look* at it?"

Jessica ran toward the living room before thinking about what she'd heard. Her long, deeply tanned and muscular legs ate the distance between bedrooms and living room in their nine long strides. Her mind flew faster than her feet. *Kids paying us back for last night? Gotcha?* No. They'd be pretending horror, not astonished curiosity. *No, this is something else.*

Jessica was tall and blue-eyed, as Nordic as a glacier, with shoulder-length blond hair, high cheekbones, and a large, cool mouth. She moved like the athletic animal she was. The muscles in her calves bounced with every long stride. She was unself-consciously naked: there had been no time to grab a towel.

Her father, Cadmann Weyland, *Colonel* Cadmann Weyland, had built the Hold as a fortress against monsters even before he understood the grendel threat. The others called him paranoid and worse, even accusing him of faking a threat as part of a power grab, even a military takeover of the colony. He left them then, and built his home on a high ledge, digging into the side of Mucking Great Mountain. Most of it was underground: cool in Avalon's winters, and warm in her summers. Light slanted in through the Hold's louvered ceiling. The living room was Paradise.

A green-tiled channel grooved the middle of the living room. The glacial Amazon ran through that, right through the living room, a foot deep and four feet wide. It had once been deeper and narrower there, but Jessica didn't remember that. It was another of those facts she had been told, and which she believed in the same way that she believed there was a solar system with a yellower star and a planet named Earth.

A gently sloped tile shelf ran along part of the stream. The rest was fenced off by a hedge that grew along the edge of the running water. The hedge was composed of plants from both Camelot Island and the far reaches of Avalon, so that the room was as much aboretum and botanical garden as living space.

Fully half those weirdly shaped plants had thorns and spines. They weren't really cactus, but resembled cactus more than they did any other kind of Terran plant. Avalon plant life needed protection. Any defenseless life-form was instant grendel chow. Some plants had other protection: the violet-petaled beauties with acid resin, tiny deep blue fruiting bulbs with astonishingly active poison, carnivorous lilies that could turn a frog-sized creature to a husk in forty-eight hours. The garden grew more lethal over the years as the children of Cadmann Weyland's Hold grew more able to cope with them. The plants came from everywhere—Camelot Island's highlands, offshore islands, even the mainland, all brought here to line the stream—and despite the garden's lethality it was beautiful.

From her earliest days Jessica thought the Hold was the most wonderful place in the world. At present Cadmann, Mary Ann, and Sylvia were in the southern thorn forests hunting specimens. The Hold and Cadmann's Bluff itself were Jessica's and Justin's for the next day and a half. A safe place despite the garden. A perfect place to begin the initiation of the Grendel Scouts. Later they would be taken to the mainland for their real coming-of-age. There were neither serpents nor scorpions in this paradise.

So who was doing all the yelling?

She was opening the front door when she saw it behind her. *Something* emerged from the downstream edge of the Amazon's emerald streambed. It wriggled under the lip of the living room's southern, downhill wall to come right into the Aboretum. Something alive. Something thick-bodied and powerful. Its head reminded her a little of a horse's, only stubbier. It pushed its way farther in. The head melded into a broad, powerful neck that grew longer, and longer. . . .

A voice behind her said: "Hot damn! It's an eel!" Toshiro knelt by the side of the Amazon to watch as the beast worked its rubbery length against the current. It splashed cold water on Jessica's bare feet as it moved past. It ignored them completely. Eventually the entire creature emerged into the living room, fully sixteen feet long, and as thick as a horse's upper leg.

The front door slammed open, and two panting children ran in. One of them was a small dark girl, Sharon McAndrews. She brandished a sharpened stick. Her mouth and eyes were wide as she watched the eel wiggle sinuously toward the living room's upstream opening. The other, a fourteen-year-old redheaded, freckled lad named Carey Lou Davidson, gawked at Jessica's chest before reluctantly returning his attention to the eel.

"Stay back," Jessica said quickly. She turned to Toshiro. "Hey, keep an eye on that thing, and watch the kids. I'm throwing on some clothes."

"But what *is* it?" Carey Lou asked.

Toshiro laughed. "I think that Mrs. Eel is just trying to get upstream."

"Spawning grounds?" Jessica asked.

He nodded. "Remember Chaka's biology lecture last month? The ecology is returning to Camelot now that the grendels are gone. This will be part of it. Hot damn!"

He was hopping on one leg, pulling his pants on, risking intimate injury in his enthusiasm. Jessica was already halfway to the guest bedroom.

She struck the room like a blond whirlwind, sucking up shirt, pants, and thong sandals without a moment's pause. She was back in the living room before the eel disappeared uphill through the northern wall.

There was a change in the location of the general hooting outside. Jessica exited, pulling on her blouse, neglecting the buttons but knotting the corners together into a makeshift bra. She almost collided with Justin.

"What do you see?" Jessica was already running.

"It's heading right up the hill. Did Dad leave any of the holocam stuff?"

"Ice on my mind! I didn't check."

Justin took off up the hill. She swiftly overtook a mob of shrieking Grendel Biters. "Stay away from it!" she shouted.

"It won't hurt us," Sharon McAndrews said. "It can't, it's too slow."

"You never saw anything on *speed*," Jessica said.

"No legs," one of the children shouted.

"Yes, all right, but stay away from it anyway, we don't want to scare it." She'd seen the videos of samlon growing legs to become grendels, but that took hours, it couldn't happen in a minute. Still— "Stay away from it."

With an ear-numbing burr, Skeeter VI buzzed up over the edge of the bluff. Jessica turned and shaded her eyes to look into the windscreen. Evan Castaneda, clean-cut, classic Latin features, was at the helm of the silver-blue autogyro. Coleen McAndrews, fifteen but looking much older, sat in the passenger seat, holocam clipped to her right shoulder.

Jessica waved Evan down. The skeeter dipped and buzzed, as if intoxicated by flight.

She hopped onto the runner at the skeeter's side, twined the seat belt around her wrist, clipped a safety line to her belt, and gave a thumbs-up.

With gut-wrenching speed Skeeter VI rose two hundred feet above the house and hovered. From this perspective, Cadmann Weyland's ranch was a miracle of human effort. Rows of soybeans and corn and alfalfa checkered the bluff, and pens for pigs and goats and the small, furry Avalon native marsupials called "Joeys."

Beneath them, the Amazon sparkled in a silvered ribbon, just catching the morning sun. Alongside it raced a stream of children who laughed and urged one another to greater effort. Justin was well in the lead.

"Can you see it?" Evan yelled above the turbine whine.

The sunlight glinted off the stream. She thought she caught a slender shadow, but . . .

"Not yet."

"Try these." Coleen handed her a comm-link optical set: binoculars with cameras linked to the colony's central computer system. "Cassandra. I'm turning the war specs over to Jessica."

"Ready, Jessica," the computer responded.

She slipped on the war specs—they looked and felt like heavy sunglasses—and was rewarded by an enhanced version of Cassandra's camera-eye perspective. She adjusted it so the right lens was transparent, and the left gave her the comm-link image.

She squinted her right eye.

Yesss . . . there be the dragon. Shimmering in the fluorescent reds and blues of the thermal enhancement, the eel struggled its way upstream. "Cassandra, display best size data."

Length: 647 cm.

Estimated weight: 27 kg.

Cassandra gave them a glowing wiggling eel track.

Jessica whispered "Enlarge." The eel stopped, then wiggled forward and back. It expanded to fill her field of vision.

"Who sounded the alarm?"

"Little Chaka or his old man," Coleen said. "One of the Mubutus picked up the river alert. Nothing this big, not ever."

Not for the twenty years we've been here, and not for—She thought about the implications. When humans arrived, the island of Camelot had an incredibly simple ecology, samlon and green slime in the rivers, Joeys and pterodons in the high mountains, and a few thorny or poisonous plants scattered about the plains. Grendels had eaten everything else. But how long had it been that way? "You know what this means? The grendels didn't own this island for thousands of years. They couldn't, the eels wouldn't keep coming back—"

"Sure about that?"

"No, but it's something to think about. Don't lose it!"

"I'll give you another," Coleen said. "What triggered the return after all these years?"

"Now, that is one interesting question."

The tumbled granite majesty of Mucking Great Mountain rose up to greet them. The peaks were constantly swathed in fog. A few irritated pterodons swooped out of their nests to investigate Skeeter VI. Humans didn't hunt pterodons. Over the two decades that humanity had infested Avalon, the great leathery creatures had lost all fear, and now considered the skeeters worthy only of derision. The autogyros were fast but clumsy, barely capable of beating a pterodon on the straightaway, and zero competition at aerobatics.

The eel continued to labor upstream. It humped painfully through the shallows, fighting as urgently as any Earth salmon ever did.

Salmon.

Samlon.

Jessica repressed a shudder.

This thing was almost certainly a carnivore—but would confine its hunting to water. It might be as dangerous as a moray eel, fully capable of taking a baseball-sized lump out of an unwary buttock, but it shouldn't be able to do anything else. It couldn't come out of the water.

Still . . . "If it had *speed* it would have used it by now," Jessica dictated. "Cassandra, database search, match that image."

"No exact match. One similar life-form, two hundred ninety centimeters in length, observed in a stream on Black Ship Island." A map flashed momentarily in her vision: Black Ship Island was a smaller uninhabited island off the mainland coast.

"Evidence of *speed?*" she asked.

"None," Cassandra replied. "No visible speed sacs, no structures evolved for cooling. Probability low to nil."

"Thank you."

"You're welcome."

Every skeeter carried a fully armed shock rifle, one of the tools developed in case the grendels ever came back. They never had, but everyone was trained to use the weapons anyway. Shock rifles could deliver numerous designer loads: chiefly a capacitor dart to stun, and an engineered biotoxin which triggered overload of its "*speed*" sacs. *Speed* was the superoxygenated hemoglobin that allowed the grendels to accelerate to over 110 km/hr in about three seconds. The toxin drove a grendel completely beserk, drunken on her own "adrenaline." A speed-drunken grendel produced enough heat to cook itself in about seventy seconds.

Evan tapped his ear. "Roger."

"What's the word?" Coleen shouted.

"Kill it. Standing Municipal Order One-four-two. On file. Kill it first, decide whether it's harmful later."

"It's got no legs," Jessica said. "It can barely function on the land. Cassandra says it doesn't use *speed*. Let's wait."

"Got my orders," Evan said ruefully.

"Is Skeeter Six still set up for dolphin transport?"

"Sure—we flew Quanda and Hipshot up yesterday."

"Great. Somebody was playing with a Ouija board."

The eel struggled up and up, blindly urgent, making surprisingly good time. Justin had kept up with it, although many of the children had dropped back by now. She patched herself through to Justin's comm link.

"Jessie here. What does it look like to you?"

"Ugly thing. Ignoring us, though. What's the word?"

"Kill it."

"What do you think?"

"Let's take it alive."

"I like the way you think. Zack's got ice on his mind."

There was a crackle of static and another voice came on-line. It was Zack

Moskowitz, governor of Avalon. *"I find that tasteless, young man. You listen to me, both of you—your father has standing orders—"*

"Our father isn't here, Zack."

"I want you to kill that thing. We don't know—"

"That's right, we don't. I'll kill it when I'm ready."

"Dammit, Jessica!"

She thumped her headset. "Brzztfplt. Gee, Zack, you're breaking up! Over." And switched her comm link off as Evan was bringing the skeeter around for a landing next to a large pond.

The skeeter thumped down on rocks. Jessica snatched up the rifle, and hopped off.

The eel humped itself over a rock break, looked at her without seeing her, and wiggled into the center of the pond.

Coleen moved a little closer, her holocamera recording the entire event. Every time the eel moved, a staccato series of computer-enhanced afterimages flashed before Jessica's left eye. Cassandra's exobiology study program was having a field day.

"Get in closer, Coleen," she said.

The eel swished back and forth through the pond's crystal-clear water. Jessica clambered up a rock to get a better view.

Beside her, Coleen whispered, "Cassandra: M-D Coleen EELTALK," opening a personal file, and began to speak.

"Eel-like. Probably carnivore. Five meters long. Estimate top speed of twenty knots. This is no infant. Cross-hatching indicates healed scars. Minimum of a year old, probably more like ten years, possibly a lot more than that. This is a mature animal seeking a spawning ground."

Justin was the second up over the rocks. The children and others of the teens were behind him. It had been an uphill jog, and despite his superb physical condition he was blowing hard.

Coleen nodded acknowledgment, and kept talking. "We can bet that it didn't spawn here. We haven't seen anything like this. Probably genetic memory. Likes the taste of the water."

"That water's glacial. It won't have much taste," Justin said.

"This is great," Evan said. "The first. The first returning land animal— oceanic?"

"Aside from a couple of the bird-thingies," Coleen said, "you're right."

The eel began to move in diminishing circles, as if claiming the pond for its own. Then it was still. The children gathered around the edge. An expectant hush settled over them.

Jessica anticipated Justin's first request, and handed her comm card to him before the words left his mouth. He sighed with pleasure.

This was something new, something that would occupy conversation for weeks—no mean contribution to their lives. For this alone, she owed the eel a chance to live.

The First would have to allow more frequent visits to the mainland. Have to!

After all—the local ecology was returning. Evidence of it was everywhere. There were three times the flora to be categorized now. The wind carried puff-balls and tiny fairy-brollies and fertilized seeds, and the Earth-native crops of Avalon were experiencing their first real competition. Weeds were a universal fact of life.

Two dozen children ringed the pool. The eel was still, then rippled, then was still again. Justin adjusted his face gear, zooming in on the minor miracle.

Something was happening, but Jessica had to get down on her knees and elbows to see it. A jellied mass began to emerge from a gland two-thirds of the way back along the eel's dorsal surface. It squirted out like whipped cream, milky with reddish dots within.

Egg sac. Thousands upon thousands of little eels. Jessica's earphone was sizzling. Zack. *"Jessica? Why haven't you killed it yet?"*

"Sacrilege," she said distantly. "The miracle of childbirth. It's an ovary thing—you wouldn't understand."

"You don't know what the hell that creature is."

"Oh, and you do, right, Zack?"

The squirting seemed to have stopped. Once again, the pool was still.

Jessica selected a load for the shock rifle. "Thirty kilos, close enough," she said softly, and turned the dial on the capacitor dart. A green light blinked on the rifle dart; the batteries in the stock held sufficient charge. Reluctantly she thumbed the arming switch.

Justin's long face was peaceful. "Now?"

"Not yet. Let's see if it's supposed to die here."

He nodded. The eel was almost motionless, merely shuddering. The rippling became regular, as if it were straining at some mighty task. Its black wet muscularity swelled and released.

Then, about one-quarter up from the tail, a puff of black appeared.

"Semen?" Jessica whispered. "Bifertile hermaphroditic?"

"Why extrasomatic?" Evan asked.

"Think about it," Justin said quietly. "In the old days, this pool might have just *boiled* with eels. They release their egg sacs. Then they release their semen. The semen spreads through the pond, perhaps preferentially fertilizing other egg clusters. Instant exogenesis."

Coleen whistled. "Wrong. I think it's blood."

"Blood?"

The eel had begun to shed its tail. A chunk of meat was separated from the main mass of the body, and blood was more plentiful now.

"All that blood in the water," Justin said. "Best evidence I've seen that grendels weren't native to this island."

Coleen ran to the skeeter, unloaded a roll of absorbent rubber sheeting, and lugged it back to the pond. She took off her shoes and socks and rolled up her pants. "I'd bet minerals in the blood are a clue to Mommy's home territory, her mating ground."

"Mating ground?" Justin asked.

"I say she's *not* hermaphroditic. Mated before she came up here. Stored up the semen, dumped it here."

"Bet."

The tail had worked its way almost completely loose now, clouding the water with blood. Only a few scraps of tissue held the tail on. They watched as those fibers tore away.

The eel swam in a lazy circle, shedding its former torpor.

"Doesn't look moribund to me," Justin said.

It seemed to notice them for the first time. It dove, wiggling fiercely beneath the surface of the water, and left the pond.

"Time," Jessica whispered, and put a capacitor dart just behind its head. It spasmed once, and then again, and sank.

"Move it!" Justin was already clambering into the water. "We don't want this thing to drown!"

Coleen McAndrews was right after him. "It humped its way over rocks—we saw it out of the water for more than thirty seconds. I think we can make it." The tarp was around the eel in a moment. The children started to plunge in with them. Jessica waved them back. "Watch out for the egg sac!" she yelled. "Stay ashore."

They rolled it out of the pond. Its skin was surprisingly spongy, and oozed water. It was the work of a moment to attach the eel and its roll of protective sheeting to one of the dolphin slings beneath Skeeter VI. Jessica clambered aboard.

"We'll get another skeeter up here," she yelled above the growing whine of the turbines. "Get us an egg sample and meet me at Aquatics."

"There in ten minutes," Justin promised. She whooped and raised her hand, and he slapped it hard. Their eyes shone.

"Got one, dammit," Jessica said.

Ten seconds later Skeeter VI was up in the air, and plunging toward Camelot.

2

MOTHER EEL

How cheerfully he seems to grin
How neatly spreads his claws
And welcomes little fishes in
With gently smiling jaws!

—LEWIS CARROLL,
Alice in Wonderland

The skeeter soared. Evan's sure hands took it up so rapidly it seemed the world deflated beneath them. The acceleration was a little much for Jessica, but then, that was Evan. Damned if she'd let *him* know he'd upset her. She grabbed the horizontal hand bar set above the instrument panel, and hoped he wouldn't notice her white knuckles.

She patched through to Biomed, down at Avalon town. "Chaka. Got something for you. Get Hipshot and Quanda out of pen number three soonest."

"Is that the eel that everyone's talking about?"

"Betcha."

"I expected something like this. We're draining the salt water out of the tank, and flooding it with the Miskatonic."

"I want to have your child. Can we have full diagnostics in five minutes?"

"We aim to please."

The skeeter dove, nearing free fall as it plunged toward the camp. The arc of Camelot, twice its original size, spread out below them. All of its corrals and lodgings, shops and quilted fields screamed up at them at gut-wrenching speed.

And there, near the Biomed dome, were the three saltwater tanks. Luckily, there were no sick animals at the moment, but Dr. Mubutu had flown Quanda and Hipshot in from the Surf's Up lagoon, giving them some privacy in hopes that they might breed. Someone tall and black—it had to be Little Chaka—was below them at the pens, but she didn't really have time to think. Evan was whooping as he dove in, thoroughly enjoying her no doubt pasty-faced reaction to his aerobatics.

Just wait, Evan, she swore silently. *I'll get you for this.*

The saltwater tanks were raised five feet above the ground and sunk six feet beneath it. The pen was drained, and the Miskatonic was pumping in at the rate of three hundred liters a minute. Skeeter VI came to a hovering halt, its tail rotors foaming the water.

Little Chaka waited on the white-tiled lip of the tanks. Jessica untied the cargo line. The roll of foaming sheeting loosened, and twelve feet of eel splashed into the shallow water. She jumped down to stand beside Chaka and waved the skeeter away.

The eel lay at the bottom of the tank, barely covered as the water level slowly climbed. "I think it's just stunned," Little Chaka yelled. He knelt next to the pen to examine the dark eel. "Looks to be moving water through the gills. Let's add a little oxygen." He whispered to his comm card. There were more bubbles from the air inputs at the bottom of the tank. "That ought to take care of her."

Little Chaka Mubutu was almost six and a half feet tall, dark-skinned but with the narrow features more often found in whites. He looked quite unlike his adopted father, Dr. Mubutu—Big Chaka. Together they were the colony's premier biologists. Dr. Mubutu was still at home, at the marine research facility west of Surf's Up.

"Nothing else to do," he said. "We don't know enough to help."

"I hope she lives," Jessica said.

"So do I. She looks tough. Leave it to Mother Nature. I'm going in. Coming?"

"Let me get my kit." Skeeter VI buzzed down to a hexagonal concrete landing pad next to Biomed. Jessica grabbed her belt pouch as it shut down. The still turning rotors fluttered her hair in all directions, but she didn't notice. She hurried into the building.

Little Chaka had the holos up and running by the time she entered Aquatics. The station's west wall disappeared as the cameras and tank sensors displayed data from the churning, foaming tank. Chaka sat in an oversized swivel chair, the keyboard on his lap. He waved toward a more normal sized chair. "What do we have here?" Chaka asked.

"You should know better than me."

"File name?"

"Mother Eel."

"Cassandra?" Chaka said softly. "Let's see what we know about Mother Eel."

"Integrating files. Done. Records now available," the computer's cool, familiar voice answered. Chaka's version of Cassandra's neutral voice had been given a lyrical New Guinea lilt.

The holo divided into two images. One remained with the eel, and the other replayed the skeeter's-eye view of its heroic spawning odyssey.

"What do we have . . . ?" Chaka whispered. He watched the tail drop off, and chuckled.

"What happened there?" Jessica asked.

"The Amazon is glacier water, poor in minerals. Mama Eel is making sure her babies have food."

"Cannibals?"

"No, this is a salmon trick, Jessica. The salmon of Earth swam upstream and died. Mama here only leaves her tail, but it's the same trick. Tail will rot. Parasites in the tail will multiply drastically as tissue decomposes. Insects come to dine. Water boils with insects and worms and such. Hatchlings have their dinner, won't they, Mama?"

Outside, the clouded sky cleared for a moment, and Tau Ceti glared through the Aquatics building's domed ceiling, dimming the holos. The ceiling polarized, and the holos brightened.

Slowly, the eel began to twitch again.

"Let's get a closer look," Little Chaka murmured.

The eel ballooned up before them. Its skin disappeared as Cassandra obligingly bounced ultrasound through the water, and then adjusted the scans. "Ah ha—"

The door burst open, and Zack Moskowitz stormed in.

Avalon's chairman was about fifty-five Earth years old, thirty-eight Avalon, and a slightly heavier gravity hadn't been kind to him. His shoulders stooped, and his face was deeply lined. The mustache and eyebrows that gave him an unfortunate resemblance to Groucho Marx were thinner now, speckled with white. Care and woe, stress and responsibility had bent him as if physical burdens.

"Jessica!" he roared. "I gave you a direct order to kill that thing."

"Why?" she asked mildly. "And by the way: hi, Zack."

"Standing Order Municipal Rule One-four-two. 'Until adjudged otherwise, all new species are to be considered hostile.' This is the first time something this large has returned to the island. It has pronounced amphibious tendencies."

"So does my niece, but that doesn't make her a grendel."

"Look at this." Chaka slid into a swivel chair, lacing his thick dark fingers behind his head. The eel's head became orca-sized, revealing a mouthful of tiny, even, sharp-looking teeth. "Mama eats small fish. She *might* take a chomp out of your leg if you tromped on her. Sorry to disillusion you, Zack, but you wouldn't be her idea of lunch."

Zack grunted, then turned back to Jessica. "I don't care," he said. "An order is an order."

"I know," Jessica said, her voice still extremely even. "Rules are rules, because we can't trust individual judgment. You can't trust *your* individual judgment." *And I was never frozen. I don't have ice on my mind.* "Zack, my father wrote most of the Standing Orders, remember?"

"You're taking advantage," Zack said. "Cadmann will be back tomorrow."

Jessica leaned forward. "What makes you think that I care? The Grendel Scouts are controlled by Second Generation. Biomed is controlled by Second Generation. This is for Star Born, not Earth Born."

"At the moment."

"The eel was spotted by—"

"—sensors created and monitored by adults. First Generation. We set up the alert and sent out the skeeter. You commandeered it, and directly countermanded my order—"

Jessica's blue eyes narrowed hotly. "Cadmann's Bluff is not incorporated into the township of Camelot, never has been, never will be, and you damned well know *why*. The eel was captured there. My father is incommunicado. Justin and I are in command of the Bluff until he returns. I made my decision based upon my authority on the Bluff and my control of the Grendel Scouts. Chaka?"

Chaka spun in his swivel chair. "Mother Eel is secure, Zack. We can put a net over the tank, if you want."

"You know damned well that isn't the issue. The issue is that you exceeded your authority. I am responsible for the security of this colony—"

Jessica's smile was hard, but her voice remained even and untempered. "And although I had no hand in giving you that authority, I have abided by the decision. Until now. But I think we can learn more about Avalon from a live creature—and we have eggs coming down the mountain—"

"*Eggs?*" Zack was furious. "I want them destroyed—"

"You are the civilian authority, and as such have control of ordinary emergencies. But this isn't one of them, it's no emergency at all. It is the normal functioning of the planet, Zack. The ecology is returning. The signs have been there for eight years. Plants. Fairy-brollies, and look what *they* grew into! No birds, but we have new fish, new insects—Zack, this is important, this is the way this island used to be. This is for a joint council, Earth Born and Star Born—"

"Adults and Second Generation," Zack said absently.

"All right, but this is for the joint council, First and Second Generations, together. Or the biology board. But it's not something for *rules*, or a panicked, autocratic decision."

"But—"

"Our world, Zack," Jessica said. "Ours, not just yours."

"It was my impression, Zack, that this was a republic—not a principality." Chaka's tone was mocking, but gentle. "And it is our world too."

Zack closed his eyes for a moment, and finally nodded. "Right, right. You're right. All right. I want a cover on the tank. As soon as your father links in, I want him informed. And we'll have a special meeting when he gets back." Zack placed a fatherly hand on her arm. She let it remain there.

"You don't remember, you can't." Zack said it with a kind of resignation, and she knew two things: first, she was about to get a dose of Grendel Angst, and second, this was as close to an apology as Zack could come.

"Things have been peaceful for a long time. We want them to stay that way." *It's for your own good, children.*

He patted her, then took another long, hard look at the eel. It was beginning to swish to and fro around the tank. As if seeking a way out. "Put a cover on that tank." Zack shook his head, and left the room.

"Ice on his mind," Chaka said. "You know what Ruth said?"

"What?"

"She said Zack sleeps in his own room. Wakes Rachael up in the middle of the night, screaming."

"Hell, I think that half of the First have nightmares. Freezing Grendel Wars." Jessica shook her head. "Dead and gone, man, dead and gone. Just like the grendels."

"Gone here," Chaka said. "Plenty of them over there. We'll have to deal with them someday."

"Or our kids will," Jessica said. "We won't have to settle the mainland for generations."

"Yes we will," Chaka said. "I'd better get the cover on that tank."

"Do you want one?"

Chaka shrugged. "It will be inconvenient."

"Freeze it, then. Don't bother."

Chaka looked at her. Before he could say anything they were interrupted by the whir of an approaching skeeter. "That should be baby bro, with the egg samples," Jessica said.

"Right. Cassandra," Chaka said briskly. "I want a life-cycle simulation."

"Where do you think this thing lives?"

"The Deeps north of Surf's Up, maybe."

Justin slammed the door open. A jar half-filled with murky water sloshed in his hands. Within floated a sample of the jellied egg sac. "Merry Christmas," he said cheerily. "Are we set up?"

"All but." Chaka took the jar carefully. He drew a few drops of cloudy fluid and placed them into an analyzer. Cassandra worked. Presently a stream of filtered, designer water began to splash into a small tank on the workbench. When it was filled, Chaka emptied the jar into the tank.

Jessica sat down next to Justin, winked at him. "Caught hell from Zack about our slippery friend."

Chaka was big, the strongest of the Star Born, but you didn't notice that when he was at work. "We'll just dissect one of the eggs so Cassandra can have a look. There. Window, please." A flood of biological and mathmatical symbols reeled past them in a small holographic window, a peek into Cassandra's mind. She was comparing the eel with other Avalonian life forms, including the dreaded grendel. And she was scanning the eggs down to their DNA. And although it was understood to be no more than thirty percent accurate, Cassandra would devise a best-guess life cycle for the beast, including preferred foods at varied points in its development.

Before their eyes the eel transformed: Now its holographic image was covered with skin, now it was a network of muscles, now it was a mere skeleton whipping eerily through the water. Now it was a jelly sac crowded with internal organs, and in the next second it was merely a nervous system, each branching node outlined in blue.

Jessica lit a cigarette. It was machine-rolled but unfiltered. The tobacco field covered less than ten acres of the twelve thousand acres of cultivated land surrounding Camelot. There had been discussion as to whether the seeds should be grown at all. Most of the Earth Born didn't smoke and hated tobacco. Some were astonished to find there were tobacco seeds aboard *Geographic*. The same debate had preceded the hemp planting.

Mankind's vices had accompanied him to the stars. Alcohol, nicotine, and marijuana existed on Avalon, likewise poppy fields and coca plants. The mountain ridges had been seeded with coffee. Pharmaceutical cocaine and morphine were too valuable medicinally. Hemp too hardy and useful a plant fiber. Tobacco . . . well, tobacco was tobacco.

Jessica allowed herself a cigarette or two a day. You'd have to quadruple that level of consumption to find clinical deterioration of lung tissue, and it had been a century since anyone died of cancer anyway. As for the other drugs . . . well, they were a part of Man's history.

"Terrible habit," Justin said. She nodded, and shook him out a butt.

The pumps made small, moist rhythmic sounds, swishing murky water about in the egg tank.

Chaka was totally absorbed: the rest of the world might as well have disappeared. Jessica said, "Listen, we'll check back with you, all right?"

Ruth Moskowitz waited right outside the door for them, a bemused look on her round and pleasant face. She was five foot seven of clean-featured brunette. Attractive, but not pretty. Rounded, but not chubby. Competent, but not particularly bright as far as anyone could tell. Ruth was on the edge of everything, and not remarkable for anything but being Zack's daughter. She stripped off her work gloves. "It's beautiful," she said.

"What's beautiful?" Justin asked.

"The eel! Tell me about it."

"Not much to tell," Jessica said. "It swam up the Amazon this morning, you know, right through the living room— Oh. The Amazon is a stream."

"I've been to your house," Ruth said. "It must have been going to the pools above the Keep."

"Yes, that's right."

"What would it want?" Ruth mused. "There's nothing up there, just glacier."

"Right again. Got to the headwaters and laid eggs."

"Ooh. Wish I'd been there," Ruth said. "It's safe, then?"

"Looks harmless enough. Chaka is looking into it."

"I bet Daddy had a tizzy," Ruth said. "Municipal Standing Order 142." She looked puzzled. "He must have ordered you to kill it, but I can see it's still alive."

"That's right," Jessica said.

"Wish I'd been here," Ruth said again. Her comm card chirped. She lifted it, listened a moment, and said, "Yes, sir. I'll ask him." She smiled uncertainly at Jessica. "Got to ask Chaka something—"

"Right. See you."

Ruth went into the Biomed building. Justin and Jessica looked at each other and grinned. "Wish I'd been here," Justin said, his voice mocking Ruth's.

"You're unkind," Jessica said, but she laughed. It was easy to laugh at Ruth.

"You're the one who forgot she'd been to the Keep. She was there more than once, actually."

"Years ago," Jessica said. "Look, you decided she couldn't be a Grendel Scout—"

"We all did. You know she'd go straight to Zack if she learned what we do." Justin climbed the ladder to the top of pen number two, and sloshed his hand in the water until Hipshot, the small dark male of the dolphin pair, approached and rubbed against it. He stroked the dolphin carefully. "What do you think, boy? Think you'll give Quanda a tumble?"

Jessica sat next to him. They looked down on Camelot.

The main colony boasted almost three hundred separate dwellings now, and another went up every month or so.

A hundred and thirty-seven of the original two hundred remained alive. Most of them lived here, in the expanded grounds of the original encampment. A few had imitated Colonel Cadmann Weyland and built permanent dwellings elsewhere on the island. More had hunting lodges and second homes near the snows. The fishing colony at Surf's Up was the unofficial domain of the Star Born, not quite a separate city, not quite permanent, a perpetual summer camp linked to the main colony by skeeters. If the comm cards were the nervous system of the colony, the skeeter autogyros, built on Earth and assembled on Avalon, were its blood vessels. There were never enough skeeters. Building more would require fuel cells, and fuel cells required palladium and platinum for catalysts; those required mines and prospecting, which required access to the mainland, but the skeeters didn't have enough range for routine operations to the mainland, and there wasn't any facility there to recharge their fuel cells anyway. *But if we had a power station and more fuel cells that could be charging over there . . .*

Everything we want to do requires two other things, Jessica thought. And as the First grew older, more and more of the colony's resources went into consumption, things the First Generation wanted, no, *needed,* leaving less for investment in the future.

I guess we're rich, she thought, recalling Cassandra's images of poverty on Earth. *Earth people would call this Paradise. And the First won't last forever.* She suppressed that thought as quickly as it came. It seemed ghoulish. *We have the skeeters, and we have the comm cards. We all have Cassandra and all the libraries of Old Earth, everything people learned before the First left it behind and brought us here. We're still one community, if you close one eye and squint a little.*

One community, but several places to live now. Jessica preferred the original settlement—the nerve center. Surf's Up was lovely and vibrant, with a slight Japanese feel to it, the domain of the Second Generation. The mountain settlement (thirty-five up there now!) was wonderful, with good skiing most of the year. In five years there would be hunting—the vegetation was established. Some of the trees were twenty years old, a new forest like nothing ever seen on the planet before. Deer and moose and bear were being released slowly into the fields and meadows. Some would survive; some would thrive. There was general agreement that when the herds were well established they should thaw out some of the frozen wolf embryos and release a pack. Exactly when was argued vigorously, and so far "not yet" won out. *That* wasn't a question that cut deep between the generations. Not yet. The generation wars were about other things.

There were 280 Second Generation "children," an average of four for every woman who survived the Grendel Wars.

Truly, Jessica thought cynically, *an heroic achievement.* And of the hundred and fifty female "children," almost half had already had children of their own, an additional seventy progeny, for a total of 480 inhabitants either immigrated or born here on the fourth planet of the star called Tau Ceti. *And for all we know, we're the whole universe. I guess that's what really eats at Zack. Dad, too. Where is Earth in all this? She never calls, she never writes. . . .*

The sounds and smells of life here were utterly routine now. Cattle grazed, dogs roamed the streets in packs—and not an ill-fed animal in the lot. Half-naked children played in alien dust ten light-years removed from their closest non-Avalonian relations.

Life went on.

The smells and sounds and sights of Camelot weren't very different from those captured in holovids of Earth. Their sun was a little brighter. From what her father said, shadows were sharper and bluer.

But the voracious grendels had so stripped the island that Man found it easy to conquer. Earthworms had defeated the local annelids for mastery of the soil. Earth crickets chirped at night. Crows had been seen to attack lower-level pterodon nests, destroying eggs in a battle for territory.

After the Grendel Wars, the Firsts had helped their imported organisms along. You could still get arguments among both Earth Born and Star Born on whether they'd given them too much help in competing with native life, but it was hard to blame those who favored the familiar Earth organisms over Avalon's. "Samlon," the grendel's larval stage, had seemed so harmless, until they changed . . . who knew what might next grow fangs and claws? So an orgy of slaughter had ensued. The creatures of Earth completely dominated Camelot, this small island corner of Avalon.

Justin stood and stretched lazily. "I'm going to see Carlos. Staying here?"

"Sure." She slipped off her sandals and pants. She wore bright blue underpants, which contasted beautifully with her long, muscular tanned legs. With barely a splash, she slipped into the tank with Quanda and Hipshot, who immediately glided over to investigate. Jessica dove under, then came up and spit out a mouthful of water. "Should only take an hour or so to get the preliminary reports. Inquiring minds want to know."

"You've been reading those tabloids again."

"The twentieth century's highest cultural achievement. Seems they spent all their time hunting something called Bigfoot, or triangulating Elvis sightings."

"Who?"

"Mid-twentieth-century pop singer. Died of fame."

"So should we all."

"On this backwater? Not likely."

Jessica vanished back beneath the surface. Quanda came up beneath her. Jessica firmly grabbed a fin, and let Quanda take her for a ride around the tank.

3

ICE ON THEIR MINDS

All happy families resemble each other, each
unhappy family is unhappy in its own way.
—Leo Tolstoy, *Anna Karenina*

Justin chuckled as he headed toward Camelot's main street. Jess amused him.
Saving the eel was just like her. Had she done it only to antagonize Zack? She
usually had several reasons for anything she did.

He swiveled aside to let a stream of half-naked boys and girls playing some
spontaneously generated variant of tag scamper past. They giggled and sang,
tripped, rolled ignoring their bruised shins and shoulders, and ran out into the
fields. The game might progress until midnight, when exhaustion, not security,
dictated an end to play. The grendels were dead. The only things that *could*
harm a human child were the dogs, and they *wouldn't*. Children had never been
safer, nor held more precious.

The streets of Camelot were broad and well paved, with private gardens
where vegetables and fruits were nurtured into bloom. Intimate hothouses and
hobby sheds were tucked along every byway.

Justin's favorite garden was behind Carolyn McAndrews's place. In neat,
furrowed rows she cultivated roses, carnations, tulips, and daisies. Within the
plastic-sheet walls of her hothouse lived Avalon's greatest—and only—orchid
collection. Human shapes moved inside the hothouse: Carolyn herself, followed
closely by a small brood of children. She had seven in all, three *fast* after the
Wars, and another four in more leisurely fashion. The latest was barely out of diapers. The oldest two had children of their own. Coleen, the youngest of the
first group, still lived at home, but lately she spent most of her time studying.
Coleen wanted to go back to the stars.

She'll outgrow that, Justin thought. He had. It wasn't possible, not now, not in
Coleen's lifetime. There was just too much to do with this world before they
could rebuild and refuel *Geographic*—and beyond that was the problem no one
could solve. Slower-than-light travel meant decades between stars. Stay awake
and die of boredom, or go into frozen sleep and risk hibernation instability. *Ice
on my mind.* He shuddered.

He saw motion through the plastic, and hurried past. Carolyn McAndrews
was coming out of the greenhouse. He was out of sight before she emerged.

Carolyn had been like an aunt to him until he was twelve or so. He had
sensed her withdrawal without understanding it. She did well with children,

couldn't cope with adults. She was damaged, and knew it. Hibernation instability if you were polite, ice crystals in the brain if you were accurate, ice on your mind if you were rude, it was all the same thing and it affected *all* of them. Justin remembered the shock when he'd found it out. He'd been searching through the computer for something else, and found closed files, and—

His parents, Zack, the adults, all damaged, all unwilling to trust their own judgment. How to survive? Think in advance, use collective wisdom. Make rules; talk them through; change them endlessly. In a crisis, follow them blindly.

It wasn't hereditary. Carolyn was right when she said "But I make good babies. . . ." Carolyn and her sister Phyllis—her late sister Phyllis, killed in the final minutes of the Grendel Wars—had gone into cold sleep as a pair of Earth's best and brightest, and wakened with their emotional stability shattered. Others had come out judgment-impaired or simply stupid.

But we don't have ice crystals in our brains, Justin thought. *We don't have to make rules and obey them blindly.* He'd been shocked when he first realized that. Now they taught it to the Grendel Scouts when they were old enough. The big secret: *the adults have ice on their minds.*

Every turn through the warren was comfortable to him . . . in some odd way, *too* comfortable. Everything on the island was *safe,* and sometimes it chafed.

In a world of fewer than five hundred people, every detail, every sight, every face becomes tediously familiar, comes entirely too readily to mind. He'd seen the next house uncounted thousands of times. It slid in and out of his mind so effortlessly that it felt like an extension of his own flesh.

The house frame was the same prefabricated rod structure employed by most of the First. Over the years, its exterior had been modified with simulated stone sculpted to imitate rock blasted and hauled from a distant quarry. Some of it *was* rock blasted and hauled from a distant quarry. . . .

The porch was broad. There was a swinging bench with a striped awning to protect it from the sun. Justin vaulted the fence one-handed, calling "Tío Carlos!" There was no answer by the time he reached the top of the stairs. He poked his head in, and looked around.

He smelled coffee.

This was every bit as much his home as Cadmann's Bluff. He used to spend two or three nights a week here. He was seventeen, eleven Avalon, by the time he moved to Surf's Up. These well-worn stones and boards still smelled like home. At Cadmann's Bluff the smell of coffee was rare; but this house always smelled of coffee.

The taste had shocked Justin the eight-year-old. Jessica and others of the Star Born had acquired the taste, but Justin never had. Coffee was bitter. Still, he loved the smell.

The house was crammed with bric-a-brac carved from stone and thornwood and seashells. Weird sculptures of grendel bone were shelved under a broad window above a row of complex topological puzzles molded of composition plastic.

There were hypercubes one disassembled to convert into Klein bottles, and Gordian knots only Cassandra could untie. Every inch of the walls was covered with handcrafted delights. Most of the incredible creative output was the product of one mind, the mind of Carlos Martinez.

On the way out to the workshop, he passed Carlos's bedroom. The bed was wide and spacious and rarely lonely. Justin's "Uncle" Carlos had married only once: he'd gone "down the rapids" with Bobbie Kanagawa. The marriage was six hours of bliss, bloodily annulled by a grendel attack.

Holotape of that awful event was required viewing. The attack patterns had been analyzed endlessly. They'd all heard the lecture, too often.

Carlos had married only once and became a widower the same day, but he had half a dozen acknowledged children. Some lived with him, some with their mothers. He was rumored to have more. You could never be sure who had been in that bed. *His gametes get a huge return on investment for making him. . . .*

The burr of a high-intensity drill grew louder, more jarring as he approached the high-domed workshop behind the house.

The path between house and workshop was crowded with sculpture. Naked goddesses cavorted with satyrs rendered in volcanic stone. Impressionistic cloud cities carved in some kind of webbed driftwood. The eruption of Vesuvius whittled from an enormous bone flown back from the mainland, years before.

Carlos was an accomplished wood sculptor before he left Earth for Avalon. Over the years he'd gained skills in metalwork, glassblowing, and odd, "found" art. He was, beyond question, Camelot's premier graphic artist. There was probably no single home on Avalon that didn't have a plaque, lamp, sculpture, or door plate signed with his rakish scrawl.

Katya Martinez opened the workshop door before he could get to it. Her faceplate and baggy coveralls disguised flaming red hair and a flawless body. She was a month younger than Justin's nineteen adjusted Earth years—or about twelve Avalonian cycles. Athletic, which made her attractive in ways that Trish, who lifted weights, never would be.

Katya's mother had died early enough that Justin had no memory of her, but he'd heard her talk about it. Three of the First had died of strokes in the space of four days, and one had been Carlotta Nolan's current love. Ice on their minds: damaged arteries in their brains held for a few years, then tore open. Carlotta had fallen dead during the triple funeral, and that made four.

Katya had grown up in this house, with no female role model or too many of them depending on who you asked, but she had never been in any doubt as to what sex she was. For years Justin thought of her as another sister, like Jessica. Then one day that had changed very quickly—

A flame-jet flared to silhouette two welders in coveralls in the workshop behind her. "Katya. How's the anniversary piece coming along?"

She flipped up her faceplate, and gave him a radiant, brown-eyed, broad-mouthed smile. It had been months since Katya and Justin had played games. "Fantastic. Dad's welding Madagascar into place just now."

"Let me get into safety gear. I'm down for a couple hours—thought I'd say hi."

Katya nodded enthusiastically and slipped past him. Justin pulled on heavy woven cotton overalls, and belted them in the front. By the time he finished, Katya was back to hand him a pod of beer. They watched each other while they drank. "I thought that you were taking the Grendel Scouts out for an overnight."

"Were, yes. Didn't you hear the alarm?"

"Alarm?" She brushed a crimson strand of hair out of her face, and sipped deeply. "Nope. What's up?"

"Big eel. Came right up the Miskatonic and the Amazon, right through the Hold. We captured it. It looks pretty harmless, but it's the first grendel-sized carnivore we've seen on the island, and it's bound to get some attention. . . ."

"Over at Aquatics?"

"Yeah." He tossed the empty pod into the trash. Two points.

"Keep me posted."

She held the door open for him. He was very aware that her fingers brushed his thigh as he passed her.

Four shadowy figures crouched around an eight-foot curved metal bas-relief of the African continent. The huge silhouette would soon be attached to the Earth globe under construction just north of Camelot's main gates. A series of overhead winches kept Madagascar in place while one man waved semaphore to the others.

Plasma torches spit as the piece fitted into place. Metal ran in glowing rivulets, and the air sang with the smell of scorched iron. Justin finished pulling his gloves on, and hurried to help.

"*Hola*, Carlos!"

"Hola, Justin. *Qúe tal? Cómo estás?*" Carlos glanced away from the model for just a moment. Almost instantly, there was a high, annoying whir. "*Un momentito—*"

The winch was malfunctioning, and the three-foot chunk of Madagascar—which weighed over a hunderd kilos—sagged.

Carlos and Justin put their silver heat-blocking gloves against the lower edge, where the metal still smoked, and lifted. The heat pulsed hungrily at their fingers, but didn't burn.

"At the top! At the top!"

Assistants screwed two large C-clamps into place, and Madagascar was realigned.

Torches sizzled. Carlos turned his face away from the intense light.

He stripped off his gloves. The major work finished, his assistants buzzed about, welding here and there, cooling with jets of water, then beginning to buff.

He held a broad, muscular hand to Justin. "Wasn't expecting you until day after tomorrow. Australia is next."

"I'll be back."

Carlos stepped away from the globe, leaving it to the younger artists. The African continent brushed his ceiling. On the wall opposite were blueprints for Australia.

"Have you got the basic mold finished?"

"No," he sighed. "That's what I want you for. Two days' work, maybe. Then he can cast it. Then . . ." He shrugged. "Almost finished. It's been a year. In another month, maybe, it's done."

Justin slapped his mentor's shoulder. Carlos was Latino, with predominantly African genetics. Even with his hair streaked gray, he was still disgustingly handsome. Carlos Martinez was Cadmann Weyland's best friend. About fifty-five Earth years, thirty-five Avalon, and in decent condition, but Justin knew that when Carlos cast an eye at the Seconds, especially the younger women, he felt his years.

There was a certain sadness in Carlos's face. Perhaps being so close to the completion of a dream? Sometimes that did it. . . .

"Qual es su problema, Tío?"

Carlos chuckled. "For years I wanted to build this. You know, the north road is going to be a crossroads one day. Gateway to a metropolis. We have Surf's Up, and the mountain colony. . . . Explosive growth soon now, as more of the Second have their children. And in fifteen years, whew."

"Terrific, huh? And how many of those bambinos will be yours?"

His smile was calculatedly mysterious. "Six that I'm sure of. Not everyone wants to gene scan, so who knows?"

"Cassandra," Justin said.

"But she will not tell."

Justin chuckled. "A little of that New Guinea flavor here."

Carlos waved a hand at the young men and women laboring in his shop. "These are my children, though. Not just Katya, but like you. Learning sculpture. Learning history. The ones who care."

"The others wll come around."

"Hope so. Now what can Uncle Carlos do for you?"

Justin explained about the eel. "Zack will want to kill it as fast as possible. Destroy the eggs."

"Knee-jerk reflex. I'll deal with him. Your father will want it studied." Carlos thought for a moment. "Might want those eggs destroyed, though. No telling what they'll hatch into."

"Eels."

"Samlon become grendels. We don't have any examples of harmful larval stage and harmless adult, but—"

"I see the point, but I don't agree. And that's the point. We think there's going to be a row over this at the council meeting, and I wanted to take a little straw vote, find out where we'd stand."

"What's the problem?"

"The problem is that it's *our* eel. It's our island, really—we're going to inherit it. And we can't just kill everything that comes up the river or flies in from the mainland. Eventually, we have to know how we fit in with this planet, or we'll be stuck here on this island forever."

"You could stay here for ten generations, easy," Carlos observed. "Plenty of land."

"We don't *want* to."

"Some of you don't want to."

"Some means damned near all," Justin said. "Starting with me."

Carlos studied him. "I don't blame you," he said at last. "Listen—I think that your father will side with you—he believes that strength is safety. And knowledge is strength."

"Are you suggesting that Zack would like to hide his head in the sand?"

"Can you entirely blame him?"

An arc of sparks jetted out, turning the floor into a summer night's sky. The stars died.

"We almost lost, amigo," Carlos said quietly, watching Madagascar. "We make a lot of noise about how heroic it all was. But listen between the lines." His eyes were deadly calm. "We almost lost."

"I know that it was tough—"

"No," Carlos said. "I didn't say that it was 'tough.' I didn't say 'it was a struggle.' I said that *we almost lost.* All of us. Wiped out. If it hadn't been for a fluke of grendel behavior—that you can drive them crazy with the smell of their own *speed*—they would have slaughtered every living thing on this island."

Carlos sat at the edge of one of the benches, and picked up a thermos, uncapping it to take a sip. He scanned the pieces of Earth strewn about his studio. There in one corner was India, mother to Man's civilizations. Suspended from the ceiling was Africa, possibly mother to Man himself. Already in place north of the colony was Europe, which had birthed the scientific method, and the Americas, creators of the technologies that had finally taken man to the stars.

In that moment Carlos seemed old, deeply fatigued; but a light flickered behind his eyes that was almost ecstatic.

"To our home," Carlos said, and took a long sip. The hair at his temples was almost white, and the skin on his forearms was loose over the wiry muscle. "I'll never see Earth again, muchacho. Earth is an abstraction to you. A place the old folks talk about. Pictures we show you, tapes we play. Dead voices of dead people. But it was our home."

"We haven't heard from Earth in twenty years!" Justin said, instantly ashamed of the mockery that had crept into his voice.

"Not a thing," Carlos agreed soberly. "And that means something different to every one of us. But back during the Grendel Wars, all that mattered was that we couldn't go home, and we couldn't win. We were all going to die, and there would be no one to bury our bones. We wanted to die here, to be a part of the soil—" He laughed coarsely. "But not as grendel shit. Anyway—at the meeting tonight, please understand why we are the way we are. If we are too protective of you, it's because you are all we have."

Justin nodded. "All right, amigo—but just remember—you can't keep making our decisions for us. And the more afraid you are, the more you had better let us grow up."

"I do remember being your age, Justin. So cocky. So . . . invulnerable. That was before Bobbie died, and there was nothing I could do to save her." He tilted his head to stare at the floor. "And you know? There was a moment there where I tasted my own death so clearly, when it was so . . . real, that I would have given up *anything*." He paused. "Even Bobbie. For another few moments of life."

Carlos took another drink. Justin caught the odor of fermentation from the thermos. "You never see yourself the same way again, amigo. You never quite get it back."

He grinned crookedly, mocking the pain in his own voice. "You're all we have left, Justin," he murmured. "And just maybe all that there is." As if aware that he had almost crossed some invisible line, he stood. "Back to work," he said brusquely.

Justin hiked a thumb at the globe. "Looking good," he tossed over his shoulder on his way to the door. He let it slam behind him.

The first comm shack had been a frail thing, tin and wood, but that was before the Grendel Wars. Now the colony's communications and computers were housed in a fortress, stone and concrete walls, massive doors, small windows. Above each door was a small room filled with boulders and rubble poised to fall on any potential invader.

The Merry Pranksters had once filled one of those chambers with wet cotton. They'd watched through videocameras as Joe and Edgar Sikes walked into the trap. The momentary shock and horror, then the laughter, man and boy waist deep in wet cotton, throwing gobs of it at each other . . . but Zack and the other Earth Born hadn't been amused. The repercussions hadn't died out for months, and now entrance to Comm Control was monitored by TV cameras and recorded by Cassandra, and you couldn't get in unless the duty watch people let you.

The communications building controlled all contact with the Orion spacecraft *Geographic* still in orbit above, the branch settlements around the island, and the automated mining apparatus on the mainland. The main communications board was also the colony's defense center, manned constantly as a human backup for the main computer defense systems. None of that had been needed for twenty years.

Rules, Justin thought as he buzzed the interior. *They set up their rules. Fine for them, but now we have to take turns standing watch with the First.* It wasn't hard duty, and privately Justin appreciated the enforced reading and study time that Comm Watch provided, but it was another point of contention between Star Born and Earth Born.

Edgar Sikes opened the door.

"Ho. Edgar, I need a favor. I have to talk to my dad."

Edgar didn't seem surprised. "No can do. Cadmann's down south, and that's as much of an address as he left us."

Edgar was eighteen, pudgy, and brighter than hell. A childhood back injury had kept him from early participation in sports, and he had the reputation of being more interested in computers than people, someone worth knowing if you needed information, but never the first to be invited to parties. He was slightly younger than Justin. They had never been particularly close, but now Edgar's father Joe was married to Justin's stepsister Linda. Justin wasn't sure what relationship that created between him and Edgar. Close enough that he could ask Edgar for a favor. "Let's talk about it."

Edgar shrugged and stood aside.

"Greetings, Justin-san."

It wasn't surprising to find Toshiro Tanaka in the Comm Center. Toshiro didn't sleep, at least not until nearly dawn and then not for long. He took advantage of that: other Star Born could get Toshiro to cover their shift at the center. Toshiro was going to sit alone and read or play computer games all night anyway, and by taking someone's shift he built up obligations. Like Carlos, Toshiro never wanted for coffee or tea.

"Greetings, Toshiro-san." Justin suppressed a grin. He wasn't completely sure how to take this new kick Toshiro was on. Toshiro was always polite, always smiled, but Justin had read about the manners of the Tokagawa culture Toshiro seemed to be fascinated with. They always smiled, even when they were about to chop your liver out. "You've told them about the eel, then? Joe, he told you?"

"A little," Joe said. "You saw it too. Tell us."

Joe was sprawled in a massive sculpture, a chair and footstool Carlos had carved from the hard, dense, twisted grain of a horsemane root system. Carlos had installed it for his own watch. Butts and boots and elbows had polished and scarred it, but Justin believed it would last as long as Avalon.

Joe Sikes was graying, slope-shouldered and a little paunchy despite his best intentions. He was one of the three heroes of the Grendel Wars, holding a place just below Carlos and not far below Cadmann Weyland himself. Justin's generation believed as an article of faith that all First had ice on their minds, but it wasn't easy to see what disability that gave Joe Sikes. The self-doubts characteristic of the First bothered him less than anyone except Cadmann. Sikes always seemed to be working on something. He was strong on industrial development, which included maintaining and establishing the mines on the mainland, and Justin had always found himself easy to talk to.

That changed, sort of, when it became clear that Sikes and Linda were much more than casually involved. Justin had never been able to justify his feeling of resentment, other than feeling that Joe was too damn old for her. *And he was First, the damaged generation.*

"Five meters of fun," Justin said. "Zack just about had kittens. 'Kill it! Kill it! You have your orders, you know the rules, kill it!'"

"Glad you didn't," Edgar said. He tapped computer keys, and the image of Big Mama Eel rippled across the computer screen. "Looks harmless enough. Maybe we'll learn something."

Joe Sikes grunted agreement. "Yeah, but we still got problems from the mainland. Give Zack too much to think about, we'll overload the system."

"No possible relationship," Edgar said. He jerked a thumb at the screen where the eel swam steadily around and around in the tank. "No way *that's* going to explode."

Say what? Justin said, "Explode?"

"Well, I agree again," Joe said. "But Zack may not. Justin, you're gonna love this."

"Yes," Toshiro said. "Most serious. Baffling."

"What in the world are you talking about?" Justin asked.

"Linda's working the new stuff up in the waldo room, let her tell you," Joe Sikes said. "We've had little problems at the mining site before. This is a big one, but maybe it's just more of the same."

"Which will do well enough," Toshiro said.

"You sound worried."

Toshiro shrugged. "Concerned. A setback."

"Hell, you're not going to live long enough to go back to Japan no matter what happens," Justin said. "So you can stop worrying."

Toshiro smiled politely.

"Well, it's true," Justin said. "Coming back with me?"

"Thank you, I am on duty here," Toshiro said.

Justin nodded and crossed the large central control room toward the green door at its far end.

"That wasn't very nice," Joe Sikes told him. He jerked his head toward Toshiro, who was now absorbed in some kind of computer game involving medieval Japanese warriors.

"Well, yeah, you're right, but it's still true," Justin said. "There's no way we'll build enough industry to fire up *Geographic* and go back to Earth or anywhere else. Not that *I'd* go. I can't figure why *he* wants to."

Edgar Sikes shrugged. "Beats me, I guess. I asked him once."

"What'd he say?"

"Roots."

"Eh?"

"Roots. Can't say I blame him. How'd you feel if you were the only white kid here?"

"I don't think I'd notice."

"Toshiro does," Edgar said. "There were four Orientals in the Earth Born, but they're all dead in the Grendel Wars. Anyway, that's what he said. I asked him why he wanted to see Earth again, and he said 'Roots.'"

The waldo room was at the rear of the telecommunications building. "Cassandra, ready or not, here I come," Justin said, and waited for the door to open. It didn't. He frowned.

"Sorry, I've been doing some reprogramming," Edgar said. "Let Justin in, please, Cassandra." The door swung open.

He was immediately assailed by a sweet-sour triple dose of Eau de Diaper. His sister Linda was seated at the robotics control panel. Her blond pigtails made her look even younger than her seventeen years. She leaned back into a thick leather chair, silvered goggles covering her eyes. She might have been asleep. A hand-carved cradle that could have been built in the fourteenth century, but in fact was a product of Carlos's workshop, stood next to her workstation. A three-month-old baby watched as if he knew what his mother was doing.

Joe *shoosh*ed the baby unnecessarily, then tiptoed over to Linda and planted a big juicy one on her lips.

Sis leapt out of the illusion sputtering, waving her hands in alarm. Then she pulled her goggles off, and sighed.

"Joe Sikes, I *hate* when you do that." She peeled off her headset, and stood to hug Justin.

"Hey, Cad," he said to the baby. The three-month-old was still fat and wrinkly, his stubby little fingers reaching out and trying to grasp a chunk of the world. His watery blue eyes struggled to focus.

Linda had discovered boys when she was fourteen, and when she was fifteen they discovered her right back. She had been extremely popular and enjoyed every minute of it, a dozen lovers in as many weeks. Then she was pregnant, and suddenly she was tired of casual sex, tired of popularity, tired of the game.

And *bang*, she was attached to Joe Sikes, elderly, slope-shouldered, hardworking Joe Sikes. Justin remembered thinking it was pure lust. His little sister was one of those rare women who became almost ethereally beautiful as she swelled and neared term. If so, lust had ripened into something more stable— but a palpable erotic haze still shimmered in the air between them. His stepsister had found a husband and lover. She had also found a friend and teacher, and under Joe's instruction was rapidly developing into one of the most capable of the Second's engineers. Now she studied—Aaron had once said that while the First had ice on their minds, Linda had integral equations on hers—worked, and nursed her baby, and the only way to see her was to come to the command center.

"What we got?" Joe Sikes asked. His forefinger traced a lazy circle on the back of her neck.

"*Geographic* relays checked out," Linda said. "I'm certain that the, uh . . . *will you stop that for a moment?* Thank you. Nothing garbled in transmission. We're getting the right data, and it still looks the same, there are explosions in the mines."

"Explosions," Justin said.

"In the mines," Edgar repeated. "Ain't we got fun?"

"That sounds—" Justin stopped. "Can't be grendels."

"Unless they've learned to use grenades," Edgar said.

"Now, there's a grim thought. Something break in?"

"Not bloody likely," Joe Sikes said.

Justin nodded agreement. The mines didn't exactly have doors. "So what is it? Machinery failure?"

Linda looked worried. Her face was thinner than Jessica's but somehow softer at the same time. Little Cad had been good for her—good for the elder Weyland, as well. At least six children would eventually call Cadmann "Granddad." Colonel Weyland doted on all of them, but Cadzie, as the colonel's first namesake, would get special attention. Justin felt a pang of jealousy, followed by an answering pang of shame.

"I'll do a show-and-tell at the meeting tonight," Joe said. "We'll want to make an emergency trip up in maybe a week." He was pugnacious and happy, and Justin didn't understand that.

"You think it's that serious?"

"Kid, this isn't a conveyor belt breakdown. Here—Cassandra, show us Mine Disaster Three." A phantasm formed above a holopad. It looked like an ant farm done in neon vermilion.

Joe set his blinking cursor where several tunnels joined in an angular lump. "It looked like a momentary flare of heat—very sharp—here in the processing equipment. And the sensors actually burned out. Weird. The entire assembly is completely jammed. The repair robots can't get to them. It's like something warped the entire unit out of alignment. Linda took a sonic profile of the entire operation. Look at the patterns of vibration leading up to the incident—"

A graph of sound patterns replaced the ant farm: the usual jagged hills and valleys produced by running machinery, punctuated by a sudden and violent pulse.

"We're going to translate that into sound. Listen—"

Chug chug chug.

Tung.

"Jesus Christ," Justin said.

Joe's lips twisted in a bitter smile. "The Merry Pranksters."

For a moment, nobody said anything. Then Justin cleared his throat. "That's a pretty nasty accusation. They've never done anything like this."

"First time for everything."

"You're just unhappy about getting wet."

"Nah, that was fun." He looked at Edgar and got an answering nod. "This is something else."

"So how could they have done it?" Justin demanded. "The only way to get all the way to the mining site is with *Robor*. Or one of the Minervas. God knows they're under control. How could they get in?"

"And that would be the point, now, wouldn't it?" Joe's usually even tones went flat and nasty. "It was impossible to carve fifty-foot buttocks on Isentine Glacier, wasn't it? And wasn't it impossible to use seismic charges to send Morse code limericks to the geological station?"

Justin restrained a chuckle, and raised a hand in protest. "That may be true—but they've never done anything destructive, and you know it. What would be the point? This isn't their style, Joe."

Joe's head cocked, and he waited.

"This isn't funny! It's just *vandalism*."

Joe patted Linda's shoulder possessively. "It was just a matter of time before they crossed the line," he said. "The point was always to get our attention, wasn't it? I know that there are certain residents of Surf's Up—"

Justin started to protest, but Joe waved him off. "You may know who they are, and you may not. That doesn't concern me at the moment. What does concern me is that this has gone far enough."

"Something goes wrong, and the first thing you do is blame it on us Star Born. We're not the only ones on this planet, Joe. If this was caused by a human being—"

"What else would you suggest?"

"Don't know. Some kind of natural phenomenon."

"Underground explosions aren't very natural," Joe said. "Edgar has been saying the same thing. Got an answer?"

Edgar shook his head. "Not me. Time to go relieve Toshiro." He strode off quickly.

"Right. Edgar can't explain it and neither can you."

Justin spread his hands helplessly. "All right, I don't think of anything, but— Suppose it was caused by a human being, why think it was one of us? You Firsts have a lot higher wacko factor."

"I remember. 'Ice On My Mind.' Someone spelled that out in alfalfa, two years ago. HI drops functional IQ. It doesn't cause emotional damage."

"Carolyn McAndrews," Justin said. *And Mom's been getting harder to live with. . . .*

"All right, I'll give you that one," Joe said. "But I don't believe it was a First, and neither do you."

Justin felt his fingers knot into fists. "Double-talk. All of you came to this planet coasting on your freezing intellectual egos. Thought you were the smartest things in the known universe. Then most of you lost a few points— some more than that. Add the Grendel Wars. Pretty high fear factor there, you know? Hey, sis—does Joe still wake up screaming? Still scaring Cadzie at two in the morning . . . ?"

"Stop it," Linda said. Her voice was coldly serious. "And stop it now."

"You're crossing the line, Justin," Joe said.

"You too," Linda said, but it didn't sound the same.

She's made her choice, Justin thought. *And it's not any of the Second. To hell with that.* "Just remember that. There *is* a line—"

"Justin—"

"No, Sis, let me finish. There is a line, and we'd better both remember it. You can say Surf's Up did this as a prank—but it's *your* side doesn't want anyone going to the mainland. We all want to go."

"So do I," Joe reminded him. "No quarrel there. Now let me give you something to think about. How do you suppose we were chosen to come on this expedition?"

"I've read all about it," Justin said. "Cassandra has the records."

"Like hell she does," Sikes said. "Cassandra has the official records, but they're dry as dust. Laddie, some of us *worked* to get here. Did you ever think who chose the colonists?"

"Well, it was a board appointed by the directors of the Geographic Society," Justin said. "So?"

"A board of shrinks," Sikes said. "Psychiatrists and social workers. Ruth Moskowitz was one of them. And they picked just the kind of people you'd expect them to."

Justin frowned. "I don't see what you're getting at."

"No, I suppose you wouldn't," Sikes said. "Let me put it this way. Damn near all the colonists were exactly the sort of people the shrinks wanted them to be. Colonel Weyland was an exception, a military man picked for his profession. Then there was Carlos. He qualified on brains, but the shrinks would never have picked him, so his father bribed the selection board. He wanted Carlos as far from the family as possible. As for the rest—" Joe shrugged. "Some were people the shrinks approved of, and some, a few, maybe more than a few, wanted to go so bad they worked at it, found out what the shrinks were looking for, and played head games."

"And you were one of those?"

"Maybe it's time—" Whatever Linda had been about to say was drowned out by the sudden wails of the baby. Linda glared at both of them. She swept her child into her arms, holding him close. "There . . . there." She kissed his wrinkly forehead. "Just stop it, both of you. I don't know who the Merry Pranksters are, but I can't believe that anyone, First or Second, would do something like this deliberately. It's not funny, it's dangerous."

"So what is it?" Joe demanded.

"I don't know. I think it's the planet surprising us again. And that damned eel has got everyone upset."

Justin searched his heart, searching for the voice that would say that she was right, or wrong. She was right.

"All right," he said finally.

Linda grinned. "Now, I can't have two of my four favorite men mad at each other. . . ."

"Four?" Joe forced his mouth into a neutral position.

"Sure, now that Cadzie is here . . ."

"And your brother, I guess . . . and Cadmann?"

"Sure."

And whoever was the father of the baby would make five, Justin thought. He could see that Joe Sikes was thinking the same thing. There was a long and awkward pause. "Linda, isn't there some way to find Dad?"

She shrugged. "Edgar might be able to. He's smarter than I am."

Justin kissed Cadzie good-bye, and went back out to the main room. Edgar had taken Toshiro's place at the main console and was splitting his attention, watching some kind of holoplay through his goggles. Toshiro had another set. Whatever they were doing it was together, and not visible to anyone not wearing the head-mounted displays. Justin thumped him on the back of the head. "Edgar?"

"Yeah?"

"About that favor you owe me. I know that my dad doesn't have his tracer turned on, but can you locate him?"

Edgar flipped the lid of his lenses up. He stood up to stretch, elaborately, fingers linked over his head. His pudgy body was an upright spear, its tip twisting in a slow circle. Edgar had hurt his back, long ago, and it had never quite healed.

"Go straight into Sun Salutation," Toshiro said. "Head loose as you come down. Hands farther back, take your weight with just your arms as you jump straight back . . . hold it . . . elbows back, down *slowly*. Now inhale, chest forward—"

Edgar was puffing a little as his head and shoulders came up, but he was way improved since the last time Justin had seen him. Toshiro's training was having its effect. Short of breath, but he wasn't *complaining*. Edgar finished the sequence, grinned at Justin while he emptied and refilled his lungs, and said, "Cadmann's not wearing a personal tracer. He disabled the tracer on the skeeter."

"Dad likes his privacy."

"You bet. I don't know exactly where his lodge is."

"Nobody does, except it's south of Isenstine Glacier."

Edgar grinned at him wickedly. "Well . . . what's in it for me?"

"First pick, next catch."

"Even stringfish?"

"No problem."

"Well, okay. Take over the watch, Toshiro-san?"

"Certainly. I relieve you, Edgar-san."

"Thanks. Okay, Justin, let's see what I've got." Edgar led him over to another console away from where Toshiro sat. "*Geographic* has images of the fuel dumps he uses. Here—" Edgar's fingers tapped silently at a virtual keyboard display. The wall in front of them turned into a vast field of ice and rock: the wasted expanse of Isenstine Glacier that fed both the Amazon and Miskatonic. Three tiny dots glowed redly. "There. About eight hundred miles apart."

"Spare fuel cells. Each cell takes him about five hundred miles. So he carries two backups, and has emergency dumps as well. That's Dad."

"Not that they're roughly in a straight line—"

"And the last one ends about three hundred miles north of the end of the glacier. Dad and Moms are collecting plants. The nearest cacti are probably six hundred miles from the south tip of the glacier."

"So the lodge is probably in this area somewhere—"

"Assuming that the straight line holds true," Justin said.

"Yeah. Well, additional evidence—"

Edgar spoke softly to Cassandra. "Cassie, I want to look at previous dates when Colonel Weyland took his tracers off-line."

"Weyland data is restricted," Cassandra said.

"Pretty please," Edgar said, and muttered something else Justin couldn't hear.

"Wilco," Cassandra said.

Edgar grinned. "Search *Geographic* satellite watch for unusual infrared spots during just those periods." He looked at Justin, face screwed up in speculation. "Ha. Has he ever made an emergency landing?"

"Last year. A rotor almost went. He was down overnight." Justin searched his memory. "And three years ago. Got caught in a bad storm. Put down overnight."

"The rotor should be on the maintenance records." Edgar muttered to Cassandra. Thermal maps of the glacier flashed by, held for the dates that Cadmann Weyland was known to be on one of his jaunts, and then rolled on. Justin watched in fascination as Edgar searched until two map images came into focus. They looked as if they had been taken from about two miles up, and on each of them, tiny heat pulses flared.

"Campfires." Edgar was utterly smug. "The dates probably match. Your dad put down overnight. First one matches the maintenance record. Second . . . ah. It was one of those nasty little solar-flare storms. Must have gotten hairy up on Isenstine."

"And?"

"Your dad took a hard left turn here. Tricky. Then . . . Skeeter range is five hundred miles. Your father carries at least one spare, and doesn't like to space his fuel dumps further than eight hundred miles apart. That probably puts him about here—"

"Give me a vegetation map," Justin said.

Cassandra displayed some of the vegetation to be found in the area. "He brought back some Avalon succulents last time. Does that narrow things?"

Cassandra searched, and came up with a twenty-square-mile sprawl that met all of the conditions.

"Not bad," Justin said. "Look for heat sources." Four little pulses of red appeared. "'Volcanic, on a cycle?"

"I've got a better idea," Edgar replied. "Cassandra—when was the last routine scan?"

Her familiar voice was warm and cool. "Eighteen hours ago, at the present level of magnification."

"Nighttime. Give me a thermal scan. Compare it to the chart we just made . . . and compare it again to . . . say, anything before three days ago, back to a month."

Edgar turned to Justin. "Does that about cover it? When was the last time your dad was out?"

"About two months."

"Good enough. So all we should have out there are some geysers, and maybe another hunter. Not likely in that little area, but maybe. Exclude all of that, and we'll have his campfire. . . ."

"He likes wood-burning stoves," Justin said suddenly. "He's got a cabin, but it'll have a chimney."

"And . . . bingo."

They were looking directly down at a mass of trees near the eastern edge of Isenstine glacier. "Camouflaged," Edgar mused. "You could skeeter right over and never see it. That fire is stone dead now."

"Dad would put the fire out. He's very serious about that kind of thing."

"So. Time for the stove to cool. Figure he left five hours ago . . ."

Edgar rolled his eyes up, and thought. "With refueling . . . the skeeters make about a hundred and eighty kilometers tops . . . he should be right about . . ." He poked his finger at the map. "Here. Give or take fifty kilometers or so."

He grinned up at Justin. "Betcha," he said, and went for magnification. *Geographic* wasn't in position, but he diverted one of the weather satellites to optical mode. Cassandra kept cleaning up the image, searching for something moving against a white background. . . .

They went in through the mountains, and past the savage crevasses of Isenstine Glacier. Justin could almost feel the cold.

And there it was, a flickering shadow. A red circle enclosed it and Cassandra zoomed in to show something that looked like a brine shrimp larva skittering across a pond. It was there one moment, gone the next. But Cassandra was on its track, now, locked on, and Cadmann was *caught*.

It was Skeeter II, its silver-blue length magnified by satellite optics. The view was from not quite overhead. It was a tiny bit of metal and plastic, a thing of Man flying across an impersonal wasteland. It carried plant samples and three of the human beings Justin Faulkner loved most in all the world.

"He'll need to make one more fuel stop," Edgar said. He laced his fingers behind his head and leaned back in his seat. His round face wore a smile of enormous self-satisfaction. "But that won't take fifteen minutes. This close to home he'll probably want to push it. I'd set ETA at about three hours."

"Edgar . . ." Justin grinned. "Sometimes . . ."

"I know," Edgar said. "Sometimes I amaze even me."

"Three hours before he shows. . . ." Justin glanced at his watch. "I want to get at him with a full report before anyone else can tell him what's happened." He squeezed Edgar's shoulder. "Thanks a lot, Edgar."

"First choice. Stringfish."

"You got it."

Justin ran out of the communications room, ideas and thoughts of saltwater eels swimming dizzily in his head.

4

MOUNT TUSHMORE

To compare
Great things with small . . .
—JOHN MILTON, *Paradise Lost*

The eastern wind turned unexpectedly fierce, burning right through the furs surrounding Cadmann Weyland's face, numbing him to the bone. It had swept across two hundred miles of Isenstine Glacier, picking up speed and dropping in temperature as it came. He shaded his face and cursed as he hauled the re-placement battery across the intervening few meters between the fuel dump and Skeeter II.

Mary Ann remained in the cockpit, her cowled face visible through the pow-dered flurries. She would wait there until the last minute before jumping out to lend a hand. She had always hated the cold.

Sylvia, on the other hand, loved it. She was locking up the foamed plastic dump shed, motions brisk and merry. "That was the last one!" she called over the wind. "We'll have to restock before we take our next run!" Then she crunched across the ice to help with the pushing.

Mary Ann climbed out of the skeeter when they were about ten feet away, and opened the battery bay. She was reluctant, but deft, and had the old trunk-sized cartridge out in about fifteen seconds. It didn't require three of them to lock the new battery into place, but it was good to have the extra hands: unsnap the used-up power cell, swing it to the side, swing new unit into place, snap on connections, slide in, lock down.

Mary Ann shut the unit, puffed a breath of condensation, and said, "Let's get out of here!"

They piled into the autogyro's passenger cab. Cadmann was on pilot's posi-tion on the right, Mary Ann in the middle. Sylvia on the extreme left was last in, and slammed the door behind her. Mary Ann cranked the air blower up to a toasty pitch.

Cadmann watched the wind gauge to get a feel for the gusts. He couldn't take off if they continued to build. The gusts punched at the little gyro, rocking it, but not so hard now. Curtains of powdered snow danced across the glacier in front of them in a somberly beautiful winter ballet.

Mary Ann interrupted his thoughts with a plaintive "Can we get out of here? Please?" She hated that little-girl petulance quality in her voice, but it was there too often. She closed her eyes and hunched forward to catch a little more of the hot air. Cadmann caught Sylvia's eye. She winked at him, and put an arm around Mary Ann to help warm her. Even with the thirty pounds she'd gained since their second child, Mary Ann possessed little tolerance for cold weather, but despite her discomfort she rarely let Cadmann and Sylvia go on these trips without her.

There were times when Mary Ann couldn't accept comforting from Sylvia, when any gesture of kindness or warmth triggered a burst of resentment. This wasn't one of them. They pushed tight against each other. Sylvia tucked a thermal blanket around them both. Sylvia's teeth were chattering, but she still managed to smile.

"Cad?" she said. "If you don't get this thing into the air, we may walk home."

He nodded without speaking, still trying to read the gusts. He patched into Cassandra on a secure line, and got a quick weather feed: no sign of the quick, violent storms that made traversing Isenstine so hazardous. This was just bad wind, not likely to get much worse. Carefully he engaged the engines, satisfied with the steady hum as the new fuel cell sparked to life. Nose and top and tail rotors spun into blurred motion one at a time, whipping more snow from the ground. He engaged the de-icers and the wiper blades.

"All right. Buckle in," he said unnecessarily. He was almost embarrassed to say that to adults. It was just a habit he had gotten into, three kids ago. The kids were pretty much grown now, but the reflex remained.

The skeeter leaned foward against the wind and began to scoot along the ice. Then, nose-heavy, it lifted from the ground, spun a quarter-turn as a gust punched them, and rose into the sky.

Mary Ann poked her head out from under the blanket and breathed a sigh of relief. "Bet it's calmer up about two thousand feet," she said.

"Bet you're right," he said. His hands were locked surely on the controls now. At eighteen hundred feet they hit low cloud cover, rocked for fifteen seconds, and then climbed up into relative stillness.

Tau Ceti transmuted the clouds into banks of gold-white fluff. The air was crisp and clear. The window didn't quite seal on his side, and a bright, Arctic thread of air whistled through, stinging and invigorating.

This was good, one of those moments that made the rest of it all worthwhile. He felt the calm descend upon Sylvia and Mary Ann as well. Here, floating above the clouds, there seemed to be no troubles. Tau Ceti IV was a world of wonders, a calm and nurturing land which would feed and shelter their grandchildren as graciously as it served them. This was a time when he could forget the internecine conflicts within the colony, and the occasional friction between Mary Ann and Sylvia.

There had been less of that for the past year. He thought . . . he *hoped* . . . they had weathered the last true storm in their triad. There were too few Western precedents for three-way relationships.

There was nothing standard about relationships on Avalon. The naked truth was that, in an almost exclusively heterosexual community, there were more women than men to bond with them. There was also no venereal disease. There was one hundred percent employment. Someone would care for the children, whatever the mother's interests and temperament. As a result, no woman need consider anything except who might make the most interesting father. There was no stigma at all for the unwed mother.

But some institutions die hard, and marriage, even such free-form versions of it as existed in Camelot, was one of them.

Cadmann and Sylvia had been friends, perhaps in love but not lovers, when the first grendel attacks shattered the colony's tranquil life and sent Cadmann off to the Bluff. Mary Ann had gone to him then, and helped build the Keep. It was as much hers as his.

Cadmann and Mary Ann had been bonded for years before Sylvia, widowed during the Grendel Wars, had joined them. Mostly, it worked. Sometimes wonderfully well. Occasionally it grated . . . usually on Mary Ann, who remembered when she had Cadmann all to herself, when no one else would have wanted him. No one but Sylvia, who was already married, back when monogamy made sense, before the grendels killed so many of the men.

They were probably two hours from the Bluff, and Mary Ann was getting drowsy. Air travel often did that to her. She leaned against his shoulder, bouncing a little in her shoulder harness. Sylvia looked across at him. Sometimes he wondered exactly what she saw. He knew what *he* saw in the mirror when he scraped his morning stubble away: a tall, gray old stranger who looked a lot like his own grandfather . . . or Manuel the Redeemer, or any of Cabell's male characters who were so surprised to find themselves old. Still strong, and unbent, but the hair crept back from his temples now. Both weather and time had creased his skin deeply.

God. Where had the years gone? When was the last time he had awakened without his back flaming at him? He was . . . he counted rapidly. Sixty-three Earth years old? There was little he could do to avoid the fact that his body was trying to shut down on him. Oh, growth-hormone stimulation, and exercise, and a strict nutritional regimen, and regeneration treatments kept the machine functioning better than he probably deserved, but the aches and pains of a life nowise tame had definitely caught up with him. There were bullet wounds, a bayonet scar . . . even a goddamn crocodile bite.

All trivial next to the wounds from the Grendel Wars. Bones smashed. The regrown leg. The pale angry tattoo left by serrated grendel teeth. And the memories that would never completely fade.

And perhaps, after all, it was best that they didn't. The grendels were gone, but there were other dangers.

"Good trip," Sylvia said. She could always sense his mood. She was forty-seven now, still beautiful, although daily exposure to the sun had roughened her skin. The mask of youth was beginning to slip, but in her case that was no tragedy. Disguise your thoughts and inclinations as you may, time eventually reveals your true nature to the world. Sylvia was a loving heart in a lively, quick-spirited physical package, a little shorter than Mary Ann, but stronger. She had borne her late husband Terry one child, Justin, and then another for Cadmann, and her figure was still luscious.

Mary Ann was Number One Wife—and she relished the distinction. Needed it. There was little in this life for Mary Ann, save being Cadmann Weyland's woman. Sylvia remained a competent scientist. Mary Ann had ice on her mind. Sometimes she could remember, sometimes there were flashes of brilliance, but sometimes she was lucky to remember the difference between the gametophyte and sporophyte stages of a fern. Once upon a time she had been a brilliant agronomist, but hibernation instability . . . for Mary Ann, the memories of what she had once been were the worst part.

She was still important as Cadmann Weyland's Number One Wife, and as the mother of strong and self-reliant children. *I make good babies,* she told herself, and everyone knew it was true. Over the years that had come to be enough. It had to be.

Home, Cadmann thought, remembering Sylvia's attempt at conversation. "I think I want to break out the east wall of the house, expand it again."

"You've got my permission, God knows."

She gazed out the window at the clear sky, and then peered down at the clouds. "So peaceful up here."

"I need these trips from time to time. Just get away with my ladies."

She reached across Mary Ann's sleeping form, and grasped Cadmann's shoulder hard. So much unsaid. So much that could never be said.

Cadmann's thoughts threatened to drift into another uncomfortable direction, and he focused back on the task of flying. Ahead of them reared a great beveled splay of glacial crust: Clay's Divide, an eight-mile seismic irregularity in the Isenstine. He grinned, anticipating the moment to come.

As the skeeter scooted over the gargantuan sheet of rock and ice, Sylvia began to chuckle. Then they both broke out hooting. Mary Ann was awake now, and smiling. The far side of the divide had been carved—by some unknown thermal device—into Avalon's own Mount Rushmore. Presented for all the world to see were four two-hundred-foot-tall sets of very human buttocks. Anatomical detail was admirably precise. Mount Tushmore was so huge that it had to be seen from at least a kilometer away to be fully appreciated.

Geographic had spotted it first, almost a year before. The general hilarity and grudging admiration was balanced by alarm. How *had* they done it? And who? Well, the Merry Pranksters, of course, but who were *they*? Justin and Jessica knew, Cadmann thought; one or the other of them might actually *be* a Prankster. But there was no way that the carving of Mount Tushmore could have been anything less than perilous. The danger doubtless added to their plesaure in the deed.

"If we knew . . ." he said finally, hovering at approximately anus-level with the second buttock on the left. A flat, petal-shaped protrusion marred the surface just below the right cheek. ". . . whether *that* was just an irregularity in the rock, or a birthmark, it might be possible to figure out just whose buttocks these were. . . ."

"But . . ." Sylvia choked, "and that's a *big* but . . . that still wouldn't establish whether the owner of said birthmarked buttocks was in fact the perpetrator."

"How true," Cadmann said. "It would be just like those rascals to display someone else's buttocks, just to throw us . . . off the scent. As it were."

"Ahem."

He spun the skeeter around and headed back north. He pointed his forefinger at Mary Ann, thumb cocked, and Mary Ann said, "I do hate to leave it behind."

About fifty miles from the Bluff, Cadmann engaged his communications link. Immediately Cassandra's familiar voice said, "There are seventeen messages waiting for you, Colonel."

He sighed. "Any of them emergency?"

"In case of an emergency message I would have initiated contact despite your request for isolation," she chided gently. "You have several priority dispatches, but no emergency."

"Hmmm . . . sort and play."

There was a beep, and before Cassandra could broadcast an old message, the air crackled. *"Dad! Are you there?"*

"Absolutely. Justin?"

"Glad you're on line."

"Problems?"

"We've had a little excitement since you left."

"Like what?"

"That would be telling. Why don't you just fly straight to Aquatics, Dad—and promise me something?"

"Like what?"

"That you'll try to keep an open mind."

"You implying I have a problem in that department?"

"First edition: Oxford-Avalonian Dictionary. Verb: 'Weylandize.' Definition: to render inflexible."

"Hah hah. Want to give me a hint?"

"I think not. See you in about twenty minutes. And first-class promise about that open mind, remember?"

"Remember."

Cadmann took himself back off line for a moment. Mary Ann was shaking herself awake. "What was that?"

"Our eldest boy. He's got a surprise for me. At Aquatics. . . ." His thumb hovered over the control panel. If he touched the switch again, Cassandra would come back on, and in all probability tell him more about the surprise than he really wanted to hear.

I'll let it be a mystery, he thought.

All right, Justin, m'boy. Thrill me.

* * *

The skeeter pad was clear as they dropped down toward Aquatics. A small crowd had already gathered around it, with another clutch of curiosity-seekers ringing one of the dolphin pens. Dolphins . . . ? Had Quanda and Hipshot finally made the beast with two backs, or whatever it was that dolphins did? But that wouldn't be a priority call—

He hovered for a moment, until the crowd backed farther away. There had only been one skeeter accident on Avalon, but that was enough. A sudden gust of wind, and Harry Siep's arm was spurting in the dust. Lucky for Harry. It could have been his head, and heads were much more difficult to reattach.

They spun down into a perfect landing. Mary Ann threw aside her blanket, and stretched like a big chubby blond cat as the rotors began to slow. Before Cadmann could open the door Jessica was there, golden and radiant, flinging it aside to buss him soundly.

Seeing her made him sigh. She possessed all of her mother's beauty, and she didn't have ice on her mind. "Daddy," she whispered in his ear, as intimate as a lover, "we've really got something."

He stepped down from the skeeter, and was immediately awash in comments from the rest of the crowd. He waved an awkward hello. As always, he had the sense that the group was *waiting* for something. Some proclamation, some reaction from him. They hung on his words as if his opinion meant more than all the rest of theirs combined. It was this as much as anything that created his intermittent need to escape, to be off in the south hunting, or fishing, or collecting plants. On such trips he turned his goddamned tracer off. Nothing but an emergency message was authorized to break through. Zack had "tested" that precisely once. No one else even tried.

Cadmann helped Mary Ann down, and she immediately turned to hug Jessica. Occasionally he suspected that there was some communication between mother and daughter from which he was utterly excluded, some dark and intimate female understanding.

At the moment Jessica was all showboat, twinkly and vibrating with secret knowledge, hugging Sylvia to give both mothers equal attention, then linking arms with Cadmann. Without another word she marched the three of them into the Aquatics building.

Justin opened the door for them.

Cadmann entered, and held his breath.

"Jesus Christ . . ." he started. He was frozen, felt the chill right down to his heels. The beast reminded him of a moray, in some ways . . . but it was a good deal larger. "You dredge this out of the Deeps?"

"Damn near grabbed it out of your living room, Dad," Jessica said. Justin quickly recounted their adventure. Cadmann stared at Sylvia and then at Mary Ann. He excused himself brusquely and went outside to break through the ring of observers surrounding the dolphin tank. He needed a look at the beast itself.

A large yellowish plastic bubble framed the tank, and several wet oily splotches on the inside suggested that the eel had attempted escape. It glided through the water, swishing hard from side to side, around and around endlessly, expending vast energy. Jessica and Justin appeared behind him.

"Does it eat?"

"Sure does. Anything that swims. The dolphins have been sharing."

"Has Big Chaka looked at this yet?"

"He'll fly in from the coast this evening," Jessica said. "Little Chaka's run a simulation."

"And?"

Little Chaka spoke from just behind him. The voice was always deep and res-onant, and a little surprising because it came from slightly above him. Only two people in the world were taller than Cadmann. "It lived in the Deeps," Chaka said, "and came upstream to lay eggs."

"It eats fish. Land animals too?"

"If it could swallow them whole. It's not built to carve out steaks. But I think we're seeing it at the end of its life cycle. This is an old creature. What passes for a liver is operating at maybe fifty percent. I think it will be dead in a year. Have to ask Father, of course."

"Could it have had legs early in its cycle?"

"Intersting idea, but Cassandra says no. The eggs are almost mature—"

"Eggs?"

"Yes, we've got samples. What she's producing are thousands of little eely things that look just like Mama. No sign of legs. I think that Mama Eel is pri-marily aquatic, and can survive out of the water just long enough to get back upstream. She really prefers salt water to fresh. No sign of *speed* sacs or anything like them. This is a pretty standard animal. Not a lot of surprises."

Cadmann heard Chaka's voice as if it came from the bottom of a rain barrel. A sudden wave of fatigue washed over him, hot and clammy, transmuting his limbs to lead. In his suddenly blurred vision, the thing in the water began to transmute. It grew legs, and its tail fattened. It reared up out of the tank with its huge, savagely powerful teeth drizzling blood, and snapped down just inches from his foot, and—

He shook his head, and all was normal again. A perfectly harmless eel swished angrily through the water. Harmless. Captured.

Swish, swish.

"So why has it come back?"

"To breed," someone said.

"What Colonel Weyland meant was why *now?*" Chaka said. "And we don't know."

Cadmann turned to stare northward toward the mainland.

"Dad, we'll have to go," Jessica said.

He nodded. The eel would start that debate again. It was time for a full-dress expedition to the mainland, had been for years. He'd always known they would have to go there.

Someday. He had no taste for it. After the Grendel Wars, he had thought he wanted that, and had made two trips to the mainland, the second shorter than the first. He had bagged a grendel with the new grendel guns, and been holo'ed grinning next to his prize.

But something had altered within him, some subtle tidal change in his bones.

If there was anything he needed to prove about himself, he would prove it here, on the island. And if there was anything that he needed to know about grendels, he would allow others to learn it for him.

He lived with awful, bloody dreams in which all of their efforts had meant nothing. In his sleeping mind, rapacious demons had rolled over the colony like a red tide, killing everything, everyone. The few dozen survivors stranded up in *Geographic* could hear the screams, and see the blood, but they couldn't come down. Couldn't ever come down. And stayed up there until they slowly ran out of food . . . and water . . . and air.

Waking, he would shrug away the dreams. He didn't want to know how narrowly sanity had been preserved. And when he thought about going back to the mainland, he wondered what would happen if another grendel ever touched him. He wondered if he could take it. If his sanity would hold.

He didn't ever want to find out.

". . . Zack," Justin said, pulling him out of his reverie.

"Zack?"

"Wants to kill it. And the eggs."

He felt an instantaneous, visceral flash of agreement, followed swiftly by the voice of reason. "As long as it's not dangerous that's not his decision to make," Cadmann said. He pointed to the tank cover. "Your idea?"

Jessica looked sheepish. "Zack ordered a cover."

"Good."

She hesitated. "We didn't put it on, until the eel tried to escape. Took three of us with poles to keep it in. Then we put up the cover."

"Not when Zack told you to?"

"No, sir."

"He had the authority to order that. Do you dispute it?"

"No, Dad, it just seemed—"

Cadmann shook his head. "Jessica, we've been through this before. Zack is chairman and governor, and we don't lightly disobey him."

"You did. You rebelled—"

"Exactly," Cadmann said. "I rebelled. Some things are important enough for that. But you don't do it lightly! I take it your researchers found the cover inconvenient—"

She looked at her feet.

"So you ignored a valid order because it wasn't convenient. Do I have to say anything else?"

"No, sir. But he wanted to kill it, too! And we found it at the Bluff, not down here!"

"And at the Bluff you and your brother had every right to do what you thought right," Cadmann said wearily. "Not here."

"It'll go to a vote," Jessica said. "Can we rely on you?"

"To approve keeping it alive? Yes." He thought for a moment. "That's not all that will go to a vote. The next question will be about the mainland, you know. We need that major expedition. Not just quick trips to initiate Grendel Scouts, a study expedition . . ."

"Yes," Justin said. "Joe Sikes thinks so too. Something's going wrong with the mining robots."

Something in Justin's tone made Cadmann frown. "Eh?"

"Don't know. Joe thinks it's Star Born. But it's not, it's another Avalon surprise."

Cadmann nodded. "And the ecology returns to Camelot. The wind blows from the north part of the year. God knows what may get rafted over here. We have to know what else may come."

"Avalonian homing pigeons," Justin offered. Jessica looked pained. "And no grendels here to eat them. We're likely to be up to our clavicles in something."

"There haven't been for twenty years," Jessica offered.

"There weren't any eels for twenty years, either," Justin said.

Cadmann frowned. "Good point. And the ecology *is* returning. Not just the eel. Why now?" He nodded in submission. "I suppose there will need to be . . . some kind of expedition."

"We can plan it on the next Grendel Scout outing," Justin said.

"Saftey—"

Justin grinned. "We can work that out, Dad. We can work it all out. We just want to know that, if it comes to a fight, you'll be on our side."

Cadmann hesitated.

"Or at least not against us," Jessica added swiftly.

Cadmann considered them both. The fear was in *him*, dammit, not in them. Fear would be a horrible legacy to bestow upon his children. And—it was their world, more and more it was their world. They hadn't asked to be born here.

Cadmann often wondered what the children—the Star Born—thought about that. Did they resent being born here, denied the heritage of Earth? Earth, the solar system, crowded, teeming with humanity, and with the crowding came rules, rules, rules— He had come here to escape the rules. And now they had rules because they couldn't trust their own damaged brains.

And it's their world, not ours.

"Open mind," he said. "I'm already bound, right, Justin?"

5

THE MODERN PROMETHEUS

God bless the King, I mean the Faith's Defender;
God bless—no harm in blessing—the Pretender;
But who Pretender is, or who is King,
God bless us all—that's quite another thing.
                    —JOHN BYROM, to an officer in the Army

The debate was already in full swing as Cadmann entered the town hall. The hall fairly shimmered with the aromas of the communal meal: mutton and turkey, bakery smells, mustard greens, and steamed corn fresh from the fields. It was a laughing, murmuring, jostling family chaos. Three hundred, nearly every Earth Born, most of the Star Born, all of the Grendel Scouts, many children. There were tables and seats for more than seven hundred, and that was a reminder of what population they had expected to have before the grendels nearly destroyed them.

The tables were tiered in amphitheater rows beneath the corrugated roof, grouped around a central stage. And on that stage a tall, stocky, golden young man stood at the podium, commanding their attention by his words and stance and very being. His voice was a master orator's. Every word from the thin, sensuous mouth cut as precisely as a razor. He was Cadmann's height, and beautifully muscled. A shock of flaxen hair fell to his shoulders. His eyes were a startling blue-green, electric in their intensity. Tau Ceti had burnt his eyebrows so blond they were almost white.

The young man's cheeks were healthfully hollow, his every motion perfectly judged as he emphasized his major points. Almost every sentence was punctuated by a cheer from the Surf's Up contingent, come inland for the weekly debate.

Aaron Tragon. Star Born indeed.

Cadmann listened distractedly as he found his way to the table reserved for him by Carlos and Angelica, the thin dark surgeon who was Carlos's most recent companion.

"—ladies in the audience will agree that the automatic tendency of most males is to assume a power structure which escalates from woman to man to God Almighty. This, at any rate, was the most frequent view of the nineteenth century—"

Cadmann slipped in next to Carlos and slapped his shoulder. "*Hola,* Carlos."

"*Hola.*"

"Hello, Dad."

Cadmann smiled warmly at his younger son. "Ho. What brings you down from the mines?"

Mickey shrugged and looked at Mary Ann, but he didn't say anything, which was typical for Mickey. He seldom talked and when he did not many listened to him. Mickey was smart enough, but somehow he hadn't learned to communicate.

Cadmann stood to hug Mary Ann, and kiss Sylvia briefly. "How's the debate going?"

"Stevens is in trouble."

"Has Aaron reached the Refutatio yet?"

"Beyond that. He's in the Digressio, and I suspect that the Peroratio will be an ass-kicker."

"I like the subject—"

Even without electronic enhancement, Aaron Tragon's voice rose up to embrace them. "—Shelley's modern Prometheus intended to steal not the flames of a distant Olympus, but those of Woman. And how natural for men, reading *Frankenstein*, to be deceived by her into believing that it spoke of a man's attempt to steal the divine privilege."

Aaron leaned forward over his podium, slamming his palm flat against the wood. "But her mother's blood ran in her! Mary Wollstonecraft, the first feminist, author of *The Rights of Woman*, was smiling on her daughter. And when Mary Wollstonecraft Shelley wrote of a man's monstrous hubris, his ego, his attempt to stitch together from chunks of dead and decaying flesh an imitation of life, what she truly illustrated was Man's fear of Woman's creative power. His vulnerability to that fear birthed an attempt to do without her altogether."

He paused for a dramatic moment. "Did not men's fear of women keep her a second-class citizen? Deprive her of education, of legal recourse, of the vote, of knowledge of the methods of self-defense, that she might remain chattel?"

Cadmann clucked to himself, and then looked across the room, seeking Zack's daughter Ruth. It took him a moment, but he picked her out. She was sitting at Rachael's side, leaning forward on her plump forearms, brown hair brushed back from her face, listening as if she were devouring every word. She was rapt, so attentive and worshipful it hurt to watch. If the girl weren't seventeen years old, he would have called it the worst case of puppy love he'd ever seen. As it was, her infatuation was just one of the colony's most notoriously open secrets.

In comparison . . .

He stole a sidewise glance at Mary Ann. She leaned backward in her chair, trying to put distance between herself and Aaron Tragon. Her mouth was drawn into a thin, disapproving line. She was nodding to herself, as if indulging in some kind of internal monologue.

So Mary Ann had a problem with Aaron. *Somebody* had to have one. Aside from Mary Ann, everyone just flat seemed to love the boy . . . then again, Joe Sikes wasn't all that fond of Aaron either. But it was a short list.

Aaron Tragon was exceptional. Good at almost everything he did. For Cadmann's money, that was an overcompensation, a positive side effect of Aaron Tragon's Bottle Baby complex.

The Bottle Babies were seventeen embryos raised totally in vitro, activated after the Grendel Wars and decanted nine months later. By then it had become clear that the fertility rate among the surviving women was quite adequate to replenish the colony, thank you, and the In Vitro project was suspended. Hundreds of embryos remained aboard *Geographic*. Aaron Tragon had been one of the first. Derik, the big redhead, and Trish the gorgeous black bodybuilder, and Little Chaka, who might be the strongest man on the planet, were also clustered up there in the first ten. They were Aaron's constant companions, and only Little Chaka seemed more than a follower.

The three of them seemed to be sharing a joke on the rest of the colony, one which they declined to share.

They were children of the colony, unrelated to anyone on the expedition, raised by everyone. With the notable exception of Little Chaka, few had bonded to anyone in particular. Mary Ann had always thought it a terrible idea. She thought they should be adopted into families, but she'd only shared her opinions with Cadmann.

Seems to have worked out all right. They seem like decent kids. Work hard. Come to that, Aaron did live with Joe Sikes for a few years, when he was what, ten or twelve, up until Edgar had the accident. . . .

"—being a man, I stand to gain little by making these claims. Being a man of the twenty-second century, in which we might have hoped that women would be loosed from their biological bondage, perhaps I could have another intent. For is not the drive to 'free' woman from her biological 'enslavement' also an attempt to lessen her importance? To steal her fire? Are we not then a breed of Prometheans? What happens to us, when this difference is reduced to a mere whim, or a matter of legal designation? I cannot say. I merely propose an interpretation of literary pentimento. As for the rest of it, I trust that wiser minds than my own will probe whatever additional truths might be found therein."

Aaron Tragon bowed massively to Stevens, his challenger. Stevens was slight, scholarly, managed the mining operation east of the colony where Cadmann's son Mickey spent most of his time. Their positions in the debate had been chosen by lot. From the wildly enthusiastic applause, Cadmann guessed that Stevens had been slaughtered.

The food service staff came around, took their orders, and brought sustenance. Cadmann relaxed into his meal, enjoying the spirited debate which surrounded him.

Carlos shook his head. "What do you think, Cadmann?"

"*Frankenstein* as a crypto-feminist tract? Not on purpose. Nobody writes a tract that good . . . that close to immortal. How did Stevens do?"

"His *Exordium* was pathetic. The *Narratio* was barely adequate, and his *Refu-tatio* was booed off the stage. Aside from that, just fine."

Around them, Cadmann noticed that women's voices were climbing a bit higher than the men's. As Tragon left the stage he joined Jessica. They embraced and kissed lustily.

They make a good pair, Cadmann thought. Aaron Tragon was brawny, handsome, fiercely intelligent, and possessed a magnetic presence. *My successor here. Zack's too? End this silly division between administration and security?*

In any tribe, there is an alpha. There had been a time when Cadmann thought Mickey would be his heir. He often wondered if he had pushed his son too hard. Whatever happened, Mickey wasn't interested in leadership.

Aaron and Linda were paired for a while. A good combination, but then something happened and Linda attached herself to Joe Sikes. An unlikely arrangement, and one that Cadmann didn't quite understand. Joe Sikes had been Mary Ann's lover before the grendel attacks, before Mary Ann had come to the Bluff to reclaim Cadmann from drunken despair. There had been nothing after that—then suddenly Joe and Mary Ann's daughter were paired, not merely paired but monogamously bonded.

Ruth Moskowitz moved toward Aaron, then back away. She had the faintly shell-shocked grin he'd expected. Good sport. *Hey, if he likes Jessica, all right.* The fingers of her right hand were twisting painfully tight ringlets in her hair. Probably pulling out a few strands. Rachael put an arm around her, and held her daughter close. *And that's another situation I don't understand, but I don't think I have to.*

Surf's Up provided dessert. A deliciously spiced crushed ice, its taste and aroma resurrected long-buried memories of childhood.

The audience decided, quite vociferously, that Aaron Tragon had triumphed in the week's debate. After a thunderous round of applause, Linda Weyland took the podium. Cadzie was bundled in a sling across her chest, and nursed contentedly as she spoke.

"Unfortunately," she began, "that concludes the evening's entertainment. What I have to say now is more sobering—and far more educational. Cassandra, *bang.*"

A glowing anthill filled the hall; it brightened as the hall lights dimmed.

Neon vermilion tunnels, dozens of them. Hundreds of bright green dots chewed at the tips, extending the tunnels, then flowed back up to the trunk of the beast. Cadmann remembered an ant farm his brother had built when both were small. These tunnels had more of a fractal look. Despite irrgularities in the topography of this mainland mountain range, the automated widgets were following a plan; you saw a symmetry, large patterns repeated in diminishing scale.

In the tip of a tunnel, light flared. A conspicuous shock wave, confined, flowed upward to a main trunk. Refining machinery flared red, then pulsed red-black, red-black.

The crowd's whispered reaction was immediate, and ugly.

Linda raised her voice above the sound of that evil wind. "Something exploded. Not high explosive, something more like gunpowder. How it got down there . . . well. All we *know* is that the refinery has shut down, and we can't correct the damage from here."

Toshiro raised a hand. "Couldn't this be any sort of normal equipment failure?"

Linda said, "Toshiro, these bore collectors are just drills and a bucket for the ore. They run on solar cells and fuel cells, the fuel cells are just high-tech batteries, they can't explode, and there aren't any fuel cells where we're having the problem anyway."

"Of course you thought about this before. Sorry."

"It's okay. But people, it really *was* an explosion, and it really *did* come roaring up from the tip of a bore tube. Cassandra, show us the interference waves."

Which wasn't a lot of help, Cadmann thought. And there was Mary Ann, delighted, proud of their daughter, and knowing damned well *he* couldn't read the patterns now flowing across the wall *either*. Mickey probably could, but he wasn't saying anything.

Cadmann leaned over to Carlos. "Did you know about this? Anything at all?"

"News to me, amigo. And I don't like the sound of it." Carlos stood and thrust his hand aggressively into the air. "Request to be recognized."

"Sure," Linda said.

Carlos cleared his throat. "There is a word which hasn't been spoken, but which I sense may be on many minds. The word is *sabotage*, and there are a thousand reasons to believe that no one here would do such a thing. This is no prank. It's the wrong style. It profits no one and it isn't funny. Before we form any opinions, I assume that arrangements are being made for an on-site inspection?"

Linda petted the baby, looked out to her husband for a moment, and nodded. "Why would it be sabotage? How could anyone have put an explosire *there*? A gnat couldn't get into those tunnels. Of course we'll go look at the machinery. We'll look, and we'll find out it was something weird. Avalon Surprise!"

Tip of a tunnel. No Merry Prankster could have crawled down a tunnel, Cadmann thought. Too narrow, and the central processing plant was a metal plug massing hundreds of tons. The mine was all nanotechnology; it had been growing in place for seventeen years. The tunnels led to it, not past it.

Cadmann leaned toward his son. "Mickey? You know mines. Any suggestions?"

Mickey frowned and shook his head. "Avalon Weird," he muttered, but not loud enough for anyone but Cadmann to hear.

As good as any other theory, Cadmann thought. You couldn't even . . . hmm. Cause a bore collector to *deposit* a charge of dynamite or gunpowder? Acquired how? From the fuel cell dump? A bore collector had been at work when the explosion happened.

It would have been a hell of a difficult prank. Would it be enough for the

Merry Pranksters that it was impossible? There didn't seem to be any other motive. The mine was the colony's metal source. Why choke that off?

Joe Sikes limped up to the platform. "Linda's right, it's Avalon Weird. Something else about this planet we don't know. Something that happens on the mainland and not here."

"And it's time to take the Grendel Scout candidates over to the mainland anyway," Linda finished for him. "I just wanted everyone to see how much trouble this was causing. . . ."

She thinks it's sabotage, Cadmann thought. *I guess I do too. "Impossible" is a challenge to the Surf's Up crowd.*

"So what should we do?" someone asked. "Can we fix it?"

"We have to go look," Linda said. "There's no point in fixing it until we know what happened."

There's that tone again. She really does believe it's the pranksters. They get their joke and the mainland expedition they want all at once. Linda hates this, and she's talked Joe into leaving it lay. Wonder if that's the right approach?

It was clear enough that Joe would prefer it was the Pranksters. That would give him the moral high ground. Joe seriously wanted to be an alpha male, particularly now that he'd hooked up with a much younger woman.

Cadmann would have stopped that marriage if he could. He still wondered what they saw in each other. Because Linda looked very like her mother, and Mary Ann had slept with Joe Sikes before Cadmann staked his claim? *Be honest. She reclaimed me from an alcoholic fog. It's her claim on me, not the other way around. . . .*

Old news. Cadmann Weyland's effector nerves didn't extend into other human beings, not even into his daughter. It was a thing he had to relearn constantly.

Meanwhile: the bomb.

It was a difficult prank, but possible. Develop your own nano-beasties. Or drill straight down from the surface to where a convenient bore collector would be in a week, or a month, if you could just work out the damned fractal pattern—

But it didn't *feel* right, and Cadmann felt the hairs trying to stand up along his neck and arms. An Avalon Surprise, on the mainland, where there are dragons. Alarum: Linda would go to the mainland with his grandson. She never left Cadzie. Mary Ann had raised her children the same way, with lots of affection and bonding.

Linda and Joe knew those mines better than anyone, and they had no clue, so what was more probable? This didn't feel like the Pranksters. It was destructive and unfunny. And if not them, than an Avalon Surprise: like the grendels.

Mary Ann's hand closed over his. "Penny?"

"Bad bargain," he said quietly. "Bad memories. I'm going to be helpless again."

"You don't like that feeling, do you?"

"Being tied to a table with a grendel in my lap. Being tied to this island while my grandson is half a world away."

"Go with them."

"I don't think they want Daddy tagging along." And what he didn't say was: *I've had enough, Mary Ann. I don't want any more excitement. I've had all I need for one lifetime. Let someone else deal with the damned dragons.*

And Linda was handling herself beautifully. She was in a spot: she had to admit the possibility of sabotage—but could only admit it to herself. She couldn't let that uncertainty infect the Earth Born. On the other hand, she had to let potential perpetrators know she knew, and hope to God they had enough sense to stop.

A fine line, indeed.

There was another general murmur, and both Jessica and Little Chaka raised their hands.

"Jessie," Linda said. "You wanted to say something?"

Jessica pushed Little Chaka ahead of her, and they both strode onto the stage. Linda and Joe Sikes retired hand in hand to their seats. Chaka strode to the podium and blinked at the crowd. "Cassandra, display my Long Mama Demo, please."

The screen behind him lit to show the eel struggling up the Amazon, flashed ahead to show it in the glacial pool, then cut to the covered tank where it glared up at the camera. "Our visitor. She's not really an eel, but that's the closest thing Earth evolved to this, a big saltwater eel."

"Sure startled me!" Jessica said. "Came right into the living room at the Hold."

Someone guffawed and an adult voice shouted. "Good thing for Long Mama Cadmann wasn't home!"

Chaka grinned uncertainly and started over. "I looked at everything Cassandra knows about eels back on Earth," he said. "It isn't really an eel, but it's interesting, eels on Earth go long distances to spawn, and that's what Long Mama was doing, trying to find the headwaters of the Amazon, following instinctive patterns that might be ten or ten thousand generations old."

"Not ten thousand," someone shouted.

Chaka frowned in thought, and Jessica came to join him at the podium. "Probably not ten thousand generations," Jessica said. "I agree, it's likely that anything that carried those genes would have been wiped out by grendels. But we don't know!"

Chaka had found his voice. "A shorter time argues that the grendels came to the island fairly recently," he said.

"And makes our point!" Jessica said in triumph. "It's inevitable, really inevitable, the natural ecology of Camelot will come back now that the grendels are gone. Sorry, Chaka."

He nodded absently. "The natural ecology will come back. Shouldn't we know more about it?"

"Won't be the same." Edgar Sikes's nasal whine came from the audience. "Can't be."

"I know, Edgar. We've seeded the island with Earth species," Chaka said. "When they mix, it'll get interesting. But we'd like to guess what any Avalon life-form will *do* to us."

"Tell us more about the worm," someone called. An adult voice.

"Carolyn," Sylvia whispered. "She sounds scared."

"I don't blame her," Mary Ann said.

Chaka didn't seem to notice the fear. He spoke eagerly. "We've only had the eel a few days. And she's just one piece of the pattern! We don't know how she interacts with other life, with climate, with grendels for that matter. We don't know what prompted her to swim upstream *now*, now when so many other Camelot species are changing their habits. We need to know what the mainland ecology is doing. Are things changing there, too?"

"And what eats grendels?" A child's voice from the back of the room. Several older children shushed him.

"Big grendels eat grendels. I've been over there," Joe Sikes said with belligerent pride. "That's your ecology, Chaka. Big grendels, little grendels, grendels that live in snow, water grendels, grendels that build dams, grendels that *are* dams. Grendels eat grendels, and they deserve each other. There aren't any grendels here, and by God we'll keep it that way, so why do we care how our stupid eel interacts with grendels?"

"That's not fair," Jessica said.

Chaka cleared his throat. He sounded more positive now. "We do have to know, Joe. What you don't know can kill you. If you hadn't known grendels need to cool off . . . ?"

There were murmurs of approval from the tables where the Surf's Up crowd sat. Linda nodded and pulled Joe Sikes back into his seat; and Joe didn't resist. *You wouldn't have dumped burning kerosene into the Amazon Creek,* Chaka hadn't needed to say, *to sear the grendels raging through humanity's last refuge.*

"We have to know," Chaka repeated, "and it should be clear there's only one way to find out. We need a full expedition to the mainland. A permanent base there. Not just trips to the highlands, mine inspections. We need a full biological team in place to study the mainland, study it *now*, before the winds carry Earth species from Camelot to the mainland, because once that happens we'll never know!"

"Now just a minute!" Zack Moskowitz half rose. "If it comes to that, we don't have to know—"

More murmurs. Cadmann frowned in thought.

"Wrong way to talk to the youngsters," Carlos said.

"We do have to know," Chaka said. Jessica nodded vigorous approval as Little Chaka stood to his full height and let his voice rise. "We must study what is there now, we must understand the natural ecosystem, or we will be caught unprepared. For the past twenty years you have ignored this truth, the truth that it is impossible to live on this planet and hide from it at the same time. I say that this is *our* world, and we don't know enough about it. It's time we learned."

There was loud applause from the Star Born, mostly silence from the First Generation.

"And we'll need all the resources, here *and* the mainland," Coleen McAndrews said. Her voice was as serious as a fifteen-year-old's can be. "To go back to the stars!"

The audience buzzed like an angry hive. There was no organized back-to-the-stars group, and no real leader, but the issue cut across the generations. *No leader yet,* Cadmann thought. *But when that girl grows up and all that enthusiasm matures we'll have another political fight. Lord, lord, why did we think we left all that behind when we came here?*

Zack Moskowitz rose. He took his place at the second podium, across the stage from Chaka. "I think," Zack said, "that an issue as important as this one should be considered as formally as possible. I propose a debate a week from today—"

"No!" Jessica stood, flushing.

"The chair hasn't recognized you, young lady."

"The chair didn't recognize you either, Zack!"

"You know that I am the chairman—"

"Of formal discussions, yes. But this isn't a regular meeting, it's an after-dinner discussion. You can't just run roughshod over it like you do over everything else, Zack. This is too important. Are you declaring an emergency meeting?"

"No—"

"Then wait for Chaka to recognize you."

Zack looked to Cadmann for support. The king appeals to the warrior, but the warrior was ignoring him. Zack stifled his protest. "Very well. I will turn the floor back to Chaka. Chaka? May I be recognized?"

Little Chaka's white teeth gleamed. "Jessica first," he said, "and then you."

Zack smiled sourly.

Jessica took the podium. "The time to decide this is now. We're already taking the Grendel Scouts over, and we've got to send a repair crew as well. It's the right time. Make this the beginning of a permanent base."

"For what?" Zack said.

"For what? To learn about our world," Jessica said. "We need toxological tests, soil tests, we need to know about parasites. The highlands would be perfect for an initial base. *That's* safe, at least."

She looked as if she had more to say, but had changed her mind about saying it. "Chaka, can we alter this format?"

"Into what form?"

"Informal debate. Allow Zack to take the opposing view, at your podium. We can then field questions and see if we can come to a consensus this evening."

Chaka yielded the floor, and Zack took his place, giving Jessica a grudging nod. "May I?" he asked. She inclined her head.

"May I ask what is the great hurry?" Zack began. "You will shortly visit the mine site. Others will carry out the Grendel Scout rituals. When you've returned we can decide what needs to be done next. Perhaps by then we will know what has gone wrong at the mines. It's probably something natural but surprising. In any event nothing need be done in haste."

"There you go, being reasonable again," someone shouted.

Zack shrugged. "I try to be."

"You wanted to kill the eel," Jessica protested. "That wasn't reasonable!"

Zack nodded. "Yes it was. The eel was unfamiliar, and we have standing rules formulated by our best experts after discussion. The rules aren't perfect, but they're the best judgments we can make."

"And that one is wrong," Jessica insisted.

"Perhaps. This time it appears to have been wrong. But that doesn't mean all the rules, or even that one, are wrong as a general case. We can't foresee everything."

"We don't have to foresee everything," Jessica said.

"You're talking past each other." Aaron Tragon stood. "I beg your pardon for speaking out of turn, but don't you see it? Governor Moskowitz is concerned that when an unexpected danger appears, we won't be able to decide what to do in time, and while it is unlikely that the delay will destroy the colony, it might. Isn't that it, sir?"

"Yes, exactly."

"But here there is no possible danger to the entire colony," Aaron said. "The people who go to the mainland may be in danger if they are careless, but the colony won't be. . . . Actually, to be callous for a moment, if there's something so dangerous on the mainland that the only way to find out about it is to have the entire expedition killed, that knowledge alone is worth the price! It will make the colony safer, not less safe. Wouldn't you agree?"

Aaron waited a moment, and when Zack didn't answer, nodded politely and took his seat.

"Arrogant little snot," Mary Ann said.

"I thought he was quite reasonable," Cadmann said.

"You would."

"Not that there is that much danger," Jessica was saying. "We've been to the mainland dozens of times now. We even take the children to the highlands. And in all that time, the only dangers have been grendels, and we know how to deal with those."

"I'm still worried," Zack said.

"Name the danger."

Zack shook his head. "You know I can't. Call it Avalon Surprise. We couldn't have named grendels, but they were real."

"But you learned how to fight grendels," Jessica said, "and you taught us. By the way, thank you. From all of us Second—"

There was a murmur of approval. "Well said," Aaron shouted.

"But Zack, you knew it would be dangerous before you left Earth," Jessica said. "But you came. You couldn't ask if we wanted to come—"

"We did think about that, you know," Zack said.

"Yes, sir, we learned all that in school," Jessica said. "And we're not sorry you brought us. But it's our world too, and we want to know more about it. Don't we?"

Another chorus of young voices in enthusiastic approval.

"Except I want a shopping mall!" someone shouted. Everyone laughed.

"And we're learning," Jessica went on. "The eel is important because it's a reminder that we won't always have an artificially simple ecology here. We still don't know when grendels came to this island. We don't even know if these were normal grendels! Maybe they were—"

"Supergrendels?" Chaka said. He grinned.

"Or stunted, stupid weak grendels," Jessica said.

"My God," Rachael Moscowitz said. "That's a horrible thought!"

"So we go find out," Jessica said. "And now's as good a time as any. A highland base with expeditions into the lowlands. Now. This year."

A swell of applause, and not only from the Second.

"Count me out." That too came from where the Second were seated, to be answered by catcalls. "Aww, poor baby—"

"Who staffs that base?" Zack had lost and knew it. "Who plans this expedition?"

"We can work that out," Jessica said. She looked meaningfully at Cadmann. "We're not fools, Governor. We want your advice."

"But not our leadership," Zack said quietly. "That's plain enough."

"We want that too, unless your leadership means doing nothing without your orders."

"We just want you to be safe—"

"If you wanted to keep us safe, you could have stayed on Earth!"

Mary Ann stood. Cadmann looked at her in surprise. Mary Ann almost never spoke at meetings.

She didn't wait to be recognized, but no one said anything. Certainly Jessica wasn't going to interrupt her. "Why do you think it was safe on Earth?" Mary Ann demanded. "It wasn't safe. Not even in the best neighborhoods. You must know that. We brought recordings."

"Mom—"

"It wasn't," Mary Ann said. "You think of Earth as some kind of paradise lost? An Eden? It was a horrible place, where all the education in the world wouldn't save you from losing your job, and there was nowhere you could go without graffiti, and smutty drawings, and criminals, and people demanding handouts and accusing you of being a criminal if you didn't give them something. Where . . . Jessica, it's safe here, really safe, but it wasn't safe on Earth. That's why we came here!"

There were murmurs of agreement from the First.

"Well, Mom, you make Earth sound more dangerous than the mainland."

"It was," Cadmann muttered. "We forgot that."

"It's still the end of the debate, amigo," Carlos said. "Jessica still wins."

"Yeah," Cadmann said. "And we'll have to plan it."

"What you mean 'we,' paleface?"

"We've got some time, though," Cadmann said. "First they go look at the mines, initiate the Grendel Scouts. Time enough for serious planning when they get back."

Jessica thanked the audience and made her way back to her father. She quietly touched his shoulder. "Thanks, Dad. Mom."

Cadmann put his arms around Mary Ann and Sylvia, drawing them in close. Mary Ann chuckled. "If I know your father, you might be taking that thanks back in a few days. He's going to put you through the wringer."

"I wouldn't want it any other way."

"Jessica—can you and Justin come up for dinner?" Mary Ann brushed a strand of blond hair out of her eyes. "It would be nice to have a family dinner. We've been gone, and you'll be going over to the mainland . . ."

"Not tonight," Jessica said apologetically. "This is going to be big news at Surf's Up. I think that I need to be out there tonight."

Sylvia looked up at Cadmann. "How long do you think it will take to set up a lowland expedition?"

"Skeeter-based? Sighting out a location? A little preliminary work." He closed his eyes, musing. "Built it around the *Robor* vehicle. A fairly quick in-and-out. I would say no more than twelve hours, preparing for a much more thorough expedition in maybe a . . . month?"

Jessica nodded happily. "You're reading my mind, Dad."

"Plans will be on Cass by tomorrow morning. Okay?"

"Finestkind."

The meeting was breaking up. Jessica and her brother headed toward each other, hugged fiercely, and collected in a cluster with some of the other Second. They headed out the door together.

A hand smacked Cadmann's shoulder, and he turned around to face Aaron Tragon.

As usual, the sheer size of the young man hit Cadmann, hard. Reminded him of a friend . . . long ago.

Ernst. First casualty of the Grendels.

As such he should have felt a touch of nostalgia, of loss. Ernst had died because Cadmann thought he could handle it. Could handle everything.

And for a moment it felt as if Cadmann were moving in slow motion, Tragon's glittering, wide smile so intense and intimate that it seemed that the other shapes in the room faded to nothing.

The full force of Tragon's personality was so strong that Cadmann had to consciously remind himself where he was. Not in the past, but here, in the present, as if he had awakened from a micronap.

"—you for backing us, Cadmann. Jessica said that we could count on you."
His smile was dazzling.

"I imagine that you'll be going over?"

"Wouldn't miss Grendel Scout initiation."

"Good," Cadmann said, and meant it.

"Not that Justin can't take care of the kids," Aaron said carefully. "Well, good night, sir. Thanks again."

Aaron turned, but before he could walk away Ruth Moscowitz blocked his path. She stared up at him in admiration. Aaron paused and took her hand. "You look lovely tonight, Ruth."

She beamed. "I thought you were just brilliant."

He touched her right hand to his lips, winked at her, and strode off to rejoin his coterie. Ruth took her right hand in her left as if she wanted to wrap it in tissue paper.

"I think I'm going to be sick," Mary Ann said.

Sylvia chuckled. "He's a nice young man. I can understand what Jessica sees in him."

Mary Ann's smile was ghastly. "Let's get home, Cad. I'd like to build a big fire in the bedroom. Get really toasty. Okay?"

"Sure."

Sylvia unwound herself from his arm, and headed off. "I want to check with Linda on her simulations. I'll be up to the Bluff later, all right?"

"No problem." The crowd was thinning now. Cadmann took Mary Ann's small hand in his, squeezed it gently. "Things are changing fast now. It had to happen."

"I . . . don't want to talk about it just now. Cad. Take me home."

6

SURF'S UP

Friendship is Love without his wings!
—GEORGE GORDON, LORD BYRON,
Hours of Idleness

Justin brought the skeeter in for a last approach to Surf's Up. He'd skidded through the mountain passes. The land road would have added an extra five minutes to the trip. The thermals coming over the mountains could be a little hairy, but there were beacons in the pass, both visual and radio, so that it was just dangerous enough to be fun. There were unofficial records for three paths through the mountains under varying conditions: on visual, on radio, blind at midnight, fog, storm.

It kept the lords and ladies of Surf's Up busy, if not out of mischief. It also drove the adults crazy.

When he called in for landing he didn't just get the usual Cassandra go-ahead. He got an audio channel, and from the background noise, the party had already begun.

He shot out of the pass at 120 kilometers a second accelerating all the way, putting him well ahead of the other Seconds racing him back from the colony. Light flooded the beach from a huge flat vidscreen twenty meters square that showed a daylit mountain scene on the mainland. He took the last few meters skewing sideways, shot straight over Surf's Up and out over the ocean, where a little night action was under way.

Justin had viewed holograms from Hawaii; Malibu, California; Australia; and other places supposed to have the best surf action on Earth. In Justin's expert opinion, Camelot Island beat them all. The water was cool but not cold, the waves rolled forever, and the surfing season lasted all year long.

Someone was riding his board in with a torch held aloft in one hand . . . no, now that he saw it more clearly, there were three of them, carrying horsemane gum torches that silvered the entire wave crest. Two girls and a guy, and one girl was Katya Martinez, lookin' good.

Sand whipped in all directions as Justin touched the skeeter down. He dismounted and ran to the open barbecue pit, kicked off his shoes, and did a kind of victory dance, screaming, "We're going over, troops!"

They howled like mad dogs, and Little Chaka hurled a beer pod. It slapped Justin just above his heart. It stung, but the pod didn't break.

He grabbed a lady and got a long wet kiss, and then grabbed another one and did it even better, then plopped down in the sand and popped the beer open.

Derik Crisp spread big beefy hands. "So?"

"So the mining machinery is down. Great timing. They've got to go over."

"Great timing." Derik grinned. "So how'd you do it?"

"Me? No," Justin protested. "Hey, that'd be real sabotage, nasty stuff."

"Sure," Derik said. "Sure." He was still grinning, but he read Justin's irritation. "Does this have to be real? Nobody had to blow anything up. Just tell Cassandra to make pictures."

Justin said, "I never thought of that. Who could do that?"

"Edgar," someone yelled.

"Yeah, but he wouldn't."

"Depends on what he's offered," Little Chaka said.

Jessica had come running out of the communications room in time to hear them. "You don't really think it's the computer, do you, Justin? Whoever did it would have to be good, really good, they'd have to fool Linda and Joe—" She cut herself off.

"Yep," Derik said. "Edgar Sikes could sure as hell do it."

"And no one else," Jessica said. "Gee, Linda's got enough generation problems without *that*." She shook her head. "And I saw Linda's files, sure, if anyone can fake it Edgar could have, but I just don't believe it." She looked accusingly at Justin. "The explosions were real; now, how did they happen?"

"Sheesh! Why me?"

"Why Edgar?" Jessica demanded. "Same reason. Who else could it be? Who could have done Mount Tushmore?"

"You wrong me," Justin said, but he had trouble hiding the pride in his voice.

"Aaron," Derik said. "Aaron Tragon could have done it."

Jessica nodded vigorously, and a lot of Justin's pride faded.

"I'm going to call them," Derik said suddenly.

"Hey now, wait—"

"No, just to talk to Linda. See if she knows anything." Derik went to put through the call.

Derik and Linda had been a thing, once, for about ten days. Calling her right now might cause Joe Sikes to shove his phone down his throat. Jessica would have stopped him . . . but others were gathering around them now. "What's the word?" someone called.

"We're going," Jessica answered. "Not just the chicken run for the candidate Scouts."

The light from the screen had been a view of the mining site on the mainland. Now it was Linda Weyland standing fourteen meters tall, holding four meters of baby Cadzie under one arm. Jessica couldn't hear her or Derik.

Aaron Tragon waded out of the water carrying a sand-colored writhing shape. The thing wrestled with him, but he had it by the blades. He dropped it onto the grill and went for a towel.

The crab struggled as it cooked. It was a Camelot sea crab. They'd found more than twenty variations already, all with a bifurcated shell and four mobile limbs, but—"This one's new," Chaka said.

"Study it quick," Aaron suggested.

There would be no rescuing the beast. Chaka knelt above the fire pit, one hand bladed below his eyes to shield them from the heat. He watched the crab move, noting the play of the joints. The crab had two wide fins for swimming, and the shell had expanded into a big aerodynamic plate. The forelimbs were agile little spears now trying to fight the fire. The armored wrist/elbow joints were almost human in their agility.

"More incoming natives. Those *wrists*. You can't help wondering if something's waking them all up at once," Chaka said. "I want the shells."

Another skeeter touched down neatly next to Justin's, and Stu Ellington hopped out. Six more came over the mountains in tight formation. Two carried firewood. One brought food from the main encampment. The others brought passengers, and the party grew until it seemed that the beach would sink under their weight.

Aaron Tragon strode among them, and slipped one brawny arm around Jessica's waist. "Well, now," he said merrily. "I think we can call that a major victory."

"Let's take a look at Dad's plans first," Jessica said. "And then we can decide how much victory we've got." She was about to pull free, reflexively. Justin saw her *decide*: she leaned back against him. They had been casual lovers for nearly a year now. Casual: Justin had never seen Jessica *change a plan* to be with Aaron. Or any other man. Sometimes he wondered—

Justin felt someone kneading his shoulders. He looked around just enough to catch a glimpse of dark hair. Long. Wavy. A face not pretty, but made beautiful by devastating eyes. Eyes to drown in, to die for. Katya. He reached back and grabbed her, pulling her close to him, and craned around to gnaw on her neck.

She was dripping wet and cold as death, and their torsos touched from ankles to eyebrows. A wave of cold washed through him, and he couldn't seem to control it. It had been a long time, and he was surprised by the strength of his reaction.

One of the other kids said: "So—who's going over?"

Derik turned the volume up and Linda's voice blasted over the beach. "We are! Joe and Cadzie and me, we're going in first."

Justin, not quite watching Jessica over Katya's shoulder, saw sudden shock instantly swallowed.

They'd spoken once, when an older friend was seven months pregnant, and Jessica had remembered this—

The adults around her were half a dozen fully pregnant women, her mother included. Jessica had been five or six, pretending to play, but listening. And the women must have been locked in a dominance game, detailing their prenatal discomfiture. Little Jessica had listened in awe and horror, stupefied by the realization that she would one day be slow, and fat, and vulnerable just like the big ones, the adults. . . .

Funny she'd remembered at all. Maybe it had happened only in Jessica's imagination. It was a story she'd told Justin when she was twelve, when an older friend was pregnant. For an instant, now, Justin saw Linda as her sister did. Trapped.

The baby Cadzie was holding her prisoner. Before his birth she was already imprisoned, heavy and slow. Now she couldn't even attend a beach party. Now she was burdened by what Cadzie needed: milk, diapers, the cobalt blue blanket, the bassinet, the conversations that wouldn't happen because everyone wanted to talk about the baby instead: the *distractions*.

A cacophony of voices was rising. "I want to go." "Me too." "Hey, who's better at making a camp than me?"

"Room for a lot of us," Justin said. "We can take, what, twenty Scouts and fifteen Seconds. And the candidates, but they come back with Linda and Joe, but still, we could really do it up right. Set up primary base on the Mesa, and a secondary down at Heorot. Do a little . . . fishing."

Jessica got into the spirit of it instantly. "Take two of the skeeters and survey—"

"Get the initial surveys from Orbit. Let Dad spot two or three likely areas—"

Aaron was into it now. "Listen—we only need three skeeters to move the blimp, but four is safer. We can set up crisscrossing fire zones for the one that touches down."

"Touches down?"

"Plants, soil samples, plant some seismic detectors, hell, we can do some serious work!"

Aaron swept Jessica up in his arms and smooched. When he set her down she gave him her very smokiest gaze, linked her arms around his neck, and drew him close for some very serious kissing, her hips rolling against him in a clear "all systems go" alert. Justin couldn't seem to look away. When they broke, she reached out and licked the underside of Aaron's upper lip. Onlookers might as well have been on Isenstine.

Aaron turned and leered at the rest of them. "'Scuse us," he said. His great, corded arms lined around her waist. He exhaled and lifted her onto his shoulders so that her belly button was inches from his nose.

Jessica giggled "Don't you dare bite—" and then uttered a shocked and somewhat dreamy "Oh!!?" as he began walking backward to his hut.

With a brief and bleary cheer, the rest of them returned to their party.

There was something in Justin that felt . . . out of place. He walked down to the water's edge and stood alone to watch the moonglade dancing in the surf. Aaron was brilliant, handsome, athletic. And wrong for Jessica. He was sure of that, utterly certain, but for no reason he knew. It was just wrong—somehow. Justin didn't much appreciate the thoughts and feelings nipping around the edges of his mind.

Katya came up behind him and slipped her arms around his waist. "What're you thinking?"

North of them, two days across a warm gray sea, was the continent. He hoped it was far enough away. He wanted to be with Jessica, but if she and Aaron were going to be together . . . maybe it wouldn't be such a good idea for him to be there.

He could hardly tell Katya—

"What if," she said, her sharp little teeth gnawing at his ear, "I took you back to my hut, and made violent love to you?"

"I'd consider that a right friendly thing to do," he said. A file flashed through his mind, all of Katya's preferences and pungencies, all of the ways she moved and whispered, her small guidances and encouragements and the many happy little bits of erotic filigree she superimposed upon a very basic act.

He hadn't really made up his mind, but she'd gone a good distance toward making it up for him. She took his hand and led it along a row of wooden huts built back from the waterline. They were lashed together with rope and stilted against the seasonal rising of the tides.

The wood was a bamboo-like shoot transplanted from south of Isenstine a decade before. The south had less direct access to water—and therefore grendels hadn't razed it so thoroughly. The bamboo-like shoots were delicious for their first two years, and then hardened into something light and strong, almost ideal for building of houses or boats. The second-to-last house in the row was Katya's. She held the door open and beckoned him in.

Social interactions were an ongoing experiment on Avalon. Pregnancy was no issue: all children were welcome. Those who chose not to become pregnant could do so with near hundred-percent certainty, and if they missed, the fetuses could be removed to an artificial womb more safely and painlessly than any therapeutic abortion in the twentieth century. So Cassandra had told them; but it had never been tested. The social pressure to have children was high, and so far every girl who became pregnant had become a mother.

There was no disease. Those life-forms had been left behind on Earth. The threats that had shaped human sexual mores for much longer than human history were missing on Avalon. In a very real sense, all Avalon was one family.

There in the shadowed confines of Katya's shack, she stripped off her clothes and stood, naked, challenging Justin with the cant of her hips. Her black hair fell softly to the tips of her shoulders. Her body was full, and ripe, and lovely.

Moonlight slanted in through the blinds, throwing bars across her as she walked to him. With many little kisses and whispered endearments, she began the process of seduction.

Jessica . . .

The thought flitted across his mind, then was gone. A sudden fierceness took him. He gathered her up in one arm and flung her back upon her bed, a pile of undulating artificial fur that purred as their weight sank upon it.

Distantly came the roar of the surf. Wave crests scattered the light of a single full moon, and bathed their bodies in pale light as they made love . . . or something like love . . . on that bed.

And as he threw his head back, panting as Katya's fingers kneaded his flesh, he stared mindlessly at the window. The moon was adrift. That was Nimue, the smaller, closer moon. You could tell time by Merlin; it crossed the sky every six days. Nimue moved too fast for telling time.

The moon looked back at him and it wasn't quite round. It wasn't the moon that Justin's distant ancestors bayed at, beating drums and singing songs, holding their newborn infants high to bathe in its light, for a thousand generations before the birth of civilization. Although it was the only sky he had ever seen . . .

It was alien to him.

There is a rhythm between human beings, as well. As steady and strong as a heartbeat is the rhythm that men and women find with one another.

And in a social service so willingly and pleasurably provided, in this brief mingling of flesh and fluids, this joining of warm moist membranes in the service of health and convenience . . .

There is a moment, near the peak of it all, when logic falls away, and breath grows sharp, when the eyes meet, and you can see *through* each other, through all the little social barriers . . .

Down, down to the place where a bit of hindbrain still thinks that this is *about* something.

Isn't this about making babies, it whispers.

Isn't this the continuation of life? And aren't children vulnerable things, helpless before the cold and the predators? And isn't this act really about the rest of your life? And your children's lives? And your children's children's . . . ?

Isn't there a part, a place, a tiny, lone voice somewhere deep inside that asks if this couldn't, shouldn't, can't mean something more? That looks into the eyes of each and every partner, and asks, in its own way . . .

Are you the one?

"Carolyn was taking care of me, not Mom. Mom wouldn't let anyone touch her. I saw her stop crying, and then she toppled out of the chair. A bunch of the grown-ups picked her up and ran her into the hospital, and I don't know what happened after that." Katya stirred in his arms. "I wasn't alone after that. They moved me right into Dad's place."

"I spent a lot of time there too."

"I remember."

"You were hell's wrath with a grendel gun." She'd beaten him in the exercises, Justin remembered. "Did Carlos start you early?"

She laughed. "Yeah."

"That outhouse we all built when we were, what, twelve?"

"About then. Geometry lessons," Katya said.

"Don't remember what we had in school that year, but that's how I learned carpentry. Katya, I must be slow of thought. Why did anyone want a classic outhouse?"

"Hendrick took a skeeter and lofted it to a peak in the mountains. Coffee pickers use it. There's not another outhouse in the universe with a view like that."

"What did it feel like? I grew up with two mothers—"

"I had a great many," Katya murmured. "Not just Dad's guests. Mary Ann and Sylvia, Carolyn, Rachael Moskowitz. Dad would skeeter off to find special rock, wood, crystals, bones; or he didn't want me underneath when he was welding. It must have been like that for the Bottle Babies, don't you think?"

"You're not like them."

"No." Katya shuddered. Why did she do that? But her drowsy voice trailed off.

He turned onto his side. She snuggled up behind him, his buttocks tucked against the furred thatch of her groin, her hand reaching around to cup the recent instrument of her pleasure.

They had never spoken of a future together.

The moon was looking Justin in the face. Not Man's moon. He listened to the surf. His surf, but not his ancestors'. Shorter, quicker waves striking with more force in the stronger gravity . . .

But moon and surf belonged to his children, and his children's children, for generations to come.

The act of love so recently performed there, in that bed, carried its own rhythm, born in the eternal search for the Now. The search to end the lonely "I." The endless search, conducted eternally, by every human being, throughout each isolated lifetime.

That rhythm was perhaps the only thing born of earth remaining to them. And when those rhythms changed to match the moons and tides of Avalon . . .

As perhaps they had already begun to do . . .

What then would remain of them?

Jessica . . . he thought one last time. Before his thoughts devolved to mist, and sleep claimed him.

When Justin woke, Katya was gone. He could hear sounds of construction on the beach. He showered in cold water, pulled his pants on, and wandered out.

The vast Chinese-dragon shape of *Robor* was undergoing a full diagnostic over the Surf's Up beach. The hundreds of separate, flame- and heatproof hydrogen pods providing her lift were individually listed for leaks, and superstructure was inspected. . . .

Robor was as large as a football field and as tall as a twelve-story building, the largest vehicle on Avalon. He could lift forty tons of cargo. The Minerva shuttles could land anywhere near a water source (although the discovery of Grendels had made that a *nervous* proposition), and also travel to orbit. The skeeters had more versatility and speed and maneuverability, but minuscule range. Only *Robor* could travel to the mainland and bring back the booty.

Robor was constructed mostly of molded plastics. The satellites that originally surveyed Avalon had revealed oil in large quantities. When *Geographic* took its hundred-year jaunt across the sky at one-tenth light speed, she brought with her three prefabricated factories to manufacture the kind of high-tensile plastics that only zero-gee processing made possible.

Robor had no independent motors. Instead, three skeeters were anchored to the upper frame in triangular formation, and hooked into the dirigible's main bank of batteries and Begley-cloth solar collectors. Their engines became *Robor*'s engines.

Robor was a favorite target of the Merry Pranksters. He had been painted with huge cartoon-whale eyes, been transformed into a gargantuan eighteenth-century Venetian gondola, and had once been transformed by a half ton of light-weight building foam into a remarkably lifelike phallus. When Little Chaka pointed out that *Robor* couldn't lift in that state, the decorations disappeared quick, but the dirigible's pronoun remained *he*.

His most recent incarnation was more innocuous, colorful . . . and oddly appropriate.

In red and green and electric blue, with snaky white mustache and huge, crimson-lipped leer, *Robor* was currently the living image of a Ming-dynasty dragon god.

The dragon hovered above the colony of Surf's Up, and in his shadow a working celebration of a kind was under way.

Justin spotted Cadmann's broad shoulders and graying hair through the crowd, and sought him out.

"Morning, father figure." He grinned. They shared a hug. "I wasn't expecting to see you."

"We're putting a rush on it. I think the eel in the Amazon and the bomb in the mine shook some of us up just because they came so close together. Inquiring minds want to know. Like, why *now?*"

"Just a moment, Dad." Justin shouted to Toshiro Tanaka. "Hey, Toshiro-san, can you go over this checklist and make sure we're not forgetting something? Thanks, owe you one. Dad, what's the report from *Geographic?*"

"Weather's fine," Cadmann said. "They're doing a critter check on the highlands and Xanadu, nothing so far. I take it you're going on this trip?"

"Sure, I'm in charge of the candidate Scouts—after all, their overnighter was kind of disrupted by all of this."

Justin led Cadmann to the main hall. Surf's Up's meeting hall was a 1960s Hollywood set decorator's fantasy of a South Seas beach hut, built of thorn-wood and foamed plastic struts. The roof would have been convincing, but the fronds were all from one mold, all identical.

Cadmann spread a roll of paper out on the table. "I think better on paper," he said, but he had computer files as well. "Cassandra, give me last night's notes, construction mode, freelance."

He spread out the paper. "Here," he pointed, "is the mainland. Eight hundred miles from here, and a good two days by *Robor*. You'll have some decent wind behind you. Coming back will be slower, but you can charge up off the mine's collectors."

"We'll hook up for recharging as soon as we land."

A small crowd had gathered to listen. Aaron slipped through the press. When he stood beside Cadmann they were almost exactly shoulder to shoulder.

Aaron was larger, but time has a tempering effect available from no other source. Aaron Tragon might be a Cadmann Weyland one day. He wasn't yet.

"Yes, there's plenty of charge," Linda said from the door. "The mine hasn't used any for a while. Hi, Dad."

Cadmann looked a little startled. "You certainly made good time," he said.

She colored a little. "Take after my dad, I guess."

Justin grinned to himself. Stu Ellington held the record for speed through that pass. She'd have been taking it easy with Cadzie aboard. Justin had already put money on her for the next Landing Day race.

Little Cad was nursing, or sleeping, or both. The cloth covering Linda's bosom made it difficult to tell which. "Dad, we've found two more maybe-type explosions in the mine record."

"Grendel guano! Are the dates significant?"

She stared. Cadmann said, "I meant, did they happen when someone might have wanted—skip it. Tell me more."

"Recent explosions, twenty weeks ago and fourteen. Low energy, like gun-powder again, way tamer than dynamite. But they didn't happen where boring was going on, they happened in the secondary processors. That machinery is very forgiving, and it just went on chugging."

Cadmann thought carefully. If sabotage, then . . . test explosions before the real thing? But the real thing had been something quite different. "Got any ideas, small bright one?"

"Some defect in the thermal unit at the secondary processor. Some contamination in the coal itself? There's a mushy look to one of the spikes, like . . . less like a single grenade than a bushel of cherry bombs."

"Coal dust?" someone said from the door.

She shook her head. "Coal dust can explode, but we thought of that in the design. If air is mixing with the dust there'd have to be something wrong in the machinery, something Cassandra doesn't see. Even something deliberate."

"Sabotage?"

She shrugged.

"Have you done a spectroscopic on the coal?"

"Yes, of course, months ago—"

"No, I mean recent."

"Joe says we can't, the instrumentation is gone. We've got to go there."

"I was thinking dynamite at the bit, but what if air was getting in?" Cadmann was looking about him, not obviously, trying to read faces.

"Possible, but tricky. We'll look when we get there," Linda said.

"All right. Bluff Two. Good moorage for *Robor*, and it's the right place for the Scouts. Make it the base, and we'll check the other mine areas by skeeter."

"What about the lowlands expeditions, Dad?"

"Remember, this is a dry run. Take three days, check everything, do your overnight with the Scouts, then you can look for a good place for a base camp. Stay alert, and pull back fast if anything unexpected crops up."

"Reconnaissance in force," Linda said.

Cadmann grinned faintly. His fingers moved across the map. "Once you're through with the Scout stuff, you can do geology with one skeeter and use another for mapping. While you do that, the Grendel Scouts stay on the Mesa with somebody steady in charge. Usual rules there. Stay high, no lowlands at all. Any variation from this order will be cause for mainland privileges to be revoked. Do we understand each other?"

For a moment Justin wondered if Aaron would give an argument, or say something provocative—he had been known to do that. But he wanted this trip too badly. Justin could almost see him sitting on his emotions, holding his tongue for dear life. Instead of smart-mouthing, he nodded.

Linda sighed. "I'm sure that whatever is wrong, we can handle it. Nothing to worry about. Otherwise," she said, "I'd never take Cadzie with us. Never in a thousand years."

7

THE MAINLAND

Its horror and its beauty are divine.
—Percy Bysshe Shelly,
The "Medusa" of Leonardo da Vinci

"Can we talk?"

Linda looked up with faint annoyance. Linda had learned what all mothers learn. *Sleep when the baby sleeps, stupid!* She'd just got Cadzie down for a nap.

"Please."

Edgar looked desperate. Joe had been worried about him lately, worried that Edgar had problems he wouldn't talk about. Joe would want to know. She sighed and pointed to the sleeping baby. "In your work room, then. Cassie, Cadzie is asleep. Listen for Cadzie. We will be in Edgar's workroom. Call if he wakes up."

"Understood, Linda," Cassandra said softly.

Edgar led the way. "Coffee?"

"Sure, thanks," she said. "I like coffee and I never get a chance to go pick beans."

Edgar gave her an evil grin. "There's one way you can get all the coffee you ever want."

"I used to do that," she said.

"Hey, I didn't mean anything."

"All right." She sipped coffee. "I do like this stuff. Okay, Edgar, what's so urgent it can't wait for me to get a nap while Cadzie's asleep?"

"Why don't I get laid?"

"What?"

He couldn't meet her eyes now. "It's hard enough asking once, let alone twice. Why can't I get laid? I must be the oldest virgin on this planet."

"You're not a virgin. You're a Grendel Scout. I was *there*. Trish Chance, the Bottle Baby."

"Close enough," Edgar said. "There was that once on the mainland. I didn't know what to do. Trish had to show me, and she hardly speaks to me now."

"Why ask me?"

He sighed and shook his head. "There was a time when I'd have given anything I had to sleep with you. You know that."

She struggled to avoid laughing, and lost. "I'm sorry," she giggled. "But Edgar, I never knew—"

"You knew," he said. "Come on, I don't know much about girls, but anybody could tell you were keeping score, making sure that anybody you hadn't made it with sure wanted to. You—unless I'm psychotic. Linda?"

"All right, I suppose I did," Linda said. "And then one morning I woke up tired of the games."

Edgar nodded, relaxing a little. "You slept with damn near everybody! Everybody but me. I figured what the hell, eventually you'd get to me just for the record. But you never did. I guess you got pregnant first."

"Pregnant and tired," Linda said.

"So I'd wait till you had the baby, and then I'd have a chance, but that didn't work because now you're my stepmother! Near enough, anyway."

Tired, and pregnant, and lonely, which didn't make sense because I could have awakened with anyone I wanted, but— "Let's just say I had a lot of friends."

If he'd been a dog, Edgar's tail would have wagged. "I've read a bunch of different names that people used to use. Hooker. Town pump. Round heels."

"Round heels?"

He laughed. "Falls over easily on her back. And *hooker,* I read about that one. There was a Union general, Fighting Joe Hooker, who had so many shady ladies following him that pepole called them Hooker's battalion—"

"Thank you for the lecture, but that's quite enough." She stopped, and thought for a moment. "But come to think of it, *Joe* knows those words, too. He'd never use them, but he knows them."

"Yeah. Wow, I never would have thought of that. Has he—?"

"Never."

"Anyway, it never happened with us. Or anyone. It's that way with all the girls. Some of them are friends, but none of them want to sleep with me, and it's driving me nuts. Why?"

"You're too eager, for starts," Linda said. "And you have a talent for lecturing on the wrong subjects."

"I tried being hard to get. That doesn't work either."

"No, of course not. I mean—"

He looked down at himself with a sour expression. "Yeah. I know what you mean."

"Then why ask?"

Edgar looked at himself. "I'm fat. I've been taking lessons from Toshiro—"

"It shows," Linda said. "More muscle tone. Better posture. Lose some weight and you'll look good. Edgar, I'd sleep with you now. I mean, I won't, but I would if I were doing that sort of thing now."

"You mean that?"

". . . Yes."

"You sound surprised."

She smiled. "Tell the truth, I *am* surprised. I hadn't thought about it until you asked me."

"So why now, and not back when you could? You're just saying it?"

"No, I'm not just saying it. Edgar, you really are attractive, but it takes work to see that." She frowned. "You *make* us work at it. I guess I mean, there's something about you that drives girls, maybe not just girls, *everyone* away, until they get to know you, so there has to be a reason to get to know you. I had one, I'm in love with your father and he loves you, so I worked at it, but after a while it wasn't work."

Edgar shook his head. It was hard to read his expression in the dim light from the viewscreens. Edgar usually kept the lights low in the rooms he worked in. "My old man doesn't love me. And I don't know what you mean—"

"He does too. Edgar, you're always testing people. Him most of all. You want to see just how much we'll put up with. Most of us won't put up with much. Why should we? But Joe does, and I had to, and you know, after a while you stopped doing it so much to me, and then I really got to know you, and you're really a pretty neat guy, somewhere down in there. Keep it up with Toshiro, and pay some attention to yourself in the mirror, and you'll look like one, too. And then you'll get all the girls you want."

"Maybe," he said, but he sounded happy.

And how much of that did I mean? But if he believes it, it might even happen that way. She was trying to think what else she could tell him—

"Linda," Edgar said. "About your kid's father."

"It's not your problem," she said automatically.

"No, but it's yours, isn't it?"

"I—what do you mean?"

"You don't know who the father is, and you're afraid to find out, because you think it's somebody you don't like."

"Edgar, that's a horrid thing to say. Maybe I don't like you after all."

"Linda, do you want to know who the father is?"

"You mean you know?"

He shook his head. "No, but I could find out."

"How?"

"Cassie knows the blood types of everyone in this colony, including the babies. She has to. Someone might need a transfusion."

"But Cadzie is O positive," Linda said. "So am I. That rules out some boys, but it leaves at least a dozen—" She saw his grin. "Yeah, I wondered. A weak moment."

"Linda, you didn't look at the minor factors. There's a lot more to blood types than the majors—"

"I know about MN factors," Linda said. "And that still leaves a dozen."

"You sure got around."

"I used to be proud of it," Linda said.

"Sure put one in the colonel's eye."

"I guess there was some of that in it," Linda said. "And showing him there was something I could do really well—"

"Why'd you stop?" He looked around, then back at her. "Yeah, yeah, Dad knows the ancient magical words that turn a lady into a wench. It's still a good question."

"I stopped because I didn't like myself anymore," she said. "And now it really is none of your business, and before you ask, no, I'm not going to sleep with you."

"I don't want you to. I mean—" He froze up for a moment, then forced words out. "Dad would— He *wouldn't* kill us, but he'd think he should. Am I right? Anyway, let's just keep it simple, because I really do like you, and I guess I like my old man, and he's so much more, since you, him and you—" Edgar stopped and took a deep breath. "Linda. If you want to know who the father is, I can find out. Cassie has more than blood samples to work with. She already knows, you know."

"She does not. I asked her."

"You didn't ask in the right way," Edgar said.

"What is the right way?"

He shook his head. "I too know the ancient magical words. I can find out. I can keep anyone else from finding out, too. Anyone but the colonel, or Zack; they can override anything I put in if they know my block's there."

"Joe thought you could do something like that. You locked him out of some of your files, didn't you?"

Edgar didn't answer at first. "Privacy is a right—"

"When you were eleven years old?"

"Well, yes, dammit! What's age got to do with it?"

She smiled. "Not a lot."

"So do you want to know? I can stop anywhere," he said. "File accesses are easy to track, anyone can do it, and you spent a lot of time looking into blood typing and paternity and estral cycles just after Cadzie was born."

"Oh. Edgar, sometimes you scare me."

"Just sometimes?"

"Yes, just sometimes. Let me think about this, okay?"

"Are you *worried* about who it is? Look, would you like me to cover your tracks so no one else can find out you were interested?"

"Oh my God, I never thought—Edgar, if someone else was—tracking my file accesses—would you know?"

"Yes. Especially if he asked me to do it for him."

"Did—who asked you?"

"Aaron. Hey, it's all right, I didn't tell him anything!" He studied her. "You think it was Aaron, don't you? You were together a lot last year. Like him and your sister now."

She didn't say anything.

"Why don't you like him?" Edgar demanded.

"Why do you hate him?"

"I don't hate him, I'm scared of him," Edgar said.

"So am I. So. Why?"

Edgar bent over as if to touch his toes. "Pretty good," he said. "Toshiro's a miracle worker. You know what Aaron did to my back."

"Edgar, Joe says you fell out of a horesmane!"

"I did," Edgar said. "It was a long time ago, when we were eleven, Aaron was living here then. Dad thought the Bottle Babies ought to have some family stability. He was even thinking of adopting Aaron."

"You must have liked that!"

"Actually I didn't hate it as much as you'd think. Not at first. Dad was pretty rough on Aaron. Said he had to teach him some manners, just like I had to learn. It was sort of fun watching Aaron have to go through that. . . ." He glanced down at the computer consoles. "Cadzie's sleeping fine," he said.

She waited.

"So one day we went for a hike, just Aaron and me. You know Strumbleberry? High and dry, with horsemane trees on top. We camped up there overnight. Next morning we saw a pterodon dive into the topknot and come out. Aaron climbed up to see what was up there. He came down. Panting. Said he could beat me to the top.

"Aaron was ten and I was eleven, but he could generally beat me at anything. But he'd just tired himself out. So I said 'You're on!' and slapped his ass and swarmed up that tree. Near the top I looked and he was right below me, but I knew I could beat him.

"I pulled myself into that mass at the top and something snapped at my eyes, a claw big enough to take my head off. I reared back and half a dozen claws like big scissors were trying to take my face off, and then there wasn't anything under me. Next thing I knew I was falling. And I remember the look on Aaron's face as I dropped past him.

"I landed flat on my back. I couldn't move anything below my arms. It hurt like I was dying. It felt like I was killing myself to fish out my comm-link card. I was sure it would be broken, but it wasn't—"

"Edgar! *Aaron* didn't call?"

"He called. He called after I did. Maybe he would have anyway. Maybe. But he didn't until I got mine out and called for Dad."

"Jesus. That's awful. But you never told anyone."

Edgar said, "I told Dad. I don't know if he believed me."

"I think he did. He doesn't like Aaron," Linda said.

"So I spent a couple of years recovering. Missed out on growing up with the rest of you. Damn near missed out on getting into the Grendel Scouts. It was *me* who nailed down what's wrong with the Earth Born. And now I can't get laid."

"And you blame that on Aaron?"

"Shouldn't I? Why are you afraid of him?"

She shook her head. "I don't know. He reminds me of my father, and that ought to be good. I'm not afraid of Dad, but—Edgar, I don't know. Let's leave it at that."

"Sure. And you're afraid Aaron's the father," Edgar said. "So you don't want to know."

"I didn't say that."

"No, you didn't say that."

"Edgar, has Aaron—has he been tracking my computer accesses?"

She was getting to know that grin. Edgar said, "Linda, he's tried, but he hasn't been able to, because I blocked access to those files, only it doesn't look like I did it, it looks like it was the colonel."

"That was a nice thing to do. You say he has tried to—to track my file accesses? And asked you to help?"

Edgar nodded. "I told him I didn't have time just then. Then he tried on his own, but I'd been there first."

"Thank you." She stood. "I think I better go look at Cadzie, and we've got to get ready to go to the mines. Let me think about this. Maybe it really is time to find out, whatever the answer is. Thank you."

His answering smile caught her turning. His proud smile. "*Wups*. Edgar?"

"Yeah?"

"I've got your attention now? You listen. You think about what I'm saying. You even work out ways to do things for me."

Edgar grinned. "Yes, Mom."

"Edgar, I can remember you losing interest in the middle of saying hello! We used to talk about it, the way you'd get bored and walk off in the middle of something. You'd be off into something else with someone else, programming, going back to the stars, what's with Earth, mainland ecology. Remember that T-shirt?"

Edgar remembered. Linda had cut a scarlet T-shirt to ribbons, so that it fell like lace across her body, dropping to her upper thighs, concealing and revealing.

She was watching him. "Got your attention, did it? I just had to know I could."

How would Dad answer? Edgar said, "I hope you sent that to Medical when you were through with it. Useful for restarting a stopped heart."

"Edgar, is there a girl you could do something for? Something nobody else has thought of?"

His face went slack. She remembered that look: Edgar, withdrawing into his own mind. "Maybe . . . I see what you mean, anyway. Linda? Thanks."

✳

Justin stopped short of *Robor*'s top foredeck. The whiff of coffee was faint, but it touched his brain from underneath. It came to Justin that Aaron Tragon was ruining the smell of coffee for him.

Before the grendels came, before the First seeded the rivers with trout and catfish, the First had scattered coffee beans over the mountain ridges. Coffee was easy to grow. It was a bitch to harvest. Coffee kept the First healthy! They had to hike into the mountains with backpacks or do without. They'd come back with as much as they wanted, plus a little more for trading. That was why Carlos always had coffee, because someone always wanted a table or bureau or carved doorway.

Aaron always had coffee because he sent someone to get it. Justin had done that when he was younger. The backpack groups always had fun, but they carried back smoked bear meat once instead of coffee, on Justin's suggestion. He hadn't gone again.

There was an inner circle at Surf's Up: the coffee drinkers. Some were addicted. Trish and Derik and (oddly) Ruth Moskowitz, and maybe even Jessica, didn't like the taste. They sipped; they made a cup last all night. If you weren't in you were out.

Justin had dropped out. Others haunted the fringes, trying to find lives, but always ready to display a cup of coffee.

Coffee smelled like dominance games. Justin was beginning to flinch at it.

Aaron squeezed his shoulder and slipped past him, and Justin realized he was blocking a door. He shrugged and followed.

The hum of the skeeters could be felt through the floor of *Robor*, but even more clearly through the Plexiglas windows at the bow. Jessica stood just behind several of the Scouts. They crowded against the windows, and fought for a place at the front. Palms and faces pressed against the Plexiglas. Morning mist shrouded the sea below them. The loom at the eastern horizon was more blue than the rosy-fingered dawn images of Earth poetry.

They expected landfall about dawn, and the candidate Scouts had been awakened early for their first look—real sight, not virtual—of the mainland they'd heard about all their lives.

She sipped her coffee from a hand-fired cup sculpted with a grendel tail as handle. This wasn't the instant stuff that her parents had drunk for the first ten years on Avalon. Coffee took some getting used to. The first beans had been harvested and ground, the first cups served, when she was just nine years old. She still remembered Cadmann's expression as he took the first sip, as if a rare and delicate mystery had suddenly been revealed to him. And her own first bitter sip, which she had spit out into the saucer.

Aaron had persuaded her to try it again, years later.

She felt large, strong hands clasping her shoulders, and shivered a little at the touch. Those hands were so strong and so gentle, when they wanted to be. They were always commanding, but usually gentle as well. She kissed the fingertips, and said, "G'morning, Aaron. Sleep well?"

"Like a baby," he said. He picked up a broad-based conical cup and sipped as he peered out into the mist. The foredeck, one of the two upper above the cargo hold, was crafted of polished waxwood. This dark, smooth timber was one of the odd strains to be found south of the Isenstine. Carlos considered it a finer grain than teak, and thought that they could get a good trade going with Earth . . . if Earth was still there, he had added soberly.

A gust rolled *Rober* to port. The guidance computer noticed and the skeeter engines made their correction. The ship righted quickly, but the Grendel Biters ooh'd and ahh'd and pretended to lurch this way and that.

"Look," Aaron said, squeezing her shoulder. "Sunrise."

It wasn't, really. It was a false dawn, the first rosy blush of Tau Ceti along the eastern horizon. The glow would fade, then minutes later grow stronger, leading into the light of day.

Some of the other Second were in the lounge, and the rest of the Grendel Scouts were pouring in. The window was floor to ceiling and wall to wall, curving slightly outward, made of plastic strong enough to take an elephant's charge. The kids could lean against it all they wanted.

Jessica undogged a deck chair and moved it closer. "Sit a spell."

"Sure." Aaron dogged the chair to the deck. He sprawled out, relaxed.

Jessica watched him lazily. He was so relaxed about everything that he did, and so totally committed at the same time. If he sat, he was . . . just sitting. If he spoke before an audience, he was just speaking. If he climbed or surfed, he was just climbing or surfing. And if he was making love, he was doing that and nothing else. It was a relief. Every part of him seemed congruent with the others. Unfragmented. Whole. And when he wanted something? But that kind of ruthlessness was natural to someone so purposeful.

Was she in love with him? She wondered that herself, and hoped that the answer was yes. Her hand stole into his, and he clasped it.

A sliver of Tau Ceti had crept above the horizon now, and the reflected radiance pierced the mainland's cloud cover. The clouds were blue-black atop and silver beneath. All the passengers were awake now. Nobody wanted to miss the first general outing in over a year, and for most of the Grendel Scouts this was their first trip ever.

Justin brought up a chair and dogged it down. "How many candidates do you think we have?"

"For a chicken run?"

He nodded.

"Six are old enough."

"Think we can find a grendel for them?"

Nasty chuckle. "Not one for each, but we can sure run a lottery."

"Extra safety, okay? Lay an extra rifle on," Aaron said thoughtfully. Jessica examined him. Aaron Tragon was not usually the man who spoke for caution.

"Why?"

"Nothing goes wrong. Not *now*. We're about to get everything that we want." Unspoken: a permanent base on the mainland, manned by the Second. The beginning of a new colony.

Even more unspoken: the *real* colony. If Aaron had his way, *he* would lead that colony. He would set the artificial wombs aboard *Geographic* pumping out a hundred children a month, and found a nation before he died. He would make the original landing little more than a footnote in the history of Avalon.

And why not? They were here to conquer a world.

The clouds were shot through with gold and silver now, and the mist was beginning to burn away. On the horizon, perhaps twenty miles distant, was the mainland. The pilots had timed it beautifully. The Scouts began to applaud and hoot and stamp their feet.

The mainland was green and lush. The mist seemed almost to change color there ahead of them, coiling and snaking around the bay that opened before them. They watched the water—dark gray foaming to blue, waves rolling in toward a rocky coastline broken by irregular reefs. The mist was heavy, oily, oozed from the ground like smoke and hovered close to it.

Jessica's heartbeat sped up, and a light sour sensation of pleasure begin to boil in her stomach. This was only her sixth trip to the mainland.

The obsevation deck was getting crowded now. Carey Lou had drawn breakfast lots the night before. He served her a tray of scrambled eggs and sliced fruit. Jessica sipped and chewed and sighed, and felt that all was right with the world.

Once of the first things that anyone noticed about the mainland was that it was more lush by far than Camelot Island . . . as if all the grendels had disappeared, but of course they hadn't. Still, farther north on the vast prairie they called the Scribeveldt, *Geographic* had seen beasts large enough to give a grendel pause. *Geographic*'s cameras showed tracks tens of kilometers long, pale lines scrawled across the vast green-brown prairie. They crossed and curved elegantly, as if some entity were trying to write messages for the stars. It was natural to call the entities Scribes, though seen from orbit they were only squarish blobs at the track endpoints, prairie-colored and nearly featureless. Scribes had to be herbivorous, but everything beyond that was speculation.

There was a forest at the edge of the Scribeveldt, and sometimes Cassandra saw, or thought she saw, fairly large animals in herds. No one had ever seen a herd of grendels, and the only thing that ate grendels was other grendels. *Robor* rose to cross a ridge of splintered rock crested with dense green and green-blue foliage. The ridge looked like the bottom row of a skull's teeth. Just beyond it the rock dropped away into a dense green carpet of valley. An old river fed by snows on mountains far to the north snaked lazily along the valley floor until it cut through the ridge to the ocean.

"Grendel hunting grounds," Aaron said. The candidate Scouts stared down at the swamps and forests. "We stay out of there."

At the side of a pond beneath, a herd of something vaguely resembling a cross between a horse and a pig drank nervously. *Robor* was only about sixty feet up now, barely ten feet higher than the tree line, so that the Scouts could see more clearly.

With a sudden, violent splash, something exploded from the water, so fast that their eyes could hardly follow what happened next. One of the beasts at the edge of the water was bowled backward, smashed flat by the awesome velocity. Probably dead that instant. The other animals fled in all directions, in a sort of galloping waddle.

But that wasn't what captured their interest. That wasn't what caught every eye in the lounge. No one seemed to breathe. Heartbeats may have frozen still.

There, perched above the torn and bloodied body of the pig-creature . . .

Was a grendel.

A voice came over the speaker in the lounge. "*Grendel kill,*" Linda said from the control room. "*We have just seen a grendel kill.*" The clear curving outer wall clouded, and a video window opened up on its right side. The death scene was replayed for them in slow motion.

The camera brought them in close. The herd of pig-beasts drank slowly and carefully. Three stood guard above the bank while the herd went down to the water, just a few at a time, in a clumsy, laughable waddle. Then, in slow motion now, the pond's surface bulged, broke, and four meters of black death exploded from the depths.

Jessica whispered, "Oh God," just as stunned as anyone else in the room. It was impossible *not* to be impressed by this creature, the most savage predator that mankind had ever faced.

Blunt snout. Crocodile armor. Blunt, spiked tail. It emerged at rocket speed, and the pig-thing died snorting water and blood. Its body deformed as the grendel struck it. It tumbled back, plowing up dust and grass. The computer, enhancing some kind of wide-angle holo view, kept right with it. Another, wider-screen angle, still in slow motion, showed that the other animals broke and headed for cover almost instantly, running fast but at normal animal pace. No animals save grendels had ever been observed moving on *speed.*

Grendel teeth had torn its victim's belly and rib cage open. Blood spurted, covering the grendel's snout. It burrowed its teeth into the wound, head deep. It ripped out a mouthful of viscera before looking around, and then up, directly at *Robor.*

It opened its mouth, and closed it in that disorienting holographic slow motion. Blood and saliva drooled away from the daggerlike teeth, droplets running down as it screamed challenge at them.

Was it the sound of the skeeter engines? Their aerial bulk? The grendel's eyes locked with them, as if uncertain of *Robor*'s distance. As if it thought they might challenge it for the meat.

It screamed a scream that they couldn't hear. Then it turned, and hooked its spiked tail into the carcass. Its tail differed from pictures of the Avalon grendels, with one big, gaudy hook almost underneath, and the shattered scar where a matching hook had been.

The pig's bleeding had slowed to a trickle. Its feet still trembled a bit. Just a twitch, now. The grendel dragged it back, down into the water.

And the moment after it sank, the recording played again at normal speed. The pig-things approached the shore; one darted in to drink; death smashed into it and tore it apart. Jessica flinched violently.

"Jesus," Aaron said. "I love those damned things."

She looked at him, and for a moment, felt something akin to jealousy. Love hadn't been too strong a word. His eyes burned. The grendels represented something . . . raw power, absolute single-mindedness . . . naked ferocity?

Some quality or gestalt that Aaron Tragon respected.

Admired.

Loved.

She had never been certain that he loved her. But she could never doubt that he loved grendels. Loved hunting and killing them, likely enough. But loved them. More, probably, than he loved anything else in the world.

How very odd to feel jealous of a monster. But Aaron can't really love grendels! I couldn't love a man who—

There was more to see: plains that sloped away from the mountains. Get a kilometer or so from running water and you saw lush vegetation and more animal life. There were creatures that looked reptilian—nothing too large, but several packs of animals that momentarily darkened the plain, then broke and ran at the first touch of *Robor*'s shadow.

Here, the brush thickened to jungle density. Her heart leapt. There had been virtually no exploration of the mainland forests. Almost no categorization of flora or fauna. Little mapping, save by satellite. Except for territory immediately surrounding the mining concerns, there had been precious little of anything.

And now . . . a lot of that was going to change.

Lunch came and went before they caught sight of their destination. It emerged from a smoky haze, mist so thick it was almost like volcanic ash. The mountain was bare and weathered, curved and hollowed, spotted here and there with patches of green until it resembled a mossy skull.

Pterodons arced gracefully through the heights: a touch of something familiar, thank God.

Jessica's hands moved by themselves, checking her rucksack, as she gazed out. This land, this whole land, was theirs for the taking. . . .

It seemed that Aaron was reading her mind. "They don't want it," he said, shaking his head as if in amazement. His strong, sure fingers dug into her shoulders. It hurt, just a little bit.

That was like Aaron. He hurt, a little. It was difficult for him to remember just how strong he was. So strong, so smart . . . so sure of himself. It was no wonder that she was in love with him. His air of remoteness only increased the temptation, and the value of the prize.

The burr of the skeeter engines grew throaty. The floor vibrated beneath her feet as *Robor* took an eastern heading, sliding along a table of mountains. It was the warm season, and everything was green and brown and yellow-blue. Later in the year, there would be snow. Farther inland there were higher ranges, but here, barely two hundred miles from the coast, was a rich supply of ore. *Robor* passed over the first mining camp. Jessica wandered up to the control center, where Linda and Joe were reviewing telemetric reports from the site.

"Anything new?" she asked. She ducked her head to fit into the low-ceilinged room. She watched the computers and screens as Linda pored over them, completely absorbed.

"Ah . . . nothing. Everything is just fine. We'll be at the site in less than an hour. Check there first, and then we can look back and check the others."

"Any additional information?"

"*Not* sabotage."

"Why?" she asked, trying to keep the relief from her voice.

"The vibration signature. It's more like black powder than any of our standard blasting compounds. If somebody was going to booby-trap our mining equipment, they wouldn't use some kind of unstable low-yield compound. They'd use something concentrated, neat, reliable. That's what I'm thinking. This is just weird."

Jessica laid a hand on her shoulder. "Oh well. You'll have your chance to inspect things close up in . . ."

"Thirty-seven minutes," Linda said.

"Then we're over Grendel Valley. Aaron should be thrilled."

8

THE GRENDEL GOD

God answers sharp and sudden on some prayers,
And thrusts the thing we have prayed for in our face,
A gauntlet with a gift in 't.
—ELIZABETH BARRETT BROWNING, *Aurora Leigh*

Old Grendel was hunting. She lay covered in mud under a mash of water and rotting vegetation. The river lay almost half a mile behind her, but the ground was soft. She'd burrowed her way up from the river over many days, clawing through the dirt, allowing the water to follow her. And here, so far from moving water that her prey must consider themselves safe, she waited.

One was nearby. Large enough to last for three days, becoming truly sweet only on the last day. A snouted thing with hoofs and big ears and large eyes. The snout quested about, testing.

Ah, gently, gently. If the wind shifted in the wrong direction, then Snouter would scent, and Snouter was fast enough to lead a merry chase. But not fast enough to evade Old Grendel, no, not even in these days of sluggish blood, of slow heats and rapid cooling. Old Grendel still had *speed*.

Old Grendel had murky memories of her youth, when she had first emerged from the water, a dim-brained beast, before a sickness caught in the high water had opened her eyes. To the degree that she was capable of such things, she felt an almost reverential awe toward those high waters. Something there made her itch, made her head hurt until she thought she would die of the pain. She could do little but wallow in her agony, unable even to hunt effectively. Even the depths of cool water helped little. But when the pain receded . . .

She could see differently. She didn't know how else to think it. In her youth, Old Grendel had seen the world in basic gradients of scent and taste, of need and satiation. Her life cycled: hunger forced *speed*, *speed* created heat, heat forced her back to water. But after the change, after the swelling of her head, and the pain . . . She'd come out of it mad with hunger, too weak to fight the lake monster, until the patterns showed her what to do. Then *she* was the lake monster, and there was prey everywhere, everywhere she hadn't looked. Hunting was easier. She used *speed* less often. Fights for territory became less bloody. She saw everything more clearly, and understood what she saw.

In those days she had been sleek, and as fast as rainfire. She was absolute death, the empress of her domain. She had given life to a hundred thousand children, and perhaps ten had survived to maturity. Those she had driven upstream to the heights, when she could. Two had tried to return, to challenge their mother on her own ground.

Those, she gutted without mercy, the killing flare in her head and in her body stronger than thought or reason, stronger by far than any rudimentary maternal instinct.

Those had been good days, and perhaps her greater intelligence was a curse. She was not what she had been, *and she knew it.* No longer so fast, so strong. Her wounds no longer healed as swiftly.

For any creature unaware enough to be caught within her kill radius, she was a flash of teeth and claw and pebble-textured black armor and spiked tail. Sixteen feet long and a quarter ton of instant murder.

But *speed* drained out of her more quickly these days, and the generated heat stayed longer. She was afraid to go as far from water as once she had.

There were advantages to the Change. A grendel ahunt is a grendel whose mind is lost to *speed.* There is no thought, only action. Chase and fight and kill, a race against the heat inside; get the prey to water, and feed. Years ago the sight of prey would madden her, would drive all caution away. It was sometimes so now, but not so often. She could think ahead, imagine the consequences of actions.

In sane moments she wondered if the tree-dwellers knew this. These wretched creatures would lure a desperately hungry grendel far from water. They darted high up into one of the thorn trees when the grendel blurred toward them, leaped from tree to tree when the grendel tore down the tree trunk.

Old Grendel remembered that she had almost died. The creatures had led her from one tree to another until she'd nearly cooked herself. She'd be chasing one and it was gone, and here was another, out of reach and sluggishly making for another tree, and the hunger and killing urge were so terribly strong. And another farther on—

She'd found the control to make for water before it was too late, before her internal organs roasted with the heat of her own *speed.* Behind her, scores of the creatures were suddenly chattering at her from every tree and tuft of grass. Long-legged and long-armed furry things made of crunchy red meat screamed their mockery. In saner memory she could see the length of their teeth . . . could see that they were also, in their strange way, hunting.

She'd stayed clear of the forest from then on. Years later, she had seen hunter-climbers feasting on a dead grendel who had been lured too far from water and cooked in its own heat. Not of her kind, that grendel. The naked red bones of its huge shoulders and forearms named it: it was of the kind that built dams. She chased the hunter-things away and ate the corpse of the dam builder.

There were things that hunted grendels, just as she hunted them. But what worked with a young grendel failed against Old Grendel. She had eaten hunter-climbers and found their flesh delicious; but then almost anything was delicious, even swimmers, even her own swimmers. Since the Change she was vaguely aware that while all food was good, some was better. Meat was better than plants, walkers better than swimmers, alien swimmers better than her own. It had always been so, but she hadn't known it.

Now Old Grendel was slow. Still a blur, but a *slow* blur, if you like. She would wait for Snouter to get closer. . . .

The snouter stopped, turned, looked up nervously. It made a flabby wet sneezy bray and turned again, bending almost double, and bolted into the trees.

Old Grendel was too surprised at the sound in the sky to give chase. The sound made her uneasy and reminded her of the Death Wind, but it was not the same.

It came from the south, filling the sky, shadowing the land. Red and green. Unimaginably huge fangs. Terror on a scale she had never known filled her body, her heart. It was a grendel of cosmic size. It was God. It blotted out the sun, its giant lips grinning at her, challenging her.

She tried to disappear into the mud. If this thing, this colossus wanted her territory, there would be nothing for her to do but die.

But she would fight! She had to fight! It came straight at her, looming like a mountain, moving not much quicker, and she felt the *speed* course through her body, preparing her for action.

The *speed* roared through her like a flame, and she couldn't move. She couldn't see how to reach the beast! Slow, slow, it didn't *have* to be a new breed of grendel. Was it challenger or meat? *How to reach it?* Fire roared along her veins and her mind was shutting down. That rock? No, that somewhat more distant log—

She lurched from the mud. Mud splashed across startled snouters. Instinctively she smashed one with her tail, curling it so that the creature wasn't hooked and caught. It screamed and lurched away, but Old Grendel ignored it and flashed onward. In seconds she reached the low end of a tree that had fallen across a white boulder. For another second she was clawing her way to a stop, skidding in a curve along the mud, while the snouters scattered in all directions. She reached the naked roots and blurred up the log and launched herself, and tried to take her bearings as she flew. The God of Grendels was too big to miss.

She had never seen anything so large in flight. Certainly she had no practice targeting such. She was falling below it. It was as if she'd jumped at a moon! Her claws were ready, she had one last surprise for the beast when it turned to snap her up . . . she'd be no more than a mouthful, but she would burn its mouth. . . .

She smacked down into an inch of shallow water over soft mud. Impact knocked her dizzy, but she clawed for leverage and skimmed a tight curve, knees and ankles buckling, across the mud for a hundred feet, then burrowed.

She was two hundred feet from where she had been, buried snout-deep in moist dirt, motionless, with only her snorkel raised. The heat was leaking from her, the fatigue too, but too slowly. At this moment the God of Grendels could have her for a snouter. Where was it? She lifted an eye.

It was behind her. Above and behind, moving away.

It was leaving! She had driven it away! She had defended her territory—

But as, pain-filled, she crawled back to the river, the image of the hideous thing filled her mind. At some time in her long, long life, she had seen something like it before.

Much farther away. It had flown. Its markings had been different then, not a grendel at all—a black back, pale belly, enormous eyes—but it might be of the same species. It had moved the same, sounded the same. It too had been vast, larger than a whole brood of adult grendels. Bigger than a cloud. She could not begin to comprehend its meaning.

She had done a dangerous thing. The huge-eyed nightmare was going where she could not, where no rivers ran, and where jungles and hunter-climbers did. But she'd followed a rare rainstorm uphill, and kept moving after it was gone, up the slope of a nearby mountain.

That was not long after the Change. With her new sight she'd felt that she could do anything. She had reached the peak of the mountain and placed herself above that *thing*, in time to see it sink down to kiss the earth.

Three smaller flying things had left it. God's swimmers? Much smaller creatures had swarmed below it. Parasites, she surmised, seeking to spread their kind. But though they showed only as dots, she could guess their size. They never went on *speed* for as long as she watched. Slow, stupid: not grendels, but prey.

Then she'd crawled back down to water. Never a drop of rain came to cool her. She was ravenous every step of the way, and she had never gone on *speed*. If she had, she would have died.

Now this, the Grendel God. If it was prey, it would feed all the grendels beneath the sky.

She'd been hungry before, she was ravenous now. *New* prey. *New* tastes. New games to lose and win, new blood to wet her snout.

New, new, new.

If Old Grendel had been able to clarify her concept of a god, she would have prayed to it. The spawn of grendels were so small, not even a mouthful. One of those two-legged things would feed her beyond her capacity. She would bury it in the mud for a day, or two, or three, until it grew sweet. Until the water bugs came and ate its eyes into raw wet sockets, and the tissues bloated with nectar. Then she would feast.

The first tinglings of *speed*, urgent and warm, began to stir her. She clamped her mind down. She was already too close to being burned out. They could hunt *her*, this New Meat, this spawn of the Grendel God. They were slow, and clumsy, but . . . experience tried to warn her of danger.

All creatures make mistakes.

Hunter-climbers made mistakes. She had cracked their bones with her teeth, and savored the sweetness within.

She wiggled back toward the river, a few inches at a time. God floated toward the Cloud Mountain, where it began to descend. Where the first huge-eyed Great Flyer had descended. No rivers ran near there. Too far. Always too far, up the rocky slopes where she could go when there was enough rain, but that happened seldom.

But all things were prey to a grendel, and all things must spawn. Its spawn would come down to water. If she could not eat the great flying creature, then she would eat its spawn.

✳

"Deadwood Pass," Jessica said. The roboticized mining camp was located on a half-mile-wide mountain pass. To the east the land fell away steeply across rocky ground to the Grendel Valley River some called the Styx four thousand feet down and five miles away. The west side of the pass was less steep, falling a thousand feet to a high desert in a mile of boulder-strewn cliff slopes. The pass was bounded by steeply rising slopes to north and south. When the First found this area ten Avalon years before, a stream had run down from the northern peak. It wasn't a large stream, but it was enough to worry the First. They had changed its course with dynamite. Where once it flowed down to the pass and then westward into the desert, now it veered to the east and fell over a series of cliffs to make spectacular waterfalls. They had installed sluice gates so that water could still be diverted to run in the old stream when Deadwood Pass was occupied.

Water meant grendels. When grendels hunted they went on *speed*. It made them incredibly fast, but it also generated heat. A grendel too far from water could cook itself. They had never seen a grendel more than two kilometers from water except in rainstorms.

Joe Sikes examined the area below with binoculars. "Base, this is Sikes. I have examined the pass and I confirm no change in water levels," he said formally.

"*Roger, Joe Sikes,*" Zack's voice said. "*Geographic confirms no cloud formations, no rain expected, all water levels at or below normal in all directions from Deadwood. You are cleared to approach.*"

"Bring her down," Sikes called. He continued to look through the binoculars, sweeping his view up and down both sides of the pass, then up and down the sharply rising peaks bounding it. "Jess, Linda, please confirm this, I see nothing." He handed the binoculars to Jessica.

She made a cursory examination and saw Sikes grimace in disapproval. *All right, I'll play your game.* She looked again, this time sweeping the glasses slowly from the western desert up to the pass, across and down to the eastern valley floor. "Joeys," she said. "I see three Joeys about fifty yards north in the shade of the solar conversion cloth. Otherwise nothing."

Linda took the glasses and looked again. "Confirm, normal, three Joeys," she said formally, then laughed. "It must be safe if the Joeys are out like that."

"*Roger,*" Zack's voice said. "*All right, you're cleared to land. Keep us posted, and stay in touch, and we'll keep an eye on you.*"

Winds constantly blew across the pass, sometimes from the west, more often from the ocean to the southeast. The small flat area of the pass was smoothed by the constant wind. Now that the stream was diverted there was little green, just short brown and purple grass, and twisted brown bushes. The area was ugly enough, but it did hold a permanent mainland base: a square shelter to hold batteries and fuel cells, a hut good for overnight, packed with emergency supplies and technical equipment; and of course the mine itself. The north slopes above the pass were covered with solar-electric conversion material woven into the flexible sheets called Begley cloth.

Jessica took back the binoculars and examined Deadwood Pass. The first thing she saw was a tubular frame geodesic dome crouching like a spider above a great dark hole in the earth. Usually steam would be gushing from the hole. Today there wasn't even a wisp of vapor. The problem wasn't here. They already knew that. They'd find the primary damage twenty feet away, in the refining apparatus.

Linda had the controls while Joe gave instructions. They were both very relaxed, very professional. Jessica remembered Linda demonstrating the same kind of intense interest observing transplanted silkworms munching transplanted mulberry leaves.

Cadzie was in a corner, sleeping. Jessica walked wide around his bassinet. He didn't seem to slow Linda down very much, or else she never showed it. She only had to plan for him . . . but how did she learn?

The refining station was just below them through the huge windows, but they spared it not a glance. They were studying its innards on two of the viewers. One was a demonstration view—Jessica had to watch for a minute before she understood—a cartoon of the station working normally.

The little mining drones churned up the soft coal, and a conveyor belt moved it, a chunk at a time, up and over to the refinery. The prefabricated refinery processed the crumbly stuff, turning it into thick dark bricks of protoplastic, the fodder of their building and pharmaceuticals industry. Jessica recognized this sequence: it was a classroom film.

The other showed the refinery setup dead and mangled. Track had lurched out of one of several tunnels, had lifted and twisted the casing of the refinery system. The damaged casing was smoke-blackened across that side. Damage inside could not be seen. Ore had piled high before the system's rudimentary intelligence shut it down.

Joe said, "I'll kiss the ass of the nerd who's good enough to be sending us *that!*" and added as an afterthought, "Unless it's Edgar."

A *real* bomb, Jessica thought. Low-yield explosive. Wrecked equipment had forced an expedition.

The eel, too, had forced an expedition to the mainland. Interesting coincidence? Jessica shook her head. No one would do that.

"Touchdown in about nine minutes," Linda said.

Jessica groped in her pocket, began pulling on tough, light gloves. "I'm ready. Eager, and willing."

"That's what all the boys say." Linda examined her big sister craftily. "You'll probably cut out after an hour or so."

"Ask Joe."

Were Joe's ears turning pink? He said, "Security check, Jess. Make sure the perimeters are secure, and none of the movement sensors have picked up anything. Then we can let the kids down."

"And get them out of my hair. We've got work to do," Linda said.

Jessica scrunched her nose at Linda, and paused to say "goo" to little Cadzie. "Pete Detrich," she said. "You were dating him for a while last spring. . . ."

Linda straightened her back proudly. "I'm not telling, and that's that."

"All right, all right. . . ."

Jessica paused at the door, and then said back over her shoulder—"Zack Moskowitz."

"Hah! His mustache tickles."

Without admitting defeat, Jessica affected a slouch, leaving the room.

Jessica climbed down a narrow spiral staircase into the cargo bay. It was vast and almost empty now, thrumming with engine vibration as they neared the ground. There were six great bay doors of molded high-impact plastic. Four were already open. She took a door next to Justin, who already had the cable attached to his belt-buckle carabiner.

"Race you!" he said merrily.

"What stakes?"

"You make pan biscuits tonight."

"Fine—or you hunt up tubers."

"You're on."

She unlatched and flung her door open. The breeze ruffled her hair, cooled her face. They were fifty feet above the low, bluish grass. Even from here it looked scraggly, surviving where the heavier brush had died for lack of moisture. She tied the line through her carabiner and braced it at her hip, right hand taking the high grip, and threw the rest of the line out over the side. Before it had completely unreeled she launched herself. She looked back up, shadowed by *Robor*'s bulk, its Chinese-dragon facade dropping away from her toward the morning sky, and laughed.

She hadn't been the first out. That was Aaron, as usual, his hours of mountain climbing serving him well. But Justin was coming down fast, and then Katya and Trish and Toshiro, the six of them like a small colony of spiders spiraling to earth. The ropes still dangled sixteen feet above the ground when Aaron reached the bottom of his line. He paused a fatal instant, and she paused watching him, and Justin snapped free and dropped the rest of the way down, hitting and rolling like a paratrooper. He came back to his feet lightly, sporting a bruised face, a shoulder stained with dirt, and a grin of evil triumphant.

Jessica didn't jump. The five of them jumping in concert could wobble *Robor*'s descent.

When it finally came within reach Justin grabbed his line and anchored it to one of the steel loops set into the ground. Katya was next down. She grunted, trying to get her cable into a ring. It wouldn't quite reach as a gust of wind took

Robor sideways a few feet. Aaron grabbed the end of his line with his left hand and stretched out to grasp a steel ring with his right. His mouth gaped into an O of strain, and she heard his shoulders creak. But will and muscle and a shift of wind brought the line close enough to the ring for him to attach the mooring clip, and from there on it was easy.

Robor's undercarriage brushed the ground, and secondary lines tied it into place. As Justin walked past her, Jessica slapped him a casual high-five.

"Let's take a look at the processor," he said. She nodded.

The flat was four hundred meters across, rocky and mostly barren. Up a short incline was a second terrace. They scrambled up the lip of the rise, and paused. Geodesic dome. A dozen yards away, a corrugated shed housed the automated processor. Other than those, nothing for two hundred meters in either direction. Nothing . . . then a rise of mountain, crested with bushes with purple-green, roughly triangular leaves. The dirt beneath their feet was scarred, treadmarked where mini-tractors had carried their loads of plastic bricks back to *Robor*.

Ordinarily the mining equipment, sheltered beneath its dome of pipes, churned merrily away. But all was silent now.

Jessica turned and looked below her. *Robor*'s dragon shape stirred in the wind, seemed almost to breathe. Its red and green stubby wings struggled to break from bondage. The lower cargo doors were opening, ramps descending. One of the mini-tractors was exiting smoothly.

Below *Robor*, and beyond, stretched Grendel Valley. Green, wild, twisted with vegetation. And through the very middle of it ran a river. The Styx. Death.

Higher up were plateaus where children of Earth could play. North and east she could see three mountain ranges. The farthest high peaks were lost in the mist. In winter even the lowest would be snow-crested, but today the air was warm and moist, the light and heat of Tau Ceti steady upon them.

Pterodons glided silkily through the peaks, more plentiful here than on Camelot. On the island they ate fish, or darted into the isolated horsemane trees to snatch eggs from a variety of Avalon crab that lived in their tops. She could see other birdlike things. Huge insects, perhaps, dragonflyish things that darted. At half a kilometer she couldn't make out details.

The air was heavy, moist and . . . well, *green*.

It smelled alive. It buzzed and hummed and crackled. The very sounds here were different, a low, heavy thrum of life. The area immediately surrounding the Styx was relatively clear, but back a kilometer or so the forest began in earnest, dense enough to satisfy any dreams of childhood discovery.

Joe Sikes trudged up the hill while Linda followed with the tractor. Cadzie, stretching and looking about, bounced in a sling across her chest.

"What's the schedule?" she asked Joe when he was close enough.

Joe was laughing. "Jess, Chaka just went past me with a kind of a glass shell on his back. It must weight a tonne. He looks like a giant turtle!"

"It's just the cook pot, Joe."

"He could get something a lot lighter. Is he just showing off his muscles?" She chuckled.

"Star Born Secrets? Well, never mind. Business first," he said. "We want to take a good look at the processor."

Now the Biters were streaming down *Robor*'s passenger ramps. Twenty kids, the youngest just eleven, bright healthy kids on their first trip to the mainland.

"Stay close together," Jessica called down. "Patrol leaders check packs." She turned back to Jose. "Justin will check and if all's clear, we'll hike in and sleep at the oasis."

"The usual communication arrangements?" Joe was smiling a little, even through his concern.

"Joe. You wound me. It's a sheer accident that those transmitters get switched off every time."

"Yeah, yeah."

Justin was climbing up atop *Robor*, and had unhooked one of the three slave skeeters. He revved its engine, then whipped it up into the air and down toward the mining complex.

"We want to get down to Paradise," Jessica said, "get things set up. If we're lucky, we can get a Run in tonight. You can handle things here?"

"Sure," Joe said. "Straightforward diagnostic and repair. We've got the tools, and some replacement parts. Everything we need to repair—the problem is: what the hell happened, and will it happen again?"

9

PARADISE

I have lived some thirty years on this planet,
and I have yet to hear the first syllable of
valuable or even earnest advice from my
seniors.

—HENRY DAVID THOREAU, *Walden*

"Fall in. Count off," Justin said.

The youngsters formed a line, oldest and largest to Justin's left, a stair step
down of heads off to the right until at the end was Sharon McAndrews, not
quite the youngest but certainly the shortest. Beyond Sharon, Jessica, Carey
Lou, and Heather McKennie formed a small group.

"One. Two." They counted down the line to Sharon, then the older Scouts,
finally Jessica.

"Remember your number," Justin said. "Now let's do it again. Count off.
Okay. Remember your number, and remember who's on each side of you. Okay,
go wander around."

The kids scattered. Justin waited a moment, then blew a whistle. "Count off!"

There was a moment's hesitation, then they began, "One. Two." "Twenty-
six." Jessica finished the count.

"Right. We'll be doing that a lot," Justin said. "Now the rules—"

"We don't need no stinking rules." Carey Lou giggled. "Rules are for Earth
Born."

Justin saw that Joe Sikes was recording everything. "Not quite," he said.
"There are times when you need rules, and this is one of them. Now listen:

"Groups of three. Never less than three," he said. "One to break his leg, one
to stay with him, and one to go for help. Groups of three or more. Okay?
Good.

"The trail is marked, orange paint splotches on the rocks. If you see red
splotches you're off trail to the left side as we go out. Green is off trail to the
right side going out. Everyone got that?"

"Red right returning," one of the smaller ones said gravely.

"Right—uh, correct. And Jessica is Tail End Charlie. *Nobody gets behind Jessica. No one.* When I look back and see Jessica I want to be sure everyone is
ahead of her.

"When either Jessica of I call 'Count off' you count off, right then, and nobody ever answers for anyone else. This isn't Camelot! There are grendels out here."

Some of the Grendel Biters exchanged knowing looks.

"Okay." Justin turned to Joe Sikes. "Latest reports?"

"All clear to Paradise," Sikes said. He didn't sound happy. "You're cleared to trek. Good luck."

"Thanks. Okay, let's move out."

Chaka lifted his pack—minimal gear, plus the glass cauldron that was big enough to serve them all—and swung it into place with a grunt. He hadn't done that a moment early. Joe Sikes shook his head and turned toward the minehead.

Justin unslung his rifle and checked the loads, then led off down the side of the pass, down north and eastward toward the green valley and the grendels. There wasn't any danger up this high. Everything they knew about grendels said they couldn't go far from water. Still, he looked everywhere, ahead, to the sides. It was his fourth trip, the third as leader, and every time there was that feeling in the pit of his stomach.

The first time Justin had come down this trail his father had been leader, and Joe Sikes had been Tail End Charlie. There had been a big fight in the council, with Zack adamant that no children would go to the mainland.

"Think again, Zack," Cadmann had said. "You have to let go sometime."

"No."

"Speak for yourself, Zack. You can give orders down here, but my family hasn't been part of your jurisdiction since a year after we came here."

"That's not fair."

"Which way did you mean that?" Sylvia demanded. There'd been a buzz of conversation and whispers as everyone remembered those times. Cadmann had predicted anger. No one had believed him. No one believed there were any dangers on the island at all. They were all sure it was pranks, or something worse, an old military man's desperate efforts to be needed. Until the first grendel attack. Then Colonel Weyland had taken his share of tools and equipment and gone up to build the Stronghold, and if he hadn't done that, when the samlon changed the grendels would have killed everyone on the planet. No one liked to think about that, not then and not now. Colonel Cadmann Weyland, warrior and Cassandra. And now *Zack* kept seeing dangers.

The trail was dry and dusty, which made Justin feel better. Grendels didn't like dry and dusty. After fifteen minutes he stopped. The two youngsters who'd been trying to keep up with him gratefully leaned against boulders. Behind him the Grendel Biters were strung out along the steeply rising trail. No sign of Jessica, but the trail threaded among boulders. "Count off!"

"One. Two." The count moved back along the trail until he couldn't hear any longer. There was a pause, then more shouts passed back up the trail. "All present."

He took a moment to raise his binoculars. They hadn't had good binoculars the first time, just the increasingly rare and valuable war specs. Those had come all the way from Earth. Once there had been fifty pairs of the computer-enhanced optical systems. Now only eight remained.

But a year ago they'd been able to schedule the time for Cassandra to build optical grinding equipment, and now they had binoculars in a variety of strengths and fields. These were 10 x 60, really too heavy for backpacking, but he could see a long way, and they worked well into twilight.

War specs were Cassandra's eyes. The First could see through those; but they couldn't see through binoculars.

Justin scanned the area below. Far down in the valley something moved among the grass at the river's edge. Almost certainly a grendel. Not much else lived that close to a river. But sometimes—sometimes there were large things that didn't look much like grendels. They never stayed still or visible long. What were they? Another kind of grendel? They didn't know, and that ate at Justin.

This was their planet but all they really knew was that anywhere there was water there were grendels. All kinds of grendels. Some made dams, some hunted farther from the river. Some lived in shallow mud, some couldn't live without submerging themselves in river water, but if there was water, there were grendels.

The river was low. The lakes formed by grendel dams were not much more than ponds, and where there had been grassland and bushes last year there was nothing but caked mud with vast cracks. And above that were dry rock and horseman trees. Grendels couldn't live in the rocky ground above the river, but Justin scanned the rocks and sand ahead anyway. Nothing there but swirls of dust kicked up by the rising wind behind him. On Earth there would be snakes. He'd seen them in films. Avalon didn't seem to have evolved the snake, and so far they hadn't encountered anything particularly venomous, at least not to humans.

"Watch your feet," Chaka sang out. He was rolling along like a juggernaut, ignoring the way the ground rose. "Justin, Carlos will want that shell if you've got room."

Now Justin saw it too, an empty shell with a golden iridescence, curled and fluted, lying in the mud like a dinner platter lost from the Sun King's palace. Centerpiece crabs were big enough to catch Joeys, the largest thing that lived in these dusty areas. Their jaws held crud and corruption but they weren't dangerous to anyone with boots on. Carlos made wonderful things from their shells.

"Maybe coming back," Justin said. His pack would be lighter and roomier too.

"Okay. Kids, pass the word back, it's on your left and *don't miss it*. The centerpiece crab evolves those shells as a mating display. He wouldn't do that if he had to see to his defenses. You see an animal get that gaudy, or a bird, you know it's because he's been threat-free for a long time."

Carrying that mucking great pot, why wasn't Chaka puffing? Nobody else could do that, barring Aaron.

Behind Justin, Katya Martinez had her binoculars out. "Ha."

"Ha?"

"Joeys. Off trail to the left, about three hundred meters ahead."

"Ah. Good. If there's Joeys there aren't grendels. Okay, kids, let's go." Justin led them onward, through the dry rocky ground. The air seemed even drier than usual, a hot dry wind blowing through the pass from behind them.

"Devil wind," Katya said.

"Devil, you say?"

"They called it a Santa Ana back in California. Air mass flows down a mountain range, you get a *foehn* wind. *Sirocco* in Europe. Hot, dry compressive heating, lots of positive ions. Makes people nervous. You feel it, don't you?"

"Guess so. You read much about it?"

"Some."

"Anything I ought to know?"

"Do you think I wouldn't tell you? Ha. See, it's getting to me, too."

The trail led down and north along one of the mountain ridges framing Deadwood Pass. Twelve kilometers from the pass there was a saddle. Their dusty trail led to the right, then steeply uphill. Dimly above they could see green trees, bushes, tall but straggly grass. Justin called a halt.

"Fall in. Count off." He waited for the responses. "Okay, listen up." He pointed up the hill. "That's where we're going. Chaka, Katya, and I'll go up first. The rest of you follow along, but stay together. Jessica will tell you when it's safe to come up." He unslung his rifle and again checked the loads, then waited until Little Chaka and Katya had done the same. He carried the rifle at the ready as he led them up the hill.

"Are there grendels up there?" Sharon MacAndrews asked solemnly.

"Not *there*," one of the older Grendel Biters answered. There were snickers.

"Never been any so far," Justin said. "Not so far."

Eight years before he'd followed Cadmann up that trail. Aerial surveys showed there wasn't anything large up there, and *Geographic*'s IR sensors had never seen anything. "So what are we worried about, sir?" he'd asked.

"Caves. The second grendel lived in a river cave," Cadmann had said, limping along on a stick carved by Carlos and a skinny new regrown leg. "We went in after it. Stupid of us, we didn't know what grendels were." They'd gone up slowly, while two armed skeeters flitted about watchfully. "We lost good men hunting that grendel."

"Looks quiet." Chaka's words brought Justin out of his reverie.

Paradise was a garden mount in a desert of dusty volcanic rock. It thrust upward from the side of the mountain range, a rocky slope that rose steeply for nearly two thousand feet. The gentle bowl at the top was a five-hundred-foot circle no more than fifty feet deep at the center. Some trick of nature had placed a spring at one lip of the dish. Water gushed up and ran down into the dish. At the bottom of the dish the water vanished into the ground, never to reappear. Paradise was a high oasis with no streams leading in or out.

They circled the mound until they came up over the lip on the side opposite the spring. Vegetation was sparse here, but most of the bowl was covered with grasses and horsemane trees. Insects flitted among the plants. One flew closer to have a look at them.

It was smaller than a hummingbird, but larger than the insects of Earth. There were two large wings as rigid as the wings on an airplane, and a blur beneath it from its motor wings. It hovered near and didn't seem afraid of them at all. After a while it lost interest and flew back down into the bowl.

At the bottom of the bowl was a tree that seemed covered with webbing. Something moved in there.

Justin scanned the bowl, first unaided, then with his binoculars. Finally he opened his communicator. "We're here. I see nothing unusual," he said.

"Roger. *Geographic* reports nothing unusual," Joe Sikes said. "You're cleared to take the kids in. Only this time try to keep the radios working."

"Sure thing." Justin flicked the channel switch. "Bring them up, Jessica. All clear."

Dusk.

"It's getting late," Jessica said. "You sure you want to do this?"

"Part of the job," Justin said. "And it won't get any earlier. Chaka? Coming?"

"Sure."

"Me too," Katya said.

"I think I should go," Jessica said.

"Nope. Someone's got to be in charge here, and that's you. Let's do it." Justin looked over his rifle. "Check your loads. Right. Here we go."

He led the way out of the bowl, over the lip, and down toward the river far below.

✳

Jessica stood at the rim and watched them until they were out of sight among the volcanic rocks. "I've got a bad feeling about this," she told herself, but she grinned, because she'd had the same feeling last year, and the year before, and it hadn't meant anything. *Mostly I just want to go with them. . . .*

She went back to the kids. They were sprawled on the grass. Youngsters that age can be energetic blurs one moment, motionless heaps the next. *Another talent lost with age . . .*

Two of them had discovered the insect life in the grass. Jessica bent down next to them and peered between the yellowish purple blades. Something that looked like a red-orange beetle was caught in a sticky webbing, and thousands of blue mites, so small they resembled a powder, were swarming over him. They stripped the beetle and carried the parts away into the rocks.

The mites disappeared, leaving only an empty blue shell dangling from a transparent web.

Damn that was fast, she thought. *Insects on* speed?

She shook her head. "All right!" she called. "Campsite is down in the bowl. Let's get to it—we've got a lot of setup before dusk."

She hauled the kids up, complaining, and set them on their way, and followed after them. But she still couldn't quite get the memory of those mites out of her mind. If a Biter laid his sleeping bags in a nest of *those* . . .

Blankets and sleeping bags, tents and cookstoves were produced, assembled, spread about. The entire camp sprang into existence like magic, a bubbling, steaming, jostling cacophony filled with busy bodies and giggling children, Grendel Scouts scurrying about on secretive missions, and Grendel Biters channeled into busywork and told to mind their own business.

Carey Lou shucked off his backpack, and looked about for a place to call home. He wandered a little away from the main camp, toward the familiar shape of a horsemane tree.

The frozen-waterfall appearance entranced him. He had spent many nights back on Camelot in the shaded comfort of the local trees, and had stolen his first kiss in their shadow. He shucked off his backpack, perhaps nurturing romantic thoughts, and stepped toward the tree.

Jessica grabbed his shoulders, and marched him around. "No." Bad idea.

"Why?"

She brushed some of the hanging fronds aside. "Take a closer look," she said sternly.

He looked, and gulped. This wasn't at all like the friendly, sleepy trees on the island. From the root to as far up the trunk as they could see, and even in the strands of the mane itself, the entire tree was infested with symbiotes, parasites, *things*.

Near the base, the greenish brown mane had turned milky, and took on the appearance of a coarse spiderweb. Something was fluttering in one of those nearby. Maybe prey, maybe predator, maybe spider. Carey Lou didn't get close. He gulped again. "Maybe that one over there?"

"These things are notoriously hospitable to local life. Give it a try," she said.

Carey Lou walked cautiously to a second tree. He looked closely: no symbiotes. Relieved but still cautious, he pulled out his rolled tent. His thin arms snapped the roll outward and it unfurled into a triangle, then popped open further: a disk, then an open dome.

Four startled Avalon birds dropped out of the horsemane tree like so many dinner platters. They caught themselves, and wheeled around the tent as it settled to the grass like a big balloon. Two brushed wings, whirled to fight. One knocked the other spinning. It dropped toward a tree a dozen meters farther out, recovered too late. The tree had it.

Carey Lou stepped close, but not too close. Jessica was behind him, fingers resting on his shoulders. The bird: she could see details, now that it was trapped. Two big rigid wings, curved up at the tips into spiffy little vertical fins. Four little translucent oar blades, the motor wings, were still trying to thrash the bird loose.

The creature's relationship to a sea crab was very clear. The rigid wings had been a bifurcated shell, way long ago. That early crab hadn't been so specialized as today's crabs.

Jessica stepped forward, reached gingerly into the web. She was ready for something like a big spider. If anything had scuttled toward her hands she would have jerked back. Nothing did, and she pulled the bird loose, holding it by one wing. The motor wings buzzed, trying to pull it away. She held on until she had brushed webbing from the fixed wings. It was too rigid to bite her, but it shivered hard in her hand, trying to twist around to escape.

"I've seen these before," she said. "Have you? Where have you seen something like this?"

She waited expectantly.

Carey Lou studied it, knowing that she wanted him to get it right. His eyes suddenly opened wide. "Sea crabs!" he exclaimed.

"Right . . . go on."

"Split shell. You know, the wings are more like a beetle's than a bird's."

Jessica released the bird. It hovered for a moment. The four blurred motor wings were splayed like legs on a coffee table. Then they tilted aft and it zipped away. She said, "Very good. The grendels don't like salt water much—so there was a lot more variety in the life-forms just off the coast. All those crab things. Strange how often the pattern has repeated itself on the land, isn't it? We've seen leaf-cutting bee-things like little crabs, and birds like crabs . . ."

"And crabs like crabs . . ."

She laughed. "Anyway—our lesson for the night—camp only in the open, and back with everyone else. Now scoot." She swatted his behind, sending him back toward the others.

She waited there in the clearing for a moment, smelling the forest. This was good. There was nothing around here that could hurt someone Carey Lou's size . . . but it wasn't a bad idea to put the fear of God in him.

A little healthy fear could keep you alive.

✳

One of Old Grendel's daughters held the river hereabouts. Old Grendel moved up a tributary. Why fight her own blood, when far more interesting prey were about? She had a score of crabs trapped here. They hadn't tried to crawl past her; they were crawling upstream, and Old Grendel followed at her leisure.

She was following the weirds.

Far above her, the daughters of God had settled out of sight. They had come from the drylands, a place Old Grendel never expected to see close up, but now they had landed much closer. Those flattish shapes with their blurred wings reminded her of the near-universal shape of the Avalon crabs. But the huge grinning Grendel God was of a different shape entirely. Perhaps the "daughters" were parasites.

And the little ones, could they be parasites on the parasites?

She could see three, four of the little ones at the edge of the cliff, looking about them, then withdrawing one by one. Now others moved downslope, slowly, clumsily. Would they come to her?

No, they were gone before they came that far. Old Grendel observed patiently. The sky was darkening before she saw them again. Five, six weirds moving back up the rocky slope.

Old Grendel believed she could reach them.

She could see the tip of a tree up there. Likely there was water.

She could have to drink until she could barely move. If her daughter caught her then, she would die. With a belly like a drum, she would have to crawl two miles uphill without ever going on *speed*. At the top she would have used up every erg of energy; she would be dry as an old bone.

If there was no water, she would die.

If anything attacked her, she would die.

Watch them move, slow and clumsy, easy prey. It was like watching hunter-climbers. Old Grendel flashed underwater and crunched down on a bite-sized crab. She would see where else the weirds led her.

✳

At suppertime there were baked potatoes, and Cajun-style greens, and a Grendel Scout favorite, a rolled biscuit-bread baked in the campfire.

And as they settled down to enjoy the feast, the kids were treated to another specialty.

With great ceremony, Aaron and Chaka tramped back in from the shadows, carrying a steaming cauldron between them. "This," Chaka announced, "is the specialty of the house. This is the real reason that we like to come over here. There's never enough of it to take back to the island." He paused, and then said smilingly: "There really isn't enough for you guys, either, but if there's any left, you can divvy it up."

The kids looked suspicious, but when the older Scouts didn't even invite them to eat, and promptly served themselves, Carey Lou shouldered his way over, poked a spoon in, and tasted.

He pronounced it delicious, and they dove in.

It was like a thick jambalaya, served over crumbled biscuit. Delicious. It was filled with things that chewed like mussel and tasted like clams or fish. Several times someone asked what it was composed of, and received only an evasive smile in return.

"Secret recipe," Aaron said, and everyone broke up laughing.

There was only a tiny helping for each of the kids, enough to whet their appetite for burgers. "Mainland Stew," they were told, was for full Scouts only.

After a little wait, Jessica inquired innocently, "Who'd like some for lunch tomorrow?"

All hands went up.

"Well," she said. "I guess we have to respect the public demand, now, don't we?"

Carey Lou belched with satisfaction. "So tonight," he said. "Tonight we get to find out more about grendels?"

"Tonight," Aaron said.

Heather McKennie leaned forward, her dark eyes intense. "They were like a feeding frenzy coming after our parents, huh? Like sharks on earth?"

One of the other kids chimed in: "Or like piranhas! I saw that James Bond movie, and they ate that women right up!"

"Blood-crazed monsters . . ."

Justin laughed. "I read up on piranhas. It wasn't really blood that triggered them. There was this guy who went down to the Amazon. Zoologist named Bellamy. Went down there and studied the little bastards."

"Why?" Aaron asked curiously.

"Well, their behavior didn't make sense to him. The stupid little buggers rip each other to pieces. Dinnertime isn't a friendly affair at all."

"Ghastly business." Katya's "upper-class" English accent was *terrible*. "Not a black-tie occasion?"

"They'd eat the tie too. Now, our barmy zoologist began wondering: what's in it for the fish?"

He dropped his voice. "So they went to the village where it happens. Where the natives throw pigs into the water, for the entertainment of the tourists. And they'd throw one of these terrified creatures in the water, and it would thrash— and the water would churn with blood. Piranhas ripped it to ribbons in a couple of minutes. Just like in the movies."

Justin was getting into it now. "And he wondered: Was it the blood? Was it? And he took a bloody knife, and slipped it into the water . . ."

They held their assembled breath.

"And *nothing* happened. Nothing. And then . . . he slipped his foot into the water."

"Jesus. What happened?"

"Nothing. And then he slipped his hand into the water—"

"Christ! Did he stick his dick in the water too?"

"I have no idea," Justin said haughtily. "I did hear that he later requested an audition with the Vienna Boy's Choir, but that was likely a coincidence." Justin gave the speaker a nasty look.

"At any rate—then he slapped the water with an oar, and they went *crazy*." He leaned back. "It was the *splash* that did it, all along. Drives 'em nuts."

Aaron nodded slowly, thoughtfully. "I bet you have trees overhanging. Monkeys or something fall in occasionally . . ."

"Yeah. Instant piranha chow."

"Well, but there aren't many trees that overhang the water, and monkeys aren't that stupid," Chaka said. "Not enough critters fall in the water, certainly not enough to affect evolution of the fish."

"So why?" Aaron asked. "What is in it for the fish?"

"Absolutely nothing," Chaka said. "It's extra behavior."

"Extra?"

"Extra. Extraneous. Useless. Something that got genetically coded with a real survival characteristic. Happens all the time."

"We haven't found anything like that here," Justin said.

"How do you know? We haven't had the chance to look," Katya said. "Not over here. We understand Camelot, but really, the grendels didn't leave much to understand. Here there's a real ecology, but they won't let us come look at it."

"They," Heather said solemnly. "The First."

"They're just trying to take care of us," Sharon McAndrews said. "Aren't they?"

"Jailers take care of their charges, too," Aaron said. "You can't be a prison warder without a prisoner—"

Sharon McAndrews frowned. "You told us that you would tell us some things. About our parents." The other kids echoed her enthusiastically, but she sounded a little nervous.

Justin, Jessica and Aaron looked at each other. "Not tonight," Aaron said softly. "Tomorrow night. But not tonight."

"Why then? Why not now?"

"Because—" Justin began.

"You sound like a First," Heather said.

"Maybe I do. But we do have reasons," Justin said. "These are things you have to learn first. You'll know before we leave here."

"Is that a promise?" Sharon McAndrews sounded younger than her twelve years.

"Sure, it's a promise," Aaron said.

They sipped their coffee, and watched each other without speaking. Unspoken was the thought: *First, Carey Lou has an appointment. He won the lottery.*

*

Carey Lou had been asleep for no more than an hour when they came for him. They said nothing. Blindfolded him and tied his hands behind his back. Thrust a rope between his teeth. Someone spoke, in a voice too gruff for recognition: "Hold on to this, and follow us. If you drop it, we leave you for the grendels."

Thank God they slipped shoes onto his feet before leading him away from the camp, out into the woods.

He had no idea how long he walked, or what time it was.

He lost track of the distance. He could see nothing, but felt every slap of brush, heard every night sound. He kept telling himself that this was calculated. This was all planned. They wouldn't really leave him for the grendels. . . .

Still, his teeth bore down on that half-inch hemp until he was certain that it would break off in his mouth.

"Shhh," Justin whispered. He adjusted his night glasses, binoculars with big lenses to gather as much light as possible, and focused in. Fourteen-year-old Carey Lou was about twenty-five yards from the edge of the water, and looked ready to soil his pants. The boy stared back at them beseechingly. His hands were strangling the grendel gun. He knew that somewhere back in those shadows was Heather McKennie, she of the cutoff jeans, freckles, tanned hide, and raunchy sense of humor. Heather, a whole enormous two years older than Carey. Heather would be his prize. . . .

If he survived the night.

"Carey . . ." She called from somewhere in the darkness, beyond the torches.

"Oh, sleet," he said, and took another step closer to the water. Twenty-three feet now.

Justin's rifle scope gave him a good angle on the pond. Aaron would be fifty feet to the north, similarly equipped. Little Chaka was farther south. All wore the modified infrared scopes. They would have barely a second to act, but that would be enough. Reacting to grendel flare was something Avalonians learned almost before they could walk.

Carey took another step closer to the water.

Burbling just beyond him was a spot already identified as a grendel hole. That meant a momma, and a flock of young'uns in the larval stage of grendel development. Samlon. They knew that upon maturation Momma would drive them out. In lean times she would eat the samlon themselves. On the island of Camelot, an entire ecology had developed—samlon eating algae, mommas eating samlon. They also knew that under ordinary circumstances, momma grendels would eat *anything* rather than their own young.

They would certainly eat tender fourteen-year-old colonists.

Jessica's voice wafted from somewhere in the bushes. "Just a little closer, Carey. . . ."

Carey, stark naked, terribly alone, looked back into the brush. He would be blinded by the torches, unable to see anything.

Justin remembered his first grendel hunt. He hadn't been alone, but there hadn't been a backup team behind him either. He'd waded into the water, going slowly, feeling stark terror, but more too. Carey would be feeling that now.

Stark terror. Anger. Fear. And excitement, because if the grendel came and he survived, he would be a man.

Naked except for the grendel gun, shivering with the cold, Carey took another step toward the water—

And then the water parted. Something glided from its depths. A black destroyer. A fanged shadow. A thing of terror and appetite, made flesh. It blinked slowly, placidly at the naked creature trembling before it, and took a lazy step.

Carey shifted his rifle at the first disturbance. The kid was quick. Skinny, but quick. Justin was already sighting—

Carey screamed, aimed, and fired. The grendel gun bucked, and a splash of Day-Glo orange splayed across the grendel's snout. The grendel *blurred*, flying toward Carey at heart-stopping speed. Carey fired again, and shouted, "Oh, sleet!"

Another long second, and the marrow had to be freezing in his veins. Perhaps the first bitter words of condemnation and a forlorn prayer were beginning to form on his lips. . . .

Then fire flared in the darkness behind the torches. Three shots almost as one. A quarter second later, a fourth shot. Then the grendel was hit six, seven, eight times, slammed by heavy-caliber slugs that fried its nervous system, turned its assault into a leaping spasm, splashing toward the paralyzed Carey, who seemed to be watching the entire tableau in slow motion.

He staggered to the left as the grendel thundered to earth. It was on its side, its projected prey forgotten now. Alive, but in an awful agony as its own *speed* sacs overloaded. A quarter ton of amphibian death clawed at the ground, screaming, chasing its own tail in diminished circles, tearing up earth and rock and grass there in the half circle of the firelight, its dying hiss burning their ears. . . .

Steam rose from its body. Its claws and tail trembled, twitched, and were still at last.

Carey turned back to look at them as they emerged from the shadows. Jessica hung back, her motion sensors wary for additional predators. They were pretty certain about this—only one momma per hole. But grendels had surprised them before.

Not *this* time, but it *had* happened.

"You . . . bastards," Carey said. Panting, he flung his rifle down on the ground. Pitiful in his nakedness, he had clearly wet himself, but was unconscious of it.

"You incredible bastards." He took another breath, and held it. This was a critical moment. He looked back at the grendel. Justin remembered the first time they had done this, and what the kid had said afterward. There had been no one to do this for *him*—he was one of the eldest Star Born, and no Earth Born even *dreamed* that something like the Grendel Run was going on. None of the Earth Born would do something so risky . . . and so much fun.

But he knew that Carey was looking at them. And the rifles, and then at the grendel. And remembering the incredibly short pause before the grendel was blown back into the water. Less than a second. Time enough to lose control of his bladder. Time enough to feel more naked and defenseless than he had ever imagined a human being could feel. Time enough to experience the incredible precision required by a kill team.

Carey looked at them and swallowed. He knew somehow that his entire reputation for machismo rested upon what he said next.

"Well . . ." He strained to sound casual. He bent, picked up his rifle. He walked toward them until he was standing three feet from Justin. He extended the rifle with his left hand. Justin extended his own right to take it—and Carey hit him, quite hard and very quickly, with his right first, just under the left ear.

Justin stumbled back, tripped, and went down.

Finally Carey smiled. "That was . . . pretty fair shooting." He watched Justin carefully.

Justin pushed himself up to a sitting position. He felt his jaw tenderly. "Got a pretty good right there, kid." And held up his hand.

Carey took it and yanked him up, then stood with his legs slightly apart, well balanced. His lopsided grin was challenging. "Hendrick's a good coach," he said. Justin nodded. No action. A great sigh seemed to go through them all, a release of tension.

"You'd have got him, you know," Justin said. "It was a good hit."

"Why the hell do you do that?" Carey asked.

"It's fun," Aaron said.

Justin frowned. "We had a kid panic once. Nobody got shot, but it was close."

"Why paint? Cassandra would know if I hit—oh."

"Heh. Cassandra doesn't know about this. Jesus, can you imagine what Zack would do?"

They all laughed.

"So who panicked?"

Justin looked at him and shook his head.

"Edgar," Aaron said.

Carey smiled knowingly.

"Got the grendel, though," Justin said.

Carey coughed politely. "Who's got my clothes? My nuts are freezing."

Heather sashayed out of the dark. "Here's a blanket," she said sweetly. The blanket was wrapped around her. When she opened it, there was nothing underneath but Heather.

Carey swallowed hard. It wasn't certain, but the good bet was that Carey was still a virgin. Well, this evening would see the end of *that* onerous burden.

Heather wrapped the blanket around the both of them, and Carey became very, very involved in a kiss. Amid the general cheering, the two of them retreated from the firelight.

Aaron grinned. "Today I am a man," he said.

"Indeed. Now. Jessica—any other ghoulies about?"

"No grendel-sized heat sources. Let's harvest some samlon."

By the time they got back to Heorot, Tau Ceti was rising over the mountains.

Mercifully, the day was set for lazing and play. Carey Lou managed to stagger to his tent and collapse. Or at least they assumed that he was collapsing. Heather was with him, and the more Justin thought about it, the more he was convinced that a fourteen-year-old libido just might be impervious to fatigue, fear, and a thorough workout by the (rumor had it) inexhaustible Miss McKennie.

Ah, youth.

The day passed quickly, samples were gathered and catalogued, lessons on wildlife and herbology were taught by the elder Scouts, and a considerable amount of skinny-dipping, impromptu tree-climbing competitions, and general hell-raising continued through the day.

When evening finally fell again, there was a pleasant air of fatigue settling over the camp. They had shared two extremely *alive* days. Carey had also learned that three other Biters had suffered as he had. He was a member of a fraternity now, and he was already relishing the thought of passing that favor to one of the younger kids in a few years. Say, his younger brother Patrick . . .

The cook fires were burning, and soon dinner would be prepared. But there was another question still on the Biters' minds, and they had pestered their elders all day long.

Finally, Aaron sat them down, not a shred of playfulness in his attitude.

"All right," he said. "There's something serious we need to talk about tonight. Tonight, it's time that you learned things."

"About our parents?" Sharon asked.

"Things about your parents. And grandparents. There are reasons why they didn't come over here. Why we're the ones."

"Why?"

Justin and Jessica looked at each other nervously; then Justin said, "When you freeze something that has water in it, you get ice crystals. They thought that they had whipped the problems, but something went wrong. They froze the crew of *Geographic*. They woke them up in shifts for various duties around the ship, crossing from Sol to Tau Ceti. And there were problems."

"Problems?" Carey asked.

"Yes. When you freeze people for a hundred years and then wake them up, chances are you've formed some ice crystals in their brains. Wake them twice, you get more crystals. Crystals rupture cells, mess it up in—" He tapped his skull. "—here."

"What did it do?"

"A lot of our parents aren't as smart as they used to be. They get emotional problems, too. Coordination. Early strokes. Just plain stupidity. At first it didn't really matter. They were still smarter than most people they'd known, and they'd chosen the island because it was safe. No problems to face, nothing they couldn't deal with. Even then, they got in the habit of talking things over, being sure they weren't doing something stupid—"

"Rules," Sharon McAndrews said.

"Rules," Justin agreed. "And that was good enough for a while. There weren't any real dangers here, none that they knew about anyway. Then, the first grendel came. They didn't understand. They had rules, and they stuck to the rules, and it didn't work, but Colonel Weyland helped them and they defeated the first grendels. They went hunting, and when they thought they had killed all the grendels, they hadn't. You know about that. What you don't know is how bad it shook them. After the Grendel Wars they stopped trusting themselves and they stopped trusting each other. They didn't work well together when the grendels popped up, and that's one of the reasons that our parents are so afraid of them now."

There was silence. Justin could see it: they were trying to find a lie in the story. But there were too many clues. They knew, they had always known. There was something wrong with Mom, with Dad. With Uncle. They had always known, but never had a label.

Now they did.

"Ice on his mind," Carey Lou said. "I've heard that, but nobody would tell me what it meant—"

"And my mother slapped me when I said it to her," Sharon said.

"Christ," Carey Lou said. "What can we do?"

"Love them," Jessica said. "They're doing the best they can. That's what we expect of you. Just love them, but do your own thinking. Including about their rules. That's why they make rules. They don't trust their own thoughts, not when they act alone. So they try to get a collective judgment on everything that can happen, and make that a rule, and then they follow the rules no matter what."

"Ice on their minds," Carey Lou said again, slowly. "Son of a bitch!"

Aaron and Trish carried a pole across their shoulders, with a dozen netted samlon suspended from it. They were singing some kind of hunting song or working song . . . "High ho, high ho, it's off to hunt I go" . . . making up verses as they approached the campfire.

Water was already simmering and bubbling in the glass cauldron. Potatoes and onions had been brought over from Camelot, but there was more: mainland bulbs and leaves known to be edible, and tasty. Some of the brighter Scouts noticed how flashlights had been focused into the cauldron, so that the vegetables could be seen dancing around in the roiling water.

There was an air of excitement, and someone ooh'd as Justin produced a wicked-looking knife and sliced the heads off the samlon.

"Look at their eyes," he said. "But for us, they would have been grendels one day, and hunted us. We killed them first. What eats grendels?" he asked. "We eat grendels."

They were as tense as an audience awaiting a magic trick. Justin figured that that was pretty close to accurate.

His blood-smeared hands gathered the beheaded samlon up and carried them to the pot, dropping them into the water.

The water foamed with blood.

"Watch," Justin said, "watch and see . . ."

Those first few trips, the Scouts had been crawling all over each other to watch and see, to look down into an inadequate aluminum pot. Once Ansel Stevens fell in and scalded his whole arm. Once there was a full riot. The pots kept getting bigger, but the Scouts still missed most of the action, until Chaka got big enough to carry this mucking great glass cauldron. And now everyone could see it all.

The three gallons of water in the pot churned. The samlon sank, and then churned up to the surface again, in a curious and disquieting imitation of life.

Something was happening. The flesh of the samlon split, and wormlike things boiled out. Scores of them. Hundreds. Pale, fleshy things churning and dying in the boiling water, turning the clear bubbling broth into a kind of thick gumbo . . . or jambalaya.

The Biters pulled back, choking. There rose from the red kettle a stench of blood.

And in a disturbing way . . . it was a good smell. Like last night's savory aroma, only stronger.

Justin and Aaron and Katya and Jessica and the other Second watched ghoulishly. The children stared at the kettle, sniffed at it. One of them fled to the entrance of the cave and vomited.

In a half hour the brew was done, and ladled into bowls. It was an evil-looking mess, filled with fragments of samlon heads and the gutted carcasses now torn into chunks by Katya's bloody knife. The dead worms and corkscrew things were bloated pinkly in death. There were little transparent crabs no bigger than a Biter's fingernail. The base stock was as crimson as tomato soup. It looked filled with insects.

Aaron held the bowl to his lips. The Biters watched him, horribly fascinated.

"Mmmmm," he raised the spoon to his lips. He blew on it. Something thick and wormy flopped over the edge of the broad spoon. He slurped it up as if it were vermicelli, making a smacking sound. "Delicious."

"Dinner," Jessica said, "is served."

10

THE FIRST CHURCH
OF THE GRENDEL

In thee, O Lord, do I put my trust; let me never be
   ashamed: deliver me in thy righteousness.
Bow down thine ear to me; deliver me speedily; be thou
   my strong rock, for an house of defence to save me.
For thou *art* my rock and my fortress; therefore for thy
   name's sake lead me, and guide me.
Pull me out of the net that they have laid privily for me:
   for thou *art* my strength.
Into thine hand I commit my spirit: thou hast redeemed
   me, O Lord God of truth.

—*Psalm 31:1–6*

Jessica rose only when she was absolutely certain that the others were asleep.
On tiptoes, she crept out of the cave. The soft purring snores of sleeping children surrounded her. She felt a delicious synthesis of maternal concern and
utter wickedness.

Aaron waited just outside the cave, and held a finger to his lips. "Shhh."

Jessica nodded, understanding the need for secrecy. This wasn't for Justin.
Not anymore—he had made his choice, and Jessica had made hers. Her heart
thudded in her chest as she followed Aaron down the path. They passed a tree,
and it wasn't until they had passed that she realized that it wasn't just a shadow,
but Trish, dark as the night. A Bottle Baby.

Trish joined them as they moved silently down the trail. Little Chaka and
others drifted into their line until there were seven in all. They came to a small
clearing near a very shallow running stream.

"Running water," she observed unnecessarily. "Everything I am, and everything I've learned says to stay away from it."

Aaron nodded. "*In mortis veritas,*" he said.

He pulled a stone away from a cairn of fist-sized, smooth rocks. Then all
seven of them were rolling away rocks, until they exposed a small kettle
wrapped in transparent plastic.

Trish produced a hot plate and a battery cell. Toshiro brought water from the
stream, and filled the small kettle.

Jessica's stomach felt light and fluttery. During the day she watched Aaron
studying leaves and plants with the intensity of a trained ethnobotanist. She

was one of the very few who knew *why* he studied so intently. Quietly, without drawing any attention to himself, he had collected the plants that he needed.

He had also collected the grendel's liver.

Speed generates enormous heat. The metabolic by-products would kill the grendel, just as the by-products of combustion will kill a fire. Its liver and bile ducts—or the grendel versions thereof—are awesome. A grendel can eat anything, and survive the products of its own massive oxidation, because of its efficient cooling and detoxification systems.

At thirteen years of age, Aaron had analyzed grendel bile ducts, livers, and other organs of cleansing with a view to psychopharmacology.

At fourteen he had created the Ritual. Since then, he had indoctrinated ten others into the mysteries of grendel flesh.

"The First Church of the Grendel," Jessica had laughed. Aaron had barely smiled.

The kettle was bubbling now, and would soon be ready. He added a few handfuls of mushroom-looking things, and something that looked like a fern. She nervously contributed her own handful, a few leaves pruned from one of Cadmann's living-room cacti. Poisonous, yes. But in very precise combination with certain plants, and the liver of a grendel that had died on *speed* . . .

She watched the stars. The same, but different stars from those beneath which her ancestors had lived and died, loved and hunted, fought and borne children. But they were *her* stars. The way to survive is to become one with the environment. The Earth Born still saw Avalon as a place of strangeness, of danger. Every one of them would have to die, the things of Earth would have to die before this planet could be truly conquered. And this ritual, as old as humanity, was the prayer of the hunters and gatherers whose lives were interwoven with the land itself. The Earth Born had come as the Europeans to the new world. Aaron said that they would have to learn the traditions of the Native American peoples in order to survive here. They could not own the land, but they could be a part of it.

Aaron dipped a cup into the brew, and lifted it steaming to his lips. "To us," he said. "To the children of a new world."

He drank. When he was finished, he passed the cup to the left, and the ritual was repeated, and again, until all of them had downed a mouthful of the sour mash.

It smashed into her gut like napalm. She broke into a sweat, her heartbeat rocketing.

For a few foolish moments she prayed that nothing would happen this time . . . then her stomach soured, and she knew there was no use in hoping. It had begun.

During the first grendel ceremony, she had vomited. Since then Aaron had incorporated acid neutralizers and buffering agents, and now the entire experience was, at least physically, much milder.

The psychoactive alkaloids were kicking in now. External sounds were fading.

It was not that they weren't there, or that she had gone deaf, it was that her focus of attention was so tight now, so utterly complete that it was as if she was staring down a long, long tunnel. There at the far end were the simmering kettle and the fire. And if she turned the focus of her attention on Aaron, she saw Aaron, and only Aaron, and if she looked up at the stars and the night sky, she could focus on any point of light, bring it up bright and tight, a hot little marble that she could almost hold in her hand. Aaron's voice crooned to her, sounding for all the world like the music of those very spheres:

"We are the inheritors of this world. We own all of this, everything that we can see, everything that there is to own. We are the strong ones. The others call us Merry Pranksters. We do what we do to test our power. To insure that we can control every aspect of this planet. And then we place a clown's face upon our deeds so that the old ones will feel no fear.

"But one day we may have to take other steps. And when we do we will have to act as one mind, as one body. As the inheritors of this world, with no barriers between intent and action. As one mind. As one body . . ."

She could hear his words, felt them slipping between those bright hot marbles. She was burning up, but sought refuge in the very fire that consumed her. Aaron's hands were on her. And then other hands. And then she was reaching, touching, tasting, consuming and allowing herself to be consumed in the fire raging within her, without her, and in the space between those bright, hot marbles in the sky.

11

INVISIBLE DEATH

Death hath so many doors to let out life
—JOHN FLETCHER,
The Custom of the Country

The children and their guardians were not quite alone. Above them was *Geographic*. In geosynch over Camelot, *Geographic* maintained a web of satellites across the continent and around the planet, and kept careful track of weather and tidal conditions. *Geographic*, the largest movable object ever created by man, had carried its cargo of frozen human begins across ten light-years, expending a cubic kilometer of deuterium snowball along the way. The deuterium was exhausted now. Its sleeve was a shrunken silver balloon, the pressure inside barely higher than the vacuum around it.

Geographic could still be moved by smaller steering rockets, but until the deuterium was replaced—if it ever was—she would remain in eternal orbit around Avalon. She was their link to Earth, and the Earth Born insisted that all of their children be taken up. "This is your heritage. You call yourselves Star Born, now see the stars."

A few came back as often as they could. Some of the Second still dreamed of crossing the void between the stars. A few even spoke of returning to Earth. For the most part, though, the children of Earth were rare visitors. *Geographic*'s corridors were empty, cold, and dark, with only a few flickering lights to give any sign that she had once been alive.

In the command center, the duplicate of the ground-based Cassandra system analyzed a planet's worth of data. She filtered it, and relayed down whatever seemed of interest.

Greg Arruda looked up from his novel as the comm light came on. "Arruda here."

"*Zack. How are things?*"

"Jesus Christ, Zack, they're the way they were the last time you asked." He looked at the console. "The board's green. No large objects approaching the oasis. Children all accounted for at last head count. Wait one—"

"*What?*"

"No panic, Zack. Yellow light from one of the close-in satellites. There's a wind coming up. Northwest wind, about thirty knots through the pass."

"*Rain? Rain means grendels!*"

"Ah . . . indicators say dry. Way dry, suck the water right out your pores. Zack, for God's sake, you worry too much. Let the kids have some time to themselves. And get to bed! I'll call you if there's anything you need to know."

"Yeah. Greg, I know you think I'm a fussy old woman—hell, you were there, you remember grendels."

"No, they slipped my mind for a good twenty seconds there. Zack, get to sleep."

Linda woke as Cadzie shifted in his blanket to search for a nipple. Half-asleep she cooed to him, and peeled back her blouse. Drowsily suspended between dream and reality, she didn't really wake up until Cadzie was sated. The morning was still dark. Light would creep across the glade in another twenty minutes.

Joe was still asleep, his strong, broad back to her. The regular rise and fall of his breathing was absurdly comforting.

They made a good team. They worked together well, and they played together well. And love was . . . every bit as good. It felt whole, healing. She could easily imagine being with this man for the rest of her life. As soon as she could be away from Cadzie for a day or two, she was going to take Joe down the Miskatonic, in the wedding ritual as old as Camelot himself. All the way down to the ocean, there would be camping, and cuddling, and long, slow, warm lovemaking, and it would be . . . wondrous.

She wrapped the infant in a blue blanket, covering all but his nose. She opened the door of the dirigible, and stretched in the breeze. She felt utterly content.

Joe had come up silently behind her and was kissing the back of her neck. Dawn was coming in now, darkness already giving way to a warm, silvery glow. The air was no longer still. Ginger and Toffee, the twin golden retrievers, were still asleep, curled up next to each other near the dead fire. There were buzzing sounds and distant calls of pterodons, and even more distant hisses, calls of the monkey-things and the imitative calls of the big spider devil that hunted them.

She turned and kissed Joe. His morning breath was sour but not unpleasant. She handed Cadzie over, patted Joe on his rump, and went to wash and dress, girding her mind for the day's business.

By the time Linda climbed down from *Robor*, Joe was already roughhousing with Ginger, pretending to bite her throat, growling and barking at her. He gathered up Cadzie and gave Linda a minty kiss. The two of them crossed the glade, dogs nipping at their heels. She never noticed that all the creature sounds of Avalon had gone away.

The machinery within the corrugated refinery shack was burnt and twisted and scummed with pink fire foam. Linda placed her drowsy son just outside the shack, in the waxing sunlight. Ginger curled up next to Cadzie like a big cat. Dog warmth, and the heat of his blue thermal blanket, would keep the boy comfortable until Tau Ceti climbed a little higher.

Joe was still examining the equipment when she returned. He looked utterly disgusted. "Morning light doesn't improve it much, does it?"

"Not a bit. Let's go ahead and make the report." She touched her collar. "This is Linda Weyland, at station three. Who's on duty?"

A second or two of silence, and then they got their reply. *"Edgar here. Hi Dad, Linda. Nobody else around yet. Ready to report?"*

Joe sighed. "Frankly, I think that we should trash it and rebuild."

"Except that it might happen again," Edgar said.

"There's that. Edgar—"

"Yes, sir?"

"Oh hell, of course you don't know anything you're not telling us," Joe said.

"They don't tell me everything," Edgar said. *"Aaron doesn't much care for me, and the others—do you still think it's sabotage?"*

"No," Joe said carefully. "I'll say that for the record. After examining the damage here at the minehead, it is my considered opinion that we don't have the foggiest notion what happened. It's another goddam Avalon Surprise."

The wall shuddered as the wind howled against the shack. "Bloody hell, that wind's come up strong," Joe said.

Linda stepped out to fold the blanket over Cadzie's face.

"Sorry, Edgar," she said. "We're picking up a little wind here."

"What?"

"Wind."

"Roger, we see that. There's a storm coming southeast over the mountains. Dry wind, no danger from grendels, but is Robor *secure?"*

"Very."

Ginger growled, coming to joint. She looked off toward the west. Toffee was fifteen feet away, staring in the same direction. They began to bark, yapping against the growing wind. A dry wind, hot. It dried her skin faster than she could sweat.

"Joe? That wind is really coming up. Double-check the moorings, will you? And get a wind warning down to Heorot."

Joe dropped a length of singed tubing, and grunted in disgust. "You *know* that they're off-line. We can get them in an emergency, but that's about it."

"All right—well, I hope they've got the skeeter sheltered."

"You know Justin. But I'll go make a check."

Linda kissed Joe, and he looked almost surprised. "I'm just going to *Robor,*" he murmured against her lips.

"Do I need a reason these days?" she asked.

"Never." He kissed her again, and started off across the glade.

"Will you guys stop the mush?" Edgar said disgustedly.

"No respect," Linda clucked. "Remember—I'm going to be your mother one day soon."

"Hey. You know, one of a mother's duties is to find mates for her offspring."

"I told you what to do about that problem."

"Sure. I'll keep trying. Linda, Dad says it wasn't sabotage. You agree?"

"Yes."

"*Say that again?*"

"Yes! I agree it was not sabotage. Edgar, that wind is really howling now, it's getting hard to hear." She put her hand across her nose in a vain attempt to filter the dust. "It's as if the coal had little flecks of dynamite—" She stopped. Some creature was howling in torment.

"*What's that?*" Edgar shouted.

"I don't know—" Across the clearing, the dogs were leaping and biting—at the dust. Joe slapped at his chest and neck and face. At first she thought it some kind of joke . . . some kind of crazy dance.

The wind was stronger now, driving a wall of dust before it. She coughed and stepped out of the shelter, trying to see more clearly. Her smile was dead on her lips, her laughing questions stillborn in her throat. "Joe . . ."

And then she screamed.

"*Linda? Dad?*" Edgar's voice sounded urgent. "*Alert! All stations alert! Base Two is in trouble!*"

She was blind before she quite realized that she was in trouble. Agony shrieked in her eye sockets, and she slapped her hands up to cover them. Blood slicked her palms, she felt the hollows where her eyes should have been, and the backs of her hands were being shredded.

The world was consumed with agony. The wind roared in her ears. She had time to scream "Joe!" and then the pain was at her lips, her tongue, and she was gagging on blood. Some mass staggered into her, and she knew it was Joe, darling Joe, loving Joe, groaning like a thing that had never known human consciousness. The dogs' barking had transformed into an endless, pain-racked howl.

✳

In Camelot, bedroom alarms shrieked, and the streets were filled with sprinting bare feet. Hastily armed grendel guns pointed in all directions, and found nothing. There was no threat to be seen.

By now the image from Satellite 16 was being piped through *Geographic*, enhanced, and relayed to Camelot's communications center. The image was expanded again, and then again, until it seemed the scene was no more than a hundred yards distant . . . but it was all a blur, just textures shifting through fog.

Hendrick Sills was first into the center. "What's the alarm, Edgar?"

There was panic in Edgar's voice. "I thought it was a dust storm! They come through there regular, no problem, but the dogs started barking and Linda was screaming and now I can't hear anything, and I can't see anything, and my God!"

"Get hold of yourself," Zack said. "Dust storm. Rain?"

"No, no rain, it's a dry hot wind, sirocco wind. Stronger than they usually get, but— Zack, I can't hear anything. They were screaming, and now they don't answer! What do I do?"

"Keep watching. Can you zoom in?"

"Trying. There, the dust is thinning out—"

The image focused. Edgar's voice dropped to a whisper. "Oh, my God." Two human shapes and a dog shape were writhing on the ground. "Dad! Linda!"

The wind howled, and under the wind they could hear a baby's wail. The image cleared for an instant. Shapes thrashed, slowed, then faded into a fog of blowing dust. Someone muttered a prayer; then the room was still. Half a world away, two people that they knew and loved were dying in agony, and there was nothing that they could do to help.

✳

Linda was beyond pain. She felt her eyes eaten away, the flesh etched from her bones.

With the very last strength in her body, her blood-slicked fingers closed on Joe's misshapen, lifeless hand. And her last thought was *Cadzie* . . .

She heard her baby crying, crying, crying . . .

And then there was nothing at all.

12

PARADISE LOST

Nature is usually wrong.
—James Abbott McNeill Whistler,
Ten O'Clock

Jessica snuggled next to Aaron in their sleeping bag. She was only half awake until the whitter of skeeter blades roused her from her reverie.

She had barely wedged her eyes open in time to see it thump to ground, landing too damn fast. Justin leapt out, and ran toward them. "Emergency, dammit!" he screamed. He was bare-chested, wearing only briefs. A surge of adrenaline whiplashed her into wakefulness. Aaron was already scrambling to his feet.

All right, so Camelot had gotten nervous. This wasn't the first time the Star Born had taken themselves off line. She knew that they'd catch hell for that one day, and just maybe that day had come. . . .

She struggled her clothes on, and hopped out toward the skeeter. Sprawled around the dead fire, the other Pranksters were hauling themselves toward consciousness.

"What's the problem?"

Justin looked pale. "Edgar rang through. He was on-line with Linda and Joe. They got cut off. *Move* it!"

The piled into the skeeter. Aaron had time to yell "Trouble at Deadwood!" to Toshiro, who was up and pulling on a knit shirt. "We're going up. Get back to camp and watch the Scouts. Set a defensive perimeter. Keep them back in the cave. Interlocking fields of fire and no mistakes."

"Got it."

Jessica buckled in. "Any sounds, messages, images at all?" she asked.

"Screams," Justin said tightly. "Just screams."

"Anything on the motion sensors? The thermals?"

Unbidden, Edgar's voice came over the radio. *"Nothing. We've got Sat Twelve locked on, and I don't see anything. I think they're dead."*

They rose up out of the glade, in toward Heorot. There they dropped down for a moment. Jessica and Aaron took the other skeeter, and she had them airborne in fifteen seconds. Their ascending spiral twisted the glade, the valley, and the surrounding mountains into a dizzying whirl.

No one spoke as the skeeters leveled out and dove, crossing the two kilometers to the camp in about ninety seconds. *Robor*'s Chinese-dragon shape leered up at them, its red fringes rippling slowly in the wind.

There was nothing. Nothing . . .

And then Jessica whispered, "Oh dear God." Bones. Human bones. Animal bones. Aaron said, "I see three skeletons. Two human. One canine." His voice still held a machine precision. He was speaking for Cassandra, for Edgar back at Camelot. For whoever might have tapped into the line, and was now sick with concern.

Her mind reeled. Grief and fear and raw hatred boiled within her like lava. Her vision clouded. She gripped the handbar in front of her as if a moment't loss of concentration would tumble her off the edge of the world.

Justin's voice was arctic. *"What do you see on the movement sensors? Any thermal flares?"*

"Nothing."

"Nothing," Aaron agreed.

Justin's voice was labored. He sounded like some kind of animal straining in a trap. *"I don't see any sign of the baby. Of Cadzie."*

A trapdoor opened in the back of her mind. She felt herself slide a little ways down, then clawed her way back up. What waited at the bottom of that pit bore fangs and claws, and was ravenously hungry.

"No sign. Not yet." And what she didn't say, what she couldn't say, was *Cadzie is barely a mouthful for a grendel.*

They hovered almost directly over the glade. Skeletons. The mining dome. A dozen yards distant, the refinery shack. The dirigible. And that was all.

Aaron snapped out the trance first. "Cassandra, replay Sat Twelve, during or just prior to the incident."

Jessica slipped on a pair of goggles, and watched while the images played. Running, struggling. A dusty windstorm. Death.

Bones.

"Oh, sweet Jesus," Jessica muttered. "That was no grendel."

"It wasn't anything." Aaron was shaken. "It was *invisible.*"

✳

Camelot was awake, and gathering in the main hall.

Carlos tore at a scrap of ragged flesh at the corner of his thumb. The satellite feed kept playing it over and over again, enhanced with thermals, to full magnification, giving the illusion that the couple was no more than a hundred meters away.

Impossibly far away. A world away.

Justin's voice came over the speaker. *"This is Skeeter Two. We are holding at seventy feet. We see skeletons. There's nothing alive down there that we can see. Nothing we can do to help them. Need instructions."*

Zack touched his collar. "Moskowitz. Did you say skeletons?"

"Yes, sir. Two human skeletons. One canine," Aaron said.

Zack was unnaturally calm. "We copy that. Skeletons. Satellite inspection detects nothing."

"Motion sensors detect nothing," Aaron said. *"And we see nothing—wait one. There is a small skeleton in the rocks about about twenty meters above the camp."*

"Human?"

"No, sir, too small. Now I see another. There are two small skeletons. I would say Joeys from the size."

"You say there's nothing to be done for Joe and Linda?"

"That's my best judgment," Aaron said. *"And there's no sign of the baby."*

Zack looked around. "Where's Colonel Weyland?"

"On the way."

"Hold off on landing for a minute, please."

There was no answer. "Please continue reports," Zack said. More colonists streamed into the hall, their voices a roiling cacophony.

"Wha—"

"The hell—"

"Will somebody tell me—"

"Who's up there—"

Still no answer. Zack lowered his voice. "I know that you can hear me. Hold off on landing until we have an assessment—" Carlos tried to imagine what Justin was feeling now. In one sense, he couldn't possibly know. In another, he understood precisely. The entire colony was family, their lives linked as closely as the fingers of a hand. But Linda was Justin's kid sister.

All of their lives, the Second had heard horrific stories. But a thousand stories pale in comparison to a single scream of agony.

The crowd behind them parted as Cadmann Weyland stormed in. He was red-faced, unshaven, and flinty-eyed. His beige coveralls were wrinkled and stained, as if he had thrown on yesterday's clothes.

He glared at the screen, his face as solid and square as stone. "What happened?"

"Something attacked the minehead," Zack said. "No one knows that."

The second image was a skeeter-eye view of the same scene. Skeeter ID number and pilot registration were etched at the bottom of the screen.

"Justin," Cadmann barked. "Who's up there with you?"

A long pause.

"Justin! Answer me, dammit." They didn't hear a sound at first, and then Justin's voice rang down to them.

"Jessica. And Aaron."

Thank God, Cadmann thought. Jessica and Justin could handle their own, but Aaron Tragon was one of the best shots he had ever seen.

"We're going down, Dad."

"Hold off on that. We're still sweeping the area."

"We don't see anything. The motion sensors don't pick anything up—"

"They didn't pick anything up twenty minutes ago, either!"

Mary Ann had made her way to Cadmann's side. Her face looked as if emotion had been pressed from it like oil from an olive. "Linda? Is Linda all right—"

Cadmann squeezed her hand. "I don't think so. Justin, you're there. Do you see the baby?"

"Baby!" Mary Ann shouted. "Justin, go find her!"

"Cadmann." It was Aaron's voice this time. "*You're wrong. The sensors did pick up motion before. Wind. Dust storm. Probably some kind of mineral powder, something that confused the sensors. We have to go down.*"

"Roger. Be careful. Secure *Robor* first."

"We will."

"Is that safe?" Zack demanded.

"They're on the spot," Cadmann said. "And without *Robor* they can't get the Scouts off the mainland."

"Oh—"

"Cadmann, what's happened to Linda?" Mary Ann wailed. "Justin, where's the baby!"

"*Father,*" Jessica said. He almost didn't recognize the voice. He had never heard his daughter sound like that before. "*I don't see Cadzie.*" Her voice was beyond ice, somewhere out in deepest space. The clearing juddered on the wall. "*Father, that's Linda down there. And Joe. They're dead. But one dog is missing, and I don't see Cadzie.*"

He was searching for something to say. What hope was there for his grandson's survival? Almost none. And yet, if there was any chance at all . . .

"All right," he whispered. "We'll keep watch from here." Then he turned, and held Mary Ann. When it came right down to it, there was really nothing else to do.

✳

Justin watched Jessica touch down without a bump, taking that last couple of inches as carefully as a man stepping onto thin ice.

Aaron dismounted, carrying a grendel gun. Jessica bore a regular hunting rifle, its safety off.

Justin hovered overhead, watching. He wiped his moist hands nervously on his pants. He strove to starve his imagination, to keep focused on each individual moment. *Now* and *Now* and *Now,* and after that, the *Now* to come.

One careful step at time, Jessica and Aaron Tragon crossed the twenty feet between the autogyro and the skeletons. After each single footstep, she stopped to sense her surroundings. There was no sound except the steady *shoop shoop* of Justin's skeeter blades above them.

Aaron's gaze locked with hers for a cold moment, and then slid past. Neither of them was willing or able to speak. Her heart thundered loudly in her ears.

Three skeletons—two human and one canine—lay in a rough circle of flattened grass, as if they had thrashed around crazily, fighting, maybe. Fighting what? Where were their clothes? Could they have come running out naked? Naked but with sandals on . . . and Joe's hat, but not Linda's woven straw bonnet.

Aaron kicked over a small rock that lay beneath the smaller skeleton: Linda's, the one with no hat. There was a tiny bloodstain under the rock.

"No blood," Aaron said. "Little spots like this, but no blood! How long since—the attack started?"

"Twenty-eight minutes since we heard the skeeter alarm," Justin said.

Aaron looked around warily, rifle at the ready, but there was nothing to shoot at. "And it was all over before we got here."

Jessica couldn't move her eyes away from the three skeletons. The bones were stripped bare of clothing and of meat, but all were in place, as when an archeologist opens a grave. Nothing had broken or scattered the bones. She picked up Joe's hat and rubbed it in her fingers. Inside the brim it looked etched, or chewed.

Bones stripped of cloth, of meat, of sinew, ready to be mounted for biology class. Eyeless sockets glared up at her. Something gleamed. "Linda's chain," Jessica said. She pointed. A chain of tiny gold links encircled the neck of one of the skeletons. The next thing she knew she was bent over, stomach contracting violently. She felt it squeeze and pump, heard her own gagging sounds as from a distance, as if that other part of her were above the glade, watching as the tall blond woman tried to turn herself inside out. Aaron laid a comforting hand on her shoulder. She very nearly hit him. She wiped her mouth with the back of her hand. *No time for emotions, you sniveling bitch.*

"Cadzie," she whispered.

"What?"

"He's got to be here somewhere. Whatever did this was in a feeding frenzy. It wouldn't have taken him somewhere else."

Stripped clean. Plucked bare.

"Where's the other dog?"

"Hope to God it ran away. Ran far enough." They headed toward the mining shack.

Her collar buzzed. It was Justin. *"What do you see?"*

"It's Linda and Joe and one dog."

Aaron's voice was flat. "We're going over to the processing plant. The . . . door's open. Still no sign of the baby. Continue to record."

"Be careful," Justin said.

"Right."

Jessica was ahead of him, rifle at the ready. The ground was bare, not even dust. Jessica stopped short and pointed.

"Another small skeleton," Aaron said carefully. "Probably an immature Joey."

Jessica reached the processing plant. The door was open. There was an aroma of burnt plastic within, and an ancient, oily musk. The door creaked on its hinges as she pushed it back.

The interior was deeply shadowed. Slivers of light slanted through holes in the roof. Her breath sounded like slow thunder.

"Nothing," she reported. "There isn't any sign of . . ." She spun at a sudden clatter behind her. Wind against the corrugated steel door. There was nothing,

nothing here at all. She heard Aaron's voice from outside. "You had better come here."

Her heart was a stone in her chest. She went outside, dreading what she was about to find.

Aaron closed the door. Behind it was the skeleton of the missing dog. Next to it was a bundle in a blue blanket. It made a coughing sound, and began to cry.

Jessica watched motionless as a tiny pink fist thrust out of the blanket and waved, more fiercely now, crying, calling for a mother who would never come. "He's alive!" she shouted. She touched the collar button, then changed her mind. Instead she ran to pick up the baby.

Cadzie clutched at her. She dropped his deep blue blanket in the dust and held him at arm's length. Cadzie was furious. Cadzie was—

She hugged him with her left arm so she could touch her collar button. "Cadzie is alive! Dad, you hear? He isn't even marked!"

"We have found the baby," Aaron said. "He is apparently unharmed."

"*Tragon, this is Weyland.*" Her father's voice, flat and unemotional, came from her collar tab. "*Would you repeat that?*"

"Yes, sir. We have found the baby. Jessica is holding him. He appears to be alive and unharmed."

"*Thank you. Advice.*"

"Yes, sir."

"*Jessica, get the baby into the skeeter and stand by. Aaron, we've got good photographs. Grab anything you think might help us understand this and get out of there.*"

"Sounds good to me." Aaron nudged Jessica. "Go to the skeeter. I'll cover you," he said. "Get inside and close the doors."

She nodded vigorously. She wanted to run, but she was afraid she would drop Cadzie. It felt good to be in the familiar skeeter seat.

"Justin, do you see anything?" Aaron asked.

"*Nothing on either side of the pass.*"

"Then I'll chance gathering the bodies," Aaron said. "But I don't get it. Something hit this camp. Fast and hard. Killed everything. Except a baby. It couldn't find a child wrapped in a blanket."

"*Maybe it wasn't hungry by the time it got to Cadzie.*"

"No, that's not it," Aaron said. "It stripped a dog next to him, right down to the bones."

"*Aaron, this is Zack. We think you should get out of there. You can gather evidence later.*"

"Agreed." Aaron ran across the dry ground to the skeeter and jumped in. "Okay, Jess. Hang on to the baby. We're out of here!"

13

EVACUATION

A monster fearful and hideous,
vast and eyeless.

—Virgil, *Aeneid*

Carey Lou was afraid. There was something wrong, and no one would talk about it. They were all calm. Too calm, so calm that their very lack of emotional expression terrified him.

Each skeeter could carry three children and one adult pilot, and under three guards, the children were escorted back up. Carey Lou was in the third group, and maybe six times he asked the same question. "What's wrong? Is something wrong?" And received no answer. Finally Aaron Tragon, big Aaron, his buddy, looked at him, his eyes like glass. Carey Lou almost felt afraid in that moment. Not of grendels or of some other bogey being out in the jungle, but of Aaron himself.

That, of course, was *crazy*.

So he asked no more questions as they carried load after load of children back up the mountain, and when it was his turn he didn't question, had run out of questions, and wanted only to squeeze into his seat, and make himself small.

Justin piloted the skeeter, for which Carey Lou was grateful. Whatever was going on, Justin knew about it. He could tell in the rigid set of his shoulders.

The skeeter spiraled into the air. Ordinarily he loved flying. But this time there was no joy. There was nothing but fear.

Why won't they tell us . . .

What's wrong . . .

They circled *Robor*. There were two pairs of guards on each side, facing away from the craft, grendel guns at the ready.

Their expressions just about froze his heart.

He had thought that *Robor* looked funny, almost comical. A big grendel. A big dragon, the biggest that ever lived. But there was nothing funny about it now. They landed behind the two guards, and were immediately whisked into *Robor*'s shadow by Jessica, who looked almost as pale and emotionless as Justin.

Again he was struck with the contrast. Jessica and Justin looked scared. Aaron looked . . . intrigued?

They ushered him up the gangplank, and into the hold, and he went to the nearest knot of kids and lowered his voice, asking, "Does anyone know what's going on?"

He found Heather, who tried to smile in memory of a magic evening. She looked as frightened as he felt. "Something's wrong," she whispered. "Somebody's dead."

Carey Lou went to the front window and pressed his palms against the glass. Who? Who was dead . . .

He remembered who had stayed behind. With her baby. The room swam.

"What in the hell was it? I *won't* believe in invisible grendels!" Cadmann squeezed his eyes shut, and massaged his temples with stiff fingers. There was a monster of a headache coming on. They'd seen every kind of grendel, and he was far too close to believing in this one, too.

There was a numb sensation in his chest, something spreading as if he had been struck there. He wanted to scream, to foam, to throw something . . . to do anything but sit here and wait. Wait as they received sketchy video broadcasts of skeeters relaying children back to the *Robor.* Wait, and pray to a half-forgotten God. "Not everything on this freezing planet is a grendel," Cadmann said, tasting the thought. It felt right: real. "We don't have any idea of what's really here. We've *got* to stop acting like grendels are the be-all and end-all of lethality."

Hendrick grabbed his arm. "What in the hell are you talking about?"

"We've been afraid of grendels," Cadmann said. "To that extent, we've probably blinded ourselves to what is actually out there . . . over there. We never went and looked for ourselves, and I think that the grendels became a kind of bogeyman." The screens showed *Robor* taking off now, safe. Safe from what lived in the ground.

Have they gathered her bones? he asked himself. *God. I hope they gathered her bones.* But of course they would. Jessica would insist and Aaron would have done it. *Thank God Aaron was there.*

He felt numb. Doors were slamming in his mind, and behind them raged fear and grief.

If he wasn't careful, a door might creak open. Behind one of them was Linda's birth. Such a small, wrinkled, bulbous thing she had been. And his first touch, his first scent of her . . . she would have been a breech birth, but for the prenatal diagnostics, and God. . . .

He slammed that door in his mind, and the one with invisible grendels behind it too. *Pure horror fantasy. You'd have to be crazy.* . . . Came up, hearing the hubbub in the room . . .

. . . and then sank down again, fighting as his eyes grew hot, and then flooded, all of his efforts to keep his tears under control as futile as their attempts to tame this fucking planet.

It was no good. None of it was any good, and he had to leave the control room, which had grown crowded.

The news had to have reached every corner of the camp by now. Razelle Weyland would be flying in from the lumber preserves, and her brother Michael from over at the slope camp. People were looking at him with an emotion in their faces that he had never seen there before: Pity. Shock. They wanted to touch him, to comfort him, but with every step he felt the shields sliding down, even as the shields around his heart crumbled.

The images were coming so fast, too fast, as if there were twenty years of tension, twenty years of fear stored up inside of him, and now that it had clawed free and claimed his youngest, there was nothing to hold back the pain anymore, and then . . .

He saw her, running up to him. Linda was just a baby, and her round and shining face, the diapers bunched up between her chubby thighs, her little chubby arms outstretched to him, her smile stretching that round little face. Her eyes so blue, her mother's eyes.

He held out his hands to her, stretched out his arms. Stretched his arms across the table, his fists closed hard on the edge, his good ear pressed flat against wood, eyelids like tiny fists closed hard around red-hot embers.

$$*$$

The trip back to the island was subdued. The children were wrapped in blankets. Some of them cried. All knew, by now, what had happened to Linda and Joe.

Jessica came to sit next to him. Justin looked at her, and she felt the oddest sensation from him. Almost as if he were a stranger, rather than her brother. His eyes weren't hot, or cold. They were just eyes. Black holes, gathering data.

Justin's hand strayed over and over again to his pistol, palm resting on it as if death might follow them into the air, come aboard *Robor* and follow them back to Camelot.

"Where were you?" he asked quietly.

"You know where," she said.

"Pranksters," he said.

"Justin—even if I had been there, right there, I couldn't have done anything."

"Of course."

"Justin—she was my sister too! Don't shut me out. Please."

"She shouldn't have been there alone."

"She was *not* alone. She was with Joe!"

"You're right. You're right." He wiped his hand over his face. And for the first time that she could remember, Jessica hadn't the slightest idea what was going on behind her brother's eyes. Was he blaming her? Himself? Imagining what he was going to say to Father? Was he thinking of the bones in the hold, all that remained of their baby sister?

She reached out to him, touched him gently on his shoulder, and was absurdly happy when he didn't brush her hand away.

Aaron came up behind her. "Jessica," he said, "I need to talk to you."

She was torn between Justin and Aaron for a moment. Then she smiled almost apologetically, and said, "I'll be right back."

Justin's gaze slid coldly from Jessica to Aaron and back again, and then he nodded, so shallowly that it was almost no motion at all. And then, in some way that she couldn't completely explain, Jessica knew what Justin was thinking.

And feeling.

She *knew* it, but couldn't *quite* make the thought rise up to consciousness.

That might have hurt a little too much.

✳

The entire colony was on the beach as *Robor* floated into bay. Cadmann drew his coat collar up around his jaw. The cold seemed more piercing somehow, as the mist rolling in off the ocean penetrated coat and shirt and skin. Around him, radios crackled. A dozen rifles were held in crossed arms.

Perhaps Death is aboard the Robor, he could almost hear them thinking. It was what *he* wondered. It was the fear that had lurked just beneath the surface of their loves and growths and actions, every day for twenty years. And now it had come home to roost.

The air was filled with the ocean's steady, rolling roar, the crackle of the radios, and no other sound at all. Then they heard the purr of skeeter engines. Out of the fog loomed *Robor,* like some great mythical beast bearing its dreadful, beloved cargo. Its gigantic red lips glistened in the mist. As soon as the lines dropped, colonists chased after them to tie them to the docking loops.

The mood was dark, probably the worse he had seen since . . .

Remember Ernst, Cadmann . . . ?

His memory didn't want to go over it again. And over it, and over it.

Someone yelled an instant before one of the docking lines slapped across his face, smashing his head back. His hands flew up to fend off the blow. His hands clasped the flagging rope as he pulled. His hands and shoulders ached. As Stevens and Carlos lent their weight to his line he reached up a trembling hand to feel his right cheek. His fingers came away bloody, and he said something ugly.

Robor touched down. The rampway opened.

14

THE TRIAL

I, John Brown, am now quite certain that the crimes of this guilty land will never be purged away but with blood.

—JOHN BROWN, *Last Statement*

There had never been much need for a formal courtroom. Most problems were handled in a counselor's office. Really severe cases, such as the time years before when Harlan Masters tried to horsewhip Carlos, were decided in the council meeting room off the main assembly hall.

It wasn't a very large room. Seven First Generation, four men and three women, sat at a dinner table with their backs to a bright window, so that it was hard for Jessica to see their faces. Everything had been done in a stilted formal manner that she wasn't used to. Like something out of an old Earth novel.

"Do you have anything to say in your defense?"

She couldn't even tell who had asked that. Probably her father. No one had slept for almost forty-eight hours, so that all the voices sounded alike, unbearably weary. The forensic reports, diagnostics on the mining apparatus, the computerized clarification of the death scene, depositions from each Biter and Scout . . . all of these had taken their toll.

"Yes," she said. "We were out of contact. I'm not going to lie to you about that. I know that it was against the rules."

"And what were you doing while you were out of contact?"

"I don't see what that has to do with my sister's death."

Cadmann's fingers were folded carefully, and he looked up and down the panel. "We are attempting to determine the cause of the disaster. Your delayed reaction time may well have been a contributing factor. If some of you had stayed behind, or been closer, or responded to your radio links . . ."

"What are you insinuating?"

"They might have tried to call you on their comm links!" Cadmann half stood. "She was your little sister. You should have looked out for her!"

"The camp was secured, dammit!"

"Yes," Cadmann sat back down. "It certainly was. I ask you again, what were you doing?"

We were sleeping it off, and I am damned if I'll tell you that. "We slept late. Grendel Scout graduation runs late, and there's an orgy after the ceremonies." She said that defiantly. "We weren't scheduled to be back earlier."

"You're right, of course," Cadmann said. "But it's a damn shame. More eyes, more rifles, you might have done something."

"Do you think that hasn't tortured me ever since we saw—what we saw?" she demanded. "Colonel, I plead guilty to the childish prank of being out of communication, but the fact is that we couldn't have got there in time to do or see anything to begin with."

"She's right," Zack said.

Silence. Somewhere outside, a tractor coughed to life. Zack said, "Can you think of anything else we ought to know? Thank you. That is all, for now."

Jessica looked defiantly from one of them to the other, and then lowered her voice. "No one here lost more than I did. No one. I loved her, dammit. Every time I close my eyes, I see her face, and I ask myself: Was there something I should have done? Is there anything I forgot? Is there . . ."

"Thank you, Jessica," Zack repeated. "I think that will be all. For now."

Jessica stared at Cadmann as if she was expecting him to say something else. Something more—anything more. She turned, and left the room.

Cadmann fought to keep himself focused on the moment. But it was all he could do to keep his mind away from that terrible moment when the oilcloth was carried down from *Robor*, and he had unwrapped it, carefully, gingerly, as if what lay within it could still be wounded by human effort.

One set of those bones had been his youngest daughter. The other, one of his oldest friends.

He had only known Joe Sikes for, what . . . ? A hundred and twenty years? And there was a thing that stood between them, but they'd recovered from that. . . .

"This is an inquest, not a formal trial," Zack announced carefully. "I do warn you that anything said here may be used as evidence in a trial if this board of inquiry decides to file formal charges. Do you understand this?"

"Yes, sir."

"State your name."

"Aaron Tragon." There was the faintest hint of a smile at the corners of his mouth. This was all being recorded, and there was no chance that Cassandra didn't know who he was, but the rules said that you state your name to begin formal hearings.

"Aaron Tragon, you were in charge of the children's expedition."

"No, sir. Justin was in charge. I was second-in-command," Aaron said carefully.

"Why do the younger Scouts say you were in charge, then?" Zack asked.

Aaron shook his head. "I guess because we don't make a big thing of it," he said. "Justin and I both know what to do, and it never came to any conflicts, so I suppose the kids didn't know."

"Or care?"

"Yes, sir, or care," Aaron said. "I'm sorry sir, but it just wasn't a big deal."

"All right, I can understand that. But you were second-in-command. You were aware that the communications cards had all been turned off?"

"Yes, sir."

"Why?"

"It was a tradition," Aaron said. "Maybe a silly one, but—this is Graduation Night, something we Seconds do, and—"

"And you don't need no stinking First listening in?" Carlos prompted.

Aaron nodded. "Something like that. We wouldn't put it in quite those terms."

"You resent the First?" This was from Julia Chang Hortha, agronomist, nurse, counselor, and a minister of the Unitarian-Universalist Fellowship, the closest thing to a formal church they had.

"Well, sometimes, ma'am," Aaron said. "Not the Earth Born so much as all the rules."

"Rules are important," Zack said automatically.

"Sure they are, for—" Aaron cut himself off. "Yes, sir, under many circumstances rules can be very important."

"But not for you?" Cadmann asked carefully.

"Not always for us, no sir. Colonel, we are of age in any civilization you had on Earth. Full voting citizens entitled to full rights, including the right to live under laws we have consented to. Aren't we?"

Everyone in the room knew what Aaron hadn't said: "laws made by people in full possession of their faculties, not by those with ice on their minds."

"You have made your point," Zack said. "But the fact remains that you consented to the rules before you went to the island. Didn't you?"

"Well, yes. We had no choice."

"Consented under duress?" Carlos asked carefully.

"If you prefer."

"All right, Aaron. Tell us what happened."

"Yes, sir. We were awakened by a panic message from the watch officer, Edgar Sikes. That is all recorded. He told us there was trouble at the minehead. He was highly disturbed and shouting.

"Jason, Jessica, and I took the skeeter after telling Toshiro Tanaka where we were going and instructing him to set up a complete defensive perimeter at the camp for the protection of the children."

"Yes. That was well done," Cadmann said.

"Thank you, sir. We then proceeded to the minehead. Again this is all recorded. When we arrived we saw no large animals and nothing that could have attacked the campsite. Linda Weyland and Joe Sikes were unrecognizable, identifiable only by jewelry. The dogs were mere skeletons.

"We were hesitant to approach the site but we had no choice since there were no signs of the baby. We then found the child alive and unhurt. Jessica took the baby and locked herself in the skeeter. When she was secured there I photographed the site and recovered the human but not the animal skeletons. At your suggestion I was as brief as possible. We returned to the children's camp. We then assisted in getting everyone aboard the dirigible and returned to the island."

"Anything you would have done differently?" Cadmann asked.

"No, sir. By the time we got to the minehead, it was far too late for—for medical remedies. They were not merely dead but—" He put his fingers to his temples and shook his head. "Absolutely nothing we could have done would have been of the slightest use."

"And there was no sign of what killed them? No clue, nothing?" Dr. Hortha asked.

"None I saw. As we got closer there was—"

"Yes?" Zack prompted.

Aaron's eyes drooped, he wasn't seeing Zack. "Motion. Yellow dust in a wind. Sir, I'm not sure I saw anything, and I can't find it in the satellite recordings. If it was there, it blew away before we could get close. But after we found the baby and before we left, I looked again. The dust was just the usual dust that always blows across the pass. It's a dusty place, more so because we diverted the stream away from the pass. I'm sure you all know that."

Cadmann looked up from his papers. "Thank you, Aaron, we both know that whatever the formal chain of command, you're the real leader of the Second."

"If so it's unofficial, sir," Aaron said. There was little expression in the face, or to the voice . . . but somewhere, back in the cave where Aaron Tragon lived, something had shifted and coiled. He was warier now.

"We also know of a group that we call the Merry Pranksters. Now, you're either their leader, or you know exactly who is, and who's part of that group."

Aaron shrugged. Now his face had no expression at all.

"And we all know that during trips to the mainland, you have private gatherings. Some of these involve the younger children and are part of the graduation ceremonies. Some do not. We haven't interfered, because it is important that you assume as many of the responsibilities of this colony as possible. Some of us understand that you really are citizens, you know."

"Yes, sir. And?"

"What I want to know is . . . were you performing such a ceremony the night that my daughter was killed?"

"Yes, sir, we were."

"Were you further away from the encampment than you had been directed to travel."

At the corner of Aaron's mouth, a muscle spasmed. "Yes, sir, we were."

"Were you out of radio communication?"

"To all but an emergency alert, yes, sir."

"And it is conceivable that Linda might have been too confused, or in too much pain, to remember proper procedure for an emergency message."

Aaron thought for a moment. "Yes, sir, it is possible. I might even think it likely."

Cadmann nodded. He could respect this boy. He was a good one.

"And you can agree that it was your duty to remain within range of the base camp, which you did not. And to remain in contact, which you also chose not to do."

"Yes, sir."

Zack interrupted. "I have another question."

Aaron regarded him almost as if he were an intruder. "Yes? Sir?"

"During this period of time when you were out of communication, were you intoxicated?"

Aaron's eyes narrowed. "Yes, sir, we were."

"And the intoxicants were not on our list of . . ." Zack struggled for a word.

"Sir. They were not on the list of recommended inebriants. But if it had been beer, or marijuana, the results would have been the same. We made a mistake. But the choice of psychoactives has nothing to do with that."

"I disagree," Zack said. "From the very beginning, from the discovery of that eel, to the discovery of the explosions on the mainland, to the way we were pressured into this operation, to your behavior on the mainland, this entire affair has been handled in an irresponsible, childish, criminally stupid fashion."

Aaron turned back to Cadmann. "Sir. Our actions on the mainland were disastrous as it turned out. We certainly broke rules. But normal safety precautions were taken, with the exception of radio links, and proximity. I submit to you that whatever killed Linda and Joe might well have killed anything else nearby. And in any event we weren't supposed to be up there that night or that morning. Yes, we used teacher plants and then connected with each other—"

Zack was unimpressed. "You mean you got high and had a sex orgy."

Aaron didn't rise to the bait. "We put the littler ones to bed first. We chose Toshiro Tanaka to stay straight and be in charge. And while we're talking for the record here, I want that record to show that the kids were our responsibility, and we met that. Not one of them was killed or hurt. They were our responsibility. Not the people up at the mine, who would have been there even if the rest of us hadn't gone to the mainland at all."

"Aaron—" Julia said.

"Yes, Dr. Hortha, I should calm down," Aaron said. "And I will. But I wanted this on the record. We met our responsibilities.

"As to what we were doing, that is the business of the Star Born. The Second, if you like that term better. But we are all adults, and the nature of our ceremonies is no concern of you Earth Born."

"I say it is!" Manny Halperin had been quiet until this explosion.

"It was a spiritual ceremony, Mr. Halperin. We have the freedom to practice what we will—"

"You got stoned and fucked your brains out!" Spittle flew from Halperin's mouth. "What the hell is so damned spiritual about that?"

"Do I have to answer that?" Aaron demanded.

"I'd appreciate it if you did," Zack said.

Aaron paused. When he spoke all of the incredible blowtorch intensity of his will was focused onto Zack.

"I didn't *choose* to come here," Aaron said, his voice so soft and low that they had to strain to hear it. "I didn't ask to be born not of woman. You brought us, and gave us a world filled with opportunity—"

"And dangers," Cadmann said quietly.

"Yes." Aaron smiled. "Dangers. You brought us here, into a situation which you couldn't possibly understand, a very dangerous situation indeed. And many of you died. Did you hold a tribunal then? Did you judge each other? Did you ask each other questions about how you prayed, on those nights?"

Damn straight we did. Cadmann wouldn't have spoken anyway—

"How *dare* you question us!" Aaron thundered. "How bloody god damn *dare* you! We are not your possessions. And I am not your child. Not the child of any of you. You made damned certain of that, didn't you? Not one of you would give me his name. My name came from a record book. The only place I could call home, the closest one of you I have to a father, is the man whose bones I picked up out there on that pass! You think you lost something out there? So did I!"

"Aaron," Julia Hortha said.

"No, ma'am, I won't calm down. Not this time! You hypocrites! You believed that because you fed us and clothed us and taught us we should be freezing grateful to you . . . well, we are. But don't tell me what god to worship, or how to worship It. It is none. Of. Your. Freezing. Business."

He had lowered himself so that both knuckles rested on the table, and he stared directly into Zack's face.

Then he stood up. "Of all of you, only Cadmann is a *man*," he said. "The rest of you can go to hell. Cadmann. You have always told me the truth. You have always spoken from your heart, not from some freezing rule book. What do you say?"

The entire room turned to look at Cadmann.

He felt small. Finally he spoke. "I lost a daughter," Cadmann said. "For reasons that are still unclear. But that was an accident, a result of another of the hideous secrets this planet conceals from us. I can't hold that against you. But you agreed to follow certain procedures. And you broke your word. We are a community, and a community must have its rules. We can't break away from that."

Aaron seemed to be hearing beyond the words, and gave the barest of nods to Cadmann. "And so?"

"And so," Zack said. "The mainland is off limits. There will be no human return there. Robotic probes will be devised to learn what needs to be learned. You'll help us design them. You'll help us ask the questions they will answer."

Aaron seemed to grow dark. "We lost one of ours, Administrator. We have a right to our revenge."

"You have no right!" Zack exploded. "Don't you understand what you represent?"

"We *decline* to represent *anything!* We're not your frozen fetuses anymore. We are living creatures, with our own wills, and our own needs! We are not your freezing children! WE are the future of this planet. You are its *past.*"

"There will be no return."

Aaron glared at them. He seemed to be on the verge of saying something. Then he nodded curtly.

"Is that all, then?"

"It is," Zack said.

Aaron Tragon turned, heel-toe, and left the room.

15

THE VERDICT

I tell them that if they will occupy themselves
with the study of mathematics, they will find
in it the best remedy against the lusts of the
flesh.

—THOMAS MANN, *The Magic Mountain*

The clouds were gray, tinged with orange where Tau Ceti licked them from beneath, at the seventh dawn after *Robor*'s return. A lone pterodon circled overhead, *skaw*ing mournfully to the misted cairn of Mucking Great Mountain. Its angular wings flapped somberly.

The early light had yet to transform the fertile fields and roads and buildings of Camelot into a community. It remained a sleeping thing, and but for the four hundred people gathered in the small graveyard, it would have seemed deserted.

The coffins were small. Not much was needed for bones. Mary Ann had asked that her child be cremated. Cadmann told her gently that that was out of the question: additional tissue tests might be needed at some future time.

She asked that Linda be buried up on the Bluff; but every member of the colony wanted to be present for the ceremony. A compromise was reached. The ceremony was performed in the colony graveyard. Joe and Linda would be buried up on the Bluff, side by side.

Sylvia held Cadzie, who was oddly quiet. The past week had been hard for him.

Cadmann looked out at his friends and family, and tried to hold his voice even. "We knew what we did when we came here. We entrusted our seed, breed, and generation to a world no human being had touched. We knew that there would be brief, but also joy."

Mary Ann clung to his arm, wan and fragile and shattered inside.

"There has been joy here, so far from Earth. There has been—" He faltered. The words wouldn't flow. "The joy of hard work, shared by friends and family. The joy of discovery, of a new land. The joy of love and birth and growth. There is a price for everything in this life, and we thought we had paid that price."

His vision clouded. "We were foolish enough to think that one generation can pay the way for the next. God has showed us that each must pay his own way through life. My daughter is gone. The man she loved, our friend and companion for twenty years, is gone." He looked out over the faces in the crowd. He knew each one of them. Had been present when many of them were born. This was their world . . .

Wasn't it?

"By a miracle, their baby, my grandchild, was saved. We have an obligation to keep that child—" Gently, softly, he took Cadzie from Sylvia's arms. "—this child safe. He belongs to all of us now. We have . . ." The hurt was bubbling up now, faster and faster and he didn't seem to be able to get the barriers up in time to stop it. "We have to keep this world safe."

He held Cadzie to his chest, felt the life in that small bundle. Smelled the fresh baby smell, and heard the small heart beating, and knew how close, how terribly close death had come to this small thing that he loved so dearly. Suddenly the ground had struck his knees. How had that happened? Sylvia was prying Cadzie out of his arms. His forehead struck Linda's coffin, and all of the things that he had never said, had thought that there would be time to say, boiled out of him, scorched him with their scorn, and turned all of his carefully planned words into a miserable slurry of lies.

And when, after a while, Sylvia and Justin helped him up, and the final words were spoken by Zack, Cadmann felt high above himself, with the pterodons, up in the clouds, watching these small, insignificant people scratching in the dirt of Avalon, burying their dead in the earth that would, too soon, receive them all.

Aaron's den was crowded with bodies and talk, and warmed by a crackling thornwood fire. Chaka pressed his big palms against the northern window, feeling the vibration as big fat sparse drops shattered against it. Beyond the deserted beach, waves rolled and crashed as if attempting to wash all trace of Man and his words from Avalon.

A tiny human shape rode a sliver of wood and plastic atop a black wave. Idiot. Probably showing off for the kaffeeklatsch that had not invited him.

Chaka turned, for the thousandth time examining Aaron's living space, speculating on what it revealed about the Starborn's de facto president. It was small, actually—smaller than many of the other Surf's Up dwellings. Not elaborate, or richly appointed.

But what it was, was *precise*, to a degree that made Chaka vaguely uncomfortable. Aaron had designed and built it himself. Every joint of wood dovetailed into every other joint with machined precision. The couches were built into the walls, chairs fitted to tables, windows slanted to give the illusion of more room and positioned to catch the maximum of natural light.

But there was something almost . . . what? Womblike? Aaron's lair was really a bachelor pad, without room for a cohabitant, no matter how often or intensely he might entertain overnight guests.

He knew, for instance, that no woman had ever slept on Aaron's narrow bed. It was too narrow for lovemaking—such intimate activity invariably took place on the living-room divan. Or the floor, or the shower, or standing up in a hammock. Aaron was nothing if not a sexual athlete. The bed was almost too narrow for sleep. Even unconscious, Aaron's discipline was Spartan.

A kitchen/dinette for meals, a living room for guests, a den for conspirators, a library for study, an exercise room for physical torture, and a bedroom for sleep, all fitted about one another like pieces of a jigsaw puzzle, in perhaps two-thirds the space of the average dwelling. Odd.

Katya made coffee at the counter along one wall, using the elaborate samovar she had installed to keep a constant supply of hot water. She seemed to be giving the conversation only half of her attention. The rest of her mind was probably evaluating the relational dynamic between Jessica and Aaron. Jessica stood next to Aaron's chair, idly fondling his hair. Not that Katya was directly interested in Aaron—any fool could see that she as in love with Justin. But a Tragon-Weyland alliance would affect Avalonian history for the next three centuries.

The monitor next to Aaron's huge easy chair looked blank at first glance, and Chaka took a moment to study it. Pale brown, with a fine texture . . . faded ornate lettering . . . and then it leapt into focus.

It was the Scribeveldt, that northeastern region of the continent which had never been seen except through cameras aboard *Geographic*. Flat and featureless, endless pampas, with one river and few streams. Chaka watched cursor points draw tracks in speeded-up motion. They made pale graceful curves that crossed each other rarely, as if something immense was trying to write messages to *Geographic*.

Chaka cleared his throat and spoke to the computer screen. "Edgar, you on?"

He was looking at the top of Edgar's head. Eyes glanced up, fell again. "Yeah."

Trish Chance's fingers clamped on Chaka's forearm, and she swung him around into a gaudy, passionate kiss. Edgar looked up again, fighting a smile. "I'm here, I'm listening. Hi, Chaka. Hi, Trish. Enough already."

"Hi, Edgar," Trish sang sweetly.

"Edgar, it's official," Aaron said, and it was suddenly clear he was speaking to them all. "No expedition to the mainland. Not even for Grendel Scout graduations. Nothing until they understand what happened."

"That's a quote?" Chaka asked.

"Condensation. Accurate, though."

"They *won't* understand until we learn more," Chaka said. "And we *won't* learn until we've *been* there awhile."

Katya asked, "Chaka? What do you think happened?"

Chaka shook his head. "Avalon Weird. It's a locked-room mystery. I don't have any ideas. Neither does my father." He caught Aaron's change of expression, and met his eyes. *Father.*

"Your *father*," Aaron said, "is as likely to have ice on his mind as any other First. Your *father* is not closer to an answer than anyone else. *They* will never find out. Something killed our friends. They won't let us go until we know, and we can't know unless we go. It's a perfect dilemma."

"I wouldn't go that far," Chaka said.

"Oh? Why not?"

Chaka sipped black coffee. "The point is, one day we *will* go back. This edict won't last forever."

"Sure, we'll outnumber them one day," Trish said.

"I won't wait that long." Jessica stood at the wet bar where Katya waited for water to boil. There was jittery energy in her stance, in her voice. "Something killed Linda. Linda and Joe, but not the baby. How can you *sleep*, not knowing what did that? You say *Avalon Weird*, you're talking about something that almost wiped this world clean of us! I have to know what killed my sister."

"Your father's the one who won't let us find out," Aaron said.

Jessica nodded. "Loyalty. Dad's big on loyalty. He'll fight Zack every step, but once a decision is made—"

"Loyalty to the king," Aaron said, skirting sarcasm only by the blandness of his expression. "A cardinal virtue of the warrior."

"Chaka Zulu would agree," Chaka said without a trace of irony. "Courage, obedience to the king, protection of the weak. Universals." He was already thinking in terms of robot probes. Earth's solar system had been explored by probes long before the first men set foot on Mars. Neat little multiwheeled bugs had crawled over the faces of Mars and the outer moons. Cassandra had to have templates. . . .

"Well, we're not bound by obedience," Aaron said. "To Zack, or Colonel Weyland, or the council, or all the icebound Earth Born at once."

"Ice, ice, ice," Chaka exploded. "Why is it always ice when the Earth Born aren't doing what we want?"

Aaron took a moment to shape his response, and Toshiro stole that moment. "The First are not always wrong. Jessica has the scar to show, and Mack what's-his-name died—"

"Mack Reinecke," Chaka said. "He was a Bottle Baby too, just younger than Justin. Most of you weren't old enough to be there—"

Aaron was listening, silent. The story would get told, no matter what he did.

"Four of the First took us on campout," Toshiro said. "Zack Moskowitz needed exercise. Zack and Rachael, Hendrick Sills, Carolyn McAndrews. They wanted coffee. And they took eight of us, the oldest children, whoever might be big enough to carry his pack. I was eleven. At that, Trish got too tired and Hendrick had to tie her pack to his own. Made Hendrick a little surly.

"So we made camp at night, and the next morning the First set us collecting coffee. We got bored with that, so they took over and we went exploring. An hour later we were looking at a pterodon nest. It was below us, across jagged rock cliffs.

"We watched it until we got hungry, and then we went back for lunch. Trish told Zack. Zack told us not to go anywhere near a pterodon nest, and Hendrick backed him. Aaron, you asked Zack what he thought would happen. He didn't know. Hendrick didn't know.

"We went off again. Mack Reinecke led us around to a place we could get down into the nest. Mack was in the nest—"

"So was I," Aaron said. "And four eggs, way bigger than hen's eggs, and leathery. I took one."

"Yes you did," Toshiro said. "And then one of the adults came back. We all scrambled away as best we could. The other big bird caught us coming up the rocks. That one slashed Jessica across the head and neck, a great gaudy scary slash. Aaron fought them off with rocks while the rest of us got away.

"It took a skeeter to find Mack. He was part eaten. The pterodons knocked him off the rocks."

"All right, Toshiro," Aaron said. "I'll even give you this. Zack and Hendrick gave us the same advice we'd give the Grendel Biters now. We acted like we had ice on our minds. We were children."

"So what will we do?" Katya asked quietly.

"Go back."

The Second looked at each other. Nobody said anything until Chaka asked, "How?"

Aaron shrugged. "Once we decide *what* we'll do, the *how* becomes a mere tactics and logistical detail. Are we agreed that we'll go?"

There was a chorus of ayes, Chaka's not among them. Aaron noticed. He raised an interrogative eyebrow. "Have we a problem?"

"Maybe," Chaka said. "Edgar is worried about the weather."

Suddenly, Edgar's onscreen attention was theirs. "There's no doubt about it, the sun is heating up, and the local life-forms—"

"Wow," Trish giggled. "How much? I mean if this is the *end* we should have a hell of a party—"

"It's not going to cremate us, Trish!" Edgar said indignantly. "You have apocalyptic tastes."

"Oh," she pouted. "Sorry."

Like hell, Chaka thought. *She's playing a game, and I can't see it.*

"It's normal variance," Edgar said. "Tau Ceti has a fifty-year cycle. We're coming up on the maximum output. More energy means more variable weather. Higher winds. Weather gets less predictable . . . say, two days ahead instead of four. I've had Cassandra mark out regions on the mainland where we could get tornadoes." A map replaced Edgar's face for a long moment; then he reappeared. The Scribeveldt was an angry red. "Here in Camelot we could get hurricanes and typhoons along the north and west coast. The ecology seems to be heating up too, but you'll have to ask the Chakas about that."

"The wild Joeys around the Stronghold have disappeared," Chaka said. "The tame Joeys were tearing up their claws trying to burrow. It was making Mary Ann Weyland crazy until she turned them loose. They burrowed in and estivated. At sea we're getting eels—"

"Eels?" Jessica asked.

"There've been over thirty eels since Big Mama," Chaka said. "Eels in nearly every Camelot stream. Father thinks the solar cycle is the trigger. More ultraviolet, and the eels start to spawn. Probably triggers other biological reactions too, but there isn't enough biology on this island to notice."

"But there'll be a lot on the mainland?" Aaron asked. "Interesting. We'd better make sure Edgar is watching that, too. Edgar?"

"Yeah. Aaron, weather problems will get serious in about four months. Tornadoes that can tear *Robor* to tinsel before you can say *shit-oh-dear.* We could do worse than to leave *Robor* in his nice safe hangar for the whole season. Watch the mainland from orbit, send some probes, let the First cool down for a year. We can collect so many good questions that it'll drive them crazy by the time the weather settles down."

Chaka waited for Aaron to destroy Edgar. He was surprised when Aaron mildly said, "Sitting on our asses isn't exactly to my taste, but it certainly makes a good default option. Can you and Chaka work up some probes for the interesting mainland ecologies? Chaka, we do this right and we'll have your *father* foaming at the mouth."

"Hell, yes," Chaka said.

"You'll work on that? Maybe you could talk to Edgar in the bedroom for a while."

Edgar coughed, seeming almost embarrassed. "Not too long a talk, okay? I have an appointment with Toshiro."

Chaka waited for the criticism, and was again surprised to see Aaron nod understandingly. "This will only take a minute. The rest of us can map out a way to return to the mainland. We'll flash it to you later for comment and refinement." Edgar winked off.

Chaka went into the bedroom and closed the door.

The room was near-silent until the monitor returned to a view of the Scribeveldt.

"Edgar," Katya said, "could be a problem."

"Asset," Aaron said absently. "The secret to life is turning stumbling blocks into stepping-stones."

"And just how do you do that?"

His grin was pure evil. Instead of answering. Aaron templed his fingers and narrowed his eyes at Trish. "I believe that you have things to do and people to see."

Trish grabbed her gym bag from the corner. "And places to go. On my way."

"Oh, and Trish—you *will* be endearingly clumsy, won't you?"

She took a step toward the door and stumbled, barely catching herself. She assumed her best poor-little-me expression. "I just don't know what's *wrong* with me today." And she was gone.

Jessica stooped to look carefully into Aaron's eyes. "And just what are you up to?"

"I *could* tell you," he said cheerfully, "but then I'd have to kill you."

✳

"*Tsuruashi-dashi,*" Toshiro barked. Edgar's mind swirled. He was staggering through that twilight zone between fatigue and utter exhaustion. He'd been marching back and forth across the hard rubber gymnasium floor for what seemed like hours but couldn't have been more than fifty minutes.

His legs were sacks of wet sand. The fire in his chest threatened to engulf him. Toshiro stood before him in white pajamas, a garment he called a *gi*, with a black sash knotted about the waist.

Edgar kept his mind on that belt. His father had earned one back on Earth. Toshiro had earned his by satisfying Cassandra's kinesthetic model of a third *dan* karate expert. Joe Sikes had tried to interest Edgar in the formal dances, the complex and challenging stances, the terrifying strikes and kicks of *Kyukushin* karate. Edgar had learned only his own terrifying vulnerability. He was as likely to perform surgery on a friend as to kill with a *mae-geri* front kick.

Now Joe was dead. Maybe this penance was a way of keeping a little of his father alive.

Edgar stood in the *Tsuruashi-dashi*, the crane stance, balanced on his left leg, the right foot tucked up on his thigh, arms spread for balance. His calf was cramping, his toes digging into mat for balance so hard that he felt his toenails ready to rip free.

Toshiro wasn't the laughing funster now. Not the talented guitarist, nor the avid surfer, or careful lover. When he donned that white uniform something else came out. Maybe he was channeling a sixteenth-century samurai. Or Thomas DeTorquemada. One of those fun guys.

No mirth shone in Toshiro's eyes, but finally he acknowledged Edgar's suffering. Toshiro softened his voice momentarily. "Do you feel the similarity between this and the yoga Tree Pose?"

Edgar's whole body trembled. Why was this so damned hard? Bruce Lee made it look *easy*. He was drowning in a sea of lactic acid. "I, uh . . . I have to stand on one leg?"

"That's the obvious answer. Look deeper."

The room was spinning. This asshole wasn't going to let him put his foot down until he answered! He was going to fall, crack his head, and his brains would run out on the mat. Maybe then the Shogun of Suffering would be satisfied. Edgar almost smiled to himself, appreciating the alliteration.

Wait. Suddenly, he had the answer. "Balance," he gasped. "I have to concentrate on the same place in my body, you know, at my navel."

"Just below your navel, and three inches in. The center of mass. In Japanese, *hara*. In sanscrit, *Manipura*. All right, bring your foot down *slowly*."

Edgar nearly collapsed, almost didn't hear the polite applause from the side of the gym. He turned and saw Trish. She was dressed in a tan leotard that revealed the curves and angles of that magnificent body more than simply nudity ever could. What was she doing here? Was she here to watch him make a fool of himself? This was only his tenth lesson. It wasn't fair!

Toshiro seemed to read Edgar's mind. "Trish asked if she could join us today. It's her fourth lesson. She's having some trouble with her stances."

Trouble? Trish? Hard to believe.

She smiled at him. He wasn't certain, but it might have been the first time he had ever seen it up close. Even when stern she was just drop-dead gorgeous. But her smile was sort of sweet, and disarmingly girlish. "Do you mind?"

"Well, ah—"

"I thought it might be a good idea for her to see a student who is better than she is, but not so much better that it is discouraging," Toshiro said quietly.

I'm better than she is? At something physical?

Suddenly, and quiet dramatically, all of the fatigue flitted away on wings of testosterone. He felt an inch taller, and his muscles—flabby and girded with fat though they were—were suddenly steel bands. Well, rubber bands. But bands nonetheless.

She stood by his side. Taller than he by an inch, and devastatingly feminine for all of the muscle now clearly revealed to view.

"Today you learn to teach what you know," Toshiro said. "Let her take her stance, and you make the corrections."

"Would you?" she asked. There was no mockery in her voice, but some part of him still just couldn't believe it.

"*Zenkutsu-dachi!*" Toshiro barked. Trish bent her front knee, and leaned forward, straightening her rear leg. She wobbled badly.

"Oh," Edgar said, and just like that his mind slipped into analytic mode. "I see the problem. Your knee is leaning past your toes. And your hips are twisted wrong, see . . . ?

Toshiro nodded approval.

The shower beat down on Edgar's back like a rain of needles, sluicing the sweat and dust from his body. It felt *terrific.* It just might have been the first time he had ever actually felt *good* after a workout. Before this, karate sessions functioned mainly to assuage guilt.

With the second half of the day's lesson devoted to teaching Trish, her wide, liquid-brown, humbly grateful eyes following his every move, he had actually gotten out of his head and done well! Maybe his punches and kicks weren't like Toshiro's—blur-fast and savagely precise—but at least they were *correct.* And Trish liked what she saw. He could tell. A karate man knows these things.

"Toshiro?" he said dreamily, working the soap into his pudgy sides.

Toshiro was rinsing. He was smooth-muscled, his body like a swimmer's. Hard, flat plates rounded by a thin fat padding. For a startling moment Edgar realized that *he* could have a body like that.

Wow.

"Yes, Edgar?"

"I really did all right today, didn't I?"

"You did fine." Toshiro grinned at him. "I think that Trish would agree with that. Don't you?"

Edgar's face felt hotter than the water beating against it. He thought about Trish again, and realized that he'd better change the subject before his body reacted too obviously.

"You figured out the karate stuff from the tapes, right?"

"Your dad was a help—he'd studied a long time ago. But mostly from the pic-tures." Toshiro's face was a little dreamy and distant. "Some of it was difficult, but I had balance from surfing. The stances you just do until your legs get so tired that the only way to keep erect is to do them correctly. Then you experi-ment, I mean, they had thermographs and electromyographs of these old karate masters going through their moves, so you can make pretty good guesses about what was going on under their uniforms, but finally you just have to make guesses."

"I think you did pretty well."

"I wish they had recorded the Grandmaster, Mas Oyama, in his prime. He could kill bulls with his bare hands."

"No." His mind swam. *Edgar Sikes, bull-killer. Master of Men.*

Toshiro turned off his shower and toweled vigorously.

Edgar followed him. "You know, you're really smart."

Toshiro shrugged. "You're the computer whiz."

"But I never realized all the intelligence that goes into learning to use your body. I mean the yoga, and the surfing, and the karate . . . it's physical smarts, but it's intelligence. You must be as smart as Aaron is. Like Trish is as strong as he is."

Toshiro looked at him, a touch of reserve leashing the energy in the black eyes. "So?"

"So why do you both follow him? He calls the shots, doesn't he?"

Toshiro paused, and Edgar thought that he saw the muscles along his jaw bunching tightly. Then his friend and teacher relaxed. "I guess I'm a little like Justin," he said. "Neither of us wants to be a leader. Justin doesn't think *anybody* has to be leader. I'm realistic, but it won't be me. Give me the sand, and the sun. And time to work on the old Samurai stuff. *Hai!*"

Toshiro's left foot whipped up and at Edgar's jaw. *That wasn't full speed . . .* Edgar was thinking and then realized that he had blocked it, automatically, with his right hand.

Toshiro smiled. "Some must be students. Otherwise there could be no teach-ers. Who wants to live in such a world?"

16

THREE SEDUCTIONS

The surest way to prevent seditions (if the
times do bear it) is to take away the matter of
them.

—FRANCIS BACON, *Essays*

Weeks passed, and a semblance of normality returned to the colony. The Star
Born mostly brooded at Surf's Up and avoided interacting with the Earth Born.
Justin stayed at the Bluff. When Jessica came home from Surf's Up, she rarely
spoke to her parents, although Cadmann tried to reach out to her.

Then, on a day when *Geographic*'s satellites warned that storm clouds were
sweeping in from the mainland, Jessica called her father to ask if she could come
for dinner.

There was no mention of any of the unpleasantness during the call. In fact,
there had been little public protest of Zack's proclamation. And that, in itself,
should have warned them.

Ruth Moskowitz adjusted her chamel's harness for a little more give around the
shoulders. The beast's name was Tarzan. All six of the tamed chamels were
males. The females were too large and irritable to domesticate, and they'd only
captured one before the expeditions into the forests northeast of Deadwood
Pass had ceased.

Male chamels were horse-size and had the exaggerated grace of a praying
mantis. They were intelligent and fast, with excellent pack instincts. Only three
of them were really *tamed*, but there was every evidence that Tarzan and the
other two might be just the first of thousands. There were some very special reasons why tamed chamels might be ideal hunting mounts.

Ruth had never seen a kangaroo, although the Chakas were thinking of developing one from the fertilized ova banks, but Tarzan reminded her of those in
Cassandra's pictures. Tarzan looked like a kangaroo with feathery antennae and
stronger forelegs. He was tan with a greenish tinge, but his back was changing
color even now to match Ruth's blue denim outfit.

Tarzan balanced himself on his strong hind legs and reached around to snap
at her irritably. She tugged her reins expertly, and spurred him with heels to the
ribs. He whistled in exasperation and galloped around the corral for the fiftieth
time that day.

She wove him in between carefully spaced stakes, wheeled him, jumped him first over a low gate and then over one three feet in height. They were into high golden grass now, and Tarzan's coat was turning to gold.

Chamels jumped oddly. They would hit the ground, sink, seem to pause for an instant, and then unwind from that deep crouch and spring into the air as if from a standing position. Their hind legs were so powerful that they landed with no shock at all. She loved Tarzan, and everything about training him.

She and Tarzan were getting into a rhythm now, speeding around the quarter-mile perimeter exhilaratingly fast, occasionally dipping into the center of the pen to try weaving and jumping maneuvers.

She was so caught up in her work that at first she did not notice a flat, regular clapping sound. Flushed and sweating, she turned in the saddle to see Aaron Tragon, mounted on a gray horse, just the other side of the gate.

"Bravo," he said, striking his palms together.

She smiled shyly, and trotted Tarzan over to him. Aaron's horse was a mare, a quarter horse named Zodiac with a raucous disposition. The mare tossed her mottled head and eyed Tarzan suspiciously. Horses and chamels existed in an uneasy truce at best.

"You're really bringing him along," Aaron said. His golden hair was tied back in a ponytail, and he wore a loose buccaneer-style shirt cut almost to the navel, crisscrossed with leather thongs. His lips were half opened in a lazy smile.

"What brings you out this way?" Ruth asked. "I thought you were out at Surf's Up."

"Man does not live by wave alone," he laughed.

"So what brings you here?"

He looked at her for about thirty seconds without speaking, and Ruth felt her cheeks start to burn. She had to look away.

"To tell you the truth, I just wanted to ask you on a picnic."

She snapped her head up. Her throat felt constricted. "Me?"

"Sure. We had a great catch last week, and we've smoked it. I made fresh bread last night, and I have enough sandwiches for a small army. You look hungry enough for a division."

She felt her heart speed up, had the terrible, crazy thought that she must be dreaming. She felt as if she were falling down a deep well, and made a powerful effort of will to bring herself up sharp.

"Well?" he asked. There was a world of insinuation in his question. His eyes twinkled. "I tell you what," he said. "I'll race you to the grove."

"Winner?" she asked.

"Takes all," he answered, and her cheeks burned again.

Edgar Sikes slept alone in his room off the main communications center. He had another domicile, out at Surf's Up, but spent little time there. Most of his personal possessions—such as they were—were here in his little cubbyhole. It was cluttered and overstuffed. He rarely had visitors. Most of the time he was in the computer center, or in his room reading. He'd been reading a James Bond metabook when he went to sleep.

Something hit his door three times, hard enough to rattle it. He sat up with visions of SMERSH assassins dancing through his head.

Trish Chance was an impressive sight. Five foot ten of brown-skinned feminine muscle, her body was almost—but not quite—a parody of the female form. When he opened the door she brushed past him, buttocks sliding pleasantly past his, as if she were dancing with an inexpert partner. She turned as if posing. The muscles in her arms and shoulders shifted and separated like the coils of a spring.

In the crowded environs of this room, she was damned near overpowering. The only girl who had shared a bed with Edgar Sikes, once and nevermore. She smiled at him, and closed the door behind her.

She wore a formfitting pair of black denims, and a white ruffled shirt so tight across the chest that her breasts threatened to explode through the cloth. She smiled at him, lips curling up at the corners like those of a jungle cat who has spotted something extremely edible.

Edgar's throat tightened until he could barely swallow. "Ah—hi Trish," he said, startled by his own daring. Why was she looking at him like *that*?

She crossed the room to sit beside him on his narrow cot. It creaked at their combined weight. He sat too, and her thigh was only an inch from his. She wore some kind of sweet, musky oiled essence. Her skin had a soft, almost golden sheen in the dim light.

Trish was part of Aaron's inner circle. What was she doing *here*? "Is there something I can . . . do for you?"

In answer she leaned forward. What happened next was so shocking, and so powerful, that when she finally pulled back it took almost a full minute for his brain to get back into gear. He had *never* been kissed like that. His experience with kissing—or anything else to do with women—was scant. Yet and still he would have wagered either kidney that no more thorough kiss had ever been given—or gratefully received—in the history of the universe.

He leaned forward urgently, hands questing for something to hold on to— preferably Trish's extraordinary breasts. She held him away gently but firmly. In that instant he verified what he had always suspected—that Trish was *much* stronger than he. Why didn't that make him less a man?

Because his masculinity was so painfully self-evident that it could have withstood anything short of a hurricane without withering noticeably; and because Trish was saying, "You're going to get everything that you want—and more." Her hand slid between his legs. She started a silky stroking movement.

He whined. He hated to hear the sound of it coming from his own throat, but undeniably, there it was. Oh, God—he hoped he didn't start to whimper and beg.

"Please . . ." he whimpered. Maybe strong women *liked* whimpering. He was in a state to try anything. Dammit, she wouldn't let him any closer. If she kept stroking like that, in another moment it wasn't going to make any differ—

She stopped, fingertips still touching. He felt like a violin string in the last moments of a Vivaldi concerto. A weird notion danced through his head: that

Trish in his room was some last legacy from what he *could not* cease to remember as a neat array of clean bones . . . from the woman who would have been his father's wife. For just this once, for Linda, he would believe in life after death.

"First," she said softly. "First I need to know what kind of man you are."

"Whatever kind you want," he said, and believed he meant it.

"I want to know," she said, and her eyes bored into him. "I want to know if you're the kind who believes in revenge."

He withered. She couldn't know why; and he was thinking again. *Not* Linda. Aaron must have sent her; nothing else could have. And Edgar Sikes did believe in revenge.

Oh God. Her hand felt so good. She smelled so good. It had been so long. He pulled back a little to see her face.

"Yes," he said. *On Aaron Tragon!*

"Good," she said, and began to unbutton her blouse. "There's something that Aaron wants you to do."

"Aaron . . . ?" he asked inanely. But then she had bent him back flat on the bed, and her hands were unbuckling his belt with practiced precision, and her left nipple was in his mouth. And all he could think of was: *I'll believe in the Tooth Fairy, or the Easter Bunny, or Dianetics . . . but not in Aaron Tragon. But Trish, Trish, you don't have to know that! Not ever.*

She knew it. Ruth could see that Aaron was reining Zodiac back, letting her win. Chamels weren't quite as fast as horses, and Aaron was a fine horseman, but by the time they were halfway across the plowed field, she *knew* that she was going to win.

She knew it. Knew it! Well, whatever his little joke was, she was going to get full measure of satisfaction from her victory. She'd make him take her to one of the notorious Surf's Up bashes, *that's* what she'd do. She would arrive with him, on his arm—

"*Hiyahhh!*" She looked around, and saw that Aaron had suddenly stopped playing, he was letting Zodiac have her way, and the mare was charging powerfully, head down, feet digging into the soil and ripping up great clots of earth, Aaron bent into the saddle, urging the quarterhorse on and on.

Ruth heard a little yip of fright escape her throat. For a time Tarzan kept his lead, and then Aaron slipped past her just as they entered the shadow of the grove, and she had lost.

She reared Tarzan around, and brought him to a halt. One thing at least— chamels could change direction or stop faster than horses. She slipped down his back and patted his muzzle, calming him, stroked the great, trembling hind legs. Tarzan stretched and folded down into a sitting position. Where shadows dappled his back, his color had begun to change.

Aaron returned on foot, leading Zodiac by the reins.

"You know," he said, "I think that chamels will actually be better for hunting than horses. They're more flexible in the brush."

"And *almost* as fast on the straight," she said.

He was very close to her. God, her whole body was shaking. She wasn't certain that they had ever been this close together. Not alone, anyway. He was breathing very hard, and sweating. His sweat smelled very . . . male.

"So," she said, a little frightened by her own daring. "Exactly what reward do you claim?"

He leaned nearer until she thought that he was going to kiss her. She moistened her lips, and tilted her face up, and when his face was only an inch away, he said: "I want *you* to serve the food."

She felt her face drop, her entire body freeze with disappointment.

Then he added: "First."

They spread the picnic blanket. Aaron handed her his backpack.

Her hands were shaking. She was trying so hard to do everything perfectly, to bring a dancer's grace to every tiny motion. But every part of her was too aware that he was watching, every inch of her skin was too sensitive, felt his touch even though they were separated by feet. She kept speeding up, and he, with infinite patience, kept reminding her to slow down.

"We have all the time in the world," he said.

She set out the carefully packed plates, and the carefully wrapped food, and the carefully wrapped utensils. "Slowly," he said. "You have to make sure that everything is in its place. Everything is exactly where it needs to be."

She nodded, feeling feverishly hot.

They ate. There was no moment when his eyes met hers, and she wanted to scream, wanted to throw the food down and throw herself into his arms, wanted to feel his lips and hands and tongue all over her body, just like she'd read in the books, seen in the holos. She longed to do the same for him. *Please God, please, let this be the time, now, here. . . .*

But her silent pleas went unheard. He continued to concentrate on his food, eating as slowly and carefully as if it were a tea party.

She watched his hands. So large and strong. They moved with such certainty. Such strength. Hands like that could do anything, could take anything that they wanted.

She thought she was going to die.

Please . . .

"Excuse me." He broke the silence for the first time in five agonizing minutes. *touch . . .*

"Would you hand me the butter?"

me. I love you so . . .

She nodded silently, and grasped the small platter, extending it to him. His hand reached out, and their fingers met.

And their eyes. And she was falling forward.

And then their lips.

And then it was everything, every moment she had hoped for, so exhilarating that even the brief, sharp pain as he eased into her only increased the impact as dream crossed over into reality. A fierce, tender, laughing, tearful, all-consuming experience.

His lips and tongue. And God, his hands. So gentle. So strong.

Hands like his could do anything. Take anything they wanted.

She thought she was going to die.

✳

Trish Chance was bored. Aaron had a plan, *sure* he did, but *right now* his plan was to do *nothing* . . . and meanwhile they were trapped on the island, unable to go to the mainland, under suspicion but forced to be polite to the First.

Trish left the comm shack wearing a wide grin. *Smile and smile and be a villain,* she thought. She didn't have to spend all her hours sulking. Edgar was an eager student—and so grateful, too. And everyone was so surprised! The comm shack was centrally located, which meant it was near everyone's place, and if Trish kept visiting Edgar everyone on the island was going to know it.

Her grin faded when she saw Carolyn McAndrews approaching with a purposeful look. Carolyn had tried to adopt Trish in the early days, when no one was quite sure how to raise the Bottle Babies. Trish had been ten years old, and eager to have a permanent home rather than the communal nursery. But not *that* eager, not in *that* home.

Now Carolyn was coming at her. "Trish!" she called.

Trish slowed, hoisted a smile into place. "Hi, Carolyn."

"Have you got a minute to talk?"

"Sure. What's up?"

Carolyn quieted as Julia Hortha and Manny Halperin strolled past in deep conversation. When they were out of earshot, she said, "I'm sorry things didn't work out for us, earlier—"

"It was a long time ago, Carolyn, and you had your own children to take care of. I can't blame you for putting them first."

"Did I? I suppose I did," Carolyn said. "It comes of—of living alone. Trish, I think you've fallen into a—well, a kind of role."

"A role?" Trish was genuinely puzzled. "What kind of role?"

"You and Edgar. And before that, Derik, and Terry—you were their first, sort of the Initiator."

Trish giggled. "I guess I kind of fell into that, yes. Edgar too." Her smile went exotic and mysterious. She assumed a thick and flagrantly faux accent. "I like to teach the young ones zee arts of love."

She laughed, then let it die when Carolyn didn't join in. "I did that, Trish. I slept with any man who didn't have a partner. None who did, at least not that I knew of, but a lot of men. And look what it got me."

Trish shrugged, genuinely missing the point.

"I'm alone, Trish."

"What do you mean, alone? Everybody likes you." *Nobody listens to you,* she thought, *but who would? Smile and smile*—"You're one of the heroes of the Grendel Wars. Carolyn and the horses."

"Trish, every man would sleep with me, but none of them wanted to take me down the rapids. Now I'm getting old, and no one wants to live with me."

Sudden understanding. *She must think she's my mother.* "Oh, that. That's not what I'm looking for, Carolyn."

Carolyn grasped her arm. Trish looked at the hand, and decided to let it remain there.

"Trish, it's a bad thing to be alone. Don't you want to belong to someone? To have someone who belongs to you? You have nothing but casual relationships—"

She laughed in Carolyn's face. "In a world with less than five hundred people, there is no such thing as a casual relationship. We're *all* family."

"Imagine yourself alone, with no defenders, at my age," said Carolyn.

Trish was incredulous. "Defenders? Defend from what? Do you think I'm going to starve in the snow without a man to protect me? Nobody starves on Avalon. Nobody goes without. And I'm tougher than I look, lady. I'm stronger than almost any man here—and men aren't any better at hunting, or producing, or anything else than women are. Didn't you get the word? There was this thing called the Industrial Revolution. That made us equals, that and Zack Moskowitz's grendel guns. And then there was birth control. Maybe your mother forgot to mention it to you."

Carolyn smiled, not a thin smile but with genuine warmth. "You might be surprised at what my mother taught me. And Trish, dear, my sister and I did win places on this expedition, and we didn't owe a damn thing to any man for that, either!"

"That's the spirit. I have to go now."

"No, wait, this is important. Trish—it's a terrible thing to be alone—"

"It's also a terrible thing to have ice on your mind," Trish said, and made as if to leave. Carolyn blocked her path, but Trish knew that she had scored a direct hit, and for the first time felt a tiny trace of remorse. She wiped it from her mind. *Who gave her the right to lecture me on morals?*

"I don't seem to be explaining this very well," Carolyn said. "I know they call me a hysteric, but there's more to this than you think." Carolyn struggled for words. "Sometimes hysterics has nothing to do with ice crystals in the brain."

Change in conversational direction, or change in tactics? "Sure, you can be scared into it. What was it that got you, Carolyn? Grendel fever? Seems to have done it for everyone else."

"No, not grendels. That was awful, but . . . it was earlier, Trish. When Ernst came out of cold sleep and he was a m-moron, and he barely remembered m-me. And old friends were dropping dead all around me. It turned out half of us were damaged and we couldn't be sure of the rest. . . . It was Hibernation Instability. Ice on our minds, we said. We were trying to be polite!" Her eyes defocused, as if she had forgotten she was talking to another person. "We were trying to be polite. . . ."

Trish had heard it before, too many times. This wasn't insulting, it was pitiful, and just plain boring. "Excuse me, Carolyn," she pushed past the older woman. "I'm almost sure I have something to do, somewhere else."

"I'm trying to help you," Carolyn said. "You're playing with something you don't understand."

"And you do?"

"I understand more than you do."

"Carolyn, I doubt that."

"I know you do. When I was your age I was sure I knew everything, too."

"And you didn't?"

"Of course not."

"But that was back on Earth. I've watched some of the old Earth dramas. I once did sixty hours straight of 'General Hospital'! That was Earth, Carolyn, and this is Avalon, and life isn't like that anymore!"

Carolyn laughed. "It never was like that, but never mind. Trish, I know this much. Men and women don't see sex the same way, and that's wired into our brains. It's not something you can ignore just because you want to. Trish, I *know*."

"Then I guess I'll just have to find out, won't I? Excuse me—" She brushed past and walked at a fast pace, too fast for Carolyn to catch up without running.

Behind her Carolyn was still talking to herself. "We'd jumped light-years between stars, the whole universe was ours for the taking, and it was all going wrong. Ice on our minds. . . ."

✳

"More greens?" Mary Ann said, too briskly. A bright and terrible smile had glazed her face during the entire visit. Only when she kept herself busy did it fall away, did a genuine mask of concentration replace it.

She served her family, bustling about as if work were the only thing that stood between herself and damnation. The very constancy of her motion was an irritant to Jessica. "Mom," she said. "Please. Let me help you."

Mary Ann turned and her expression was diamond-clear and hard, and just as emotionless. "No. No dear. I think you've done enough, don't you?"

Cadmann sat next to Justin. Without anyone saying anything explicit, a line had been drawn in the house.

"I was in the Arboretum earlier," Cadmann said. "I noticed that some of the cacti stems are broken."

Jessica shrugged.

"Do you know anything about that?"

"Not particularly." She avoided his eyes.

"I've been told that a powerful hallucinogen can be produced from its leaves."

"Really?"

"Yes. Katya said that once. I believe that Aaron is the real expert."

Justin felt his stomach knot. The subject had been approached from a dozen different directions over the past weeks.

Sylvia was very quiet. Mary Ann had politely but firmly excluded her from most of the kitchen duties. She smiled and whirled, bringing pans of biscuits and rolls and an entire wild turkey to the table. She had worked since morning to prepare everything, and she would probably be clearing the table, washing dishes and cleaning up until after midnight. Then, perhaps, she could fall exhausted into her queen-size bed, and cry herself to sleep. Justin wanted to comfort her, but he couldn't. No one could. Cadmann hadn't slept in her room since the funeral.

After steaming wedges of French apple pie, Jessica excused herself, and went into the guest bathroom.

"It's been good to have you here," Cadmann smiled.

"That goes for both of us," Sylvia said. She paused. "Has it put any strain . . . ?"

Justin gave a long, sour exhalation. "Surf's Up is pretty well split right now," he said. "Aaron's *koffeeklatsch* has pulled pretty tight. A lot of grumbling."

"They'll get over it," Cadmann said.

"They think I'm consorting with the enemy."

Cadmann laughed. He tamped his pipe down, lit it, and took a long draw. Then he slowly exhaled aromatic smoke.

"Everyone makes his own choices," Cadmann said.

"Except in the sense that Aaron suggested: we didn't decide to come here, and there's no place for us to go. So John Locke's implicit social contract doesn't really apply to us, does it?"

Cadmann chuckled. "You've been studying again. Damn nuisance, an educated son." He tapped his cigar against the ashtray, and his big sun-browned face wrinkled in exasperation. "Where is that girl?"

Almost on cue, Jessica reappeared. She smiled uncertainly.

"Well—it's been lovely. If I'm not mistaken, I hear Aaron's skeeter."

Mary Ann appeared in the kitchen doorway, apron flapping. "It's a good surprise, seeing you. We'd like it more often."

"You're always welcome," Sylvia chimed in.

Mary Ann looked out the dining room window, a vast northern expanse of clear, seamlessly cemented plastic rectangles. The clouds were darker now, and the first drops of rain spattered against the plastic. "Are you sure that you won't stay the night? The storm looks serious."

Cadmann nodded. "Cassandra says that it's a big one. The first of the season. There's always a free room. The bunkhouse is available if you and Aaron would like your privacy."

"No, thank you." She wrapped a woolen shawl around her shoulders. "Justin—are you sure you're staying?"

He nodded. "Yeah."

A decided coolness there. Cadmann thought that she was about to say something, but at the last moment, just smiled.

The door opened, and big Aaron stood framed by the darkening, cloudy sky.

He had aged since the return from the mainland. The last of his boyish qualities were gone, replaced by a rangy, impenetrable quality. "Cadmann," he said.

"Aaron." They shook hands, hard. Aaron's eyes were frozen. Before now, Cadmann had always had a sense of who lived in there, back behind the blue eyes. Now he didn't know. From time to time he wondered if he had ever known.

"Are you ready to go?"

Jessica nodded.

Aaron kissed Mary Ann's hand, and held it for an extra moment, gazing into her eyes as if trying to make a connection of some kind.

Then they were gone.

The skeeter rose up into the orange-black sky. Tau Ceti was near the horizon, and night would be upon them within minutes.

"Did you plant it?" Aaron asked. His big square hands were calm and certain upon the controls.

His hands were always sure, she reflected. Always calm and strong.

"Yes. It will trigger in—" She looked at her watch. "Eighteen minutes."

"I love it when a plan comes together, don't you?"

Jessica was silent.

They swooped down toward the colony.

Chaka saw the way Edgar's face lit up when he saw Trish Chance. It fell as he saw Chaka in her shadow. Little Chaka smiled and held up a satchel. "Coffee too," he said.

"Excellent," Edgar said, and ushered them in with wobbly grace. When his head turned away, Trish mimed Chaka a shrug. Did Edgar delude himself that he and Trish would be making the beast with two backs during this critical period?

Not likely. Aaron had ordered a storm and put it in Edgar's charge. Chaka said, "I'm here in case you run into a glitch. If 'Dragonsnatch' has to be aborted, I'm one of the not-many who can do that. Got an outlet?"

"There."

Chaka pulled out fine-ground dark-roasted coffee, a flask of milk, mugs, and an espresso-and-steamer device, which he plugged in. He measured water and coffee and set the thing running. Edgar Sikes wasn't in the kaffeeklatsch, any more than Ruth Moskowitz was, but both had tasted coffee. Ancient tradition spoke that a nerd must have caffeine. Aaron might sometimes follow an ancient tradition, if it amused him.

And Trish was rubbing Edgar's neck and shoulders, flirting, maybe, but doing a damn good massage too. Chaka had felt her magic touch. She stepped back as Edgar stretched, yoga fashion.

"Looks good," she said.

Chaka asked, "Didn't you used to have a bad back?"

"Broken. It's healed pretty well. Toshiro's taught me some yoga." Edgar sat down and summoned up a hologram, an abstraction, it seemed . . . no, it was a hurricane in infrared, as seen from *Geographic*. They'd beamed it to the National Geographic Society on Earth, a complete recording of another world's major storm. "This was from last year. I'm going to jazz it up a little. Chaka, I'm ready for that magic fluid any time."

The coffee was beginning to flow. Chaka filled the cups with milk. He was thinking, *Toshiro's a good man. He's teaching me karate*— But Chaka shouldn't say that even to Edgar, and if he said it in front of Trish, Trish would tell Aaron.

Many things involving Aaron went unsaid. *Nobody on the planet is stronger than Aaron, except Little Chaka Mubutu. So when we go to the mainland, I carry the cook pot. If a grendel came among us, the last man to use a weapon would be Little Chaka. Someone would have to protect me . . . someone like Aaron Tragon. Little Chaka doesn't compete.*

Little Chaka doesn't know how to fight.

The steam jet howled like a fighter jet. Trish jumped: her back was suddenly plated like an armadillo, and she turned with her eyes bugged. Chaka loved doing that . . . but Edgar never even twitched. When Chaka had the chance to look up, Edgar was moving a whirlpool of cloud over a map of Avalon.

"We want it where people can't see it," he said. "Or can't see it ain't there. So. But the fringe, here, that'll raise hell around *Robor.* This arm we'll taper off a little . . . there . . . matches what Cassandra's predicting. Now here's how it looks from Surf's Up."

Surf's Up was being torn to pieces. Anything lighter than a blockhouse was already gone, fragments floating in the huge waves, or flying through the air.

"Like it? Here's the view from Cadmann's Folly. . . . Nope, they'll see it isn't there. Okay, watch this." He had the whirlpool, the view from orbit. It bent east a bit, and shrank. Back to Cadmann's Folly— "And that matches the Cassandra prediction, which she based on my data. Aaron's too antsy, Chaka. This is the easy part."

"Damn," Trish said. "You're really good."

Edgar preened. He was, and everyone knew it, but he had something else going here.

Trish likely hadn't found Edgar Sikes impressive. Chaka knew her style, and it was domination. But here and now, Edgar Sikes was no schmuck, no mere decoration for a woman. This was Aaron Tragon's wizard, and a wizard makes a risky servant.

"Hey. Chaka? Do you know about a crab that lives in the tops of horsemanes?"

"Sure."

"I wondered why the grendels didn't eat them all."

"Grendels never did *climb* the big horsemanes. They knocked down smaller ones and ate them. Anything that lived in the top of a big one of those might survive. These do. Dad's studied them. They breed by getting the attention of the pterodons, who see a wiggle of prey in the top of a horsemane, and dive, and get eggs on their feet."

Edgar's fingers were still molding the shape of a hurricane. "What brought it to mind was my back. When Aaron and I climbed that tree. Raced for it. I was winning. I got just in reach of the top, and something with teeth flashed right at my eyes. I dropped right past Aaron."

He watched the hurricane raging at the hangars. Nodded to himself. He said, "I was a long time healing. Cassandra was still relearning the old medical techniques she lost to Greg's fire. Trish, Chaka, this should do it, and it's set to go. I should be on duty throughout."

"Then we'd better get on the stick," Chaka said. "Here." He'd made Edgar a second cappuccino. Trish set it down for him, and kissed him. Chaka watched that for a bit, then stepped outside.

17

EDGAR'S STORM

But the king covered his face, and the king cried with a loud voice, O my son Absalom, O Absalom, my son, my son!

And Joab came into the house to the king, and said, Thou hast shamed this day the faces of all thy servants, which this day have saved thy life. In that thou lovest thine enemies, and hatest thy friends.

—2 Samuel 19:4–6

Hendrick Sills winced as he glared at Cassandra's view of the coming storm. It was a nightmare swirl of reds and blacks, pressure zones and cold fronts, sweeping down from the north. Within a few hours it would be hammering the island, the worst storm in a decade.

The onboard barometer had yet to drop far, but fat raindrops were splashing against the windscreen. The dirigible was anchored down tight, and he was making a final check of all compartments. Make sure that all equipment is secure, triple-check the mooring lines, and then scoot to shelter.

Toshiro Tanaka scrabbled briskly up the chrome ladder connecting the command deck with the cargo hold. He saluted, half-seriously. "We're secure, sir," Toshiro said. Good kid. They were all good kids, really. Pity Zack had landed on them so hard, but it was for their own good.

"All right," Hendrick said. "I'm getting back to camp before that storm hits. You probably don't want to stay aboard—it won't be fun if the wind picks up."

"Aye, aye."

Hendrick left Toshiro there in the control room, and climbed down the ladder to the main leve. He paused at the door, trying to remember if there was something, anything that he had left undone. It felt as if there was *something*. But he couldn't put a name to it.

Oh, well . . .

He climbed down the gangplank. The great reptilian bulk of *Robor* loomed above him. Clouds were gathering, but it still didn't look like a nightmare of a storm. You could never tell about these things. Better to trust Cassandra.

He hopped into his skeeter and revved it, spinning up into the darkening sky. He dove at the mountains, whipping through the passes, hitting each beacon in turn. Despite his odd feeling about the storm warning, the air *was* choppy. He didn't want to have an accident.

There were no guards at the main supply depot. None were needed. Technically, there were no guard duties anywhere in the camp.

But on the other hand . . .

Twenty years ago, Cadmann Weyland had taken dogs, and supplies, and a skeeter, and begun his own encampment up on the Bluff. On two other occasions, colonists had emulated him, starting branches up in the eastern mountains without formal permission. All three incidents had followed disagreements, arguments, harsh words at Camelot. The Star Born were certainly upset, and there was precedent for, well, freelance requisitioning.

So in the evenings, it was not uncommon to find Earth Born busying themselves at special duties around the livestock, the landing pads, the central supply depot. . . .

Tonight Carolyn McAndrews had drawn the short straw.

She counted cartons of Concord grapes shipped in from the eastern drops.

She heard something behind her, and turned. The warehouse was shadowed, and she touched a button on her belt, turning the lights up. "Zack? That you?"

The administrator had been in a couple of hours earlier, for a sour exchange of opinions. Zack had been irritable, stubborn, and unreasonable, wanting tomorrow's ledger results yesterday. "Zack?" she called out. "You know, you're not going to get things faster by bugging me every couple of minutes, you know?"

No reply.

She walked down the narrow corridor. She could *swear* that she had heard something back there. The camp was relatively quiet, folks settling in for the evening. She could hear rain beginning to patter against the roof, and the wind was picking up. Good weather for putting your feet up in front of a fire, and—

A shadow detached itself from the others along the corridor, a small female shadow, and Carolyn felt sudden, swift joy. "Ruth! What brings you out here?"

Ruth smiled hesitantly. There was something different about the girl. Carolyn had noticed it in the past week. She walked a little differently, combed her hair a little more carefully. Rachael had noticed it too, she was certain, but there had been no conversation about it. Carolyn was pretty sure she knew what the telltale signs meant, and it was hard to repress a grin.

Welcome to the other side, sweetheart. Who was he? Was he nice to you?

"Hello, Ruth. What do you need? The avocados have turned ripe—"

"I'm sorry," Ruth said. Her face had changed. The smile had been a mask. There was sorrow and fear there—and something else. Excitement.

Carolyn had only a moment to think: *Ruth?*

Then light exploded behind her eyes. Pain, so abrupt it barely had time to register before she fell over onto her side, unconscious.

Trish dropped the grendel gun to her side. She stepped out of concealment and stared at Carolyn with eyes that were cool and unconcerned. An hour of sleep, and she would be as good as new. The capacitor darts had been very carefully adjusted.

Ruth stood with her hands clasped very tightly together. She looked white as a ghost.

"You did fine, honey," she said. "Just fine."

She gave a low whistle. Little Chaka and Derik emerged from the shadows. Chaka bent to roll Carolyn out of her contorted position and push her purse under her head. He looked at Ruth and might have spoken, but set to work instead.

Little was said in the next few minutes, although much was done.

Hendrick was twisting through one of the last mountain passes when he caught a glimpse of something traveling north, in from the main encampment. Two skeeters, locked for heavy cargo, carrying a pallet of some kind. It looked heavy.

They were lost in shadows before he could see anything else.

Hendrick triggered the radio. "Hello. This is Skeeter Six. Skeeter . . ." He checked their IDs on the dashboard display. They were Skeeters VIII and XII. Eight was registered to the kids at Surf's Up, the other to the main encampment. He felt mild curiosity. "You guys better get settled in. Looks like a bad one."

Aaron Tragon's voice came back. "Thanks for the warning. We'll be down in twenty minutes. See you when this mess is over."

"Roger and out."

Hendrick headed in toward camp.

Carlos Martinez wandered into the main communications center. Edgar Sikes was the only one on duty, and that bothered Carlos. The boy had grown more introverted since his father's death. He tended to hang out at Surf's Up more, and talk to the First a little less, perhaps. But the big change was that he had become an absolute workhorse. Burying himself in his job, as if it were his only salvation. And since most of the communications center could be handled by one energetic operator, he spend an inordinate amount of time alone.

Carlos stood in the doorway, watching the screens as they displayed images from the various satellites. *Geographic's* skeletal framework hovered just above the blue mist of Avalon's upper atmosphere. From another angle, Tau Ceti was just sinking below the horizon.

Another image was of gathering storm clouds, swirling just off the subcontinent. It was almost hurricane dimensions, possibly the storm of the decade.

So far, only a few droplets.

"Edgar?" he said quietly. "*Muchacho,* aren't you pushing yourself a little hard."

Edgar almost jumped, he spun around so hard. "Carlos! Give a guy a heart attack, why don't you."

Carlos chuckled. Edgar was definitely working too hard. But why so jumpy? On the other hand, with a storm *that* large coming in, nervousness was easy to understand.

"Everything battened down on the coast? The waves could get pretty rough."

"We're okay. We can pull up into the foothills if there's any problem."

Carlos nodded. "Do we have a live feed from Surf's Up?"

"Well, yes, but they control it. The Star Born have their secrets, Tío Carlos. They'll let us know if they see a problem."

Carlos nodded, and ordinarily would have let it drop, but something was nagging for his attention. What, then? "How about *Robor*? That's on our line, not Surf's Up."

Edgar switched in an image from one of the coastal security lines. Rain was falling out at the beach. *Robor* looked secure, and in the night vision its dark, dragonesque bulk swayed ponderously in the increasing wind. Everything *looked* secure. The side door opened, and a man hurried down the gangplank. Hendrick Sills. Carlos shrugged. "Well, amigo, if you're happy here, I guess we're happy to let you. When did you get in?"

"About five this morning."

"Long day." Ah, that *smell* was what was twitching at his mind.

"I like the work," Edgar said.

"Goes better with coffee, doesn't it?"

"You should know, Tío Carlos."

Carlos nodded. "I'll see you later."

Carlos left the bungalow. Outside he looked up at the sky. The sky was drizzling, but not as badly as it had been at the beach. He adjusted his collar.

Hendrick must be more immune to rain than he was, Carlos thought. Hendrick hadn't turned his collar up as he came down the gangplank, out of shelter of *Robor*.

He walked back toward his studio, mind already drifting toward the work to be done. He wondered where Edgar got his coffee. Even if he was in hiking shape, and that *would* be nice, Edgar had still been too busy—

A skeeter's low roar bent down on his head. He stopped, looking up at the sky, and let the rain patter against his open eyes. He blinked.

He looked back down, at the buildings around him, their shadows melding with . . .

Shadows. *Robor*'s shadow was darker than the surrounding night, and it stretched on the ground as if Tau Ceti had yet to disappear below the horizon.

But Tau Ceti had set. It didn't make sense.

The skeeter had landed. Carlos wanted to ask the pilot about the weather out on the coast. He was two-thirds of the way to the landing pad when he met Hendrick Sills coming the other way.

He blinked. There was no way in hell . . .

"Hendrick," he hailed, raising an arm. "When did you leave the beach?"

"Twenty minutes ago?" Hendrick wiped water out of his eyes. "Why?"

Sunset. There was still light. Hence, the shadow. But it was a darker video image, hence Edgar had tampered with it.

"Was it raining out there yet?"

"Not much. A few drops."

On the screen, it was pouring.

Alarm bells were cascading in Carlos's head. "Something's wrong," he said. "Was there anything unusual about the beach? Or *Robor*?"

"Nothing. Battened down nicely." He thought. "I saw a couple of skeeters heading toward the beach. Carrying heavy cargo. Thought that was a little odd, considering the storm coming in."

"Bad one," Carlos said cautiously.

"Supposed to be."

As if on cue, the rain died to a light patter.

"Let's go over to supply central, see what was so damned important."

Carolyn McAndrews had made it to her hands and knees. She was shaking her head like a big, sick dog. "*Mierda*," Carlos said. "Hit the alarm."

Carolyn said, "Ruth mm. Moss. Sorry," dropped her head, and tried to vomit.

The rain was picking up as Carlos ran across the camp. The alarm buzzers sounded, and colonists were pouring out of their houses. "Someone robbed Supply!" he yelled as he raced back to communications. "Get over there. Help Carolyn!"

His mind buzzed. Who? Why? Jesus . . . what was going on?

He made it into Communication in another twenty seconds. Edgar saw his face and turned his chair from the screen, his lips pursing in an unhappy whistle.

Carlos grabbed the pudgy boy by his shirt and lifted him up out of the chair, pivoting and slamming him into the wall. "What in the hell have you done?!"

Edgar's lips worked without producing any sound. Carlos hit him, quite hard, with his right fist, in the center of his fat little mouth.

Edgar licked his lips. He waited, politely it seemed, to see if Carlos would hit him again. Carlos held back, somehow. Edgar said, "Something killed my dad, and Linda too. You Earth Born have been trying to track it down with computer games. It can't reach you from the mainland, whatever it is, so it's all very, very safe, but you must have ice on your minds to think you can—"

"We're trying!"

"Do you think you know computers better than I do, Tío Carlos?"

"Don't call me Uncle. No, I don't."

"Joe Sikes and Linda Weyland are still dead. Whatever killed them is still running loose. You can't find it with computer games. You need data for that."

"Jesus." Carlos wiped water out of his face, and hit the communication board. "Cassandra."

"Yes, Carlos."

"Patch me to Cadmann."

"There is interference on that frequency."

"Speculate."

"Artificial origin. It seems that someone has deliberately scrambled that frequency."

"*Cabrón!*" he shouted.

Blood bubbled from Edgar's nose, but in his eyes was a quiet challenge. Edgar had pulled it off. The mad genius had faked a fucking storm, right down to the rain swept image of *Robor.* Supplies had been stolen, and the communications link with Cadmann had been broken. Precious time was lost. What else did they have planned?"

"*Dios mío,*" he said. "They're stealing *Robor* to go back to the mainland, aren't they? Aren't they, you little shit!" Edgar didn't answer. *Something* had to get through the boy's armor. "You've taken back the mainland for Aaron Tragon!"

That stung, maybe. "Oooh, no," he said, and stopped.

Zack and Harry Siep appeared in the doorway. "What's going on?" Zack asked, staring at Edgar.

"He'll tell you," Carlos said. "Tell them all about it, *bizquerno,* or I'll break every soft bone in your head. I'm going for Cadmann."

Carlos jumped into Skeeter III and pushed the button—and nothing happened.

He jumped out and tried Skeeter I. Nothing. They had sabotaged the skeeters. He threw his head back and screamed frustration to the clouds.

Wait. Hendrick had just come in. It was likely that the saboteurs hadn't had time to damage his machine. He tapped his collar. "Hendrick. What was your skeeter number?"

There was a moment's pause as Cassandra routed the call, and then Carlos heard: "Number eleven. What's going on here?"

"We've got big troubles, that's what. Get a posse together. I'll be back in touch in ten minutes."

Carlos raced across the skeeter garage, and found XII. He punched the button, uttering a short prayer of gratitude when it coughed to life. He taxied it across the garage and revved, gathered speed along thirty feet of paved runway, and took off.

He wiped his forehead, only it wasn't rainwater now, it was sweat. Where was the radio blockade? "Hello. Cadmann. Come in, Cadmann."

Nothing. No reply. "Calling command center. Can you hear me?"

"Loud and clear. What's the problem?"

"The problem is that whatever this interference is, it's on Cadmann's end."

He had gained the altitude he needed to dive down toward Cadmann's Bluff, hitting the red line. The engine couldn't be cool yet. Hendrick had barely brought it in. He rose up over the edge of the Bluff, and dropped down to land off-center on Cadmann's skeeter pad. He hopped out and had made it halfway to the house before Cadmann met him at the door. "What the hell is going on?"

Justin stood behind him in the doorway.

"I've got to talk to you," he said. He didn't want to say what he had to say in front of Justin, and that made him feel even worse.

Cadmann nodded and said, "I'll just be a minute."

And closed the door behind him.

"Listen," Carlos said as soon as they were alone, "Edgar fixed the weather re-port to get us off guard. Supplies have been stolen. Most of the skeeters have been disabled."

"Is *Robor* secure?"

"No way of knowing. Communications are sealed—we couldn't even contact you."

Cadmann ran, yelling back at Justin, "Bring the other skeeter down, Justin. We've got trouble."

Cadmann was at Carlos's skeeter before the blades had stopped spinning, and Carlos could do little save hang on. Below them, he saw Justin rev up the other skeeter, and take it into the air.

"Justin. Can you read me. Testing. Justin."

"Static clearing up now." Justin's voice crackled and then clarified.

"Cassandra. Interference originating from the house? Please track my mes-sage to Justin, and its rate of reception, and give a probable epicenter for dis-ruption."

Cassandra barely paused. "The main house."

"Thank you very much. Justin. Get down to the colony. Pick up Cheech, and get someone on skeeter repair. We need shock rifles. Meet me at the beach."

They aimed the skeeter into the wind, and flew northward. The distant mountains laughed at him.

Jessica looked back toward the mountains as if expecting that any moment they would part, and her father would appear.

Aaron's hand touched her shoulder. "Jessica. It's time to go."

The loading was done. Radio messages from the main colony were sheer chaos. It would be hours before any effective force could be mounted against them. They had prefabricated huts, weapons, and a year's worth of food for twenty people. They had all of the instruments and apparatus needed to found a research station. There was mining equipment on the mainland.

Jessica carried her bags up the gangplank. *Robor* was theirs, by stealth and by subterfuge. She had planted the disrupter in her father's house. By the time any-thing could be done, they would be far from land. Any negotiations could be carried out by radio.

It was bad. In some deep sense it was even wrong. But the Earth Born had left them with no options.

The door slammed behind her. On the roof of *Robor*, the skeeter engines whirled to life. *Robor* lifted from the ground.

"Edgar," Cadmann mused. "He set it up before we took him off watch. He's got them monitoring the lines. All right. Cassandra. Code Beowulf. Are personal code lines corrupted?"

"Code Beowulf acknowledged. Voice pattern Cadmann Weyland acknowledged. Request second password."

"Ragnarok."

"Acknowledged. Your line is secure. Standard emergency frequencies are not under my control."

"Thank you. Secure the message to Justin Weyland."

"Can you trust him?" Carlos said nervously. "He might be a mole."

"Not in him," Cadmann said darkly. "This is Jessica's doing. And Aaron's. But Justin's not involved. I know it."

They swept in through the mountain passes, and looked down onto the half-deserted village of Surf's Up, the rain-drenched swept thatch roofs glistening in the clouded moonlight.

Some small figure pointed up at them, but then they were over the water and swinging south to the dirigible dock.

"What are you going to do?" Carlos asked nervously.

"Talk some sense into them, I hope." He cleared the ridge of coast, and saw what he feared—a black emptiness where *Robor* had once nested. Waves crashed against the sand, and the concrete pad was completely empty.

"Damn." Cadmann swung the skeeter north. Carlos cleared his throat. "Cadmann—we're low on fuel," he said. "We need to go back and get a new cell."

"We can't," he said grimly. "We don't have time. We're the only ones, Carlos. If we turn around, by the time we get to the colony, and switch batteries, and get back out here—they'll be out of skeeter range, and that's *our* only link to the mainland. It's now or never."

"And to the mines," Carlos said absently. "But is it worth what this will cost, compadre? They are our children."

"They're running without lights," Cadmann said under his breath. "Cassandra. Can we have a trace on *Robor*?"

"I'm sorry," she said coolly. "That information is not available at this time."

"Damn!"

"Damn indeed, my friend," Carlos said quietly. "We're almost out of juice."

The rain pelted against their windows, and wind buffeted them. The storm might not have been Edgar's fictional typhoon, but it was no summer breeze. Lightning flashed at the horizon. A fist of wind slammed into the skeeter, knocking them sideways, and Cadmann almost lost control. His knuckles were white on the wheel, and he cursed under his breath.

There was nothing to be seen below them but blackness. "Getting altitude isn't going to help us. If the engine quits, we can autorotate, but we won't glide."

"Let's do it anyway," Carlos said mildly. "It will give me a few extra seconds to pray."

"If you want to confess all the sins on *your* conscience, you should have started last Tuesday. Nevertheless . . ."

Cadmann started to climb.

18

ROBOR

Nothing except a battle lost can be half so
melancholy as a battle won.

—Arthur Wellesley, *Duke of Wellington*

It was a power relay switch. One piece, carefully removed. The problem had to
be diagnosed, and new parts brought from Electronics. No real vandalism, just
a twenty-minute stall.

Justin was airborne, with Zack and Hendrick beside him. He was almost blind
with anger. The entire camp was in a frenzy, and there was just no telling what
could come of this."

Zack looked at Justin for the tenth time. "And you knew nothing about any
of this."

"Not a goddamned thing, Zack."

"According to Cassandra, someone placed a very powerful disrupter in your
father's house. More delay tactics. Who could have done a thing like that?"
Zack's voice was cracking.

Jessica.

"I don't know, Zack. And I won't make irresponsible guesses."

"No, I don't suppose you would."

They headed into the mountain passes.

The alarm buzzer sounded. They had only a minute or two of juice left in the
fuel cell.

Cadmann flicked on the radio. "This is Cadmann. Skeeter Twelve, calling
Robor. We are almost out of fuel, and cannot return to land. Please advise us of
your position for emergency landing."

Nothing. He repeated his message, and then sat back, arms rigid against the
wheel, listening to the static.

Jessica heard her father's voice, and then heard it cut off. She ran down the
corridor, just in time to see Trish turn away from the controls. "What was
that?"

"A bluff," Trish said. "And not a very good one, at that."

"What did he say?"

"He said that his skeeter was almost out of fuel, and asked for permission for
an emergency landing."

Jessica's mind spun. It was a bluff. It had to be. A freshly charged skeeter had more range than that. *But what if it wasn't freshly charged?* Christ . . . .

"Trish . . ." she began.

"Aaron ordered radio silence," Trish said flatly. "And that's what we're going to have."

A shock wave hit Skeeter XII, and they jolted to the side. Wind and rain and an ugly laboring in the engine all mixed together. They plunged about three hundred feet before Cadmann managed to regain control. Carlos wiped his hand against the windscreen, clearing away condensation, peering out. It was hopeless. There was nothing to be seen.

"I'm sorry," Cadmann said—

A flash of lightning, very close by, too close. It split their universe, blinded them, and Cadmann let some inarticulate sound of effort and anger and fear escape, and they plunged so low that they were momentarily out of the clouds. Another flash of lightning and—

"I see it!" Carlos yelled. "Damn it! Two o'clock. *There.*"

An arc of fire rolled along the underbelly of the cloud, lightning swelling in its belly. And there, gliding like a great dark predator, was *Robor.*

Cadmann gritted his teeth, and took the skeeter up into the cloud again. "We can make it," he said.

"If we don't, can I quote you?"

They rose up above the flat top of *Robor,* and Cadmann hit the lights. They were dim, all emergency power draining to the batteries, but enough to illumine the top. There were docks for four skeeters up there, and three of them were in place.

"All right," He said. "I'm setting her down. You take the right-side mooring cable, I'll take the left. If either of us makes it, we're safe."

The engines quit.

"See?" Trish said, laughing. "No SOS. It was a bluff."

Jessica stared at the control panel, and then looked out at the storm. A bluff. She hoped it was a bluff. She freezing *prayed* it was a bluff. Otherwise . . .

They slammed into *Robor's* landing deck just as another lightning flash tore a hole in the sky. *Robor* jolted, and then stabilized. Its gyros would compensate, and keep the deck level. It was slick, though. They skidded for three feet before coming to rest.

Cadmann wrapped a mooring cable around his arm and reeled it out. He hopped down to the deck. The wind slammed into him, and Carlos was out the other side with the right-hand cable. There were docking rings countersunk in the deck in numerous locations. The trick was finding one.

A violent shudder struck *Robor,* and the skeeter started sliding again. Cadmann backed up, slipped to his knees, slid across the deck and toward the edge.

The damaged strut collapsed, and the skeeter slid across the plates, right at him. He screamed as he went over the edge, the skeeter right on top of him.

Carlos was on his hands and knees, and his face smashed against the metal sheeting as the skeeter behind him crashed onto its side. He knew in that moment that he was going to die.

It pulled him toward the edge, and his knee hit the anchor ring. He scrabbled for it in the darkness, and found it, flipped it up, and clipped the line into place. It snapped taut in the next instant, and behind him he heard a scream, and a grinding crash, and he knew that Cadmann had gone over the side.

He was on the verge of muttering a prayer when he heard the groan.

"On my way!" he sang. He followed the cable to the wrecked skeeter, and climbed around it, finding handholds every step of the way. He came around to the other side and heard a thump. He peered over, and saw Cadmann hanging there, the cable tangled around his arm.

Jesus. "Cadmann!"

His friend looked up at him. Stunned, not injured. Weyland shook his head, like a water buffalo trying to clear itself, and looked down at the ocean, black and slow, far below him, and then back up at Carlos. "Help me," he whispered. And Carlos extended a hand to him, and helped him up.

Trish found Aaron in the main galley, supervising as the crates were hauled up from the hold and opened. Provisions, and equipment, mostly, and he had chosen well.

"We've got a problem," she said. "We've lost power in engines two and three. We're running on a single engine now."

Aaron's head snapped around. "What?"

"It's true. Five minutes ago. We lost two and—"

Her collar speaker crackled. "Trish. We just lost engine one. We have no power."

"What in the hell!" Aaron seemed to grow, his face reddening, and his entire body growing even as they watched. "We'll be blown back toward land, dammit!"

"I'm afraid so. We have the rudders and stabilizers—"

"I'm going up," he said. "Something is very wrong up there."

Carlos slapped Cadmann's shoulder as the first trace of a human figure appeared over the side of *Robor*.

The wind howled around them, and Cadmann had to scream.

"Get back, dammit. I have a grendel gun, and I'll use it."

"Cadmann?" Aaron yelled back cautiously. "Damn. How did you . . . ?"

"Power of human stupidity. Just get back down."

"We'll crash if we don't have our power, you know that."

"No, you won't. I'll give you engine one again. You are going to use it to turn around, and head back to land. And then you are going to put down."

"Cadmann. Your daughter died. We *have* to do something. We have to find out what it was, or her death will be for nothing."

Cadmann was tired and sore. His shoulder throbbed. "Listen to me. We can't talk about that now. I don't have any choice but to turn you around. Let's not let this get any worse than it is."

"Worse than it is. All right."

There was a flicker of movement behind him, and Carlos suddenly screamed, his entire body arcing, Cadmann spun and fired at a figure against the clouds. The grendel gun bucked in his arms. He fired a dart directly into Toshiro Tanaka's chest. Toshiro's hair flew out in a corona, and his teeth clamped on his tongue. Blood shot from between his clenched teeth and his hands lost their grip on the port access ladder. His body arced backwards and he fell screaming and twisting, to the sea far below him.

"Toshiro!" Aaron screamed.

Cadmann, cursing, checked Carlos. He was fine. Damn damn *damn!* The children had dialed *their* grendel guns down to stun. He had been too damned tired, too trigger-happy.

And Toshiro Tanaka would plunge two thousand feet to the water below. And from that height, the water might as well have been concrete.

"One dead, Aaron," Cadmann said. And he could barely speak. His teeth were chattering, and not just from the cold. "One dead. Let's end this."

"You killed him, Cadmann," Aaron said. "He's dead, and you killed him. Why don't you tell your people about how you did this to save lives. All right. We're turning around." Aaron climbed back down. Cadmann collapsed against the wet cold plate of the deck and closed his eyes, feeling the rain pelt against his skin.

PART II
GRENDELS

Which way I fly is hell; myself am hell;
And in the lowest deep a lower deep
Still threatening to devour me opens wide,
To which the hell I suffer seems a heaven.
—JOHN MILTON, *Paradise Lost*

19

VICTORY

Nearly all men can stand adversity, but if you
want to test a man's character, give him power.

—Abraham Lincoln

The whole colony was assembled in the meeting hall. In a few places entire families, First and Second, sat at one table, but most of the Second sat together and away from the First. By accident or design they had chosen tables on the highest tiers on the speaker's left.

There was no entertainment tonight. The circles of conversation went abruptly quiet when Zack Moskowitz came in from the adjacent council room. He was followed by six others: five of the First and Katya Martinez. Zack went to the podium. Katya came down from the stage, looked up at the other members of the Second, and went to sit at the table with Cadmann and her father.

Justin barely saw her. Carlos smiled at her, then looked up at the Second. "Montagnards," he said.

Sylvia looked the question at him.

"From the French Revolution," Carlos said. "The Jacobins sat in the highest seats in the meeting hall. They called that 'the Mountain.' Katya, are your friends contemplating bloody rebellion? Guillotine the *ancien régime?*"

"Not that they told me," Katya sat between Carlos and Justin, across from Cadmann. Cadmann was flanked by Sylvia on one side, Mary Ann with the baby on the other. Cadzie was wrapped in a dark blue blanket.

Cadzie blue, they were calling that color. The blanket was an exact copy of the one wrapped around Cadzie at Deadwood Pass. There were hundreds already, and more being claimed as fast as they could be manufactured. Mary Anne had wanted to keep the original, but that was being analyzed as no bit of synthetic wool had ever been analyzed in human history, and she had to settle for a duplicate.

Invisible death had stripped every living thing at the minehead, Avalon crawling and flying crabs, Avalon Joeys, the scrubby bushes, Earthly mammals, Linda's straw hat, leather belts and cotton cloth; everything but one baby. Was it the blanket? The color, the scent, the texture, the inorganic origin? The cocoon geometry of a blanket encircling a baby?

Dark blue flashed here and there in the meeting hall. Nearly every nursing mother had an Orlon blanket in Cadzie blue.

191

Katya took Justin's hand for a moment, and looked up toward Jessica. Jessica conspicuously was not with her family, but with the Second, at Aaron's table on the Mountain. It was a large table, with room for Edgar, Trish, and Chaka, and, surprisingly, Ruth Moskowitz. Katya thought it over. She could ask Justin later.

"What did you decide?" her father asked her.

Katya shook her head. "Zack wants to make the announcement." She looked from Carlos to Cadmann, then at Justin. "It's all right."

Zack Moskowitz was at the podium. "This is an official meeting of the members of the Avalon Colony to hear the decision of the special commission investigating the death of Toshiro Tanaka, a member of this colony," he said. "I call this meeting to order."

There was a hushed and expectant silence.

"The commission has unanimously reached the verdict of death by misadventure," Zack said. "For those without a legal background, this means that it was an accident. A majority of the commission has also determined that no further action is required, and the case is therefore closed."

There was another moment of silence. Then Carolyn McAndrews stood up "*Missster* Chairman! This wasn't a misadventure! The boy was killed as a consequence of his own criminal actions! He had accomplices. They should be punished! All of them!"

There were a few scattered murmurs of approval, and a couple of shouts of "Sit down, Carolyn!" One of the Second said, loudly enough to be heard all over the room, "Ice on her mind."

"The commission considered that, Carolyn," Zack said evenly. "The suggestion was rejected."

She looked around for support and found none. Her children were looking at her strangely. Sharon McAndrews had been at a second-tier table with other Grendel Scouts. Now she came down to Carolyn's table and put her arm around her mother.

"You'll be sorry," Carolyn announced, and sat down with infinite weariness. Sharon hesitated for a second, then sat next to her.

There was a stirring at the tables of the Second. Trish was standing. Posing, Katya thought. "There should be a trial, all right," she shouted. "But not of us! Mr. Chairman, I charge Cadmann Weyland with murder! You Firsts have been telling us what to do, treating us like children or slaves all our lives! Now you've killed Toshiro Tanaka, and you think you're being generous when you don't charge the rest of us with murder?"

"You're out of order," Zack said.

"Is she?" Carey Lou Davidson demanded. The others at his table, all recently graduated Grendel Scouts, applauded. "I know we won't win a vote, but we would if there was any justice!"

Trish had been sitting next to Jessica. Jessica Weyland's head was bent, face half-hidden. Trying to make herself invisible, Katya thought. What kind of grief was that girl buying? Justin looked as embarrassed as Jessica did. Katya massaged his neck one-handed, but he didn't look up.

Twice now, Jessica had entered her father's home to commit sabotage or theft. Now she sat with her father's accusers. She hadn't yet alienated all of her family, Katya thought, but she seemed to be working on it—

Katya saw Aaron reach around Jessica to take Trish Chance by the wrist. He whispered in her ear. Trish nodded and settled back in her chair.

"Vote!" Carey Lou shouted.

Aaron Tragon stood. "Mr. Chairman, may I be recognized?"

Zack hesitated, then nodded. "The chair recognizes Aaron Tragon."

"Mr. Chairman, with your permission—" He turned to Carey Lou. "Sit down, please."

"I still say—"

"No, you don't say," Aaron said. "Sit." There was ice in his voice. Carey Lou sat.

"Thank you. Mr. Chairman—Uncle Zack—everyone here regrets what happened, and it is utterly pointless to portion out blame. Yes, we tried to mount an expedition to the mainland. We made a lot of mistakes, but we didn't kill anyone—"

"You just shut up!" Mary Ann shouted.

Cadmann shook his head. "Let him finish," he said softly.

"But—"

Cadmann took her hand. "He can't hurt us. Let him talk."

"We didn't kill anyone, but Toshiro wouldn't have died if we hadn't acted as we did," Aaron was saying. "I think the commission has acted very wisely. 'Death by misadventure,' they said, and death by misadventure it was. The important thing is there shouldn't be any more misadventures!

"We still have to go back to the mainland. It's more important than ever," Aaron said. "You all know that Tau Ceti's flaring up. Another Avalon Surprise, and already we've seen changes. Eels. Weather. Edgar says there'll be more—" He glanced down the table, waited for Edgar's nod. "You've got more on that, Edgar? Good."

"Mr. Chairman," Julia Hortha said.

"Please," Aaron said. "I'd like to finish."

"You have the floor," Zack said.

"It's doubly important to understand what happened to Joe and Linda now," Aaron said. "We need the supplies from the mines, and it will take years to find and develop new mine sites as good as the ones we had." He had been speaking directly to Zack, but now he turned to include everyone in the room. "We're all concerned because there aren't enough raw materials. If we don't get a new supply we'll be making hard choices soon enough! And in case anyone doesn't know, there are no suitable mine sites on Camelot Island, and the only mainland sites anywhere near as good as Deadwood Pass are far in the interior or down at levels where grendels live. Deadwood has both organics and metals. It will take years to bring a new site up to the production we had from Deadwood Pass."

"But Deadwood's a wreck!"

Aaron didn't look to see who had spoken. "Yes, but not a *hopeless* wreck. There's a lot of machinery there. We could have it back up to production in a few months."

"How do you know that?" Hendrick Sills asked.

"Edgar Sikes helped me direct Cassandra to do a study," Aaron said. "Edgar?"

Edgar Sikes stood. "The minebit mommy isn't that badly damaged. It's not at the tunnel nexus, it's backed off into a side corridor. The programming might have got shook up, but Cassie's got a duplicate on file, and that's unharmed. I looked. Ask for Operation Restore Deadwood. It's all there, at least in preliminary—"

"I've looked at much of it," Zack said from the podium. "I think he's right about that. I'm not sure I share his conclusions, but even if we picked another mining site, we'd have to move that *entire* minebit factory—"

Katya leaned close to Justin. "He's got it all worked out, hasn't he?"

"Pretty much," Justin said.

"Which makes it more important than ever to understand what happened at Deadwood Pass," Aaron said. "But we will never understand that in isolation. Whatever killed Joe and Linda doesn't live up there. We won't know what it is until we understand far more of Avalon's ecology than we know." He turned to face Big Chaka, who sat with his son down among the First. "Sir, don't you agree?"

Big Chaka stood. Standing, his eyes were at a level with Little Chaka's. "I do agree." He and Little Chaka nodded in unison.

"Everyone in this room regrets what happened to Toshiro," Aaron said. "Death by misadventure. The misadventure was this senseless distrust between First and Second, Earth Born and Star Born. If Toshiro's death has any meaning at all, it's to serve as the end of that! Mr. Chairman, I move that volunteers go back to the mainland, to reclaim the mines and more, to claim what is our own. Let us honor Toshiro's memory by completing the work we should all be doing together. I so move."

There was a moment of silence; then Big Chaka said, carefully and distinctly, "Second."

✳

Trish relaxed, stretching unobtrusively, merely listening. Toshiro had taught her more about relaxation than she would ever have learned on her own. She was going to miss him terribly.

The vote was going Aaron's way. They'd be returning to the mainland with the blessings of the First . . . with obvious exceptions. Aaron himself looked relaxed, almost sleepy. What in hell did he have in mind? It was only for her own amusement that Trish had accused the First of murder. Then Aaron had reached behind Jessica's bent head and taken her by the wrist and, irresistibly, pulled her close enough to speak directly into her ear.

"Trish dear, I've got everything I want here. If you throw it away for me I'll kill you." And he smiled reassuringly and let go, let her settle back in her seat.

He means that. What does he think he has? Trish watched Edgar watching Aaron. They'd known each other since childhood, raised for some years by Joe Sikes, while Trish was bouncing from family to family. . . . What was going through Edgar's head? Trish kicked a shoe off and reached under the table with agile toes. Edgar jumped, then grinned at her.

". . . Weather," Zack said. "Aaron—Edgar—maybe you haven't seen what happened at Surf's Up? It looked like your movie hurricane turned real. Edgar, for twenty years Camelot got weather like California without the goddamned quakes and the rioters." Zack was pleading. "What's going on? I looked through your Fimbulchaos file—"

Aaron nodded at Edgar. Edgar stood up. He'd started to do that anyway, Trish noted, but the illusion would be that Edgar obeyed Aaron.

And Edgar let that notion stand. "Cassandra, give us Fimbulchaos." He didn't wait for the computer's response. "Citizens, for over a billion years, life on Earth has been studying the sun. Astronomers have six thousand years of records if you allow the Egyptians. Three hundred years ago, the sun had only been around for a few million years, because God hadn't invented fusion yet. . . ."

Cassandra had two suns floating beneath the communal hall's high ceiling. As Edgar talked, the two shrank to stars; more stars blinked alongside.

"Two hundred and fifty years ago they found resonant shock-wave patterns in the sun. Sol is ringing like a great bell. About the same time, astrophysicists first detected a supernova by the neutrinos blasting from its core, so all the telescopes on Earth were pointed at the Large Magellanic Cloud before the light even reached Earth. It's two hundred and forty years since we sent our first probes over the poles of rotation of a star. The thing is, almost all of that study was of Sol. Sol! We had twenty, thirty years of close observation of other suns before *Geographic* left Sol. What we know about Tau Ceti is pitiful."

One bright star expanded to fill the dome. A wedge of the fiery globe disappeared, and a dissected star rotated for Edgar's audience.

There were little pockets of conversation all through the hall; Cassandra was amplifying Edgar's voice above background noise. "Tau Ceti runs a fifty-year sunspot cycle, *maybe*. We've only seen about twenty years of that, so it's really just a guess. We can detect shock waves in Tau Ceti's interior. They're a lot like Sol's, but the cells are bigger, and the surface storms where the shock waves meet—Cassandra, my Fimbulchaos Sunspot Four—they're more violent than Sol's." Flame arced out from Tau Ceti, hundreds of thousands of miles before the stream bent back to kiss the surface. "They're getting more energetic as we near the peak of the sunspot cycle, but they don't reach as far out as Sol's would. Tau Ceti's got more powerful magnetic fields.

"What's happening to Avalon's weather is this. The sun is hotter, and the corona is *way* hotter, and it's reaching farther into space. It's heating Avalon's outer atmosphere. The atmosphere expands. That sets up jet streams going west, and turbulence pockets too. The Avalon ecology is trying to cope with the hurricanes, increased ultraviolet and some higher-energy radiation. Not everything has evolved to survive that. Some of what the Chakas have been finding just breed like mad and then die—"

He caught Trish's eye on him, pretended he hadn't, but she could see his belly flatten as he stretched to play with the cursor. Edgar was looking good. She grinned, waited . . . he glanced her way, and she casually crushed her plastic cup, flexing her arm muscles. He stuttered, just for a moment.

She tried to catch him as he made his way out of the meeting hall. He was surrounded. Everyone wanted to talk to Edgar Sikes.

This was a drag. Even if Edgar *was* loving it. Trish thought it over, then went to Little Chaka and borrowed his code and key.

When Edgar got back to the Sikes house, Trish was in the bedroom, cross-legged on the water bed. She turned off Disney's *Aladdin* as he came in.

He smiled, showing no surprise. "Are we granting wishes tonight?"

"There's always a catch, remember?" Trish stood as if levitating. She looked around and smiled. "You've been working."

He said, "Maybe a little," but it was pretty clear he had been doing a lot of work on the room that had once belonged to Joe and Linda. The big ornate bed Carlos had given them was gone, replaced by a classic water bed. Linda's pictures were gone from the walls as her clothes were gone from the closet. The adjoining room had been Cadzie's nursery. Now it was filled with computers and workbenches. The open door to the bathroom showed that it too had undergone a transformation. The small living room was nearly empty, with some weights and rolled mats stowed along one wall.

The surprise was that except for the computer room everything was neat and clean. *Was that for me?* "I like it," Trish said. "You're looking pretty good yourself, Soft One. Drop your shoes. Let's do some sun salutations."

He followed her into the living room and took the Tree position, "attention" in military parlance.

In five minutes he was gasping. She made him slow down, stop to breathe when he needed to. He studied her stance and tried to correct her.

"Hold that pushup pose. Your ass comes up more, your spine *exactly* level. Now go down with your elbows *back* along your ribs."

"You can't do that."

"Hell no. But I can stand on my head," he said.

"Without a wall?"

His teaching amused her at first. Then she began to understand that he actually knew more than she did. Edgar was a fast learner.

He'd learned some self-control. When she'd first started coming here, he'd have leaped at her within seconds of getting her into a room with a bed. Now— He was antsy at first, but then, she hadn't been around for a week. She felt curiosity and anticipation. Edgar remained eager to please, and it was flattering to think she was probably the only human in the universe who could get Edgar's undivided attention even for a few minutes.

He was smirking at her upside down.

Edgar had a father. Trish could nearly imagine bonding to one human being, or two; never needing to guess the thoughts of a townful of people, each of them in control of a child's life. One human being, all-knowing at first, later his teacher, later nearly his equal. Now his father was dead, stripped to the bone, murderer unknown.

Had he loved Linda too? More likely worshipped her.

The First knew of his betrayal, and many would not forgive; and Edgar lived and worked among the First in Camelot.

Trish had wondered if he would survive at all.

Edgar's breath became uneven. He came out of the headstand slowly, one leg horizontal; toes touched the floor; he knelt.

Trish rolled out of her headstand. "That must have been two minutes. Soft One, I'm impressed."

"Don't come down so fast. One leg straight out, then the other, then touch down. We done? Want some coffee?" Edgar asked.

"You've got coffee?"

He smiled.

"Later." She rolled to her feet and had her shoulder in his midsection before he could quite decide to evade. She stood up with Edgar over her shoulder. He was laughing. She rolled him, still laughing, onto the bed. "Now I'll show you why it's a good idea to warm up first. Get your heart pumping, your blood flowing. Soft One, do you really want to get on top?" She rolled them both. "Just one wish. Just one at a time."

Later she followed him into the electronics room and watched as he ground fresh coffee beans. "Smells different," she said.

"Darker roast," Edgar said. "Different beans, too, these are from higher up the mountain."

"Interesting. Who got them for you?" Under the omni-oven was a small terminal. The screen caught the corner of her eye.

Edgar's grin faded as he said, "Couple of Carolyn's kids. You know, the First were treating me like dog meat for a while. But Cassandra isn't nearly as, as *agile* without me plugged in, and they're starting to realize it. It wasn't me that whacked Carolyn—"

"It was me." RUTHFIX, said the top of the screen. Trish couldn't read the smaller print below, but there wasn't much.

"Ah? Anyway, with Dad gone they've got some interest in keeping me happy.

Even if they don't trust me." Edgar poured boiling water into a glass cylinder, pushed a metallic filter grill steadily down from the top to strain out the grounds, and poured two cups of coffee.

She smiled faintly as, both naked, they sat down at the breakfast table. His cleaning project hadn't got this far. There wasn't a square centimeter of horizontal surface showing. Trish perched her cup on a stack of printout. "They'll have to trust you now, what with this expedition. For that matter so will we."

"We?"

"The expedition. Aaron."

"Oh. Of course you'll be going. *Aayeee!*"

"I'll be back once in a while. Or you could come with us—"

"No, that doesn't work," Edgar said. "Even with getting in better shape I wouldn't be much use camping out. Better I stay here and watch out for you."

"We'll have a base. Let us get set up, then come over." She grinned. *Aaron will hate that. He doesn't like me having so much control over our wizard. But it's more than that, there's some real bad blood between those two. He just plain doesn't want Edgar happy.* She let her grin spread into something else, a sultry smile copied from an old movie she'd seen. It had turned Robert Redford on, and it was having the same effect on Edgar.

"Who all's going?"

She kept her eyes fixed on his as she shook her head. "Not entirely sure. Aaron, of course. He'll be in charge. Me."

"Why you?"

"It's where the action will be," Trish said.

"Action. You mean power games."

She shrugged.

"War specs," Edgar said suddenly. "You won't have anything to hide from the First this trip—right?"

"I'd say so," Trish said cautiously. "Aaron might have something. So?"

"So you can give up binoculars and go back to using war specs. Get me over there and I'll maintain the links with Cassandra."

"There you go." Trish said. She stretched elaborately, as she did before she made love, and made sure Edgar saw her doing it. Now she was sure she had his full attention. She moved closer to him. "What's your interest in Ruth Mosko-witz?"

Blindsided, it took him a moment to remember the terminal. He said, "Something Linda . . . no, never mind *that.* Have you noticed what Aaron's doing to Ruth?"

"Somewhat. He thinks we need her—"

"Nah. He wants her involved. Implicated. Because she's Zack Senior's daughter. He's going to hurt her. I wondered if there was a way to fix it."

"Why?"

"Linda once told me I . . . never get to know anyone. I guess I'm getting to know you, Trish, but you, you're bulletproof. It's hard to see you needing help. If Ruth keeps rubbing up against Aaron Tragon, she's damn well going to need *something*."

That was crazy. Edgar could barely help himself. . . . Trish dismissed it. "You know *Aaron* better than I do, I bet. What was he like when he was a kid?"

20

SCRIBEVELDT AND EDEN HILL

All nature is but art, unknown to thee;
all chance, direction, which thou canst not see;
all discord, harmony not understood;
all partial evil, universal good.

—ALEXANDER POPE

THREE MONTHS LATER

Little Chaka watched, as his father took another careful step toward the winged creatures they called birdles. Cane first, then left foot, then right—all slow and smooth and deliberate.

Three birdles clustered about a low bush whose persimmon-sized fruit had turned from blue to red within the last two days. Only then did they begin to attract the flying crustacea. With the deepening of summer, bushes and leaves, plants and grasses all through the forests were changing color, ripening, exploding into a thousand hues of gold and red, and deep, fertile green. Horsemane trees infested with a hundred varieties of parasite and symbiote blossomed as if offering welcome to a hundred more.

The largest birdle—a big purple flying wing with spiffy little white wing tips—swiveled an independent eye toward Big Chaka, now only a dozen meters away. Big Chaka was a small man, barely cresting five feet in his tallest years. Time had crowded, shrunken, grayed him, spotted his dark face. His close-cropped, tightly coiled hair receded from his temples, and he needed corrective lenses to read and a cane to walk. A small, unwieldy pot belly swelled the front of his shirts, and his hands trembled when he wrote in the journals he had kept for nearly a hundred and fifty years.

But he could still move slowly and smoothly enough to approach animals more closely than Chaka would have believed possible. He was still Avalon's premier zoologist. And he was still Dad.

The birdle watching Big Chaka began vibrating its motor wings. Its foreclaws anchored it to a branch, and the branch began to quiver. A high-pitched whistling whine rose up. The other two birdles stopped eating and began rustling as well. They gripped branches with two forward claws, but the little paddle-shaped wings aft blurred with their vibration. The whine became louder and louder, until the trees rustled with it.

Little Chaka wasn't alarmed, not even when the call was taken up distantly by first one, and then a chorus. Communicating threat? Summoning help?

Big Chaka retreated a foot, and then another foot, and the birdles began to calm again. They returned to their meal. The distant droning died away. Silence returned to the forest.

An almost boyish grin wreathed Big Chaka's face as he stumped back to his son "Not exactly a colony, too much independent action for that. More like small family clusters—maybe three to six. Possibly three sexes, or two fertile and one neuter to watch the nest while the others forage, like Avalon Type Six sea crabs. We'll get samples later."

He linked arms with his son as they walked back uphill. "And you call this Eden?"

Little Chaka nodded. "It's where we take the Grendel Biters. There are things they need to learn about this planet, and this is a good place for it."

"I can hear running water. Are there grendels?"

"Always assume grendels. Trust me. We don't take chances. But there is a good overhang between us and the river here. The clearest path for a grendel to reach us is over a kilometer of bone-dry upgrade. We have motion sensors strung every twenty meters—nothing larger than a Joey can get up here without alerting us, and we have good people on the grendel guns. They're death. It's safe." He frowned. "Of course, we thought Deadwood was safe, too. But nothing bad has ever happened here."

Big Chaka nodded. "Things are changing, though." He squinted up at Tau Ceti, a fuzzy ball through high clouds. "Things are changing." He walked carefully along the path. Every few feet he stopped to inspect a leaf, to study a scavenger insectoid hauling away a carcass five times its size, to scrape away a sample of fungus and deposit it in a glassine envelope. Then he made notes in his log, and photographed the sample lying on the open pages of the logbook, with the place he'd found it as background.

"You know," he said, thoughtfully, "I wish that you could have been on Earth. Then you would understand the wealth spread out in front of you. Everywhere you look, all you have to do is reach out your hand, and there is a new creature, a new plant. Something new, something new." With that faraway expression on his face Little Chaka thought he resembled a wrinkled black Buddha. "Earth had . . . run out of *new*."

He smiled crookedly. The smile broadened as he spotted a tiny corkscrew tree growing in the shadow of its parent. "Oh!" he cooed. "A perfect duplicate of its parent—except see, it's a lefty, its trunk spirals in the opposite direction. . . ."

He was that way as they headed back up to the mine, hobbling here and there, studying this, commenting on that—never complaining about the distance or the grade, although some of it must have been exhausting. Chaka's emotions were torn. On the one hand, he was still nervous about the entire area. On the other hand, it was wonderful to see his father every day, exploring with him, and hearing him lecture, just as he had day after wonderful day when he was a child.

They were three kilometers from the mine, far enough around the first bend in the trail that they couldn't be seen. Big Chaka sat down on a rock and loosed one of his shoes.

"Tired, Father?"

"No, I think I have something in my shoe. Son, tell me about this base camp you're setting up."

"Well, it's not so much me setting it up—"

"I know. Aaron seems to be in charge, and I have noticed that he needs no advice from my generation." He inspected the inside of his left shoe. "Of course, he wasn't offered much advice by Colonel Weyland."

"I noticed that."

"You and everyone else." Big Chaka sighed. "Inevitable, I suppose."

"Dad, it's no big deal."

"Not to you. Of course not. But to us— Son, when we first came here we ignored Cadmann Weyland's warnings, and we were very nearly wiped out. Since then we've got in the habit of consulting him."

"Your talisman," Little Chaka said.

"Talisman, wizard—of course he is none of these things. But I am told you have decided on a location for your base camp. Indulge me by telling me of it."

"Sure. It's something over two hundred kilometers northeast of here, in the mountains but there's a large flat area. No big streams but a lot of springs and little streams. The flat is a meadow."

"Yes, I know the area," Big Chaka said.

"Sir?"

"From the maps. It looks dangerous. There is a forest nearby."

"Only a small forest, but it's a forest. Tender leaves. Very edible. Dad, there are Joeys in the rocks, and ground animals in the forest. I don't think a grendel has ever been there."

"It will put you right at the edge of skeeter range."

"Until we get the solar collectors set up," Little Chaka said. "But it faces south, and we've got big rolls of Begley cloth. We'll get it spread out, and there's sunlight most days. It won't be long before we generate enough power to recharge the skeeters there." He rubbed his hands together. "Then we can do some real exploring. Another hundred and fifty kilometers and we're at the edge of the Scribeveldt!"

"That I envy," Big Chaka said.

"Well, you could come with us—"

Big Chaka laughed gently. "You know better. I would not be welcome among your friends." He put his shoe back on and fastened it. "Be careful, son. We don't know what killed Joe Sikes and Linda Weyland, but we are very sure of what killed nearly every one of us during the Grendel Wars. Don't be so concerned about an unknown danger that you ignore a known one. Now we ought to be getting back—" He stopped to look at a colorful lichen. "In a moment."

*　　*　　*

Little Chaka was still a little nervous about these side trips. They were too far from Deadwood's reinforced Kevlar shelters for his comfort. But Big Chaka won that argument, as his father usually did.

On their first day at the mine site, he had wandered far afield, to the very edge of the tree line. "Chaka," he had said. "Look at the density, only five hundred meters from the death site. Nothing has razed this. There are Joeys in the trees, and birdles, and these little insect fellows. Whatever killed Joe and Linda also ate the dogs. Ate all of the organic material in their clothes. It was a freak occurrence. In truth, this is probably the safest place on the planet now—this particular lightning won't strike here again for quite a while." When his son seemed unconvinced, he added, "If you're worried, carry a couple of Cadmann's survival sacks with you."

"I'm worried. Grendels can't bite through the Kevlar, but a bite could still crush a bone—"

"You have grendels on the brain. You studied those skeletons as carefully as I did. No pressure had been applied. No broken bones. No tooth marks. Scrapes, yes, something scraped the meat from the bones, but it was small, not the teeth of a grendel. Whatever killed Joe and Linda was no grendel—unless that grendel had cooked them for hours and then sucked the meat off the bones."

Chaka grimaced at his father's morbid imagery. So what was the danger? The Kevlar sacks should theoretically protect from an acid cloud, or . . . or whatever the hell it was that had killed their friends. The current guess was something biological rather than chemical. A memory stirred in his mind, something from an old science-fiction novel about giant protozoans lurching out of the swamps of Venus to digest unwary space folk. There were movies of large bloodsucking monsters among the stars.

He didn't really believe that, but invisible death had eaten two members of his family under Cassandra's very nose, and the only clue was traces of *speed* on the bones. *Speed* meant grendels, but how? A fascinating puzzle, if only it hadn't been real.

They made good time the rest of the way back to the mine. His father accepted little help, even when sweat beaded his brow and the breath whistled in his throat. Long before dusk they found themselves hiking up the final approach. The hum of machinery was clear at half a kilometer—repair and restoration were well under way. A thin stream of smoke and screams of tortured metal told that some large piece of equipment was being ripped out and refitted. His father was blowing a little on the upslope, but Chaka had released his son's arm and was stalking bravely up the side of the hill.

Little Chaka was bouncing like a balloon. Free at last! He had forgotten what it felt like to climb around in the mountains without that damned cook pot on his back.

Sylvia Weyland waved her arms as they came up over the rise. Smelting metal was a sharp tang in their noses. Cranes and scaffolding hovered about the new mine shack. A dozen workers bustled about, carrying, loading, crafting. A new and stronger shed was being erected, and Sylvia, biologist turned engineer, was the week's gang chief, and would rotate back to the mainland with the arrival of *Robor*.

"How was the walk?" she yelled.

"Great!" They were a little closer now, and voices could be dropped. Sylvia looked tired and a little sweaty, but satisfied. She and her crew worked fast. Two new steel frames had been fitted into place on the structure that would house permanent, grendel-proof shelters for mines and miners. Atop it was an antenna to serve as a backup relay for communications between the mainland and the base camp Aaron called Shangri-la, now under construction two hundred and fifty kilometers away.

"I'm not seeing as much of the local biology as I'd like," Big Chaka complained as she approached him for a hug. "My son is just too protective. I'm not a child."

"We're just taking the mountain back," Sylvia said. "Our resources are still split. Let's just say that we'll all feel a lot better when you've categorized more of the life around here, but there are unavoidable risks attached. You're the only father Little Chaka has; is it surprising he's a bit"—she grinned—"possessive?"

His father looked up at Little Chaka owlishly. "It wasn't so many years ago that I carried you up into the highlands on my shoulders. Now, you could carry me, and with less effort." Then he smiled. "I suppose that every man wants his son to grow up. Mine just grew up a little further than most."

Little Chaka glowed with pride, touched with only the slightest tinge of sadness. He was just beginning to *really* understand that one day his father would no longer be there to talk to, to share with.

But until that time, he could give thanks that they had had so much time together. That they had been able to share so much.

The *Robor* misadventure had not damaged their relationship beyond repair. He wasn't certain how he would have withstood that. Even now, there was a slow coiling of anger and resentment and self-contempt surrounding the whole issue. Self-contempt for allowing himself to be talked into it. Resentment toward Aaron Tragon. Anger, unresolved and smoldering, over the death of Toshiro.

But if his relationship with his father had been damaged . . .

He didn't want to think about that. He would have felt far more self-contempt. Far more resentment.

Far more anger toward Aaron.

He wondered, somewhat darkly, what he might have done about that. But he had to get back to Shangri-la and plan the expedition to the Scribeveldt, and there was no time at all for such thoughts.

✳

The Scribeveldt was a vast oval of highland plain that began at the foothills 220 kilometers northeast of Shangri-la Base Camp, and stretched for over two thousand kilometers to the north and east from there. A long, sluggish river that someone had dubbed the Zambezi ran from north to south a little to the west of the plain's center line. It was a river with few tributaries, and effectively divided the Scribeveldt into two unequal portions. Both parts of the veldt were covered by thick grassy stalks that grew up to waist height, and were sometimes covered with tiny yellow flowers.

It was called the Scribeveldt because when they first examined it from orbit it appeared to be covered with cursive alien script written in broad lines with faded ink, close-mowed curving stripes that approached each other, merged, then diverged. They *had* to be animal tracks. For the past year the trails had hardly come together at all, as if they were deliberately avoiding each other.

The Scribeveldt ended in a forest that covered the foothills. A few year-round streams ran through the forest, none more than a few inches deep. The Scribeveldt and forest had been examined from orbit for years, and one thing was certain; there were a number of animals on the veldt and within the forest, but except for a narrow band near the big river, there were no grendels.

*

The hunting blind was at the edge of the forest. Jessica quietly pushed aside a wisp of brush that obscured her view and peered out at the peaceful herd of chamels grazing quietly a half kilometer away. Her war specs magnified them until they seemed close enough to touch.

One of the male chamels raised its head and looked right at her. *Clever little sucker, aren't you? You can't see me or hear me. Do you smell me?*

He had a gazelle's grace and the thin, sensitive neck of a giraffe. His feathery-gray, insectile antenna trembled in the still air, sniffing. Would it alert the other eleven? Human beings were new to the mainland, but chamels often reacted with fear-and-flight response to any new stimulus. So far neither the males nor the heavy, rhinolike females nor the three St. Bernard-sized "pups" had panicked.

Jessica lay in her blind pit as Cassandra analyzed the image in the war specs and bounced data to Shangri-la 150 kilometers away.

"Do we want it?" she whispered.

"*I'm drooling.*" Chaka's voice was eager. He was in one of the other blinds, probably out of direct sight of the herd, but his war specs could display Cassandra's downlink. "*Protective coloration's almost perfect.*"

Jessica checked: naked eye, war specs, then naked eye again. Damned good. What did the chamels do? Scan the environment with their noses, and adjust the protective coloration for a potential predator's perspective? The creatures were less conspicuous than their own shadows, a perfect predator-proofing strategy.

Strange, Jessica thought. *We aren't just thinking about grendels any longer. There are other things out there. We've got to lose a whole generation's worth of bogeybeast stories, or we'll never survive.*

"There are winners. Fast, and strong, and senses are sharp. Hungry, too. Haven't stopped munching leaves since they arrived."

Chaka's voice was thoughtful. *"The trick will be keeping the herd together. We want to protect the family dynamics, if we can."*

"Cassandra," Jessica whispered. "Note the brush, and the type and quantity and maturity of the leaves being eaten. Special note of the grazing patterns of the little ones."

They'd had to add modules to Cassandra in order to keep up with the flow of data. That had sparked yet one more debate: should their computer power be used for information processing or manufacturing? It was settled only when Zack took the side of the Second. "We can live without more consumer goods, but we can't live without knowledge," he'd said, surprising many of the Second. Everything was so new, so rife with possibilities and problems. Love her as they might—Avalon had little tolerance for errors.

Aaron's voice: *"The net is ready. Repeat. The net is ready."*

She grinned. This was going to be fun. A week of preparation. And now . . .

"On my count," she said. "Three . . . two . . . one . . . go!"

Four balloon-tired dirt trikes exploded from meticulously constructed blind pits. The twelve chamels whipped about, startled and outraged to find they weren't Avalon's only masters of camouflage.

The beasts took off toward the east. Jessica revved her trike, hit a mound of earth, and exploded up into the air. She slammed down with a spine-jarring bounce. The roar of the hydrogen engines, the exhilaration of the chase, her own adrenal flush all dizzied her deliciously.

The chamels were wheeling like a flock of birds. Jessica spun around the outside to head off a move eastward. Chamel defensive strategy would keep the pups in the center, actually making them easier to herd.

Hooves and wheels churned up clouds of yellowish dust dimming Tau Ceti. Jessica fell slightly behind the herd as they thundered now toward the northern horizon. She cleared her throat of dust and said, "On track, Justin."

"We're ready for you."

The brush here was harsh and scraggly, unappetizingly brown except for tufts of tough purple grass. Even as she watched, the skin coloration of the beasts began to shift to match the sparse foliage.

Beautiful.

"Two klicks from target," she yelled. "Keep it tight!"

※

Justin wheeled the skeeter around the outside of the herd and drove a stray male back to the center. The chamels traversed a long stretch of brown gravel.

They changed colors wildly as the terrain changed, and from his aerial perspective it seemed the ground itself was flowing like a river. It was easier to track the herd by dust cloud than by direct observation.

Everything was right on schedule. "In position. Have visual contact with corral."

"*Yippie-yi-oh-tie-yay.*" Jessica's voice. He knew she was grinning.

✳

Jessica dropped her plaid bandanna across her face as she cut toward the middle of the herd. They parted for her like the Red Sea. As the trike jolted through the grass, making almost sixty klicks an hour, she could reach out to either side to touch a chamel. Damn, they were beautiful beasts! Fast, strong, agile—and intelligent. The pups darted through the herd seeking pockets of adult protection. The trike's roar blended with the steady rolling thunder of their hooves. They wheeled left to avoid a log, and she jerked her handlebars to follow.

A commotion to the right: Aaron Tragon, mounted on Zwieback, the chamel Ruth had tamed for him. They burst out of the trees just ahead of the herd.

The herd wheeled, confused for a moment . . . and then followed.

Jessica yelped her pleasure. Damn. He had been right *again*. Chamels were extreme olfactory sensitives. Pouches on Aaron's mount carried an overwhelming dose of chamel pheromones. *Whammo*—Zwieback became an instant alpha. Their herding instincts and trainability boded well. Chamels were an odd hybrid of horse and ostrich, with wide, fleshy mouths and thin, strong legs.

The trike jounced savagely as they crossed the last rise. Ahead of them was the corral, seven feet tall and a quarter kilometer around.

"All right. Let's keep it tight, keep it tight—"

It was hardly needed. The chamels followed Aaron through the open gate. Jessica turned aside at the last second and the chamels charged past her into the pen. Once inside they realized they were trapped. They snorted and tossed their heads, but there was no way out but the gate, and Chaka was already swinging that shut before Jessica could dismount and dash over to help him.

She ran up the short ramp leading to the edge of the corral.

The new twelve had joined fifty chamels captured over the previous week. The new ones snorted restlessly, but even as they did, their skin changed color, matching the beaten ground beneath their hooves.

Aaron swung off his mount, and grabbed for the ladder.

He slipped, and fell back to the ground. Jessica's fist went to her mouth. For a moment, fear locked her into immobility.

The adult chamels reared back: unmasked, Man's smell was very different from their own. Two of the adults turned their backs, and began to kick.

She had seen this behavior before. A ring of chamels to protect a pup, the heavy, hard, sharp hooves striking out over and over again. It wouldn't work against a grendel, but cameras had watched the creatures surround a bear-sized predator and literally kick it into pulp.

Aaron scrambled up to the ladder, spun as one of the hooves caught him alongside the shoulder, and leaped upward. He got two rungs up before another hoof caught him in the thigh. He grunted but kept going, and was out of range a moment later, lips curled into a satisfied smile. She could see where his jeans were dusted and cut by the striking hoof.

Chaka helped him up over the top, and he thumped down heavily. He swept Jessica up for a big, warm kiss, then gave a victory wave to the circling skeeters.

Dust fluttered about them as the skeeters touched down, and the penned chamels brayed even louder.

Jessica climbed up the ramp to look down at them. "Get along little doggies," she sang to herself. "It's your misfortune . . ."

"All right!" Justin said, slapping his hands together. She jumped, startled—he had made his approach silently. "What's left on the chart for today?"

"We've done enough work for today." Her back still ached from digging trike pits, but she had to love him. What an eager beaver. It was getting easier to relate to Justin. The bad times, at least the really bad ones, seemed behind them.

"I think we've got time to lay for the spider devils. What do you say?"

She peered up into the sky. Tau Ceti was still bright and high. "We've got five hours of daylight. Have a spot in mind?"

Chaka raised a huge finger. "How 'bout the heavy patch, about two klicks from where we trapped the chamels?"

"Some folks would say we were too close to water," Justin reminded him.

Jessica laughed. "Older folks, I'd bet."

"Yup."

Chaka waved nonchalantly. "We'll use motion sensors and a backup team. Thermal, if you want them, Justin."

"Well . . . the spider devils seem to like the area. Grendels would eat them if they could catch them." He pitched a rock off across the horizon. "I guess we can handle it."

Jessica slapped him on the back. That's *my unbrother.* "Sounds like a plan."

As Justin and Jessica ate lunch a pair of skeeters rose and swept away toward the east. Another came in with a load of chamel chow.

"Quite an operation," he said.

The fences were already sealed again. Unlike the main camp, here there were no passive boundaries—but they did have an electrified fence, twenty-four-hour guards, movement sensors, and a fortified, grendel-proof shelter.

The shelter was Quonset-hut-shaped, and certified grendel-proof by Colonel Cadmann Weyland. Jessica felt an odd mixture of security and disgust when she remembered the way he had tested the crystal-filament-reinforced plastic constructions. . . .

✳

Blackship Island was gray and rocky, just a spur, really. It held one of the relay stations constructed between Camelot and the mainland. A skeeter pad. Emergency supplies. A stormproof shelter.

The waves shot foam high into the air where they slapped up against the rocks that day. Jessica looked up at her father where he sat beside her. His face seemed as gray as the rock, as gray as the sky.

They had said little to each other since the day she planted the disrupter in his home. The day she had betrayed their relationship.

Two skeeters flew in from the north, their flight patterns carefully timed and synchronized, one flown by Evan Castaneda and the other by Aaron. Cargo hoists with specimen slings hung beneath each skeeter.

Jessica's heartbeat accelerated at the thought of what was about to happen.

Cadmann spoke casually. "Let's have Skeeter Seven first." Aaron's craft hovered overhead, and winched down its load.

Eleven feet of fang and gray scales and claws and spiked tail lay in that sling. A grendel. Type 6 was the color of gray mud; otherwise not very different from the now extinct Camelot grendels, but with a down-turned double hook at the tail . . . and a solemn, brooding mouth, where holos of the Camelot horrors showed a demon's grin. Chaka strode up to it, hunkered down, and peered into its eyes.

They were open, staring, sightless.

Or were they? Could anyone really say what was happening in the depths of its quasi-reptilian mind? They knew enough to be certain that a few volts of electricity trickling through its sleep centers would keep it quiescent.

"The jaw," Chaka said. "The hinges. See what I meant? Its bite gets more powerful leverage than the Camelot grendel, but it takes a smaller bite."

Her father was holding his breath as he examined the grendel. Given any excuse, he would kick the grendel, shoot it, inflict some indignity upon it that would be one one-millionth as devastating as what had happened to him all those years ago.

But it wouldn't happen—her father was not a man for futile gestures. The grendel slumbered on.

Chaka nodded, and Cadmann waved the motionless cargo back into the air. Aaron raised it, and then dropped the bundle down through a hatch in the prefabricated dome. If this test went well, these domes would eventually dot the mainland.

This dome was twenty feet in diameter and seven feet high, made of prefabricated sections that slotted together in minutes. They had spiked and chained it into the rock.

Cadmann cut the line. Skeeter VII spun away and landed on its triple size pad. Aaron bounded out, his long, tanned face intense.

"Any problems?" Cadmann asked.

"No. Not really," Aaron replied. A slight edge of anxiety belied his words. "She's been on ice for seven hours, waiting for your call. Cassandra identified the grendel hole, and then we just trapped the bitch."

Bitch? Jessica thought. *He's never called a grendel bitch before. He said that for Dad.*

Cadmann nodded. "All right. Let's do this."

Skeeter II swung into position. Its winch distended, to lower a second grendel into the shelter. They detached the wire.

They sealed the shelter, closed the door, and bolted it shut. Skeeter II landed.

Jessica noticed Cadmann's expression. No doubt about it, he was enjoying this. "Shall we go?" he asked.

There was no hesitation. Chaka climbed in with Evan. Cadmann and Jessica chose Aaron's skeeter. The autogyros retired to a prudent distance.

"Cassandra," Cadmann said. "Visual."

A square of holographic window opened. Suddenly, they were peering into the dome.

The two sleeping grendels were curled in their nets, looking almost peaceful. The larger one was gray, the smaller a mossy greenish brown. That one was a Type 3. Her tail was a crown of spikes. Her long toes were built for climbing trees. Unusual: most grendels couldn't climb.

She looked to be easy meat for the gray.

Cadmann cleared his throat. "Cassandra," he said. "Please record all angles."

"Yes, Cadmann." It seemed to Jessica that Cassandra's voice sounded just a little like her mother's.

"Terminate current."

"Yes, Cadmann," Cassandra said.

Cadmann took a deep breath. He seemed very peaceful.

"Trigger *speed*," he said.

A small aerosol can on the inside of the dome began to spray a pink mist.

Speed was the grendel secret. It was an oxygenating agent rivaling rocket fuel in potency, a chemical secreted in sacs in the grendel's back. Grendels running on *speed* burned energy faster than any creature born of Earth.

And the smell of *speed* was the smell of a challenger. It triggered a territorial response, a hyperexcited combat readiness more powerful than any mere hunting mode. It drove grendels insane.

The can hissed as its contents were released.

Above the dome, the humans hovered in their skeeters. Waiting.

The smaller grendel woke first.

They watched its eyes widen. Its tongue darted in and out twice.

"It *should* have flashed." Cadmann sounded puzzled.

The green grendel should have flown instantly to the attack. Instead, the first thing it did was retreat, banging into the wall, thrashing and hissing. It scrabbled, seeking a way out, finding none. Finally, it turned and faced the larger beast, its spiked tail raised a little from the ground almost, like a scorpion's.

"That's very odd," Aaron said quietly. "It almost seems to be thinking, doesn't it? Judging the odds?"

"It knew it couldn't win," Jessica said.

Cadmann looked at them from the corner of his eye, but said nothing.

Then the gray grendel woke.

Its eyes snapped onto the green one, and in that moment the smaller grendel sprang.

The screen became a blur of blood and fang. Blood clotted the camera. They could see nothing.

"Cassandra. Aerial view." From above, the walls shuddered and shook, but held.

"Take us down," Cadmann said.

By the time that they touched down, the screams from within the shelter were almost as loud as the rotor.

Cadmann took his rifle down from the side rack, and examined the charge. Lethal.

The noises from the shelter were dying down now. One last sobbing roar rose to a hissing crescendo. Then there was a *crack*, followed by a series of wet crunching sounds. Then a single, dying hiss.

Jessica stared at the holographic image. "Good God."

"When two tigers fight," Cadmann said, "one dies, and the other is crippled. Chinese proverb." The raw *satisfaction* in his voice frightened her.

Aaron nodded. "What now?"

"Open the gate," Cadmann said.

Aaron approached the dome. Scarlet oozed from between the cracks at the bottom of the dome. Something within the dome made a rhythmic wheezing sound.

"Open it, dammit."

Aaron unbolted the door, and swung it open.

The air thickened with the blended stench of *speed* and scorched alien blood.

The interior of the dome was smeared with viscera. The smaller grendel was reduced almost to chunks. The larger had been ripped open. Her intestines spilled out in gray coils. She bit at them, snapping and chewing with a blunt, bloodied snout. She made crying sounds.

The grendel raised its head unsteadily, staring directly at Jessica.

Jessica raised her rifle and shot it once in the head with an explosive dart. With a short, sharp, ugly sound the grendel's head splashed open, spattering blood and brains for meters in every direction. The ruined body quivered once, and then was still.

Cadmann peered inside, and nodded in satisfaction. He slapped the outside of the dome.

"Every joint held," he said calmly. "This dome is officially pronounced grendel-proof."

Jessica bent over and vomited.

21

THE ROUNDUP

Nature is often hidden, sometimes overcome,
seldom extinguished.

—Francis Bacon, "Of Nature in Men," *Essays*

Justin sometimes felt as if he were tap-dancing through a minefield when he talked with Jessica. There were subjects that were simply taboo: Her relationship with Aaron. Her relationship with Cadmann. Her relationship with Justin.

Ouch.

Katya had come over with a plate of beans. She pinched him again.

He let his pensive mood fade. "Hi, Kat."

She bowed, and sat next to him. Her flannel shirt rubbed against his shoulder. Tau Ceti was particularly fierce, and the distant mountains wavered in the heat.

But this was safe—at least from grendels. Their distance from water guaranteed that. Whatever other dangers lurked out there . . . well, that was another question.

He drew a little horseshoe in the dust with his toe. "All right," he said. "Twenty-five klicks west. Jungle starts there, but it's mostly fed by underground streams. The closest surface water is still eight kilometers distant. Lots of slow-moving ground animals, so we figure it's a grendel-free zone. We're going to find the spider devils. The question is the proper means of capture. Any suggestions?"

All three of them stared at the crude map for a few minutes, then shook their heads.

Little Chaka strolled over. He looked larger than life, and dusty, and extremely happy. No question why! In the last month he had begun the generations-long process of categorizing the life-forms on the mainland, shipping samples back to Camelot a dirigible-load at a time. A labor of love, the beginning of a life's work.

He said, "Father has some ideas about the spider devils. The first thing is . . . we're going to have to lose one of the piglets. . . ."

"Ahhh."

"And I was just getting attached to the ugly little bastards," Justin said.

"Well, go find the ugliest one and say your good-byes. By this time tomorrow, it will be an ex-piglet."

Jessica bounced up to plant a kiss on his cheek. "Rest time is over. Let's go and take a look at this."

"They're up there," Chaka said.

The sound sensors picked up the web spinners as they chattered to each other. Jessica, Justin, and Chaka were eighty meters to the east, as close as they could get without scaring the creatures away. It was plenty close enough to let them pick up the chittering and constant, oddly sensual singing.

"All right," Chaka whispered. "Let the piglet go."

The snouter looked confused. It carried enough tranquilizer in its belly to stupefy a battalion of grendels; but the membrane holding the toxin had not ruptured. It also wore a collar of Chaka's design. A needle ran from it into an extremely sensitive cluster of nerve endings in its snout.

When the cage door lifted, the snouter sniffed freedom and set off running. It got five steps when the first jolt of pain clobbered it. It flopped over onto its side, and wobbled back up as if it couldn't quite believe what had happened to it. It tried running north again, and got another shock.

Down it went.

"Meanie," Jessica whispered.

"That's me," Chaka agreed heartily.

The snouter turned and ran south. It got another eight paces before Chaka zapped it again. It fell over as if poleaxed.

Now one very confused little snouter, this time it tried to walk west, toward the trees. It got six paces, and then stopped—sniffed as if asking the air a question.

"That's the direction," Chaka agreed. "Nice snouter." If it hared off line, he zapped it, but softer this time, and it began going right where they wanted it.

It stopped just short of the trees.

"He's making visual contact with the spiders," he said. "Or vice versa. And there goes the music." It was louder now, and pitched lower, almost echoing the snouter's snorts.

"What do you think?" Justin asked. "If an animal is raised or nurtured by its parents, what are the chances that it is conditioned to respond to something that sounds like its mommy's voice?"

"The spiders are singing it a lullaby," Jessica laughed.

"How quaint."

The snouter hardly needed prompting. Dazed, it wandered into the forest one halting step at a time. It stopped to nibble on something green, then took another couple of steps, and trotted happily into the forest.

Justin's war specs automatically followed the creature until it was swallowed by trees.

"They'll be focused on the kill," he said quietly. "Let's get a little closer."

The brush had a jungle flavor to it, fan-shaped trees and spiky bushes, a dense tangle of greens and yellows. They crawled forward to a new position, where they could see through the tangle of brush. Justin suddenly heard a snort of pain and betrayal, of sudden, massive fear.

The snouter was caught in a web. It was thrashing and twisting frantically, to no avail at all.

Justin focused in. The strands were green and white, and apparently quite strong. The snouter made a frantic, heroic effort and almost tore itself free before something dropped on it from above. Something broad and fibrous: a net, or a coarser version of the web.

Helpless now, it rolled over onto its side and quivered.

They moved in from the shadows. One, two, three, four, five . . . six black stick-figures. Justin had wondered if they would be yet another Avalon crab, but they weren't. In motion the web spinners did look like great spiders, with small torsos, tiny heads, and four long, long limbs.

"Perfect," Chaka said.

The things were closer now, and the snouter had ceased struggling. They sang, and the song was hypnotic, in perfect tune with the snouter's own sounds. Calming. Dreamlike. Almost anesthetic.

"Jesus," Jessica said. "Kill it, will you?"

Chaka laughed. "You have no sense of drama. Cassandra. Trigger the implant."

The snouter heaved once, massively, crashed back down, and was utterly still.

The largest spider devil came a little closer, probing. It didn't seem to like the sudden stillness, but the nearness of fresh meat was too much for it. It descended, sank fangs, and went to work. The others followed, and the scene turned into a general feast. An entire colony of the spider devils was home for dinner.

After five minutes, Chaka stood. "Let's go," he said. "Motion sensors?"

"Nothing larger than ten kilos. No sudden shifts in wind."

"All right. Let's go."

Rifles at the ready, they entered the forest in a modified wing formation.

Spongy loam underfoot. Smells of camphor and lemon. Everything seemed to smell more vibrant than the colors that exploded around them. The forest canopy wasn't particularly high here, but every tree limb was ripe and heavy with leaves, and vines, and fruit . . . or things that looked like fruit.

Just out of Justin's reach hung something purple and bulbous, like a cluster of fused grapes, or a blackberry. He reached out and prodded it with the tip of his rifle, and it dissolved into a colony of marble-sized purple leggy things that swarmed up the branch to re-form a few feet farther away.

He wondered what would have happened if he had touched it with his naked hand.

That wouldn't be possible right now. They wore lightweight membrane suits that covered their entire bodies with a thin, tough barrier impenetrable to all but the most determined attacker. An entirely reasonable precaution: Chaka had already categorized at least twelve deadly plants and identified three toxic species. Small things, with a biotoxin about a dozen times stronger than a wasp. Not lethal to an adult, they would still grant a few days of truly memorable sensation.

A couple of lizardlike things perched on branches. Unclassified. Cute. Venomous or worse.

They were in the clearing now. The light slanted down through the trees, giving a louvered effect.

"Motion sensors?"

Jessica checked a wrist sensor. "Nothing for a hundred meters."

They knelt, and examined their take. The snouter was both withered and half-devoured. The spider devils had first sucked his juice, then ripped him apart.

They lay on their sides, motionless. Their faces were tiny but manlike, lips slightly parted. One, the largest, lay on its back. Its legs closed feebly on Chaka's tongs when he prodded it.

"Alive." He picked it up and examined it. The four legs quivered. Legs and torso were covered with straight black hair. These were mammaloids, Joeys, though evolved in a drastically different direction. Wet-looking lips drooled something thin and milky.

"Close your mouth while you chew," Chaka said, and unfolded his basket to drop them in one at a time.

"All of them?" Justin asked.

"Sure. They might be some kind of hive mind. Might not even be able to survive separated. I'll get them ready to ship back to Father." He grinned. "Of course, they may have ice on their minds."

Jessica and Justin examined the web. She was scraping goo from what seemed to be an enormous mat of thin vines, and putting a bit of it into a sample bottle.

"What the hell is it?" Justin asked, scratching his head.

"It looks like a lattice of leaves," she said. "They chewed up the connective fibers, leaving just this heavy venous stuff. Then they coated it with something sticky, probably a biological exudate."

"So it's not a true web."

"No. They're interacting with the environment."

"A bit chancy. They're vulnerable to the quality of the materials."

"No more than a beaver," Chaka said.

"Why would a tree want to make something useful to a spider devil?"

"Maybe they furnish the tree with high-energy droppings."

Her sample bottle had everything that it needed, and she snapped it shut. "Let's get out of here. I don't feel all that comfortable here."

"Come now. The woods are lovely, dark and deep."

"Yeah, right. But I have promises to keep."

"Right." They unclipped a rod from the side of the basket, extended it, and threaded it through loops at the top. Chaka hoisted it over one shoulder, and Jessica took the other end. Justin kept his rifle at the ready, movement and thermal sensors tuned.

And they encountered no problems at all, all the way back to the trikes.

*　　*　　*

The *NickNack* was a much smaller version of *Robor*, a cargo mover ballasted by hydrogen sacks, large enough to carry a dozen people and small enough to be powered by a single skeeter. It was reliable so long as they didn't run into bad weather.

Cigar-shaped, it hovered above the animal pens. The spider devils were frozen, the dozens of plant and insect specimens neatly and safely stowed away. They would easily survive the eight-hour trip.

Eight hours as the pterodon flies. On the other hand, to paraphrase the old joke, if the pterodon had to walk and herd a group of recalcitrant chamels, it would take twelve times as long.

"Aaron will be back by morning," Jessica said. "Then we can start them moving. Cassandra? Map."

A contour map showing a quarter of the continent opened in the air before them.

"Close on our position, Cassie. Good enough. Group, we need to water the chamels daily. We need to clear the water holes of grendels before we get to them. Trikes, horses, and skeeters are the ticket. We leapfrog ahead. Should take four days. Any questions?"

Jessica leaned back against the log. She could hear the chamels snorting in their pens. The males bonded readily to horses doused in chamel scent, and the larger females would follow the males. Her stomach buzzed with adrenaline. A new adventure. What they had fought for, bargained for . . .

Died for . . .

She sloshed her coffee down on the ground, and stood. "Let's get a good night's sleep tonight, and get started early."

"Aye."

"Aye."

The fences, the generators, the shelters, and a cache of weapons would be left behind. Eventually, there would be supply stations all over the southern tip of the continent. Forty-eight hours of juice in the fences, and enough weapons to make a hell of a stand before help arrived, with help never more than twelve hours away.

She high-fived Chaka. "Good job."

He grinned broadly. Chaka was just happy to be totally swamped with specimens. He wandered off to search for new fronds to tag.

Jessica and Justin remained by the fireside. Silences between them were strained these days, ever since . . . what had happened. But that was the chance they had taken. If anything he seemed more uncomfortable about it than she did. And that, she decided, was appropriate.

"Looking forward to the week?"

"We'll see a lot of territory," he said.

"Good find," she said. "The females make good meat, and are decent beasts of burden. The males are as fast as racehorses. Good stock.

"Imagine a hunt," she said. "Some kind of camo shirts and pants, and riding one of these beauties. Sneak up on anything."

"I've thought about it for weeks." Justin stretched. "Well, I think it's that time. Big day tomorrow."

"Big day."

He left without a backward glance. Jessica hunched her knees and stared into the fire. For all of her life she had treasured countless long, intimate conversations with Justin. She missed them more than she could have dreamed.

And yet . . . what she had done . . . what they had done was right. The only thing she regretted was Toshiro. He of the gifted hands and strong, golden body . . .

He had made his choice. As Justin had made his.

As her father had made his. And the colony theirs.

The fire crackled, grew higher and warmer, and then slowly began to die. It was well after midnight before she felt sleepiness to match her fatigue.

✳

Justin woke at the stirring of the horses. For a bare moment he was disoriented, unable to remember where he was. In his father's house? He sat up in his bedroll and washed his face from a canteen. On the mainland every camp away from a base would be a dry camp. Tau Ceti was showing a bare sliver of red to the east, and the air was pleasantly chill. The prairie was silent, and the creatures that took the place of insects on Avalon were quiet.

The path ahead was clear. Three days' ride to the foot of the mountains, some through grendel country, but they had the technology to deal with *those*. Grendels wouldn't dictate their route. "First one up makes breakfast," someone called. Justin grinned and poured powdered eggs and water into a pan. Others were stirring. Chaka came over to watch the dawn with him. "Morning, cowboy."

"Yippie-yi-o-tie-yay," Justin said.

"Do you see any problems in working with Jessica for the next three days?"

Justin glared at him.

"I know that there have been some—"

Justin interrupted him. "Listen. She made her choice. It wasn't totally right—but it wasn't totally wrong, either. I made my choice. We have problems. But she's still my . . ."

He thought about it. A dozen possibilities flashed through his mind. "Family," he decided. "She's my family. We'll work it out."

An hour later a skeeter buzzed in from the south. Justin frowned when he saw Aaron climb out of the cabin. He felt a flash of unreasoning dislike, even hatred burning at the back of his brain.

Aaron. *Everything that is good here would have happened anyway. Eventually. And everything bad—you brought. You always knew how to make the games come out your way, didn't you?*

Jessica, still tousled but beautiful, went to meet him. Aaron embraced her, then cast a radiant smile in Justin's direction. "Top of the morning, sir."

"Love sleeping on the ground," he said. Aaron roared as if it was the funniest thing that he'd ever heard, and slapped Justin's shoulder. "All ready to go?"

There was a chorus of ayes.

I'm not being fair, Justin thought. *Sour grapes. Selfish.* And part of his mind whispered, *You could have been the leader if you'd wanted to be. But you wouldn't do it, and now Aaron has that and Jessica too.*

NickNack was already out of sight. Skeeters went along to assist in herding the chamels. Two hundred chamels, and ten horsemen to keep them under control. Shock prods and tranquilizers for the uncooperative.

Aaron grinned widely. "Head 'em up! Move 'em out!" he shouted.

Someone answered, "Rawhide!"

The chamel pen was made of nylon netting strung from poles. Two electric lines kept both chamels and predators away from it. Chaka opened the gate as Justin mounted a roan mare from the remount pool. *They call it the remada,* he thought. The word, like most everything else they knew about cattle drives, came from recordings of Earth television shows.

Aaron stood in his stirrups. "All right, we have thirty klicks that's never been explored on foot," he shouted. "The skeeters will scout it for us, but stay in threes! Stay together, stay alive. Nobody gets hurt, right? All right, let's move."

"Heeyah!" Katya had ducked under the pen's netting. She waved her arms and shouted to drive the chamels out.

The males moved with light, birdlike fast-twitch motion, scenting the air and looking for an opportunity to escape. One made a dash eastward. Justin kicked at his horse and again wished for spurs. They weren't needed, but there was something about boots and spurs. He laughed and dashed after the stray, caught up and swatted it with a stun wand. The effect was astonishing. It dropped exactly where it was, quivered, and changed colors twice. Its huge eyes blinked three times, and an enormous tear rolled out of one. Then it scrabbled up onto its haunches, and it looked at him accusingly, as if to say, "You beast!"

He prodded it back toward the herd. It returned slowly, damn near dusting itself off first, its dignity untouched. It humphed like a society matron.

Jessica reigned up next to him. "Shut your mouth," she said. "You'll draw flies. Well. You certainly made a fan there, didn't you?"

He rolled his eyes, chucked his mount, and kept them moving.

Tau Ceti rose steadily in the sky, but the air remained cool. They were close to the equator, but heading into the high country, and this was winter in Avalon's northern hemisphere. In summer the high desert might be a blasted heath, but it was tolerable for now.

In fact, it was downright pleasant. There were vast beds of poppylike flowers, and twice he hopped off his mount to snag samples for Cassandra's information banks. Her major task was cataloging and analysis of all data on mainland animal, vegetable, and mineral forms.

This is the way to tame a continent. You have to let it take its crack at you. Some die and merge with the new world. More are born to take their part of the future.

But all this would have happened, in time. Toshiro died because Aaron was in a hurry.

The way was lazy and long, the sun and the dust and the cool breezes were intoxicants. The chamels sang songs of sadness and loss. He tried to whistle their repetitive rhythm.

Chaka rode up next to him. He rode double with Wendy Powers, who often shared his bed.

"This is the life, eh?"

"No worries, if that's what you mean."

"Right. *Hakuna matata*," Chaka said.

They rode together for a while, in silence. The chamels lowed and sang. The rumble of their hooves on the hard-packed dirt was a music all its own.

Wendy shaded her eyes with one hand, and with the other pointed at an irregular mound, man-high, a hundred meters to the north. "Another one of those bug hills," she said.

Chaka nodded. "I've counted a dozen so far. Little flying crab things. Industrious buggers. God, Dad would love it out here. So much to see."

They passed another klick or so before Wendy spoke again.

"Do you ever wonder what's happening on Earth?"

"Sure. I guess. No way to know, though."

"They just forgot about us. That's what I think."

"Probably a bookkeeping error," said Justin.

Chaka snorted and pulled his horse away. Before he did, Wendy swung athletically onto Justin's mount, and wrapped her powerful arms around his waist.

They rode silently for a while, and then she said, "Just like Clint Eastwood in *Rawhide*."

"Yeah. But the Indians didn't eat you."

"You wouldn't know that from watching the movies, that's for sure."

She was quiet for a while, and then said, "When are you and Jessica going to forgive each other?"

"Taking up Julia Hortha's habits?"

"No, I'm really worried about you two. And don't change the subject."

He shook his head. "She made a fool out of my father. And then made him a killer. Not easy for *him* to forget something like that."

"Not easy," she repeated. "But hasn't there been enough trouble?"

"Are you trying to make peace?"

She kissed his ear, and blew in it warmly. "Would you accept a peace offering?"

"How do you spell that?"

"Any way you want."

He laughed.

"You know," she said, "I'm not that different from you. You have a foster father, who you love. I love a dream—that's what I have instead of a family."

"The whole colony is your family," he said gently.

"That's the same as having no family at all. Aaron is my family. Aaron's dream. If mistakes were made, they were made on all sides. We've got to let them go."

"You guys. In some ways, you Bottle Babies seem like . . . one big body with two dozen legs and a dozen heads. Sometimes it seems as if you don't care about anything but each other."

"That's not true, and you know it. I fight with Stu Ellington all the time. Well, almost all the time." She smiled at him, and patted his cheek. "If you're interested, you know where to find me, tonight," she said.

She hopped off the back of his horse, and trotted effortlessly back to where one of the trikes was rounding up a stray female.

Justin hunched forward into his saddle. There was some truth in what Wendy said. There had to be a way of putting things back together. If he didn't see it at the moment, it might still be real.

Jessica nodded hello as he pulled up to the rear of the herd.

"Nice country." He felt cautious, and guilty about the caution.

"Beautiful." No other words followed.

"Jessica," he said—

There was a security buzz on his collar, and he cursed. "Yes, Cassandra?"

"Weather reports have shifted. There is now a sixty percent probability that heavy fog will shroud your intended camp site."

"Is that right? Damn. What would you expect the temperature to be?"

"As low as fifty degrees."

"How close is the nearest running water?"

"Twelve klicks."

Twelve klicks. Too damned close for comfort. Pity—they had chosen a beautiful site, near one of the wells. Shower facilities had already been erected, but . . .

Safety before comfort. We need a different route.

Even as he thought it, Aaron's voice was in his ear. "You heard Cassandra," Aaron said. "We should change course. Those in favor of taking the Mesa route please signify."

"Aye . . ."

"Aye . . ."

"Aye," said Justin.

"Motion carried unanimously. Let's do it. Skeeters Two and Six—start flying in supplies."

The air grew chill. The chamels labored upward. The fliers scouted ahead, then came back to lift trikes up to the top of the plateau. Two stayed, two others came down the trail they were climbing. Chaka and Derik pulled up next to Justin and revved their trikes. "How's it going?" Derik yelled. He held out a stick of beef jerky.

Justin said, "Nominal," and bit off a chunk. The chamels struggled up the boulder-strewn path. Their hides were a dusty gray now. It was beautiful to watch them change. They were like terrestrial chameleons with a touch of . . . well, of *speed*. Everything on this planet was sped up just a touch. Magical. The pace was fast. The trick was to keep pace, to think, to move, to *feel* just as quickly.

Aaron was right about that. They had to match the rhythms of the planet. Trying to impose Earth's rhythms was a losing proposition. They should stop counting in Earth years . . . though the change would be a major hassle.

One of the young chamels stumbled, its long and deceptively delicate leg turning badly. It slid back a few feet, and could have fallen. Justin was off his horse in a moment, and behind it just a moment before its own mother got there.

He felt a horseshoe ridge of hard flat bone close on his shoulder, hard.

Chaka came in with the shock prod, and Justin said "No!" and met her eyes squarely, and kept pushing. She backed away, put her great head behind her child's butt, and pushed.

Together, they got the calf up the defile. She sniffed around her child, and the bruised leg, and seemed satisfied. She eyed Justin suspiciously, got between Justin and her offspring, but somehow . . . somehow seemed less hostile now.

"Trying to gain their trust?" Derik asked. "I suspect that's a waste of time. They're just meat, right?"

"Not so sure," Justin said. "There are lots of creatures we can use for meat. I think that these things are pretty smart, and they've got a hell of a natural advantage. How about hunting? Ever think of that?"

"Hunting. On a big chameleon?" Derik liked it.

The mesa's top was hard and flat. The trail lay across it for nearly a hundred kilometers before dropping into lowlands again. Grendel country. They would skirt the river that carved that valley, then climb back again to the base camp Aaron had named Shangri-la. Exploring, Justin said aloud.

The northern wind whistled. Something hit his face. *Cold rain*, he thought, then corrected himself. *Sleet*.

"Flash storm," Evan said in his earphone. Justin could hear the burr of Evan's skeeter in the background. "Just like the ones up on Isenstine. Secondary camp is only five klicks. We're already setting up. You'll be here in an hour, I reckon."

"Sounds good." Prefab corrals, fire, chuck wagon. This was the life.

✳

The daughters of God, two of them, settled on the mesa.

Old Grendel watched from below, from the shade of a deep forest, fifteen kilometers from open water. The weirds had veered away from the river. They never came very close to open water.

Yet they needed water. A tiny rivulet trickled from the heights. It wouldn't cool Old Grendel on the naked rock slopes; but there would be water on the mesa, enough if she was careful. She sniffed snow on the wind.

Many nights ago the weirds had come down from their heights. Two or three tens of them had surrounded and killed one of Old Grendel's daughters. If those were prey, they didn't know it yet.

The river crabs were long gone, the local hunter-climbers had learned to ignore her, and Old Grendel was hungry. If she couldn't find prey in a day or so, she would have to attack the weirds.

They were an awkward long way away, but the hill above them showed trees; it would likely have water, and cover for Old Grendel. Water or no, with the coming snow to cool her she could get above them. It looked like she could hit and run. Creep close. Seek out a loner. Go on *speed*, hook the loner with her tail, drag her to the cliff and let her roll while Old Grendel moved straight down into the stream.

Then watch. No need to go back right away. Would the loner call for help? Would she live long enough to do that? Would help come? What would they *do*? She was as interested in that as in a quick meal.

Weirds. The more she saw, the less she knew. The little flyers were *not* daughters of God. Rigid creatures with wings so fast they blurred to invisibility, they resembled the ubiquitous pattern of the Avalon crab, though God looked nothing like that at all. God was slow and wingless. She floated like a bubble, a bubble that changed its appearance, attempting to hide itself like puzzle beast. God couldn't move without the little flyers to push. God had a true daughter, a smaller floating thing pushed by *one* little flyer.

There was cooperation here, as among beaver grendels and other species too. Was it possible that God had tamed, enslaved her own parasites?

And the little prey? The weirds rode God's little flying symbiotes like an infestation. Old Grendel knew about symbiotes and parasites. Some tiny life-forms would weaken or kill a creature; some would make it stronger. She had wondered if there was a symbiote that would open a grendel's mind . . . but it would be too small to see.

Old Grendel had followed the weirds hundreds of kilometers. She lost nothing in so doing. The river-laced meadows that had been her kingdom for most of her life were one vast swamp now. For two years, ever since the sunlight took on that spooky tinge, the rainfall had been increasing. The dammed lakes overflowed; water covered the flats. Old Grendel had left the southland to her daughters, and good luck to them. She would follow the weirds, upstream.

One branch of the river came near their primary nest, the heights where God customarily dwelt. The main river branch ran here, where Little God carried supplies that fed the weirds.

From the moment her mind opened, Old Grendel had known how much more there was to know. There was this about the weirds: no other grendel, no other *kind* of grendel had studied them like she had. When Old Grendel understood the weirds, they would be her prey alone.

✳

The wind had picked up, and was already blowing the first small flakes their way. The chill was noticeable despite their cheery campfire. "Chamels should be all right." Chaka had slipped into a fur-lined jacket. "We've observed them as high as ten thousand feet, and at temperatures ten degrees lower than anything we're likely to get tonight."

"Good." Justin said, "There was something about that calf, and the way it looked at me. I'd never seen that in one of them before."

"Well? What do you think?"

"I think that there was somebody home. Dog-smart, maybe. I don't know. I liked it. And the way the mother nipped at me, and then seemed to understand what I was doing. I can't help the feeling that it was aware. A little. More than those males we had back at Camelot."

Skeeters had whirled in and out for the last hour. Supplies arrived from Shangri-la. All but a dozen of the herders took the opportunity to go back to the base camp for a shower and a night's sleep.

Jessica came into the firelight with her arm around Aaron. The giant's laughter boomed loudly enough to fill the entire territory. He had won. The First had lost. He sat at the fireside, and lifted his voice against the driving snow. His voice was baritone, and easily penetrated the driving wind:

> "In fourteen hundred ninety-two
> This gob from old I-taly
> Was wan'dring through the streets of Spain
> A-selling hot tamal-e . . ."

Everybody knew the words, and began to sing along with the refrain:

> "He knew the world was round-o
> His beard hung to the ground-o,
> That navigating, copulating,
> Son-of-a-bitch Colombo . . ."

Justin was quiet, but Jessica caught his eye. They shared a smile, and at her urging, he joined in.

> "He met the Queen of Spain and said:
> 'Just give me ships and cargo
> And hang me up until I'm dead
> If I don't bring back Chicago,'
> He knew the world was round-o . . ."

Katya came up behind him and slipped her arms around his waist. He leaned back and looked up at the stars, at the constellations.

"Still pretty much the same as they were for my great-grandmother," Katya murmured.

"Yep. Ten light-years doesn't go as far as it used to."

> "For forty days and forty nights
> They sailed the broad Atlantic
> Colombo and his lousy crew
> For want of a screw were frantic . . ."

Katya was working her hands under his clothes, giggling breathily. It was getting harder to concentrate on the song.

Why qualify that, Justin thought in a happy daze. Truth was, it was just plain getting harder.

> "They spied a whore upon the shore
> And off went coats and collars
> In fifteen minutes by the clock
> She made ten million dollars . . ."

By the end of the song (in which Christopher Columbus returned to the Old World with an impressive assortment of New World microorganisms), Justin and Katya had retired to their sleeping bag. He protested that he was actually much too sleepy to be of any service to her. Her clever sculptor's hands soon made a liar of him. Within a few minutes, he found himself rolling on a warm and familiar tide, one that swept him slowly to the peak, and then dropped him swiftly, but gently, into the fires below.

And finally he lay at the edge of sleep, enfolded in Katya's arms. He murmured, "Thank you, ma'am," into the hollow of her throat.

"You're welcome, sir," she chuckled dreamily, and somehow managed to effect a curtsy right there in the sleeping bag.

She said something after that, something about wondering if there wasn't a river the two of them could find, here, on the mainland. He gave her some kind of answer . . . river equals grendels, you little idiot. . . . And the next thing he knew he was dreaming of childhood, of games with Jessica and Aaron and Chaka.

Games that Aaron always seemed to win.

22

GHOSTS AND WEIRDS

Take, for instance, a twig and a pillar, or the ugly
person and the great beauty, and all the strange and
monstrous transformations. These are all leveled
together by Tao. Division is the same as creation;
creation is the same as destruction.

—CHUANG-TZU, *On Leveling All Things*

Downslope, motion in the falling snow. Old Grendel held her breathing slow
and even. The snow was melting on her. She was cold, and that was a rare thing.
But if *speed* flowed in her arteries now, she would die.

Again, the flurries rippled. Old Grendel raged. The weirds were hers. But she
was alone, she had always been alone, it was the way of her kind. She could do
nothing but observe. There were grendels in the snow.

The snow grendel waited with her sisters. The fires within them were banked
and cooled by a mantle of snow, so that the smells of courage and danger were
faint. Cold One knew there was meat hereabouts. She knew it by its smell.

These were the ones who could vanish. A puzzle beast could stand only a
speed-sprint away, meat for the taking, and be gone in the next instant, neither
seen nor smelled. But puzzle beasts could be taken if the wind was in your face.

Ordinarily she didn't like sisters nearby. But puzzle beasts would feed all, and
in fact her sisters gave her a better chance in the hunt. While the prey scattered,
fleeing the others, *she* could lie in wait and pick one off. She'd done it in the
past.

Puzzle beasts, and something else: she could smell them too. The weirds were
here. The world was turning weird, and these were part of the weirdness. They
too were chameleons of sorts: they tottered on two legs, but they could change
their skins, and they could ride floating or flying things, or puzzle beasts, or creatures as fast as grendels on *speed*, that smelled of tar. *Caution.*

Slowly, she inched forward.

✳

Justin came awake in two stages. In the first stage he was halfway between sleep
and wakefulness, and still aware of his dreams. He dreamed of dancing fire, and
of snow smothering the flame.

Then the dying flame began to whinny, sounding much like a chamel. A chamel terrified almost to death.

He popped awake almost instantly, his hand curled around the grendel gun at his side. "Get the skeeters up," he yelled. Katya was dressing and rolling out of the sleeping bag at the same time, out of the tent in less than ten seconds.

He crawled out and scanned the chamels. Whatever had frightened them was still in the outer darkness, far enough away that it hadn't triggered the movement sensors, but they still whinnied in terror.

His collar beeped. Cassandra. "Five grendel-sized masses moving toward the camp. Alert."

He slipped on his war specs. Cassandra automatically gave him thermal and starlight scope. Nothing. A mantle of snow covered the ground, and more drifted from the sky. Was there really anything out there? Dammit, they were fifteen klicks from open water. . . .

The chamels ran in circles. When they got to the edge of the pen their electronic collars gave them pain for their efforts—but the pain was nothing compared with the terror. They screamed. Their hooves threw up small bits of snow.

Snow.

Freeze me blind. "Cassandra," he whispered. "I want a weather report."

"Mild storm front moving in from the north."

"Where is the largest body of water south of us?"

"A lake approximately twenty kilometers south."

"General comm circuit. Everyone, up and at 'em! Grendels coming. The wind has carried our scent and the storm has let them get here. Grendels in the snow! General alert!"

"Right," someone answered.

"Perimeter defense," Justin said. "War specs on thermal. Auditory updates to everyone else, on the minute. We better use local nodes—don't risk bouncing the signal topside in this weather."

More information, but less computing power for resolution. It would probably balance out.

"Get our best pilots *up*. Katya, get airborne." She was a superb pilot. This would be her most severe test.

He checked the charge on his grendel gun. She wasn't the only one who would be tested today.

✳

Jessica pulled the chamel pup back into the herd, got it to huddle against one of the females. Her war specs revealed four heat-shapes crouching in the outer darkness. They were waiting. Cooperating? Or did they merely tolerate each other when there was meat to share? The chamel scent was strong enough to attract every grendel from here to the river. End it now.

She touched her collar. "I don't want to wait for them," she said. "This thing will get out of control. I say that we go find them."

"I like that idea," Aaron said. "Skeeter One, Skeeter Six. Let's go hunting."

✳

Justin adjusted his war specs. They were synchronized with the rifle sights—making not quite a smart gun, but close to it. Visual, enhanced infrared, and motion-sensor data was coordinated with the rifle in overlapping lines of pale green and red. When the images aligned he had a lock. And the grendel was moving.

There! Grendel flash, alignment—

It ran straight at him, faster than he'd believed possible, faster even than the grendel images in their computer training classes, faster than a living thing could move, and it was coming for him, hot death on the move.

If he hadn't been prepared for it, if he hadn't trained for it in computer simulations a thousand times, he would have been caught flat-footed. *Damn* but it moved fast, and straight for him. Every instinct told him to run—

The sights were aligned. He fired. The capacitor dart, traveling at twice the speed of sound, hit the grendel and dumped its juice. The grendel's nervous system *flashed,* and its brain was a char, even though its legs carried it on into the herd. *Physics supersedes biology.* The chamels scattered, but inertia carried the grendel into the herd, and one chamel went down under its bulk. Even in death the grendel closed its jaws on the chamel's throat. The other chamels ran until their collars brought them to a halt. They bleated their terror.

"They're coming in!" Derik screamed. His sleeping bag was next to Justin's, and now he was standing just to Justin's left. "Here they come!"

The snow spumed up in crisscrossing lines. Grendelflash. At least six. Justin sighted, locked, fired—a clean miss. He blinked and the grendel was a hundred meters closer, nearly atop him. Lock! He fired again, and Derik fired also. One of the darts struck the grendel dead into its throat. It ran on toward them. Physics supersedes biology—

Justin rolled one way and Derik the other. The grendel plowed through the center, right where he had lain. Its legs scrabbled in the air as it made a terrible pierced-boiler squawking sound.

A skeeter flashed down from above. Aaron was belted into the doorway, and had mounted a gun there. Armor-piercing rounds stitched across the snow, then along a grendel from tail to head. Blood sprayed the snow. Everyone expected a second grendel to attack the wounded one. They had seen that in recordings made in the Grendel Wars. A grendel was wounded and the others turned on it, sometimes generating a frenzy. It didn't happen here. The other grendels charged onward.

Hungry, Justin thought. *Hungry, and wary, and they cooperate! The snow keeps them cooled off, and they cooperate.*

Christ.

Skeeter VI. Katya's voice. *"Grendelflash south-southwest."*

"Targeting?"

"Negative."

"Jessica? Can you engage?"

"I've got it."

Justin had never been happier to hear her voice. She was to the south. He and Derik had the east, Chaka the north. Who was to the west? He didn't know. *Nothing I can do anyway. Hold my sector, and hope the others hold theirs. This is what Dad meant about the First. They had to trust each other—*

Skeeter II buzzed close overhead. Katya's voice: *"We've lost visual. We've got Cassandra reconstructing our infrared images. The storm is interfering with transmissions. I'm not sure our onboards—"*

There was a moment in which the sound rose to a crackle, and then it died out. Dammit. Justin heard it overhead, coming in too low. The snow increased, another flurry driving itself against him, and he cursed. He couldn't see anything.

The earphones crackled again. "Trying to see—"

And then—

✳

Stu leaned out the door of Skeeter II. Too much was happening too quickly to let him keep the whole camp under observation. He wasn't worried. They had grendel guns far better than the ones the Earth Born used to win the Grendel Wars, and the Star Born were better trained, had better reflexes than the First. They'd rehearsed this in simulation, skeeters and Cassandra and the gunners operating together to bring maximum firepower to bear.

That was in simulation, but this was different. Here the weather kept Cassandra blind, and he was nearly so, and his heart pounded and he sometimes forgot to breathe. He peered into the snow, but he couldn't see clearly.

"Stu, where the hell are they?" Justin's voice yammered in his earpiece.

"Bring it down a little closer," he told Katya. "Justin needs help."

"Right," she said. "Uh—I can't—"

"Yes?" he shouted.

"Nothing. I'll get in closer."

✳

The meat milled right in front of Cold One, but the stink of death was in the air, and an alien chemical reek. There was much that she didn't understand here.

She bucked and snapped at a sister next to her, receiving a warning snap in return. It might have turned into a death match then and there, but for the meat—so *much!*—and for another thing. Others of her kind, others of *her own brood* had died here, and the stench of *speed* and grendel blood filled the air.

The air was filled with smoke and thunder as her sister burst open, spewing blood and bone and shredded flesh and *speed*. Something like blind panic hit her. She couldn't begin to comprehend what had just happened, but she had once seen the sky flash with light, *rainfire,* and that light climb down from the clouds to strike a tree. The tree had burst into flame.

And this was something close to that. The meat! The meat! So much of it. Yet the world was turning upside down, and she smelled death in every wind. The world was changing. Hell was coming, and any strange thing might be worth her life.

Like this: looming abruptly out of the sky was a burring thing that Cold One had only glimpsed between flurries, a birdle big enough to eat grendels, its wings invisible on *speed*. It swung down, then drew back as if suddenly aware that it had come too close to earth. A threat! A challenge!

Speed flooded through her body. A grendel would attack what it feared.

✳

Justin saw Katya's skeeter come in low, circle, come back even lower. The sound and pressure of its rotors bore down on them and swelled until they filled the entire world. Suddenly it was only a few feet over his head. "Sleet!" he yelled, reflexively flinging his hands up in a doomed attempt to ward off disaster.

Katya was already trying to correct. The skeeter headed out into grendel territory, and began to rise.

"God," Derik said. "They're going to make it—"

✳

The skeeter struggled to gain altitude against the wind and snow. The low power light winked on as she threw full power to the engines, but the skeeter tipped downward and fell. "Stu—we're going in," she had time to say.

Snow exploded, a white cloud against the windshield. The skeeter didn't want to respond to the controls, and a pale shape was coming at her eyes. She screamed and crossed her arms in front of her face as jaws came across the ship's nose. The grendel smashed through the front viewscreen. The skeeter banked violently to the left, and she lost all control. The skeeter fell into the snowbank. She had time to hope that the fall would crush the grendel, but then the rotor caught and threw up a shower of snow and dirt, and they cartwheeled forward and over, crashing down nose first. Her harness straps dug into her flesh but they held.

"Stu—" she shouted. "Stu, it's not dead!"

Stu wiped blood from his eyes. He'd lost his grendel gun in the crash. Up forward the slim torpedo head and much of its body were halfway through the shattered left-hand windscreen. The jaws opened and closed. Snow heated by the internal heat of its *speed* steamed up from its snout and jaws. Those jaws snapped closed no more than a meter from Katya's face.

The grendel had been stunned by the fall but now it was coming awake. It was like a scene from one of their recorded Halloween movies, a serpentine ogre coming back from the dead. A long strip of the windshield's frame had torn loose and partly eviscerated the grendel. It left a trail of hot blood and steaming intestines as it inched toward Stu. The stench of its dragon breath was nearly overpowering.

Katya screamed. The thing whipped its head around and stared at her as if affronted by her noise, her motion, her very mortal fear. Stu saw the grendel, impaled, dying, work its way in through the window, saw its jaws close on her head. He closed his eyes, and wished that he could have closed his ears as well, the terrible cracking-ice wet crunching sound, the sudden explosive stench of blood and brains. . . .

He blinked, hard. Katya was still alive, the grendel hadn't reached her yet. He threw off the quick-release buckles and dived forward. He screamed "Hey!" and swung his fist, connecting solidly on the side of its head. He felt his knuckle break against its armor, cursed and swung again, at its eye.

It roared, deafening in the confined space, and turned to snap at him.

Stu screamed, suddenly registering the insanity of what he had done, and jerked his safety webbing loose. He rolled out of the skeeter, spilling into the snow, and kicked the door shut behind him. The enraged grendel was coming through the Plexiglas windscreen. Ignoring the hysterical Katya, it pounded its way through the Plexiglas of the door and flowed after Stu like a shark through water.

How could the dying beast move at all? Stu staggered flailing through the snow. He'd left his gun . . . he never would have had time to reach it, but how could it still move? It flashed into *speed* and was on him. He'd gone no more than a dozen meters.

✳

Justin was moving even before the skeeter struck the ground. The snow was driving now, a sudden flurry that blinded, but it would confuse the grendels as well.

"Justin!" Derik yelled behind him. He didn't care. Katya was in mortal danger, and there was no way that he could leave her to die.

He pitched forward into the snow and peered out through his goggles.

Feasting, near the skeeter. He recognized Stu's jacket.

Justin clamped his mind down on nausea and fear and grief. Business now. Mourn later. *Think.*

That grendel was busy. It looked to be dying, ripped open, for that matter. It might even warn others away: its natural territoriality would protect Katya for a few moments.

He heard Katya whimper, and almost lost his resolve. Almost. There was a plea, a cry of *"Justin! Help me!"* He felt it reach right under his logic, and twist.

He remembered what Carlos said about his bride, up on the cliff. That he had never forgiven himself. That he had learned something about himself at that moment.

Justin could pull back to the safety of his encampment, and let whatever happened happen. Wait for the storm to abate, or for the grendel to finish its meal, and decide what to do about the whimpering woman.

And find out whether or not he could live with it, later.

Closer.

"Justin—" Katya screamed.

And—

Grendelflash.

Memory: the Learning Center, the domed building in the very center of the colony. Cadmann sets four-year-old Justin in a bucket seat in the hollow of something that looks like a big half-eggshell. Cadmann sits down next to him, touches a button.

Now they're next to a river. It's a cartoon, not real at all, and everything is moving slowly.

Suddenly, something ugly pokes its head out of the water. Not real ugly: comic-book ugly, exaggeration ugly, with pop-eyes and blacked-out broken teeth and an idiot expression. If a grendel had been in Dumbo's circus, this would be it.

Cadmann pushes a button, and a green ray shoots the ugly thing. It rolls over, thrashes, and kicks its legs. It holds a daffodil between its stubby paws.

Justin claps, delighted.

"Now your turn," Cadmann says. And he's laughing, but little Justin wonders at a queerness in the sound. Daddy wants something out of this.

The thought passes. Little Justin takes the control. This is *fun.*

At twelve, the virtual game is a regular thing. Every week Cadmann takes him. Every boy and girl in Camelot competes in the Game. It is simple. There are hunting simulations. Climbing scenarios, mining expeditions. Simulations all. They form teams or play alone.

And at some point in the Game (and there might be a dozen other objectives within a game) there will be a grendelflash.

Every week for years, a different component of skill has been nurtured. Instant response. Aim. Relax under pressure. Multiple targets. Automatic scanning for a second, third, fourth predator. On and on.

The intent is to groove one neurological response pattern. Cadmann has told him:

The grendel depends upon its speed. But unless you have been foolish indeed, you will have a second or two before it is on you. We will train you to respond in less

*than two-fifths of a second. We will train you to bring your weapon to bear, to evalu-
ate risk, to fire twice in precisely the correct pattern. It will be a reflex, completely unconscious. We can give you this gift.*

You will survive.

Pale death came at him in a whorl of snowspray. Justin's hands moved faster
than his brain could follow, lining up with perfect coordination. The thing
accelerated to over 120 klicks an hour in the time it would have taken him to
blink. If he had blinked. But that was training too. *Calm breath. Don't blink. Fire
twice.*

The first bullet tore into the grendel's throat, carrying enough shock to drive
it sideways, off line, so that he wouldn't be bowled over by its charge. The second was an incendiary round, heat for the heated, to jolt the beast across an
invisible metabolic line.

It reeled back, torn, bleeding, dying. Its eyes locked with his, its feet splayed,
bright red blood staining the snow which whirled and pelted between them.

Grendelflash, left! He shot it again, between its eyes, and tore off the top of its
head. He spun left—

The grendel above Stu was gone. *Not* gone: he caught its madly whipping tail
following it into a snowbank.

Someone fired from behind him, twice. Derik. Justin said, "Hold off."

"Why?"

"All the other grendels are hamburger." Justin was still taking it in. A mistake
in judgment here could be terribly embarrassing.

Stu's ravaged corpse lay in a pit in the snow. The grendel had been terribly
injured; he'd seen its intestines hanging in coils. Its spraying blood, nearly boiling, had melted cubic meters of snow. Three or four more dark pits led to the
snowbank: more splashed blood. The grendel had disappeared into snow *there*,
and Stu's two exploding bullets were interlocked pocks right in the middle of
that; but Justin had seen snow shift to the right, and now he saw it shift again.
The grendel wasn't moving now—huddling, he thought—but the heaped snow
was melting.

Justin said, "I'd like to give Chaka an intact corpse."

"It's still dangerous."

"Sure, we have to kill it, not study it. Do I hear the voice of Zack Moskowitz?
Cover me."

Rifle at the ready, he ran to the skeeter as Derik covered him. Katya was cow-
ering in the back, somehow wedged behind the seat. Her arms were wrapped
around her chest, and a rictus of terror distorted her face.

She looked at him without seeing. He put his hand across hers. "Come on,"
he said. "You're safe."

She clutched at his hand. He bent to the floor of the wrecked skeeter, picked
up Stu's grendel gun, and wrapped her hands around it.

✳

And that settled *that*. The weirds did cooperate.

Speed was seeping into Old Grendel's blood despite all she could do. In all her life she'd never seen anything like this. The Cold Ones too could cooperate, it seemed, when there was prey enough to feed all. But against the weirds—

The last of them had fled. The smallest, she hadn't even tried to kill anything. The small Cold One had watched, and now, steaming with *speed*, was fleeing up toward the highest snowbank on the hill. Toward Old Grendel, buried in snow but for snorkel and eyes.

Old Grendel smashed into her flank, sank teeth just ahead of her hind leg, and ripped flesh away. The snow grendel, turning with the impact, smacked sideways into the snowbank. In a blur of snow she clawed her way out, but Old Grendel was a blurred hot streak, receding.

She went straight downhill in the shadow of a gully. The weirds would not see her. Dying snow grendels and their own wounded would hold their attention. She was running over heaped snow, but the snow stopped at the trees.

Short of that point, Old Grendel turned and rolled. Snow was not enough— she really wanted water—but this would do. She spun across the snow, exhila-rated, boiling with *speed*. Her roll stopped in a snowbank. As the snow began to melt, she looked back for the first time. The snow grendel was far above her. It lurched toward her, on *speed* but terribly clumsy, spraying blood from her flank.

All grendels had that in common: on *speed* their hearts churned like the motor wings of an Avalon birdle. They lost blood *fast*. Old Grendel let the *speed* seep from her blood. She crawled backward now, over snow that melted at her touch, backward and into the shadowed forest. The snow grendel floundered after her, slowing; obscuring her track.

Would the weirds bother to track the last snow grendel? They might. Weirds left *no* question unanswered. If they looked, they would not find Old Grendel; only her prey. If they did not, a day from now the snow grendel would make fine eating.

Old Grendel was beginning to believe. God had not trained her parasites. The answer was madder yet.

As meat the weirds were no longer interesting. The weirds had enslaved God. Old Grendel intended to learn how to do that.

23

CONQUEST

Now what about those incidents in which some person seems to go beyond what we supposed were the normal bounds of endurance, strength, or tolerance of pain? We like to believe this demonstrates that the force of will can overrule the physical laws that govern the world. But a person's ability to persist in circumstances we hadn't thought were tolerable need not indicate anything supernatural. Since our feelings of pain, depression, exhaustion, and discouragement are themselves mere products of our minds' activities—and ones that are engineered to warn us *before* we reach our ultimate limits—we need no extraordinary power of mind over matter to overcome them. It is merely a matter of finding ways to rearrange our priorities.

In any case what hurts—and even what is "felt" at all—may, in the end, be more dependent on culture than biology. Ask anyone who runs a marathon, or ask your favorite Amazon.

—MARVIN MINSKY, *The Society of Mind*

The storm blew out and the sky cleared. In those two hours Aaron had used the remaining skeeters to round up the male chamels, while Justin established a defensive perimeter complete with motion detectors.

That work kept them busy for hours. When it was over, when the last reluctant chamel was restored to the herd, the Star Born returned to the grim reality of torn, bloody snow, and the tarp-shrouded body of their friend.

Justin knelt beside the tan shroud, brooding. "I know you, Stu. You'd want us to remember that our defenses worked."

Aaron nodded agreement. "When the Earth Born first encountered a grendel, it was a massacre. This was just war. We only lost one of ours."

"One too many." Jessica's left boot toe dug at a bit of dark, gummy snow. The head-shape beneath the tarp was misshapen. Even draped, the body seemed . . . broken. Shrunken.

"Does anyone want to say something?" Justin asked.

Katya nodded, and bowed her head slightly. "Stu." Her breath plumed from her mouth like a whisper of steam. "You *died* for me." Justin rose and put his arm around her shoulder. She clung to him.

There was a long pause, everyone expecting someone else to speak first.

There was no sound but the wind, the distant skeeters, and the lowing of the chamel herd.

"Do we send him back to Camelot?" Jessica finally asked.

"No." Aaron's reply was unexpectedly fierce. "He came to take the continent. Let him be buried here, where he fell. We'll mark the spot with stones, and let Cassandra record it. Send him to wind and sky and sun."

"But—"

Aaron wasn't listening. "His real monument will be at Shangri-la, the place he helped to build. This is our land now. All of this. Not Camelot, not Surf's Up. This is our land."

The midday sun melted enough snow to expose an eviscerated grendel corpse—Stu's killer. Aaron fired a biotoxin load into it, and it didn't twitch. Then Skeeter V set down carrying Jasper Doheny and the expedition's chain saw. Chaka moved in with the deadly humming wand. He began his autopsy with a beheading.

Now he pulled at torn skin, measured teeth and tail, jotting everything down in a little notebook. "You know," he said quietly, "the interesting thing is that they didn't just *tolerate* each other's presence. That would have been remarkable enough—but they actually seemed to *cooperate*."

"That's a pretty depressing thought," Jessica said.

"Alarming is more like it." Chaka wiggled the broken jaw, then ran his hands over the misshapen, not quite symmetrical skull. "The ability of grendels to organize . . . at all . . . implies a level of intelligence or social organization which we haven't experienced before. That's going to take a lot of thought."

Justin squeezed Katya's hand. She had clung to him almost continuously for the past hour. "What do you suggest?"

"Let the snow cool the head a bit more, then get it back to Shangri-la and freeze it. Then back to Camelot on the next transport. I want my father's opinion of the brain."

Aaron nodded. "The kind of thing that they'll love. A puzzle." He ran a hand over his long face. "I've had enough of this place," he said grimly. "Let's get the hell out of here."

✳

Old Grendel had seen them taking a snow grendel apart, treating each part in some different way. They had eaten none of it. Uneasy, she had moved downhill.

The snow grendels had frightened the weirds, and they were far too likely to investigate what they feared. Old Grendel didn't consider it safe to spy on them. She stopped and buried herself above the corpse of the snow grendel she had killed. Watching that should be safe.

The daughters of God rose into the air and flew east.

The puzzle beasts moved west in a great mass, with weirds all around them.

The weirds were going . . . were gone. They hadn't found the last snow grendel. Old Grendel circled wide, looking for traps and spies. There were several of the little boxes the weirds sometimes posted where the view would serve a spy, and Old Grendel would not pass in front of those.

Presently she settled in to feed.

The weirds didn't know everything. Old Grendel was oddly reassured.

※

The herd was moving again, and they were making good time. Justin could see an edge to the plateau. Beyond, never yet seen by the naked eye, was a savannah covering a third of the continent. They were as far as any human had been from Camelot without actually achieving orbit.

After the skeeters had buzzed in to take away grendels and human casualties, Katya swore that she was steady enough to drive a trike. Twice now she'd spun up next to Justin to blow him kisses. A bandage covered half her face, with a blue slash and stitches underneath, twisting her laugh into something wild.

She can hardly wait for nightfall, he mused. *All of that* my hero *stuff. Should be . . . interesting.*

He wondered, then, if she'd have nightmares. After what she'd been through, another woman might have been catatonic. But he'd be there to hold her.

Skeeter scouts found the route of descent from the plateau. It was checked first by horseback, and then by chamel. The herd descended a thousand feet to the grasslands. It was flat down there, a vast tabletop that seemed to run forever, brownish green growing gradually greener with the descent. A wide brown river meandered in S curves. Here and there were patches of trees.

The descent took five hours. There was still enough day left to make a few kilometers before camp.

The grass was almost waist high, blue-green, and rich. The trikes plowed furrows in it as they jetted around.

Justin's mare chewed happily at the grass. Analysis had showed it would be digestible; they wouldn't need to bring much animal food in by skeeter. Justin leaned down and plucked a strand, took a tiny bite, and tucked it back between his rear molar and his gum. It chewed sweet-sour, not bad at all.

In the future, this would be cattle country. Trikes zipped about, stopping here and there to make recordings and snip samples for Cassandra to muse over later.

The computer whispered in his ear. "I see an odd flower. Turn to the left again, please."

He did, and couldn't see what Cassandra was talking about. But, "*There* we are. Would you get one of *those,* please?"

The herd was behind him, and if the computer wanted something, he was going to have to get it now, before hooves and teeth destroyed it.

The flower was in the middle of a patch of blue grass, and there was a buglike thing crawling around it.

"What is it, Cassandra?"

"Closer . . ."

He got closer, and suddenly saw something of real interest.

The beetle was tearing at a fibrous bulb on the plant. The bulb, on the other hand, seemed to be made of an interwoven web of fibers . . . and some of the plant's fleshy leaves was composed almost exclusively of those fibers, but pointed skyward.

A tiny lizardlike thing, not much larger than the tearing insect, climbed the stalk and attacked the leaf. Almost immediately, the leaf began to change color, from fleshy red to blue, oozing a blue exudate.

The lizardlike thing tried to escape, but the exudate had it caught. The fibers stirred. They wound about the lizard, catching it tight. The lizard's struggles slowly bowed the plant, and the leaf bent and turned upside down.

Fascinated by the process, which had taken no more than five minutes, Justin took another look at the beetle, still working hard at the other leaf. It was in there now, and it was . . . eating something.

"Wow," he said. "Cassandra, what do you see?"

"A microecology that needs study," she said calmly.

"I see a scavenger hijacking a flesh-eating plant," Justin said for the record. "Pretty sneaky, I'd say."

"Sample, please."

Justin shook the plant, and the little bug suddenly noticed him. It turned—and spread disproportionately large jaws. It couldn't have been larger than his thumb, but the wings trebled its size. It shot off toward the horizon so fast it nearly disappeared.

Faster than hell. So fast that . . .

"Cassandra." He didn't like the stress in his voice. "Was that bug on *speed?*"

"It is possible," the computer said. It sounded like an admission.

"I believe we have found another *speed*-using species. Correlations? Conclusions?"

"Observed data indicate this is a scavenger. No other conclusions valid with existing data."

That made him feel a *little* more comfortable, but not much. He summoned a trike to take the specimens.

"Skeeter reports a large animal in your vicinity, south-southwest of you, Katya."

He and Katya putted along in the two-seater trike. The loss of Stu weighed on all of them, but especially Katya. She had clocked over a thousand hours with him in that skeeter. It had to hurt.

Her night had been filled with bad dreams. This morning she didn't remember. She was brisk and perky, as if she'd slept better than Justin.

They had buried Stu where he fell. They all wanted some kind of ceremony, but Aaron didn't agree. "We will remember him at Shangri-la," he said. Stu was a Bottle Baby, never adopted. No relatives among the First. Aaron and the others were the only family Stu had, and they let Aaron speak for them. . . .

Now they were taking back the trophy, their only intact grendel head. *A poor trade.*

He found his hand creeping to cover hers. She widened her fingers to accept his. The small motion seemed somehow more intimate than the times she had welcomed him into her body. Her eyes, golden with flecks of green, sparkled at him. The bandage was still in place.

"Let's take a look," she said.

Justin said, "Cassandra, give us a local scan for grendels."

All of Cassandra's considerable eyes and ears were suddenly concentrated on the area. A relief map glowed on the hologram stage, blank at first, filling in rapidly.

There were no grendel-bearing water sources short of the river thirty-five klicks away.

They would avoid the river. The herd would water tomorrow. Their skeeters would have plenty of time to clear out the water hole before the herd arrived. Now, where was Cassandra's "large animal"?

Justin popped the clutch and headed out toward the site, south-southwest. The grass grew higher than his head. He tried to keep one eye ahead and one for the little holostage where Cassandra had given them a skeeter's-eye hologram.

It showed a cleanly geometric trapezoid, pale brown on a baize background. An Avalon crab, Justin thought, seen from nearly overhead. Where were the legs? They must be underneath. That looked like tufts of hair along the edges. And he ought to be getting close.

He could see pterodons circling overhead . . . and nothing ahead. He was seeing through a curtain of grass. Then he wasn't, because they'd driven out of the grass into a neatly cut lawn. He grinned, speeding up, enjoying the view. High grass to left and right. Still he saw nothing of a mystery creature, until Katya spoke.

"We're looking at the aft end. Justin, we've found the Scribe!"

Scribe? Perspective came. It was almost half the horizon, a geographical feature moving slowly away from them. It was camouflaged, but that wasn't it. He hadn't seen it because it was too big!

Katya was laughing at him. He'd gasped like a dying man. Justin said, "Cassandra, sanity check. Could this be the Scribe? The thing that draws paths we see from orbit?"

"It leaves a path identical to the Scribe tracks," the computer said. "Absent conflicting data this is a valid conclusion."

They moved closer. No sign of eyes, this side of the beast. Not much detail at all, just the edge of a tremendous shell, the color of bare earth, moving slowly away.

It didn't waddle. It cruised. In its wake the grass stood a few inches high, dotted with truncated haystacks two feet tall. Droppings?

Something like a tremendous flattened crab slid up to one of the heaps, moving no faster than the Scribe itself, and over it without a pause. A juvenile?

Talking to himself, talking for Cassandra's records, Justin drove the trike into the grass again. Three pterodons were circling high above him. He rode half-blind through the prairie grass, swinging wide around the now invisible beast. "Don't want to startle it," he told Katya, and was suddenly whooping.

A small fist whacked him between the shoulders. "What?"

He could hardly speak for laughter. "Pictured it rearing up. Pawing the air. Don't mind me."

He must be far ahead of it now. There was a stand of horsemane trees, uphill. He pulled the trike into their shade, turned off the engine, and waited. The pterodons were still with him. A fourth came to join them. One peeled off and flew toward the Scribe.

A thing that size . . . it wouldn't try to plow *trees* under, would it?

They were on a slight rise, three kilometers ahead of the chamel herd. Down below them, now more than two hundred meters away, was the largest creature that Justin had ever seen in his life. A crab . . . clearly derived from a crab shell, like the Avalon crabs, like the fixed-wing birds. But you could build a city on its back! Or a village anyway . . .

In fact, a pterodon was landing on its back to join more than two dozen others. Five merged circles, a communal nest, sprawled along the front of the shell.

A deep blue line ran across the front of the Scribe at the level of the grass. It seemed to ripple. Lips, or just a lower lip . . . maybe.

Otherwise nothing about the beast was in motion. It slid along like a raft on a wide river. Any motion must be taking place beneath the shell. Others of its kind, Avalon crabs and bugs and birds, made do with four motive limbs and endless ingenuity in the shapes of their shells.

Katya rose from her seat, lifted a pair of war specs, and gave a low whistle. She nudged him, and passed them over.

The beast was even more impressive when seen through the glasses. As large as—"Cassandra, is this the largest animal we know of?"

"Negative. The blue whale is larger. This is comparable in size to the largest of the herbivorous dinosaurs."

"Thank you." The edge of the shell dipped to become skids or skis. A half-dozen snouters grazed placidly along one flank. The beast was as large as half the main colony, and flat. It must have nearly the mass of a blue whale, but it was flatter, and wider than it was long.

There: eyes. Justin had thought they'd be higher. They were bedded in the long blue lips, too low to give the Scribe a decent view. He zoomed on one eye, and it was looking back, examining Justin and Katya, utterly unconcerned.

It wasn't until Justin focused the lenses more carefully that he saw what Katya was excited about.

There were grendels hanging from the shell. Two . . . no, three distorted grendel-shapes hung from the front and side of the shell, like hanks of hair. Mummies, not quite skeletons, but long dead, he judged.

Katya was saying, "Looks slow. Let's take a closer look."

The Scribe continued on its placid way as they approached. Five pterodons rose to circle above them. Snouters scurried away around the curve of the stupendous beast. They didn't seem terribly worried. The little Scribe, if that was what it was, hadn't been afraid either. But those dried corpses were grendels!

"Cassandra," Justin said, "backtrack."

The trike's little holostage sprouted a relief map of the locality. Cassandra recreated the beast's path as it meandered among similar paths in the grasslands. There were other curves and loops of lighter grass on the flat prairie background, and they crossed only rarely.

"How close does it get to running water?" he asked, but he saw the answer as he spoke: the path dipped to touch the river, and lingered there.

Cassandra said, "Quite close, and frequently. The path often parallels waterways."

"Does it enter known grendel territory?"

"Affirmative."

"Thank you," Justin said. "Hallelujah."

"There are things that aren't afraid of grendels," Katya said.

"Obviously. Not this creature, not its young. Not the pterodons nesting on its back."

"And the snouters?"

"Don't know. Maybe they stay on the veldt when Momma Scribe drinks."

Justin stood up on the seat of the trike to watch the creature. It drifted like an island, placid and unconcerned, as if it had never been threatened in its life. Indeed, it was difficult to imagine what could harm such a beast.

He raised the binoculars and focused on one of the mummified grendels.

The four mummies looked about the same state, the same age. That might have been a coordinated attack, for all the good it had done them. Each was hanging by its tail.

"Its defenses seem to be passive," he said. "Its sheer size, and something about the shell that traps grendels."

Katya asked, "Some sort of mucilage?"

"More like Velcro. Maybe. I want to see." He levered himself off the trike and walked through the high grass toward the Scribe. He pulled his microphone aside and told Katya, "You could put a castle on this thing. Come, I will make you Queen of the Scribeveldt."

The shell was all pentagonal plates, like shields a couple of feet across. Shields, and white tails hanging between the edges, here and there. *Bones?*

Cadmann had spoken of Roman army shields: the warriors held them in a closed array, each warrior's shield guarding the man next to him, in the days of swords and spears. Roman shields would trap enemy spears . . . like Velcro, he'd been right about that.

Katya said, "Not a castle. Tents. A pavilion, a summer palace. The serfs will have to wear special shoes."

"Yeah, wouldn't want to hurt the shell."

He was vaguely aware of a skeeter's buzz, far-off and insignificant, and almost didn't register it until he heard the voice in his earphone. *"What in the hell are you doing?"* Jessica asked.

"I'm getting closer," he said. "This thing could care less about me."

"You don't know that." Her voice was irritated.

"It's good to know somebody cares," he said.

✳

Jessica brought the skeeter closer and watched Justin and Katya approach the mountainous Scribe. The lawn behind it stretched to the horizon. It was easy to imagine such an herbivore trolling the entire continent, perhaps looking for a mate, collecting a herd of animals who hid beneath its shell for safety.

It was impossible to imagine a carnivore of equivalent size. Even blue whales, while technically carnivores, were passive filtration feeders. The malevolent Moby Dick had been their little brother. So Justin was probably safe. Probably.

Still.

She was irritated. She wanted to be mad at him. He had sided with Cadmann against them, against Aaron, and was a traitor of sorts, dammit. And he wasn't really her brother, for all the talk about two mothers and a dad. Justin's father was Terry Faulkner, he wasn't related to Cadmann at all, and yet he'd sided with the colonel against the Second. She wanted to stay pissed at him, but hated the way her chest hammered in response to the visual input.

Dammit, dammit, dammit. Only Justin and . . . and Aaron. Only the two of them could drive her this crazy.

He was twenty feet from the creature now. Its eye, a spheroid four feet across with a black iris, its tiny-seeming eye was on Justin and it just didn't care. To Jessica he looked so small. She could see his point. He was nothing in comparison to a beast such as this. Why should it pay him any mind whatsoever? And yet . . . and yet . . . *Avalon Surprise.*

The pig things snorted and ambled away. They were rooting around in the grass, moving when they had to stay ahead of the Scribe's long blue lip.

She brought the skeeter in for a closer look, and the snouter looked up, more alarmed by the whirring, flying thing in the sky than it ever was by Justin's presence.

"What are you doing *now?*" she demanded.

"Getting close-ups for the record. Jess, Chaka is going to absolutely love this! I'm looking at the bones of a grendel's tail, with a couple of vertebrae still attached. The rest of it could have fallen off years ago. The spikes on the tail are caught between the edges of the plates of the shell. It catches their tail spikes and they can writhe themselves into a coma for all the good it does them. These bones, they're cracked—"

"Cassie!" Jessica howled. "Where are your safety overrides?"

"Working," Cassandra said, and went silent.

It came to Jessica that checking *all* of Cassandra's protective measures might be the work of months, or lifetimes. "Cancel that last question. You hear me, Cassie?"

"Canceled. Justin is safe by my current parameters," Cassandra said. "I have backtracked this creature over the past year. It is not an aggressor. Grendels do not survive in its domain. I find no other local predators thus far."

Current parameters. "When were your current safety parameters updated?"

"Eighty-seven days ago."

Three months ago. Edgar had been fiddling with Cassandra, likely at Aaron's instigation, giving the Second more freedom to explore.

"Might as well join the madness," she said, and brought the skeeter down a hundred meters away from the moving mountain. The Scribe didn't look able to move quickly, but she didn't want it accidentally changing course and crushing her skeeter.

She was glad to see Katya up and around and looking so damned chipper. She didn't completely agree with Justin's choice of women, but what the hell, she didn't really have anything to say about it, did she?

The wind came cleanly through her lungs as she jogged toward them through armpit-high grass. The rapidity of her approach seemed to attract Momma Mountain's attention, and it turned its eye sluggishly toward her. Taking her time. It was impossible to imagine something like this having any potential for speed.

Justin was only ten feet away from it, playing his camera over four sets of trapped bones. One was no more than several joints of a grendel's tailbones. The others were distorted mummies.

It seemed clear what had happened. Momma Mountain had approached the river to drink. Each grendel in turn, or all together, had made a suicidal charge and gotten stuck. Each had thrashed . . . that one seemed to have actually torn some of the plates loose, but it had done it no good. It hung limply, its bones cracked, as if it had shattered itself in those final convulsions. As if it was too powerful to live.

The great herbivore's lip rippled steadily, mowing two-meter-high grass.

"We have to see what's going on under there," Justin said. "Drop a camera—"

"Harden it," Jessica said, as if they'd been talking all along. "It'll get chewed up."

"Yeah, hardened, with a light—"

"A *little* light. Camera set for low light."

"Right, it must be permanent night under there. We don't want to blind . . . a whole damn ecology under there, I bet. Cassandra, we need that camera. How long to make one up?"

"That will depend on priorities. The practical answer is that I can fabricate it in Camelot and put it aboard the next supply shuttle."

"Tell Edgar."

One of the pig things came close, evidently emboldened by the nearness of Momma Mountain. Jessica took a step toward it, and it scampered away.

Justin's expression was hard to read. He said, "Watch this."

Katya echoed that. "Watch this," she said, nearly glowing with pleasure as Justin crouched, extending his hand. It held a handful of balled grass. He was very still.

At first the snouter just stared at him, but then it came close, and then closer, and then she couldn't *believe* it, but the thing was eating out of his hand. It had actually begun to lick his hand when it suddenly shook its head, startled at its own boldness, and backed away.

Justin brushed his hands off on his pants.

"What was *that* all about?" she asked.

"Dunno."

"You taste like a meat eater," Katya said, and licked his ear. He laughed, and put his arm around her.

Jessica found herself feeling enormously irritated. "Well—is it safe to bring the herd through here?"

"Safe as houses."

"We've got a water hole up ahead. Half a day." She didn't know why she said the next thing, but she did. "It was mapped as a grendel hole last month. You want to be in on the kill?"

"Sure." He kissed Katya briefly. "Katya—you take the trike, I'm going for a little skeeter ride."

Katya looked at Jessica, smiled, then pulled Justin around for a real honey of a kiss, long and deep and sincere as hell.

Jessica decided that she *definitely* didn't like Katya.

The long, low sweep of the hills tilted and tilted again as the skeeter bobbed on the air currents, carrying Justin and Jessica to the east.

"Well," Jessica said finally, after about five minutes of silence. "It certainly seems as if the two of you are getting along well."

"Well, somebody's got to be a sex object around here. Jess, how about calling them 'Harvester' instead of 'Scribe'? Now we know what it is."

She grinned mildly, her hands tight on the control. A flicker of evil intent tickled the back of Justin's mind, and he decided to push onward. "I think maybe she's feeling her age. You know, some women feel that if they haven't had a child by twenty, they're missing out somehow. Ridiculous, of course."

She glanced at him as if to say: *Do you think it's going to be that easy, bud?*

"Personally, I think that a woman's got until at least twenty-five. What about you and Aaron?"

She snorted. "Oh, you know better than that—"

"Well, you wouldn't even have to carry the child yourself. You could donate an egg, and he could donate a sperm—I assume it would only take one, I mean, as staggeringly virile as Aaron is. . . ."

"Oh, shut up."

"But *Geographic* has everything that you'd need. . . ."

They were passing a stand of trees, and coming up a river that ran into a lake. It was a sparkling ribbon of blue beneath them, girded around with trees. She hovered, and Cassandra produced maps to show where grendel-sized heat sources had been spotted during earlier flybys, but they only confirmed what her father's training and Jessica's imagination were painting.

Open water equals death.

Jessica had grown quiet. The skeeter's steady hum was the only sound. They were alone up there, hovering above the grendels.

"Cassandra," she said quietly. "Shut down."

The privacy circuit, inviolate in the camp, went into effect. No one could hear them, no one could eavesdrop on them. The circuit was dead.

Jessica put the skeeter on autopilot. They were alone in the universe. She turned toward him. "We really haven't talked much since . . . that night, Justin," she said.

"Been busy. Everything happened so fast."

"But we didn't talk about how we felt. We always used to talk about that. I miss those talks."

He tried to smile, but it flickered out. "You don't need my approval. Never did."

"No. But I need you. Dad won't talk to me. Even when we tested the shelters, he barely spoke to me."

"Jess, you betrayed him twice in his own home! When Trish yelled for Dad's head, you were sitting next to Trish, not Dad. You won't be back until somebody's funeral!"

Her cheeks flamed. She wouldn't look at him.

"So you can't go home again. The question is, can we get him to talk to you? Over a comm card, or in the meeting hall? And that's a *maybe*. He was *suffering* after Toshiro—after he killed Toshiro."

"We all were."

"Was Aaron? I didn't see it."

"How could you say that?" Her cheeks reddened. She had to remember that this flight, this conversation, was *her* idea. "Toshiro was one of Aaron's closest friends."

He said carefully, "Sometimes I think that Aaron doesn't have any friends."

"How could you say that? You've always been his friend."

"Have I?" he asked, softly. "Look at what happened. Dad is stalemated. The First don't give us orders anymore. We can have anything we want as long as we carry those damn blankets everywhere. All because Dad shot Toshiro."

"You have a point?"

"I've spent too many nights thinking about this," Justin said. He hadn't told anyone this, not even Katya, and it suddenly felt like he'd been carrying a live grenade in his chest. "There wasn't any way Aaron could lose! The plan was to take *Robor* to the mainland. If nobody comes after us, we win. But suppose someone comes. Suppose Dad and Carlos die at sea because Aaron's left orders not to do any rescue work, or suppose Carlos drops dead because Toshiro fires a lightning bolt through him. It's hardball then, with Aaron in charge of a war. If Dad or Carlos kill someone, Aaron gets the moral high ground. Even if Dad forces *Robor* back to Camelot, Aaron gets what he wants. It's a *cause*, then, and the First would have to start talking again, and Aaron is one fine debater."

"How could you say that? How can you *think* it?" she whispered again, astounded.

"All right. Answer me a question: Would you have a bottle baby? Would you take your egg and someone else's sperm, and raise it in one of the incubators?"

"Of course. . . ."

"Then why haven't you?"

"I have had eggs removed," she said, suddenly bitter. "In the case of my death, my percentage of the wealth will go to raising my child. I have listed possible donors—"

She looked away from him suddenly, and her cheeks flushed again. Suddenly, wildly, Justin wondered if his was one of the names on the list. "But as long as I'm alive, that's something I would like to try on my own. Someday. Not now."

"Not now," he echoed.

"No." She combed her hair with her fingers. "Justin, what this is all about is the chance to declare a truce. What do you say?"

He thought about it. There were so many things that he wanted to talk about. But all of them faded into insignificance when compared with what really mattered—his relationship with Jessica. Here, with the two of them, it seemed more important still.

"Truce," he said. And held out his hand. Hers was firm, and dry, and warm.

24

MISTRESS

> What we call a mind is nothing but a heap or col-
> lection of different perceptions, united together
> by certain relations and suppos'd, tho' falsely, to
> be endow'd with a perfect simplicity and identity.
> —DAVID HUME

The builders lived in groups of six to eight, rarely more than ten. The lake was
their world, and the lake was of their own making. They were fast and black and
muscular. They could strip a tree in minutes to create new timber for their constructions.

They were still slow in comparison with the other, the queen who lived downstream from them.

Sometimes the queen came for the prey in the lake. Sometimes for the swimmers themselves, the young builders.

Once, many Turnings before, one of their number had challenged the queen
for supremacy.

The queen had become a whirlwind of death. So had the builder and two of
her siblings. The fight was vicious. It tore a hole in the dam itself, so that water
and precious food slopped over into the river below. But when the fight was
over, the three were dead.

The queen was barely wounded. The survivors tasted her anger in the water,
the *speed*, the urge to kill them all. Most of them were on shore now, braving
other danger so that the queen would not taste them in the water; but she could
see them. Somehow she withheld the death that was hers to give.

No one had challenged her since.

Now she was back.

She swam upstream as she had before, crawling over the dam, never straying
onto land. They smelled her in the water. The water carried a scratching sound,
not loud, but audible everywhere in the lake, and every builder's nose and eyes
broke surface. They saw the great wedge-shaped head emerge with something
alive in her mouth.

The queen had come.

What the queen was doing was part of a pattern warped out of true. The light
was turning weird. Something tremendous had been floating in the sky for days,
never responding to challenge, nor interacting at all. The wrongness in the

world encroached on the lake itself. They could taste changes in the water and air, changes that rang down in their bones.

The queen knew it too. She had made four trips in as many turnings of the sun, and each time she had carried a similar burden.

Not for an instant did they forget the queen's blinding speed. She moved slowly, carefully, and the builders watched with respect.

Between the queen's teeth she held a live swimmer. Not one of the queen's own children—but another builder child, from another stream and another lake.

She had brought three of these, tired and feeble but alive. One had died from the distance the queen had carried it between water holes, and damage from the great, serrated teeth.

The queen set the newcomer in the water. It floated for a moment, then began to twitch its tail, then to move.

And the builders slowly, carefully approached it. It began to swim. They nudged it along. The other young butted it, but the builders were a friendly clan. Even during the best of times there would have been no challenge.

Change was coming. They must keep to the water, for the Death Wind seemed to be everywhere these days. The builders were distracted; they would not challenge the queen's guest.

The queen slipped into the water, gliding like death. She vanished beneath its surface, and came up with one of the lens-crabs that lived in the builder-made pond, a prey-creature. It flipped and flashed just once.

The queen moved like the owner of all creation, smoothly through the water, along the length and breadth of the lake. The very Lady of the Lake.

✳

"Did you see that?" Justin said, astonished.

"Would have been hard to miss. Cassandra?"

"I have recorded all of it."

"What do you make of it?"

"Please narrow your question."

"I seem to be looking at some kind of grendel social interaction," Justin said. "I know that's ridiculous, but there it is."

Jessica nodded. "The grendel brought those others—those huge hands! They must be specialized to the task of building dams—"

"Beaver grendels—"

"Brought them a sacrifice. I thought that it was food of some kind. Apparently it wasn't. The beavers gathered around and helped to guide the baby—that's almost certainly what it was—around in the pond until it could swim by itself."

"Grendels cooperating in a snowstorm. Grendels carrying the young of other grendels in their mouths. What in the hell were our parents dealing with on Camelot?"

Jessica's right eyebrow went up. "Retarded grendels?"

"Right. So what do we do? We can destroy this entire ecology—"

"Not on your life."

Jessica took them up another two hundred feet. "Cassandra. Route a message to Shangri-la and Camelot. I want an alternate path. This is the first such ecology we've found, and I want to preserve it."

"Checking now," Cassandra said.

Jessica raised her right eyebrow again. "Do you have any objections to that?"

"No, I'm with you," Justin said.

"I was wondering if you thought that it was a little flaky. You know, grendel cult and all of that?"

Justin was looking down out of the side of the skeeter, at the shimmering water hole far beneath them. Within it, there was a world that none of them had ever known.

"No. Whatever is going on there, it would be an absolute sin to destroy it."

Jessica twinkled, and squeezed his hand. For the first time in months, he felt that they were operating on the same frequency. She nodded her head happily. "Thank you," she said. And then, impulsively, leaned over and kissed him on the cheek.

His cheek burned, and he wasn't completely certain that he understood why.

Cassandra said, "Your alternate path is approved. You will head west by fifteen degrees—"

The second water hole was smaller. They'd found a grendel carcass lying seven meters away from the water's edge. They'd left it untouched. Justin lay thirty meters farther out, flat on his stomach behind a bush, and examined the scene through war specs.

"What do you think?" he asked into his mike.

Jessica answered from her vantage point in the skeeter above. *"I think that the grendel who owns the water hole got into a fight for supremacy. It must have been something to see."*

"All right. Hit it."

She brought the skeeter in to five meters above the water and dropped a wad of cotton scented with *speed*. Alien *speed*, guaranteed to make a grendel crazy.

Justin watched. The skeeter throbbed. The water lapped at the edge of the pool.

And nothing else.

"Try it again," he whispered, and she did. Splash. And then nothing.

The sound of his own breathing grew almost unendurably loud. There was something wrong here.

He stood. Justin tucked his war specs away, and approached cautiously. "Keep scanning for infrared. No grendel sign?"

"None," she said *"We've scanned that water hole. There are samlon there, but no adult."*

"Then the old adult was killed. How long ago?"

He examined the corpse. It was torn and flattened, but he noted some fluttery motion around the edges. He backed up, then tore a branch from a nearby tree to use as a lever. He lifted the grendel's jaw. "Scavengers," he said. "Like the one I saw earlier. Bugs."

"*They're not bugs,*" Jessica said.

"I know, they're obviously related to crabs like half the life on this planet." One of the scavengers flew up as he exposed it. The motor wings buzzed violently. It circled his head, then settled again. "Jessica, this carcass is just seething with these things. Cassandra, are you recording?"

"Affirmative. This is a new life-form."

"I'll get a sample." Justin lowered the grendel to the ground and took out a collection box. The grendel's hollow eye sockets stared at him. A beetle emerged from the left socket and flew away to the south with a harsh burring sound.

✳

The chamels had been watered and grazed, and were settled down for the night. Tents had blossomed around the water hole, and a defensive perimeter was established.

Aaron was off at the other fire with some of the kaffeeklatsch, and Jessica felt glad of it. Her reconnection with Justin was still fragile, still needed time to cement—but there might not be time after all. Katya snuggled up to him. Jessica tried not to feel anything, but she couldn't help watching. The two seemed to have settled into a rhythm. There were subtle turnings when either of them moved, subtle responses of body language when either spoke. They were more than lovers. Quietly and without fanfare, Justin and Katya had become a couple.

The firelight danced across them, as Jessica sipped her hot cocoa. At the second fire, there was singing, and Aaron's strong voice rose above the sound of the guitar.

Justin looked up at Jessica as she left the fireside, and smiled. He was happy. They were brother and sister again.

There was no reason for the odd sadness that she felt. Perhaps it was the loss of Stu. That had to be it.

"I'm going over to the singing," she said. "I don't think that I'll be missed too much."

Katya's head was against Justin, and she grinned up. "You and Aaron have a good evening, you hear?"

Jessica nodded.

Only thirty feet of space separated the two fires, and in crossing she passed the chamel pen. One of them nuzzled up against the wire that confined them. The wire carried a light charge. If pressure was applied, the charge grew stronger. The fence was portable, and bundled to swing beneath a skeeter.

The chamel nuzzled at her. She stopped to stroke its long, delicate neck.

She looked back at her unbrother. Justin and Katya. A good couple. Katya was quieter. She would bond more quickly. The two of them would probably start making fat babies. That would be a good thing. Justin needed to be a parent. He wasn't like her, not at all.

She looked over to where Aaron was strumming his guitar, head tilted back in song. He was golden, Apollonian. Her head swam at the thought of him. He was so strong. So . . . perfect. He made her ache. Just listening to his laugh, watching the way his head rolled back when he sang, when he tossed his hair . . . she wanted him inside her, she wanted to feel the enormous power of his body, to feel the fire that drove him igniting her.

But when she looked at Justin and Katya, she saw a gentle thing, a softness. Not at all like the driving hunger that she felt from Aaron. Jessica went and sat next to Aaron. After a while, she laughed, and sang along.

They made love, and as usual, it was perfect. Perfect. Her body had exploded more times than she could count. As usual. The perfection of their union was . . . almost predictable. As if he had direct access to her nervous system.

If anything was missing, it was the experience of exploration. With Toshiro there had been a constant *unfolding* that was lacking with Aaron.

"What are you thinking?" Aaron whispered.

Jessica felt the hard flat plates of his stomach muscles against her back. His left arm circled her waist. His right thumb made slow lazy circles around her right nipple. Waves of pleasure washed through her. "Don't," she said.

"Don't what?"

"Don't . . . that."

The pressure stopped. "Okay." He paused. She felt his heart beat against her back, strong and slow. "What are you thinking?"

"That I feel more connected to the dream than I do to you, Aaron."

"Is that so bad? I read somewhere that love isn't two people looking at each other. It's two people looking in the same direction."

She had to smile. "I read that too. But sometimes, sometimes we have to look at each other, too."

He rolled her over, and gazed directly into her eyes. "You don't think that I look at you?"

"Maybe," she said. "I've gone along with everything that you wanted. And I've given you everything that I have to give. *I betrayed my father for you.*" Oh, God, it was true. It wasn't true until she said it. "I need to know how you feel. About us."

He took her hand, and placed it between his legs. Immediately, he began to stiffen.

She gave him a light squeeze. "Not that. Not . . . just that. I know we turn each other on. That's easy for us."

"Love, then?"

"I don't know."

She snuggled her head into the crook of his shoulder, saying to herself, as loudly as she dared, *Yes, love. Call it love. Please, call it love.*

He pulled up the blanket, tucking it under her chin, and sat up effortlessly.

She could almost hear the gears grinding within his mind. His eyes stared out at the mountains on the horizon, and the stars above them, and she imagined that he could count them all.

"I've given you more than I've given anyone, Jessica."

"I know," she said. "Am I asking for too much?"

"No," he said quietly. "But you might be asking the wrong person." There was something that she had never heard in his voice before. A moment of self-doubt?

"There's something I've always wanted to ask," she said. "Was it hard for you? As a child. Not having any one family?"

Suddenly his lips curled in a merry smile, and she knew, *knew*, that his next response would be prefabricated, that the moment of truth had evaporated. "It was rough sometimes, but the roughest part was not knowing which family to stay with on a particular night. Every door was open," he said, and laughed. "They were all my family." And he laughed again.

The doors were open, to come in or to go out. But anyplace you can walk away from isn't home. You didn't have a home. Flit from one family to another, never deal with anything you didn't want to deal with. "Weren't you afraid that someday there wouldn't be a door open?"

"No. Why? I didn't do anything wrong, I was always who they wanted me to be." He turned and kissed her, more softly than she could ever remember. His perfect hair glowed in the moonlight, his mouth gentle upon hers. "This is our land, Jessica," he said. "We fought for it, and we are the ones to tame it."

"I know," she whispered.

"Our children will own this land."

His hands were soft on her arms, but she didn't try to squirm away from him. Somehow, she knew that it would be useless. His eyes trapped hers, and something within them terrified her.

"Our children. Yours and mine."

He'd said it. Suddenly, thoughts, feelings, sensations that she had never allowed herself to feel began to blossom within her, and she could feel it, feel where a child of Aaron's might grow within her, a void that opened like an awakening eye. *Yes.*

"Yes," she said. "I would love to carry your child."

"No!" he said fiercely. "You don't understand. The children of our bodies, yes, but we can have *perfect* children. Perfect. They can have everything, every advantage. We can control their nutrients, their prenatal education . . . everything."

His whisper was harsh, and his hands grew stronger upon her arms. "We can have a dozen, a hundred children at a time, and seed this entire continent with them."

Her hand stroked his cheek. From the dark of her hindbrain she felt the hope rising. "But we don't have to do that. I'd be happy—"

"No!" And her hand froze where it was. "My children will be perfect." He blinked, and then smiled, almost shyly. "At least, as perfect as we can make them."

Permission. She didn't have to be pregnant. Swollen, clumsy, imprisoned. . . . But a tiny part of her had awakened, and was watching him, sensing something wrong.

He babbled on. "They will be our children. And they will own this land. You ask me if I love you. Can I come any closer than that? Do those words mean anything to you? Anything at all?" His weight was on her, and Jessica tried to fight. *No.* She wasn't ready emotionally. There was too much . . .

Truth?

In the air between them. She needed a moment to prepare herself, to slip back into the comfortable shell of sensuality she understood so well, nurtured by Sir John Woodruff and the Perfumed Garden, and the Quodoshka and the manuals of Taoist sexuality, and the erotic works of a world left far behind. But this moment wasn't one of the complex, artistically perfect couplings she had known with Aaron Tragon. This was something too damned similar to rape. She could call out, and it would stop—but so would any link between them. His was a need so deep that it burned. The hands on her, the mouth upon her, the thighs, hot and hard, that forced her legs open were somehow vulnerably, endearingly clumsy.

This wasn't the man she knew and loved. This was almost a boy, a boy who needed something that she couldn't quite bring herself to give.

And so he took it.

And took it.

And she pushed at him, and tore at him, and came to the edge, but didn't quite call out for help. And Aaron held her more tightly than he ever had, more insistently, his body one driving urgency.

He arched, and flushed, his face suffused with a kind of ecstatic, incandescent madness, his eyes, looking off to the horizon as he spasmed, seeing . . . what? What world of spires and mazes? What cities and glorious constructions of the far future? What world-girdling belt of roads and skyways that he might never live to see, but which children unborn might inherit?

Or did he see something else? His god, the grendel, perched upon a kill, perhaps his own torn corpse? And was this moment, and all of the other moments that they had had together, nothing but a means of staving that moment off, of giving it some kind of meaning?

Did Aaron and her father share the same nightmare?

And was that why she loved them both?

Aaron collapsed atop her. His breath was hot and sweet, his hands curled up around her shoulders, his face tucked into her breast, his breath hot against her. She stroked his head and whispered to him, and knew that something had changed between them. She wasn't certain what, or what it would cost them. She knew only that there *would* be a cost, as certainly as Tau Ceti rose and set upon both Man and Grendel.

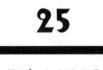

25

ASIA MINOR

O mistress mine, where are you roaming?
O, stay and hear, your true love's coming,
That can sing both high and low.
Trip no further pretty sweeting,
Journeys end in lovers meeting,
Every wise man's son doth know.

What is love? 'tis not hereafter;
Present mirth hath present laughter.
What's to come is still unsure:
In delay there lies no plenty;
Then come kiss me, sweet and twenty,
Youth's a stuff will not endure.

—William Shakespeare, *Twelfth-Night*

They were calling the Scribebeast "Asia."

"It's not *that* big," Jessica giggled, but Ruth's name stuck anyway.

Aaron had made time and commandeered the *NickNack*, and all to come see Asia. He'd brought Ruth Moskowitz and both of their chamels. Justin wondered what Jessica thought of that. He hadn't seen her in two days.

Ruth and Aaron rode Zwieback and Silver along the Scribe's long blue lip. One great eye was tracking them.

"Not there," Justin said into the comm card. "Aaron, see me? I'm on the rise east of you, with four tall horsemane trees behind me. Asia will go around the trees. You'll get a great view of the life-forms on her back. . . ."

Why bother? They were halting now, both chamels, much too close to one of the great eyes. He hadn't really expected Aaron to take suggestions.

Anyway, were they really in danger? Asia flowed like a continent across the savannah. Or like a crippled old woman; you *could* observe motion. Justin sighed and raised his war specs. He and Ruth would get here eventually. It was nearly lunchtime, and their lunch was on its way, packed in the belly of a skeeter.

Even the chamels didn't seem nervous. One great eye gazed upon them, and that would have had Justin twitchy. Ruth gaped in delight and awe.

That didn't surprise Justin. But Aaron was doing that too: mouth open, face empty. Had any human being ever seen him like this? He suddenly turned Zwieback and trotted toward the hill. Ruth followed, belatedly.

Over the next hour most of the survey team gathered on the hill, skeeter, trikes, and all, to watch the passing of Asia.

The trees were festooned with wet blue blankets.

The Earth Born insisted that Cadzie-blue blankets must go everywhere humans went on the continent. It was nearly their only demand, and not so onerous as all that; but the blankets didn't arrive clean. Mothers borrowed them first. Babies lived in them for a few days. The Earth Born never had to wash their baby blankets; they just sent them to the mainland.

And the survey team had finally had it with the smell. They'd been washing blankets in what had been a grendel lake and was now a samlon reservoir. Clean blankets would dry while Asia passed.

Pterodons were wheeling above the Scribe; more held station above the watching humans. Ruth presently said, "Justin? The birds?"

"I pointed them out to Little Chaka. Then I had to listen to him lecture."

"They're eyes for the Scribe!"

"That's what Chaka thinks. The Harvester can't see *through* grass, but she can look up and see where the pterodons are. Early-warning system. If something came right *at* an eye she'd see it when it got close . . . what the hell would she do then, *dodge?* For that matter, what would a Scribe be afraid of?"

"A cliff?" Ruth glanced sideways at Aaron, but he maintained his silence. "She'd see a cliff before she went over. And the pterodons would show her where water was, wouldn't they? Where there's water, there's carrion. Where there are grendels, they'd fly higher."

"I don't think Asia gives an icy damn about grendels," Aaron said. "Ruth, a million years from now we *still* won't have found a bigger land beast."

"Breeding," Ruth said.

Justin frowned the question.

"How do Scribes find each other?"

"Maybe they're hermaphrodites."

Ruth shook her head. "Maybe, but—"

"Or maybe baby Scribe beasts are the males," Aaron said. "That's how grendels work it."

Jessica remembered what it had cost the First to learn that samlon were not only immature grendels, but were all males. They became females when they made the transformation from a fishlike swimmer that lived largely on pond scum to the adult amphibious omnivore.

"But think, the paths cross," Ruth said.

"Or used to cross," Justin said thoughtfully. "Cassandra, consider the Scribe beasts. Is it likely that the crossing patterns of their paths is random?"

"There is negligible probability that the crossings were caused by random walks," Cassandra said. "I record seven cases in which the paths altered to approach each other. This is from records of past decades. At present the probability that the paths will cross is under ten percent."

"They're avoiding each other now?"

"It would so appear."

"Son of a bitch," Justin said. "First they cross, now they don't. I betcha Ruth is right, the pterodons guide them, and now they're steering them *away* from each other."

"Why would that be?" Aaron demanded.

"Avalon Surprise!" Ruth shouted in glee. "Actually, I think it's got something to do with Edgar's variable star. The weather's changing, and the Scribes—"

Aaron wasn't listening. He was staring out at the Scribe beast.

Justin joined the group who were loading food on the tables. Cold snouter meat, turkey and turkey eggs, vegetables and heads of lettuce from Camelot. The mainland crops weren't in yet. A glass cauldron of water was beginning to boil. Katya and Little Chaka zipped open a bag that held water and three wriggling samlon, and tilted them into the pot. Chaka chopped rapidly with his wand of a chain saw at a stack of root vegetables, then threw them in in handfuls.

Aaron said, long and low, *"Wow!"*

The edge of Asia's shell was scraping the rocky outcropping at the foot of the hill. Aaron stood at the hill's crest, not eating. Justin, with a turkey leg in his hand, tried to guess what Aaron was seeing. He'd never before heard Aaron say *Wow*.

The rippling blue lip was nearly hidden. They caught glimpses. . . .

"Wow," Justin repeated softly. He turned and shouted, "Hey!" Heads turned. "The lips!" Justin shouted. "The lips are the only soft part of the beast! Everything else is armored. *Why don't the grendels tear into the lips?*"

Little Chaka left his place at the soup pot and came trotting to look. Justin cried, "Chaka, it's Cadzie blue!"

Aaron whooped and began running. Justin saw him snatch the chain saw from its place on a flat rock.

Chaka looked down, nodding. "Poison, likely enough. There are life-forms on Earth that signal like that, with some distinctive color. Snakes and insects and such. 'I'm poison, get away.' Sometimes it's a bluff. Yes, that would . . . that would do it. The baby's blanket."

Aaron slowed as he approached Zwieback. Zwieback didn't shy; Ruth had trained him well. He spoke to the beast, then swung up. Zwieback began to move, to run. As he did, he faded from view. Justin watched, shaking his head and grinning.

They all stood at the edge of the cliff. Ruth was horrified. Justin was trying to find admiration in himself for Aaron. Admiration was all around him, at any rate, for the flying man on the nearly invisible chamel. Aaron rode straight toward the leading edge of Asia, then turned sharply to ride along her endless prow. The great eye of Asia watched placidly.

Aaron reached out with the slender wand of the chain saw, and slashed, and leaned far forward and snatched. He rode away waving half a square meter of blue flag.

Chaka said to Justin, "Camelot has your photos, you know. Cassandra has the view through your war specs and Katya's. If that's Cadzie blue, it's a wonder Cassandra hasn't told us."

Justin shrugged. "Cassie's got ice on her mind too." The computer program had been damaged in the first grendel attack. Recovering most of its memory had been the task of years. Lost medical techniques were still killing people.

Asia was just beginning to react. Her eyes closed. Her prow dipped to the earth, closing her off to the world. Now she was all earth-colored shell, a shallow butte sparsely covered with nests.

Aaron pulled up whooping, just short of the dining table. The dead Scribeskin, taken with an edge of twenty-second-century sharpness, was only two or three millimeters thick. It was already beginning to wrinkle.

Aaron swung down, holding the swatch of blue high in one hand. Ruth was there. He swept her into his arms. And kissed her hard.

Ruth whispered in his ear.

Aaron froze. Then, "Wonderful!" he said cordially. "Your family will be so pleased!" He strode past her. Justin saw the shock on her face, and wondered for an instant, but he *had* to watch as Aaron let the slice of skin settle like a veil across a tree spread with Cadzie-blue blankets.

Justin turned away to hide the grin he couldn't stop.

Yes, it was Justin's idea. And if Aaron hadn't done something, Justin might have had the credit for solving Avalon's murder of Joe Sikes and Linda Weyland. But Aaron had stolen his thunder . . . and it had blown up in his hand.

Against the Cadzie-blue blanket, the thin piece of Scribeskin was conspicuously pale. The skin was the wrong color. Anyone could see it. Heads were shaking; Aaron was furious.

Ruth . . . Ruth handed Silver and Zwieback over to Katya, then spoke in low tones to Little Chaka. She pointed to Skeeter II, and then again toward distant Shangri-la. Chaka nodded. Ruth sat down next to him and stared at the ground.

✳

It was a gorgeous, brilliant morning at Shangri-la. Clouds raced across the sky in streamers. The breeze was stiff and warm; still air would have made it an oven. The light . . . well. Dawn light had been different when Ruth was a child. Less dazzling, less . . . active? And Sol was even *cooler* than Tau Ceti, they said. . . .

Less than two hours by Little Chaka's skeeter, and she was back at the base camp, back in a world where she didn't have to ache every time she looked at Aaron Tragon.

Horsemane trees stood huge and ancient along the eastern edge of the plateau that held their base camp. A ladder rose along the bare side of the biggest and oldest tree. Big Chaka held the ladder's foot. Little Chaka, at the top, reached around the bare side of the trunk and probed with a stick at the mane. A bit more than halfway up the tree, something hidden was nipping at his stick, short-ening it in three-centimeter bites.

The Chakas might not have noticed a pair of long-armed crabs in the tree's peak. Three now, each as big as a small dog, leaned out of the brilliant green foliage as they peered down at the intruders. Ruth fished for her comm card without taking her eyes off the crabs.

Then she relaxed, because Edgar Sikes was on the far side of the tree with his face wrapped in war specs, and both Chakas were looking up. Edgar must have warned them. He was twitchy about top crabs, wasn't he? These *might* be related to the Camelot variety—

Something fell slantwise from the sky. It smacked into one of the top crabs and knocked it free.

Trees hid the rest of the action, and Ruth mewed in frustration. Her hand was on the phone now, and she put it to her mouth and ear and—

"Cassandra! Did you get that?" Edgar's voice.

"I have views through Chaka Junior's war specs and yours, Edgar. Processing."

"Yah!" Edgar ran for the mess hall. Saw Ruth. Ran over, snatched her wrist, and continued running. Startled at first, Ruth let him pull her, then laughed and tried to pull ahead.

She was barely keeping up. And some masochistic part of her didn't want the exhilaration. She had *earned* her pain, dammit, and . . . oh, what the heck. It felt good to run. You couldn't mope when you were running.

They passed over the drawbridge, ran past the open gate of the electrified fence, guard dogs yipping their greeting. Past a happy maze of half-erected build-ings: bare wooden beams, naked iron struts, plastic shells, drop-clothed wire frames.

The mess hall was a rounded half-cylinder on the main square. It was con-structed of fabric on semicircular struts, sprayed with quick-setting foam. It was the first building erected, seven months before, and had served as both dormi-tory and cafeteria for weeks. Serving trays were an arc along the back. The big holostage was unfolded in its center, and Ruth made for that. Edgar was puffing, but heyyy, Edgar used to be a cripple!

Trish Chance, eating alone at the far end, stared at the intrusion. Edgar sang, "Trish!"

"Don't have time, Edgar. Got to catch the Veldtbound skeeter in about fifteen minutes. Hi, Ruth."

"Make time, this time, just this once," Edgar said. "Cassandra, you done?"

"Twenty seconds."

Trish had lost interest.

It was hard to believe the rumors: that Edgar and *Trish* were lovers. Trish didn't act like it, and she was *nothing* like him. Ruth said with some diffidence, "Trish, he's really got something."

Trish smiled one-sided, finished her breakfast cereal in a leisurely fashion, and came over just as Cassandra turned down the lights. Then they were look-ing through a blur-edged window at a stand of horsemane trees.

The recording wasn't particularly sharp; a war specs headset wasn't that good. Top crabs leaned from the thickly grown treetop, waved menacing claws at the oblivious man below.

"Slow motion, Cassie," Edgar said.

It all slowed like a dream. Little Chaka looked up—

Even in slow motion, the predator was still falling like a grendel on *speed*. Cassandra paused it in flight: a triangular airfoil with sharp horns jutting from the forward corners; eyes on stalks just inboard of the horns; oversized oar-shaped motor fins aft.

Then motion again. The eyestalks retracted; the marauder slewed sideways in the moment before it impacted one of the treetop crabs. One horn smashed directly into the shell, piercing it. The impact flung the top crab into space, threw it free of the horn.

The top crab hit the ground hard. The predator corrected its spin, pulled up, skimmed the dirt, wheeled around and was on the dying crab. It flipped the crab over, ripped away the ventral shell and began to feed.

"That was from your POV, Edgar. From Chaka—"

Big Chaka made his slow way into the mess hall with his son alongside. "Hello, Ruth. Trish. Edgar, you get that too?"

"Yessir. You show me yours, I'll show you mine."

"Cassandra, if you will oblige."

"Chaka Junior, your view was from underneath." Close view of a horsemane tree's bare trunk, a stick probing the green mane. Something small and mam-maloid was snapping at the stick with long mini-hyena jaws, glaring through Cassandra's magic window with murderous eyes. Suddenly the view swung straight up. A variety of Avalon crab was studying them, its arms waving rest-lessly, claws snapping.

Pause. "Observe the claws," Cassandra said. A cursor arrow indicated the top crab. "Here they're much longer than on our two Camelot varieties. Chaka, shall we designate this—"

"Sikes's Top Crab Number One," Big Chaka said firmly. Edgar looked around with an unbelieving grin. Ruth smiled to see it.

"As you wish."

Motion resumed. Something smashed into the crab, knocked it into space, clung for a moment, then separated . . . and it all froze. The cursor arrow moved to the predator, which from underneath was nearly featureless. "Here the claws are recessed, almost invisible, and the mouth likewise. The eyes were retracted. Now—" Motion: the predator was spinning out of control. Eyes emerged, then paddle-shaped fins adjusted: its spin stopped in an instant. Paddles played as the creature dropped. Canards emerged in front. It actually brushed the grass pulling up, swung back like a guided missile, and—braked.

Its claws were airfoils, canards. Retracted, they fit recesses that faired the crab shell into a smooth hull. Its mouth was startling: huge and square, not just a mouth but an air brake too. The thing hovered for an instant, with claws extended and mouth wide, then dropped onto the dying top crab. It was the claws that did the work of ripping the shell open and tearing the meat into gobbets.

The view shifted: Cassandra was running Edgar's view again. A reincarnated top crab chittered from a treetop. Something dived from the sky in slow motion. . . .

Trish Chance said, "Ruthie, when you *do* talk, you're worth hearing. Guys, that was fun, but I'm off to see the Scribe."

Ruth glowed. And didn't notice Trish's overdone wink, nor Edgar's nod.

"The Scribe. I've only seen it on the holostage," Edgar said. "Is it as awesome—?"

"More. They're calling it 'Asia.'"

But the enthusiasm had leaked out of her, and Edgar noticed. "Aaron's still out there?"

"Yeah. Did you hear? Aaron thought he'd solved the killings, Linda and Joe. He didn't, and he's *furious* . . ."

"He's there, and you're here. Anything happen?"

She paused awkwardly. Then: "I told him I was pregnant."

Edgar stared. Gently he asked, "How long?"

"I've only known for about two weeks. It was that long before I got up the nerve to ask Cassandra."

"What's he think?"

"He said, 'Your parents will be so pleased.' Then changed the subject."

"He'll never be Father of the Year, but he'll try to keep your dad happy. There were too many close votes on personnel," Edgar said. "Lord knows Zack would rather French-kiss a grendel than trust *me*. Camelot got hit with one of those weird flash-typhoons last week. Zack walked into the comm shack drenched. I said, 'It seems to be raining,' and he went for a second opinion."

"Is *that* why Aaron keeps me around? Some of the time? Nobody talks to me but you, Edgar. I know I don't own him, but when Jessica's around it's like I don't even exist."

He nodded. "No. You don't own him. But that's no reason for him to treat you like sleet, either. Ruth, I'll shut up any time I'm told to."

"Oh, no, Edgar."

"Okay. Do you really think you were needed to distract Carolyn McAndrews?"

She looked away. "No." And began moving away.

"Course not. Carolyn would have let Trish walk right up to her." Edgar followed. "So it follows that Aaron didn't have to seduce you just to get your help stealing *Robor.*"

She seemed astonished. "No!" Then suddenly grinned. "But he sent Trish to *you.*"

"Sent Trish Chance to distract me. Then I think he told her to stop. Trish doesn't take orders worth a damn, you know."

Ruth had reached the coffee vat. She drew two cups and tried to fill them, still without looking at Edgar. The vat was empty. "We're going to seed coffee in the hills around Point Ten," she said.

"Below where the snow grendels popped up?"

"Yeah."

"That's a kicky notion. Snow grendels were bad enough without coffee nerves. So, have you told your parents?"

"About what?"

"About the plans for a coffee crop," Edgar said gently.

Ruth looked up, smiling bravely. "About the baby, you mean. No. I haven't told them."

"How long since you last talked to them?"

"None of your business."

"Right." Edgar plucked the two cups out of her hand. "Come with me."

He walked away without looking back. Ruth dithered, then followed. Followed him into the big tent that belonged to Edgar and a junkyard of computer equipment, and the little cappuccino device that had been with him since the magic hurricane.

He made cappuccino in silence save for the earsplitting shriek of steam jetting into milk. Ruth took the cup from him and said, "I'm sorry. I don't *mean* to shut you up."

"Okay. When?"

"Once since we got the go-ahead to come here. I couldn't stay in Camelot, Edgar. The way they looked at me! But Aaron took me with him—this far—and it wasn't that I wasn't taking Mom's calls, it was just I was always somewhere else. I talked to her once. A month ago. But Dad never calls. He talks to Aaron and says to say hi."

"You could call."

"I should call. I know I should call."

"Better talk to your mother first. Colony psychiatrist, she'll have a good idea how your dad will take it."

She nodded. "I should call."

"Take your coffee with you."

She didn't move. She sipped, not looking at him. He asked, "You don't want me listening, do you?"

She considered. She said, "Yes."

26

DEMONS

No one who, like me, conjures up the most evil of
those half-tamed demons that inhabit the human
breast, and seeks to wrestle with them, can expect
to come through the struggle unscathed.
—Sigmund Freud, *Complete Psychological Works*

Cadmann Weyland slammed his fist down on the table next to the chair. Coffee
splashed on his pants and the rug. Rachael, Zack's wife and the colony psychologist, shook her head ruefully. "Cadmann—all the way from Fafnir Ridge to end
up on my throw rug? What a waste!"

Cadmann dropped six paper napkins on the spreading stain and put his foot
on the napkins. "I'm sorry. I really am. Rachael, I just don't feel right. I haven't
for months."

"Years," she said quietly. "Almost a century now."

He didn't turn to look at her.

"None of us have really been ourselves since we left Earth. If we didn't have
hibernation instability, we worried because we might. And if we managed to
convince ourselves that we didn't, then we had to worry about everyone else.
We had to change the entire design of the colony to provide failsafe mecha-
nisms. Backups to backups, in case somebody, somewhere ended up with an ice
crystal we didn't count on."

"We did a good job," Cadmann said.

"And then the children were growing up," she continued. She was playing
with a desk hologram. It rotated in front of her, a puzzle consisting of a blue
globe and wires and a box of sticks. When she touched a piece it flashed. When
she moved her finger to another location, the piece moved with her. She made
a mistake, and the blue globe fell to the ground and shattered. It re-formed in
the air above the desk, and she continued.

"We passed our fears to our children. But they were ours, not theirs."

"Not all of them," Cadmann said.

"The nightmares?"

He nodded. "We never talk about them, not really, but the children know
that their parents wake up screaming. They *know.*"

"But you're not dreaming of grendels now, are you?"

A professional question, and he answered as a patient. "No. I dream of the
night up on that dirigible. When Toshiro climbed up behind me. When I

turned, and fired." His eyes were tired, and his voice. He felt as old as God. "But I dream Toshiro is a grendel. He's about to eat Ernst. Nobody sees it but me."

"They had no right to take the dirigible."

"Well, no, but by their lights they did, Rachael. They could even believe they had a duty. We denied them the right. And we had no justification for that. Not really. They are what we used to be!" He threw his head back and laughed bitterly. "God, I remember what it was to be their age. Young and dumb and full of cum. Ready for anything, and eager to handle it. That was what we were! What we *all* were! And what did we turn them into? Pranksters. Carving buttocks onto ice cliffs. Hacking into Cassandra. Flare-surfing off the coast. We gave them no useful place to put their courage. We called them cowards and weaklings. And they *know* it's something wrong with *us*."

"Cadmann . . ."

He spun. "Did you see the attack on the mesa? Did you see Cassandra's playback? Six grendels. *Six adult grendels*, and the kids took them. One boy died. One grendel got away. Completely hostile weather conditions, a new attack pattern. *One loss.*" The pride in his voice was something that she hadn't heard in him since the night on the dirigible, and she let him go on.

"Those are our children. *They* can take that land. Not us. We deserve to stay here. And they had to show us. They had to force the issue, because God knows that *we* never would have."

She had managed to extract a stick from the blue ball, and it was delicately balanced. So far so good . . .

"What did you want to talk about, Cadmann?"

"Aaron." He spoke the two syllables flatly. "Aaron bothers me."

"Aaron," she said. The blue ball fell and cracked. A chick emerged, grew to adulthood, flew to the floating nest of sticks and laid a blue egg.

Rachael asked, "Why?"

"I talked with Justin about that before they left. I've talked to everyone that I could, except you. And now I have to do that. Something is wrong. He was the author of a situation."

"Yes?"

"When he took *Robor*, there was no way for him to lose. I don't mean lose the dirigible, I mean . . . he thought more deeply into this than any of us did, understood in advance every move that we could make, and probably had a way to counter it. At the end half of humankind would be on the mainland, and all under his command."

"And you're feeling intimidated?"

Cadmann shook his head. "He wins. But only if he's ready to sacrifice . . . well, a scapegoat to be named at a later date. I mean, Toshiro was his friend, and his death just played right into the scenario. *Anyone* could have died in that slot. Not just one, but several."

Rachael sat back. The blue ball slipped free of its final constraint, and spun happily in the air before her.

"Cadmann—what are you saying?"

"I'm not saying, I'm asking. Is there something wrong with Aaron?"

"Your wife thinks so."

"And Joe and Linda did," Cadmann said. "Not many more. You don't, do you?"

"No." A long pause. "What is it you suspect?"

"I keep wondering if there might not be some connection to the artificial wombs. To the way they were raised."

"You're worried about some supersociopathic patterns?"

"Yes," he said, and his voice sounded small, even to him.

She was studying *him,* he thought. Afraid of *him.* "Cadmann—you were in combat. Didn't you have to face the reality that some of your men would die in a military action?"

"Of course."

"Couldn't Aaron see it that way?"

He frowned. "I suppose. You know, I never thought about it that way."

"We don't call you a sociopath just because you're capable of taking casualties to further a cause."

"You don't now," Cadmann said. "But I recall when that's precisely what you called me, and for precisely that reason."

"Cadmann—"

His smile was thin, and he spoke each word slowly and distinctly. "You've kept records on every one of us. From the very beginning, on Earth, when we were chosen, to the discovery of hibernation instability, to where everyone thought I murdered Ernst—"

"Cadmann—"

He brought his face closer to hers. His expression of cynical amusement hadn't changed. "And you decided I was crazy. Right there in the clinic, you staked me out for the grendel."

"We didn't know about grendels!"

"But I did, and I told you."

"Cadmann, that was a long time ago."

"Yeah. And I can never, will never forget that night." He straightened and smiled, this time more genuine, but still very distant. "Want to talk about night-mares?" He sat carefully, his eyes never leaving hers. "All right, let's talk night-mares. I'm the only one on this planet who has ever come face-to-face with one of those things and survived. Close enough to kiss it. Close enough to have all the time I needed to imagine it tearing me apart. I have dreamed of it killing and eating me ten thousand times. Unless I completely overestimate you, you've talked to Sylvia and Mary Ann about me, just as I've talked to you about Mary Ann. And it's *all* gone into Cassandra."

Rachael sat pointedly silent.

"I want the files on Aaron."

"For what purpose?"

"I don't know, exactly. Look, we both know he'll do nearly anything—maybe not nearly—to reach his goals. So I want to know more about what those goals are. What's he really up to?"

She shrugged. "You're the security chief. Tell Cassandra it's an emergency."

"I thought of that," Cadmann said. "I probably can bully Cassandra into giving me your files. I'd rather do it officially with your cooperation." His calm slipped a little. "Please. My son and daughter are over there. The children of the women I love most in this world." He dropped his head. "Mary Ann is just holding on, you know? And she's shut me out. . . ."

"Excuse me?"

Cadmann looked out of the window, across the fields, to the biology building, up to the stone stack of Mucking Great Mountain, where the pterodons wheeled in eternal mist.

"We haven't been man and wife since the day Toshiro died. She just *pushed* me toward Sylvia."

He paused, as if waiting for Rachael to say something. The silence stretched almost another minute.

"I thought once . . . that what I wanted was Sylvia. But not like this. Mary Ann gave her love to me. And now she can't let me in." He lowered his voice. "There's something about her now. Something . . . translucent. It is as if I can see light through her. As if she barely wants to be here anymore. Like she's not even certain why she is holding on."

"And you think you can help her?"

He nodded.

"By showing her she was right," Rachael suggested. "Aaron is a monster, and only she knew."

Cadmann looked up. "I hadn't thought of it in—"

"Ruth's pregnant."

"You've talked to her? Good. I worried about . . . that. How long?"

"Two months, she thinks. Cadmann, I'm not supposed to ferret out all your secrets. There has to be privacy. I haven't— Aaron could *keep* his secrets, but now he's probed my daughter! I'll look. Maybe I'll tell you what I find, and maybe I won't."

Cadmann stood up. "Thank you," he said, and walked out the door before he could say more.

Rachael Moskowitz sat behind her desk.

Her body felt tired, but her mind was very much alive.

Of all the Earth Born who had been frozen at Hecate Town on the Earth's Moon, stacked aboard *Geographic*, thawed and refrozen for tasks aboard *Geographic* during their trip across ten light-years and two hundred years of time, and finally thawed for the last time on Avalon's alien soil . . . only Rachael Moskowitz knew herself undamaged. Only Rachael *could* know that. And that was both a blessing and a curse.

She wasn't certain about Cadmann. What he had been through was traumatic, but it was long ago. A man like that ought to have put it out of his life, but he hadn't. None of them had really been able to put the Grendel Wars behind them.

"Cassandra," she said. "Aaron Tragon. Psychological evaluation file."

✳

Cadmann took the skeeter up and into Mucking Great Mountain, toward the fortress that, years before, had been Mankind's only bastion against the grendels.

Now it was vines and crops, pens for those animals of Earth and Avalon that could exist side by side. The mountain stream brought ice-cold water into their home, and nurtured their fields. Then it joined the Miskatonic, to bring life to the entire valley.

He spiraled the skeeter down to the landing pad with hardly a bump. Sylvia joined him at the pad, her golden hair flowing behind her. She looked like an angel.

She kissed him lightly. Before Cadmann could ask the question, Sylvia said, "She's sleeping."

He nodded. He slipped his arm around her waist, and they walked into the house together, through the fragrant living room.

In the center of the house was the common bathroom, with the big triangular tub and the steam-shower.

Once upon a time he might have had daydreams . . . two women that he loved, both married to him . . . it was easy to let erotic fantasies run wild. But it had never really worked out like that.

In the second and third year of their three-way relationship, there had been some gentle explorations of the sensual potential. Massaging, and group dancing, and even sleeping three in a bed on cold nights. But it became clear that this was happening out of Mary Ann's attempt to be what she thought he wanted in a wife, and not from any urge on her part. And so he had called a halt to it.

There were more occasions, once on Christmas, and once on his fiftieth birthday, when he found himself bedded by both of his beloved. But they were tolerating each other's presence; there was no genuine joy in the intimacy. And knowing that Mary Ann would do almost anything to keep her man happy, he began to see it as a variety of child abuse.

The three of them kept separate bedrooms, and there was a gentle ebb and flow of interest between them. He would visit their rooms, or they his, and the spontaneity of it consisted of offerings and acceptance or rejection earlier in the day. That situation had continued for years.

Within the last four months, Mary Ann had lost all interest in lovemaking.

Sylvia ran her fingers through Cadmann's hair, and gazed at a scar just at the hairline, a faded, faint white line just barely visible to her eyes against the fringe of gray and black. "I don't think I've ever seen this scar before."

She was close to him, the slowly ebbing heat of her still warming him, as it always did. In every way she was a comfort. "I'm not sure," he said.

"Right here." She brushed it, and then blew a little warm air along it, ruffling his hair. "I can't imagine why I never saw it before. . . ."

"There's a first time for everything. That one is a memento from Zimbabwe. Shrapnel. My hair hid it. Until recently."

She sighed and cuddled closer. "Oh well, the women in my family go for that increasingly high-forehead look."

"Hah hah."

"No . . . really. You lucked out."

They were quiet then again. The twin moons were both high, and their light silvered the bedposts.

"What did Rachael have to say?"

"She'll look." He traced a line along Sylvia's neck, and then clasped her shoulder firmly. He kissed it. "I wanted to thank you for how you've been with . . . Mary Ann," he said.

She pooh-poohed him. "For what? I haven't done anything."

"I know that you look at it that way. That's one of the reasons that I love you."

"Just one of them, though."

"Just one."

They lay quietly together, and listened to the sound of the Amazon, and the cooing of the Joeys. Clouds drifting in from the east. Later, they would obscure the moon, but not now.

"Are you thinking about the kids?"

He nodded his head. "And about myself. About who I was, when I started this trip."

"The journey here?" she said, knowing that wasn't what he meant.

"No. The whole thing. Is that a sign of getting old?"

"What?"

He laughed at himself. "Not asking complete questions. Wishing that there was someone who could read your mind."

"No, that's infantile behavior." She bit his chest lightly, nibbling with sharp teeth.

"Well, that's a relief."

"I'll bet."

"What I meant was that I think back over my life. Everyone I know is dead, or here on Avalon. Ghosts."

"It doesn't help that they've never contacted us," she said.

"Never. Not for eighteen years. Christ. What happened back there?"

"I can feed the files in. Want to see them?"

"Christ. It's been so long. Sure. Go ahead."

Cadmann sat up. He turned a physical switch that gave the computer access to his private bedroom, and said, "Cassandra."

It was said that Cassandra should be allowed to see everything at all times, that her security was absolute. Cadmann had to laugh. There was no electronic security in a world that contained an Edgar Sikes. There were only mechanical barriers.

"Please play back the most recent communiqué from Earth."

"Loading now, Cadmann," she said.

The wall in front of them dissolved.

There was a blast of music, and then a sound of laughter. The words A MESSAGE FROM EARTH floated there in neon, garish red.

And there followed a kaleidoscope of images:

Art exhibits in Milan. Starvation in Beirut. The inauguration of the United Nations Presidium. Images of sports. A string of faces, name-dropping at grendel speed. A play with a London background. Some chitchat from the outersystem colonies.

Each of these could be expanded upon and investigated, and they had been, endlessly. The play was detective fiction with missing clues. The inauguration might be fiction too, given that the Secretary-General was a dead ringer for the sixties' Richard Nixon. Ballet in lunar gravity had become a strange new sport. Even the familiar sports events followed complex new rules, never described. The sound bites were no more interesting than the photo opportunities.

Ultimately, there was just nothing there.

It was like the *Encyclopaedia Britannica* as designed by social scientists. There was emotion, but no real information. And the emotional inference was a culture so fatuously delighted with itself that it was blind to the efforts of unspeakably vast and numerous generations of men to get them there.

Sylvia toyed with the images, trying to find something new. Stopping and moving forward, and stopping again, and finding nothing. Nothing at all.

And then a human shape walked through the dancing light.

What Cadmann had taken for another image from the Earth message was his wife.

Mary Ann was naked, her head down as if she were sleepwalking, her swollen, ungainly limbs more pitiful when not covered by well-cut cloth. She raised her face, and stared at them, and the impression of near sleepwalking was still strong. "I . . . I heard music," she said. "Sounds. Street sounds."

Cadmann reached out and turned the video down. There was a little-girl quality to Mary Ann's voice that he recognized. She came and sat on the edge of the bed, staring at the images. She pointed into the midst of them, an image of the Canadian Rockies.

"I've been there," she said. "I grew up not too far from there."

Cadmann and Sylvia were silent.

"I'd like to see them again one day," she said, and then waited. There was no comment from either of them, and Mary Ann suddenly seemed to understand what she had said, and her hand went over her mouth.

"Oops. I guess I can't do that, can I?"

"We could go virtual," Sylvia said softly.

Mary Ann nodded. "I'd like that. I'd like that very much," she said. And she curled up at the edge of the bed like a cat, watching the images playing in the air in front of her.

Cadmann said nothing, watching Mary Ann. She didn't move again, didn't speak, but her eyes were open. And she just watched.

And finally, Sylvia's hand stole into his, and they watched until, at some point, he fell asleep.

✳

Dawn came slowly to Camelot. There was no excitement, just another day, one of an endless stream of days. There would be a single difference, perhaps. *Robor* was anchored over the main aerospaceport, shadowing it, and was being loaded now.

Zack oversaw the loading, although the kids from the eastern encampment were actually in charge. It was, as were most things dealing with the mainland expedition, a joint venture.

Rachael approached him. "Zack," she said, "Cadmann made a rather unusual request. He wants to look at Aaron's records."

Zack's round, sallow face grooved with thought. "Is he all right?"

She evaded. "He's concerned about the dirigible incident."

"He's not making any trivial request, love. What's itching him?"

"Well. The entire ectogynic issue. "

"We went over all of that a long time ago."

"And we don't talk about it much anymore. I know."

Zack walked unsteadily over to a tree stump and sat, resting his hands on his knees. He drew a large red bandanna from his pocket, and wiped it across his face with a hand that trembled.

"I think that Carlos is taking the Minerva up to the Orion today. We want to check the main systems. Why don't you invite Cadmann along, and we'll have a place to talk."

She nodded her head.

27

GEOGRAPHIC

Pretty joy!
Sweet joy but two days old,
Sweet joy I call thee:
Thou dost smile,
I sing the while
Sweet joy befall thee.

—WILLIAM BLAKE, *Infant Joy*

The Minervas were the fusion-powered landing craft brought from Sol system. Once on the ground they had served as primary power plants until the mines had produced enough materials for the fabrication of the solar-collector material known as Begley cloth. One Minerva died in the Grendel Wars. The others were used to visit the ship that had brought the children of Earth to their new world: the *Geographic*.

Late in the morning, Cadmann skeetered in with Sylvia. "Mickey's up at the house with Mary Ann," he said quietly.

"How is she doing?"

Cadmann's face was dark. "Not well. Worse than I expected. It is as if something was just taken right out of her. Linda's death was a near final thing, and then the business with Toshiro—that was a last straw of some kind. I can't say that I don't understand it. I just regret it. Regret everything."

Zack nodded.

He helped Sylvia out of the skeeter.

Cadmann went to Carlos. "*Hola.*" Carlos smiled at him lazily, stretched a little, and nodded his head. "A good day for hiking, eh?"

"A very good one."

The Minerva was a 160-foot long delta-winged aerospaceplane. Its dock was the artificial lake northeast of the colony, but it could land on any body of water. The Minerva's power plants would dissociate lake water into hydrogen and oxygen to use as fuel. Together they had made almost four hundred round-trips to the Orion craft.

That couldn't last. All of the original equipment from Earth was aging fast. One day another Minerva would fail. When the last Minerva failed, as it must, the human race on Avalon would be grounded until they could build an industrial base capable of taking Mankind back to the stars. Depending on priorities, that might take a hundred years. Knowledge alone wasn't enough. Spacecraft require specialized equipment.

They strapped themselves into the worn seats. There had been fifty, but now there were only nine. The others had been removed: more cargo space and less weight.

Carlos watched his friend ease into the pilot seat. The position was more symbolic than real: Minerva was controlled by a computer. *And that's the way it is*, Carlos thought. *We sit at the controls, but we don't run the colony anymore. I wonder if Cadmann feels that way. Probably not.* Cadmann was a strange one. He was bothered, he was troubled, but as long as there was a definite purpose to his life, he moved with all of the old intention and force. It had grown harder over the years to find a purpose to animate him, to give him a sense of meaning and potential contribution, but he still felt needed.

Or had until the *Robor* incident. Now, there seemed no way to console him. The death of one of the children . . . There was no word for the sense of loss. And Carlos, for all of the years of knowing Cadmann, couldn't say that he understood the workings of his friend's mind.

"Cassandra. System check."

Cassandra slowed her processes down to give Carlos a system-by-system check of all of the component parts of the Minerva. She stopped in the middle to flash a schematic, saying, "I have identified a burn-through spot in the right rear attitude cluster. I would suggest repair during the next maintenance cycle."

"Is it safe for today?"

"Yes. Fractional chance of failure, and two backup systems."

"All right. Power up sequence. Destination, dock with *Geographic*."

"Two hundred and nine seconds to liftoff," Cassandra said. Lights flashed on the control board. "Ground tests complete. Engine ignition in one hundred and seventy seconds." They waited. Then pumps whined, and they felt the steady roar as the engines lit.

"Power-up complete," Cassandra announced. "All systems go."

"Take us up."

"Thirty-five seconds to liftoff," Cassandra said.

They waited again; then they felt the first motion. The Minerva slid across the water faster and faster, and suddenly they were aloft. The nose tilted up until it was almost vertical. Clouds broke across the nose; then the sky was baby blue, gradually darkening. The roar seemed to originate inside him, shaking and stirring him, giving him a wild and joyous sense of freedom unmatched by anything else in his world. He loved it.

His weight eased. A whisper of thrust continued: though the oxygen and hydrogen tanks were empty, the fusion plant remained. With that he could reach the planets. Once you're in orbit you're halfway to anywhere.

He glimpsed *Geographic* twinkling ahead.

"Docking sequence initiated," Cassandra said.

Carlos unlocked his chair and spun it sixty degrees around. Cadmann was resting with his eyes closed. Sylvia's hand rested softly in his. Zack was engrossed in a holo data-management module display, probably some inventory list that needed to be vetted for the hundredth time.

They needed someone like Zack. Thank God it didn't have to be Carlos Martinez! That, Carlos decided, would have been a genuine waste. But *someone* needed to put tomorrow on an even par with today.

He, Carlos, enjoyed the present far too much.

✳

Geographic was nearly history's largest work of man (the Zuider Zee still held the record) and was certainly and by far the largest movable object. Though a mere skeleton of its former size and mass, it was still impressive as hell. Cadmann could remember the young man he had been, flying up from Buenos Aires to *Geographic* for the first time, one of a shuttle group of twelve. The first inspection of a genuine interstellar spacecraft was so different from the simulator sessions they had all suffered through.

It had been the culmination of a dream, a grand adventure at the end of a lifetime of adventures, something so beautiful, so rife with possibility. . . .

It was too big. And it was going to take them someplace too far, and take entirely too long to do it—and they had worked to be there. If they had had regrets it was far too late to voice them by the time they were aboard.

"I was thinking . . ." Cadmann said. "Why did we come out here?"

"What are you talking about?"

"You know what I'm talking about. Not what we say to the children. Not the myths. Why are we really here?"

Zack glanced up from his figuring. "What *do* you mean?"

"Why is it that all of us were willing to risk our lives. Our histories. Not one of us had enough family or friends to hold us to Earth."

"I brought my wife with me," Zack said. "So did Joe Sikes and some others."

"Think, now. We weren't the smartest and bravest, even though that's what we told ourselves." The Minerva was sailing through a sea of stars, the bright blue haze of Avalon below them. "We were the ones willing to leave it all behind. To go."

"Speak for yourself," Sylvia said. "Terry and I wanted to come here. We worked at it. Worked hard. A lot of us did, Cadmann—for that matter so did you."

They felt a gentle jolt as the padded docking tubes engaged, and inflated. Docking with *Geographic* was like an act of slow love, a reunion with an old and dear friend. She had seen them through so much, and seemed to be waiting to discover if they would need her again, ever. The air always seemed to change flavor now, at this point. Just his imagination, no doubt.

"Top floor dungeon," Carlos said. "Jewelry department, leg irons, neck irons—"

Rachael and Zack were out of the Minerva and swimming down the lines leading to the *Geographic*'s main lock. A curved door sealed behind them, and they were in a womb of steel and ceramic. Another door opened, and they were in the main corridor.

The ship smelled faintly musty. Twenty years of near desolation hadn't changed that, and they had never quite gotten that smell out of the ship. Two hundred people living in close proximity for a hundred years will do that—even if ninety-five percent of them are asleep at any given time.

They heard a voice from deeper in the ship, and Carolyn McAndrews hailed them. She was followed by Julia Hortha and Greg Arruda. There was always someone aboard because *Geographic* served as an orbiting machine shop for maintenance of the observation satellites, and Cassandra and her maintenance and repair robots couldn't be prepared for everything. There was never a problem finding volunteers to keep watch for a week, and for many it was a plum assignment, a chance to get away and meditate in near isolation. Carlos had, of course, taken advantage of other aspects of *Geographic*. He had taken many tours well stocked with female friends. He hadn't quite tired of the null-grav amenities, but he was slowing down.

Carolyn swam down the lines effortlessly. Although her bulk was growing more and more ponderous, she moved with an uncanny grace, here where her weight was that of thistledown.

"Good to see you," she greeted them. "It was only just getting lonely up here. Lots of time, and old cubes to sort through, but . . . well." A strand of her washed-out brown hair floated away, got away from her, and she chuckled and swept it back into place. "How are the children?" she asked.

"Fine," Carlos said. "But they overwater your plants."

She patted him on the chin, and kissed him lightly. "Thank you," she said. "Now—you want the computer room? Are you going to want privacy?"

Cadmann shook his head. "No. Get in on this, Carolyn. You were as much involved in Aaron's raising as anyone."

"More than most," she said. Then she closed her eyes, and blushed a little.

"This was Aaron's creche," Rachael said. "We can trace down anything, forward or backward. Cassandra, give us Childe Aaron One."

The holostage began to play out a series of images. Every image of young Aaron, from infancy onward. They were virtually a time-lapse display, carrying him through to toddlerhood.

Cadmann watched absently. "Who are his parents?"

Rachael looked uncomfortable. "As you know, the sperm and egg samples were chosen both from the members of the colony, and the frozen contributions of those who didn't make the trip for one reason or another. There are representative samples from all the basic genetic groups and cultures of the world, but all flawless. We could be picky. The idea was that some children would be raised by the colony as a whole, without any specific parental attachments. It was one of the theoretical bases of the colony, an experiment in shifting the primary bonding imperatives of a child from a pair, onto a concept or system. As you know, the experiment was begun in earnest after the Grendel Wars, and was terminated four years later."

Carolyn McAndrews smiled and said, "We were making enough babies."

"You always had doubts," Zack said. Carolyn nodded. "Maybe we should have listened." *Ice on her mind,* he didn't have to say. Nobody would have listened to Carolyn; which was a bit odd, because Carolyn had been one of the genuine heroines of the Grendel Wars. No one could quite remember when they had stopped listening to her.

Rachael said, "The project was terminated for other reasons."

Cadmann was looking out into black space. Carlos saw only his back. He asked, "Problems?"

"Stuff that came through from Earth, maybe a year after we left. There were files on the Bottle Baby research. We didn't get anything else for years. *Geographic's* last received signal was a light-speed communiqué ten years after we left. Garbled. It took quite a while to reconstruct it," Rachael said. "There was research that implied that the creche children had a more difficult time bonding. They had all been adopted into loving, supportive homes—where parents had waited years for children, but due to fertility problems were forced to utilize artificial wombs.

"Sure, problems, Cad. There're always problems. Statistically significant? Maybe. Some kind of academic dominance game was going on. Those can get nasty. I think some of their theories got sent and some got buried. Numbers, too.

"One theory had to do with the endocrinal flux in the uterus. The numbers we *got* suggest that the actual ebb and flow of biochemical products as the mother is awake, asleep, afraid, hungry, tired, sexually stimulated, whatever . . . is a form of communication between mother and child. It's another nutrient . . . an emotional nutrient, if you will, as important as blood or oxygen."

"I thought that all of those things had been duplicated."

Rachael shrugged. "It's still an art form. When you try to create a computer program to simulate the messages that a mother sends to her child, you have to remember that it is a feedback loop between the mother and the fetus. Thousands of fetuses were studied, and the ways that their mothers responded to them were recorded, and a refinement of everything that was learned was created for use in the creches."

"So?"

"So? A camel is a horse designed by committee. There is a difference between the clumsy elegance of the human body and the sophisticated, intellectual choices made by a committee of experts deciding which endocrinological experiences are good for baby. They tried to round out the experience. *This* mood swing was inappropriate, *that* orgasmic response pattern was a biochemical form of child abuse, a mother experiencing *anger* is damaging her child. The liberals swung the profile one way, the conservatives another. Too many morphemes. Too much adrenaline. Chill those kiddies out."

"Ouch."

"Hindsight. But the program may have been too *bland*. Didn't place enough of an imprint on the children, leaving them a little too vulnerable to their environment."

"What happened on Earth?"

"Not much. A statistically significant increase in emotional problems among those children. A slight indication of an increase in sociopathy. But remember something—each and every one of those children was in a loving home, one where the parents had waited for years to have a child. They had far more love and attention than average. It is interesting to note what might have happened if such children had been placed into average home situations."

Cadmann still didn't turn. "What about ours?"

"There was nothing about that from Earth—we thought that giving them love would counteract any potential problems."

The image of Aaron continued to age. From time to time the program would lock on a particular sequence. Aaron climbing a mountain. Young Aaron kicking a soccer ball. Aaron visiting Edgar in traction. Aaron debating. Aaron defeating Edgar in debate. Aaron teaching a class in woodcraft to a group of Biters. Aaron hiking, moving quickly past a not yet injured Edgar Sikes. They were surrounded by a universe of Aaron Tragons.

Rachael said, "It worked—in general. Quite well in some cases."

"For instance?"

Zack leaned forward. "Children from genetic groups conditioned for group raising of children. Little Chaka, from New Guinea, for instance. Toshiro Tanaka. But I know Rachael worried about Aaron, and Trish Chance, and a few others."

"Everyone in the colony participated in the nurseries back then," Rachael said.

"I remember, " Sylvia said. "That was a real labor of love."

"When the children were older, they were shared by the colony as well. On through their teens. Every one of them had a dozen parents, every colonist had a dozen children. This was one of the reasons that the sexual freedom in the colony was so fluid."

"Well," Cadmann said, "we didn't take any diseases."

"True," Rachael said. "But the other idea was that all pregnancies were desirable. If a particular mother or father didn't want to have the child at that time, the fetus could be removed and frozen, or carried to term in a host uterus, or an artificial womb. They could be thawed when the mother or father was ready for the responsibility, or adopted by a particular set of partners—"

"Or they could be adopted into the general colony. We tried that far more often than they were adopted by specific parents," said Carolyn. "I did what I could to . . ." She trailed off.

Rachael sighed, and removed her glasses, rubbing her temples hard. "You asked me yesterday to look into Aaron. I have. I wish I'd done it sooner, before Ruth got so involved. I found some things which disturb me."

Cadmann asked, "What kind of things?"

On the holostage Aaron had grown older. Aaron and virtually every woman of his generation, at one time or another. Aaron on the mainland, one of a troop of Grendel Scouts led by Carlotta Nolan and Cadmann Weyland.

"He has great leadership potential, but . . ."

"But?"

Rachael said, "If the combination of ectogynic origin and lack of specific bonding and imprinting hit anyone hardest, it was Aaron Tragon. I think that he has bonded not to the members of the colony, but to the dream of colonization itself."

"What's wrong with that?" Sylvia asked.

Aaron's image, larger than life, stared down at them, immense, serious, intent.

"I don't mean that he has an idealistic view of what this colony should be. I don't mean that he has the kind of gung-ho conquer-the-universe attitude that we had to have to get onto *Geographic* in the first place. I mean literally that dream itself, the dream of spreading across the mainland, the planet. The entire Tau Ceti system itself. Of Mankind taking the stars and remaking them to Aaron's wishes. That dream is his mother and father, his reason for being. That dream was what this was all about, remember?"

"I . . . remember." Cadmann was thoughtful. "But his debates . . . sometimes they seem almost conservative. Back to nature? Live-with-the-planet sort of speeches."

"Well, I don't think he wants to strip-mine the planet. He wants to *people* the planet. Our technology is advanced enough to live in harmony with Avalon— there is no need to produce more children than Avalon can handle."

"And second?"

"I think that Aaron Tragon stopped showing us his true face a long time ago."

The image of Aaron at twelve appeared, duplicated itself along the walls.

Rachel looked from one image to another and sighed. "Aaron believes that the original colonists have abandoned the dream. Betrayed it. I think he is internally rather than externally motivated. I think that he might have little true contact with anyone. I think that Aaron's sense of love has only to do with goal accomplishment."

Carolyn smiled, a flash of what she must have been like a hundred years ago. "Of course that goes beyond sociobiology."

"A little. But none of that makes him dangerous," Rachel said. "Or does it? And my daughter is in love with him, and pregnant by him, and sometimes I can't remember I'm a psychiatrist."

Carolyn put her arm around Rachel. They stood together and looked at the Aaron images.

Cadmann shook his head. "What disturbs me is the entire dirigible incident. He had us. From the first moment to the last. We were set up beautifully. But there was something so . . . so utterly cold-blooded about it that . . ."

"That what?"

"That it makes me wonder who Aaron Tragon really is. Who's really alive behind his eyes."

"You ought to know if anyone does."

"Me? Why?"

"Because he probably bonded more to you than anyone else. It's clear he thinks of you as his father."

"I—" Cadmann hesitated. "I was going to say I hadn't known that, but I suppose I did. He was always finding reasons to go places with us, and it wasn't just that Justin and Jessica were his friends. But I don't know who's in there, Rachael."

"I've told you most of what there is to know."

"No," Cadmann said. *"Who were his parents?"*

Rachael looked uncomfortable. "All right. It's not as if it was actually security sealed. It was more a general colonial agreement. I guess I just feel uncomfortable. It was under my own code—that was why you couldn't access it." She cleared her throat. "The father was from Earth. A Swedish mathematician of Russian extraction named Koskov."

Cadmann seemed to relax, Carlos noticed. As if he had expected—and feared—another revelation altogether. "And the mother?"

Rachael looked at Sylvia. Sylvia colored, and the psychologist nodded.

"That's right," she said. "Aaron Tragon is your son. It was your egg."

"Justin's half-brother," Cadmann said quietly.

"Yes. If there had been any danger of Aaron relating to one of his sisters, I would have said something. I keep track of such things . . . but it never came up. Jessica isn't his biological sister any more than Justin is."

Sylvia was very quiet, still, her mind off in some unreachable place. "Aaron and Justin."

"What do we do now?" Rachael asked.

"I think we go to the mainland. On the next dirigible."

Sylvia curled onto her side, still floating an inch or so off the chair. "I never held him," she said quietly. "I never told him that he was mine, that I would watch him and care for him. That he was the most beautiful thing in the world. The most precious child in existence."

"Probably no one did," Rachael said. "We should have done that. Aaron, and thirty others. Belonging to no one but each other. No wonder they started their cult. They had to belong somewhere."

"Who is living in there?" Cadmann asked.

"I think that we need to find out," Carlos said. "I think that we need to find out now."

28

TITHE

An honest God is the noblest work of man.
—Robert Green Ingersoll, *Gods, Part I*

"Home tomorrow," Justin said. Aaron nodded, and accepted a cup of coffee from him. The valley was swollen with mist, and it rolled across them almost sleepily.

Justin had taken the early-morning shift.

Aaron sipped at the coffee. "We're going through the main valley. We have a couple of choices there, you know."

Justin nodded. "Here be grendels. They're too far from the main camp to do us any great harm."

"But the herd will come close enough for trouble."

"I say we take the long way around." Justin scratched in the dust with his toe. Trees, hills, a stream. "If we take the southern route, we can avoid the problem."

"We do, on the other hand, have to ford the stream. No choice about that."

Grendels were death in the water. The smartest thing to do was to kill every-thing grendel-sized before the eventuality even arose.

"So," said Aaron. "What do you think?"

"This planet was here before we came, and it will be here after we're gone. I don't think we can kill everything we don't like. There has to be another way, and I want to find it."

"I agree." Aaron marked a position upstream from the fording spot. "What say we seed the water with a freshly slaughtered steer? Draw the grendels up. We won't get them from further down—that's another grendel's territory, and there is plenty of food. Grendels don't fight unless they have to . . . especially the mainland varieties."

"What do you mean?"

Aaron was thoughtful. "We never really studied grendel interactions, grendel behavior, beyond basic hunt and attack patterns. But doesn't it seem that these grendels can actually think? Plan? Observe? They're intelligent—much more than the First told us. They were here long before we were. I think that one day we may be able to communicate with them. . . ." He stopped, and laughed. "Just dreaming, I guess. Let's get on with the day, huh?"

What was it with Aaron and grendels? It gave Justin goose bumps. Aaron was sheer death in the grendel-shooting games, as if the cartoon grendels saw Aaron and just fell over.

✴

Old Grendel slept.

The prey that lived in the lake would feed her until the end of things. She had eaten well the previous day, and in these times of long sleeps and quiet days, a single major feeding could last her ten to fifteen days before hunger grew unendurable.

She occasionally roused from dream, disturbed by the daughters of God flying overhead. Their hum was the sound of the Death Wind. It frightened her down to her core, made her hunker down into the water and watch, just watch.

Change was in the air. The light was hallucinatory; everything felt evanescent, transitory, tissue-thin. She sniffed the thousand scents of lesser life-forms preparing themselves for the end of everything. Some began a madness of breeding; some avoided breeding entirely; some changed color or shape, or migrated, or entered a sleep from which even a grendel could not rouse them.

You couldn't think, couldn't plan for the end of everything. But, drowsily, Old Grendel was trying . . . when the smell of blood snapped her fully awake.

Three times within the past several days, she had followed such a scent. Each time she'd found a dead puzzle beast floating in still water. After she had allowed it to ripen for a day or two, it tasted just fine. Last time, when she returned to her favorite resting spot, she noticed that large numbers of animals had passed her way: many puzzle beasts, a few of the two-legged weirds.

The weirds flew through the air in humming flyers, the daughters of God. They walked; or they ran almost as fast as a sister on *speed,* riding strange shells that smelled of tar and lightning. They combined too many different smells in one. They didn't eat their own young. She knew this because she had come close enough to their nests to watch them.

She had tested their defenses. They knew where she was before she could smell them. If she came close enough to make out distinct aspects of their behavior, they became alarmed. Twice they sent flying things in pursuit. But when she retreated, they did not attempt to engage.

She found their rules of combat not entirely dissimilar to her own. They could move fast. They were hunters. They hoarded their young.

Could they be a kind of grendel? There were builder grendels, and the great flat unmoving grendels of the north, and the snow grendels she'd had to fight twice in her life, and the kind that laid her swimmers in a stranger's pond. . . .

In her youth, Old Grendel had wandered far during the rainy seasons. Wanderlust and curiosity were somehow linked to the days when her head had nearly burst. When the pain faded it left behind a new clarity. She began to see ways that the world fit together. She developed a hunger of a different kind, that pulled her toward the blurry edges of the pattern that was the world.

She followed the water.

When she found water already stocked with one of her own kind, she fought. But if the taste in the water was alien . . . Two dissimilar grendels could share the same water. They snarled and snapped at each other, but managed somehow to keep the terrible *speed* under control. They could tolerate each other's presence, if each knew that to begin was to end.

The weirds, now. Were they some new kind of grendel?

The smell of blood from upstream was strong; but Old Grendel moved downstream by a little, away from the blood. She coated herself with mud, and burrowed deep. She extended her snorkel to breathe. And she waited, and watched.

✳

Chaka brought Skeeter II low in over the river thirty clicks south of Shangri-la. There was a grendel there, but no point in killing it. An empty ecological niche would merely attract a younger, faster monster. So he let sleeping grendels lie, and so far the arrangement had been a good one.

Three times before, they had lured the grendel upstream with a slaughtered carcass. They had watched via camera. The first time she had dragged the meat back to her lair. Unsatisfactory. So they'd chained the meat to the ground. The grendel had to devour it there, and she did, after examining the area.

And the third time they had taken their herd across in safety, because the grendel was busy eating. They had, in a matter of speaking, tithed to the grendel god. Aaron had insisted on it, and Chaka liked it as well.

Today Chaka swept the river with his glasses, and saw nothing.

"This is Skeeter Two. We have no contact at all."

"None?"

"Nothing grendel-sized is moving. No heat source. I don't like it."

"And the river is running with blood, isn't it?"

"The ox was alive when we chained it in the river. We numbed it, sliced it, and let it bleed to death. I'm telling you, it should have done the job."

"Wait ten minutes," Aaron said.

Chaka wheeled around. This was a good life. There was beauty, and endless discovery and growth. But it required vigilance. His life had always required vigilance. Since the first time that he had become aware of the difference between himself and the other children, he had been vigilant.

Since the first time that he had formed the union with Aaron and Trish and the others, he had been vigilant. *The price of freedom is eternal vigilance.* Who said that? His father?

He pulled his mind back to the task at hand.

Chaka had been adopted, mentored by Big Chaka. Big Chaka was from America. Little Chaka's seed had come from New Guinea. Still, there was a connection, and it wasn't the odd African name. Chaka smiled to think of it, and looked forward to the visit from the mainland, for the sloping shadow of the big dirigible, and the cargo and people she would bring.

He checked all of his meters. "Cassandra?"

"Negative, Chaka," she said.

Damn. There was just nothing warm and willing to move down there. At least—nothing that could be lured by blood. He had long thought that grendels were more intelligent than anyone gave them credit for.

"All right," he said finally. "Let's dump *speed*."

One of the other skeeters dropped *speed* pellets into the water. They dissolved almost instantly. The water seethed with scent.

"Let's see," Chaka said.

✳

Old Grendel was in agony. The smells of blood and *speed* were overwhelming. She wanted to meet these strange creatures on their own ground, to *learn*.

There was so much that was new about them.

But she couldn't do that. Her whole self wanted to *attack*. If she came near them, she would tear them to pieces, or they would kill her. She would learn nothing. All she could do was fight against her own deepest instincts, feel the *speed* boiling within her, and lie buried in the mud and the silt and wait.

And dream.

She remembered a time when she had no dreams.

She remembered when the world had become so strange. When the colors and shapes and smells became *patterns*. Agony came with the change. She had suffered for a full cycle of seasons, and there were times when she was so sick and crazed that she completely forgot what it had ever been to feel well and whole. And then . . . and then her head felt heavy. Swollen. On the far side of agony came an awareness, a *newness*.

That was when she began to remember things. To think of the images that came at night, and wonder where they stopped and the world of food and fear began.

That was when she found she could tell the *speed* to stop, to go away. When she began to master the hidden essence of herself. That was the beginning of everything.

She knew that something had happened. And she knew that she wanted to pass this something on, a gift for her own young.

Perhaps once a year, she would chase down one of her own swimmers. Quite a chase it would be, too. How was a swimmer to know that the ballistic shape swooping through the water didn't mean to eat it? Every similar memory ended in water clouded with gore. But once a year the jaws would close more gently.

A swimmer could survive out of the water for almost an hour, and she moved carefully through the dusk, briskly, but never hitting *speed*. If its skin grew too dry, she would vomit a little water over it to keep it comfortable, and continue.

The water tasted different to her here. When she came here, it felt better. And when she brought some of her young, when she made certain that they lingered in this watery place, it felt best of all.

And some of those swimmers that she brought to this place felt the same strange call.

One had died. Her head swelled, as with her sisters before her, but the pain never dwindled, and her thin scream stopped only with death. She was too old, Old Grendel decided. The bones in her head had gone rigid, and expansion below the skull had split it. Old Grendel didn't make that mistake again.

The ones who had not been to the headwater smelled different. They were stupid. They would challenge her for territory when they were not a third her size, when they hadn't even fully grown into *speed*. She tore them to pieces without a second thought.

The favored ones: she watched them grow, and presently chased them down the river. Most she never saw again.

But sometimes . . . when the weather was dry and the water levels dropped, when there weren't any ponds or marshes to support them, some of them came back to challenge her.

She remembered killing many—but allowing others to flee back downriver. She didn't know what happened to them, didn't really think about it in the way that a human being might understand memories, but she felt a distaste for killing them. Ordinarily, in killing there was pleasure.

The water was buzzing against her skin, pounding in her ears. Old Grendel came back to herself in a flash of terror. Then she recognized the vibration of approaching hooves.

The water was running clean, the taste of *speed* was fading. She sensed that first. Then she retracted her snorkel, and slowed her fire so that her oxygen would last longer.

The hoofbeats were upriver from her. She could hear everything. The smell reached her a few moments later. Puzzle beasts, the ones who could change their look and scent. A herd of them! She loved the taste of their meat, and the joy of solving the puzzle they posed; for the world was a pattern, and puzzle beasts could hide within it.

Again, her juices began to flow. It was almost too good to believe, too good to allow to pass.

But she could smell more than a score of weirds. Weirds were dangerous. She could hear it coming, *rumble-roar-splash,* and she smelled a stink of lightning and heat and volcanic chemicals: one of the dead things, the shells that the weirds grew so that they could run on *speed.*

The herd pounded through the river, until the thunder of hooves diminished. Then Old Grendel slowly, cautiously raised her head from the water, and looked. They were moving away, to the east, toward the larger encampment.

She could get closer, and would. The sun was past its zenith. The day was cooling. She could make it to another spring, one which she had discovered on a foray in the rain. It was a long way from her native grounds.

29

CHILDREN OF THE DREAM

Moribus antiquis res stat Romana virisque.
(The Roman state stands by ancient customs,
and its manhood.)

—ENNIUS, *Annals*

Two rows of electrified fences greeted them as they drove the herd toward
Shangri-la.

A sheer granite expanse of mountains rose behind the base camp to the
north, solid and impassive. Handholds and supply caverns had been cut into it.
These could also serve as shelters in an emergency. There was no deep running
water to the north for nearly two hundred kilometers. The closest deep water to
the camp was the river twenty klicks east—well beyond ordinary grendel range,
except in rainy seasons. In winter and rain they would have to take special precautions.

The sights and smells of a healthy, active camp assailed them as they rode up,
singing and enjoying themselves.

Justin waited for the first fence to shut down and the warning lights atop it to
blink off. Two attendants swung the gate open, and welcomed them in.

"How was the trip?"

"Except for Stu," he said soberly, "it was great."

Long faces, nods of understanding.

A drawbridge spanned the horseshoe trench between the two fences. There
was no way in or out save across the double pits, by skeeter, or up the mountainside. Every corner of Shangri-la was protected by automatic sensors with
links directly to Cassandra.

A single electrified fence surrounded the forty acres of experimental farmland
beyond the main encampment. The electric fence was lightly charged at all
times, but the computers could switch to higher voltages in an eyeblink. Watch-
dogs roamed freely, their collars keyed to the fence's frequency. Irritation
increased in direct ratio to their nearness to the fence. After the first week, the
collars had been turned down. No dog had been hurt.

The growl of tractors, the laughter of children greeted them.

Justin moved to the far side of the drawbridge, and let the chamels through.
The herd hardly protested anymore, as if the snow grendel attack had broken
their spirit—or proved the good intentions of their new masters.

The sounds of happy laughter were evidence of the one thing that had caused
the greatest debate between the generations. The children.

Clearly, the Star Born had the right to bring their own children with them. Although there had been debate, there were no solid grounds to deny it.

So the age of consent was set at sixteen years. There were a few Star Born between the ages of ten and sixteen who had been allowed to accompany older brothers and sisters. This was for individual families to decide.

The outer gate swung closed, and the spotting skeeters buzzed over the main pads.

Four skeeters had gone out on the run, two weeks ago.

Three returned. Justin shook his head. *Snow, dammit.* He hadn't thought about that, and Stu was dead, and Katya came *that* close. But . . . they had taken out five grendels with a single casualty.

The first grendel to enter Camelot had killed seven, and wounded many more. One grendel had nearly devastated the entire colony. But that was twenty years ago.

They were learning. They would have to learn even faster.

The chamels were herded through the second fence, and across the second drawbridge, as Justin swung down off his horse.

The rotors on her skeeter were still revolving as Katya jumped down. She spotted him as she stopped at a data post and uplinked her flight records. Then she ran at him, thudded against his chest. He threw one arm around her, feeling . . . protective?

It wasn't the kind of feeling that he had for Jessica. Perhaps that was familiarity. Family. It felt good to have Katya next to him—

"You need a refresher course," he said.

He was holding a marble statue.

She said, "It wasn't my fault."

"Tomorrow, the playtent. We'll shoot some virtual grendels together. I'll spot—"

"Spot me *nothing.*"

The camp was all prefabricated buildings, squat one-story jobs with spacious windows and red roofs. The streets were wide, with enough room to play or wander. Herds of dogs and a few older kids ran in the streets. It was like Camelot made new. First the area was sterilized with flamethrowers, then Earth grasses were planted.

Then the dirigible created a series of supply depots along the way, along the rock islands dotting the ocean between Camelot and the continent.

One step at a time, until the proposed camp site was supplied and protected. Only then did the human beings enter to construct fences and buildings.

Jessica and Aaron ran up from the side, laughing, Chaka and Trish behind them. "Me for the mess hall," Aaron called.

Justin agreed heartily. Dinner sounded great.

Justin felt comfortable in Shangri-la. There was nobody older than twenty, and everything was made to their specifications. It was like a larger, wealthier version of Surf's Up.

When they entered the mess hall there was a roar. They hoisted Aaron up on their shoulders and carried him around the room, and he was handed a huge flagon of beer. Conversations were conducted at a yell: the walls throbbed with an Abo-Asian jazz fusion performed by computer wave-table synthesis from scores and themes they fed to Cassandra. Someone had dubbed that the Shangri-la Symphony Orchestra.

It was raucous, and it was home.

Posted on the walls were the totals for the week's work quotas. The entire encampment, the eighty-five of them over here from the island, was broken up into six teams, each with their own duties and responsibilities. The discipline and organization was taken over by internal teams. There was play, there was revelry. There were biweekly orgies. But God help anyone who didn't meet his quota, or was too drunk, too drugged up or sexed out to take his security post, or till the fields. It wasn't an economic system for the ages, but within this small community where everyone knew everyone else, it worked well enough. There was enough to eat, and there were some luxuries, and everyone could spend at least half time on interesting work.

That night's service detail brought in the food, and the conversation died to a gentle roar.

"Well, what do you think?" Edgar asked Jessica.

"I think it looks great. More paint on the inside, and a few more decorations. The most important thing is the new buildings."

"Most important thing is that all of the quotas are met. The dirigible is coming in day after tomorrow, and we want to be certain that we're ready."

"What's the tally?"

"Nine tonnes of refined ore—Deadwood is running fine. Zack should be happy."

She noticed that the conversation had died down. Everyone understood the question behind the question.

Edgar Sikes said, "Nobody has the remotest idea what happened in Deadwood Pass. We've analyzed from every angle. Whatever killed Linda and Joe was just *gone*. We haven't a clue. We shipped in a grendel-proof shelter and sealed it and installed air tanks. It should stop anything."

"Best bet?"

"Eh. Some sort of gas cloud," Edgar said. "Volcanic origin, something that acted like an acid."

"But wasn't an acid?"

"Certainly didn't leave acidic traces. But that's the way it acted, and that's what we have to assume."

He dipped his finger in water and drew on the table. "Look here. The best guess we have is that the wind blowing up over the mountains carried a pocket of caustic gas with it. It hit them before they had any chance at all."

"And Cadzie?"

He bared his teeth. "Don't *know*. Best guess is that she sealed the baby in the blanket. The acid cloud passed before it could leak in. But Aaron's sure it was something alive, something that veers away from Cadzie blue."

"Sealed it airtight? Against something that ate the flesh from their bones, and left no trace? You believe this?"

". . . No," he said. His plump, babyish face was tight with frustration. "But I don't believe in an invisible monster either!"

"Monsters from the id," someone sang.

"Oh, shut up. Anyway, we've combed the area. Dirt, rock, and soil samples. We found nothing out of the ordinary. The usual decomposed leaves, crushed rock, animal droppings, and general crud that makes dirt anywhere."

"Animal droppings?" Chaka asked, his interest roused. "What kind of animal?"

"We don't know," he said. "Not turds, more like a fine dry mist of concentrated shit sprayed over everything. Aaron was *sure* it was something alive. You hear about that?"

"Yeah."

"The Scribe has a blue lip. There are other Avalon plants and animals that use blue to signal *poison*. I found four in Cadmann's garden at the Stronghold! We looked hard at that slice of skin Aaron cut, and it really *is* poisonous. But Cadzie blue is a darker color."

Chaka brooded. "Dammit, Edgar, it's such a *neat* notion." He suddenly grinned. "And Aaron is so *massively* embarrassed."

Like wind passing over a wheat field, heads turned toward Aaron . . . who was apparently half-asleep.

Edgar said, "We have a piece of the lip itself. We have views through several sets of war specs. We have Justin's flash photographs. Cadzie blue is *darker*."

"Why don't you let me take a look at that stuff you collected?"

"Well . . . all right, Chaka. Right after dinner?"

Chaka smeared a trace of the dropping sample on an analyzer sheet, and ran it into the kiln.

"What are you looking for?" Justin asked.

"I don't know. But Pop considers it to be the largest threat to the colony."

Aaron nodded. Somewhat to Justin's surprise, Aaron had wanted to come over, had cut his participation in the revelry short.

Columns of numbers danced in the air as the computer began its analysis.

Aaron ran his finger through the air next to the column. "Phosphorus, carbon. Lots of nitrogen."

Justin asked, "As much as you would expect from a carnivore?"

"Sure. Urea—"

"And this stuff, it's what a mammal would turn urea into. Unless it's a hominid," Chaka said. "This matches what we know of Avalon biology."

"Not grendel, though?"

"No, not grendel. *Way* less water, for one thing." Chaka muttered under his breath to Cassandra, and the images of the droppings expanded. "It's like dust. And . . . there's more than one kind here. Lots of animal life up there, nothing very large."

"Could be barking up the wrong tree."

"Wrong damn *forest*. I can't tell anything until we match the droppings with the animal samples that we have currently, and keep going. We might be able to determine a phylum. I doubt if we can get closer than that."

"Hell of a riddle," Aaron said. He looked troubled. "I know what I want to do. I want to take a look on the west side of that mountain ridge. There's something over there. Volcanic? Organic? Don't know. But something on that mountain somewhere killed two people, and I want to find out what it was."

"What about Stu's funeral?" Justin asked.

Aaron nodded. "Tomorrow morning. But before *Robor* arrives. Stu was Star Born, and we'll mourn him privately."

All eighty-five of Shangri-la's Star Born were crowded into the main recreation hall. The eighty-sixth was buried out on the Scribeveldt, his grave marked by a pile of stone as tall as a man, and recorded to the centimeter in Cassandra's files.

Katya walked somberly to the southeast corner of the rec room, and placed a foot-tall wooden plaque against the wall. With eight clean hammer-strokes she nailed it to the wall. On it were two lines of etched letters. The first read: STU ELLINGTON. Beneath it, GREATER LOVE HATH NO MAN.

There was another plaque on that wall. TOSHIRO TANAKA. REST WELL, SENSEI.

She returned to the front of the hall, and stood beside Justin.

Aaron Tragon stood before them. He wore a dark shirt and pants. His flaxen hair lay down around his shoulders. He gazed out at their assembled faces, and began to speak.

"Most of those who have fulfilled this duty before me," he said, his voice swelling to fill the room, "have commended the institution of the eulogy. It is good, they have said, that solemn words should be spoken over our fallen friends. I disagree. Acts deserve acts, not words."

Someone behind Katya said, "Amen to that."

"But I can offer no act to equal that of Stuart Ellington. So it is with apologies to our fallen friend that I offer only words. We cannot understand Stu's sacrifice merely by considering the life he saved, or the life he lost in so saving. We must look to the sacrifices made to conquer Avalon, the world which we have inherited, with all of its terrors and treasures.

"Twenty years ago there came from Earth a group of men and women who dreamed of Humanity's destiny among the stars. These courageous folk were willing to invest their lives in that dream. And all of us here descended from that dream."

There were quiet nods of agreement.

"Most of you were born into the world through the bodies of your mothers, children of Love.

"But others of us—like me, like Chaka and Trish, like Stu—were children of the dream itself, brought into the world by mind and force of will. Mind and Heart together have inherited this world. . . .

"Stu enjoyed his garden, and his mathematics, and his flying. God, how he loved his flying. The true wealth of Avalon is found in the fact that pleasure motivates us—not the pain of lesser cultures. We don't have discipline on Avalon—we have hunger. Hunger to grow, to learn, to share. We are lovers of beauty, of wisdom, of knowledge. We differ from the states which preceded us in regarding the man who holds aloof from public life not as 'quiet' but as useless. Together in debate and action we have created every aspect of this world, and of that, we may be proud.

"For we are at once the most adventurous and the most thoughtful human beings who have ever lived. But there is a price for the wealth, the opportunity, the beauty which fills our lives. Stu paid that price. More of us will pay it. We may pray to be spared his bitter hour, but remember his sacrifice and hope that if your moment of duty comes, you may discharge it as nobly.

"It is because of this nobility that I do not mourn. For I know that we have been born into a world of manifold chances, and that he is to be accounted happy to whom either the best life, or the best death falls. The two are joined inexorably as one.

"There is only a plaque to celebrate Stu here. His body belongs to the soil, to the cycle of life. This whole planet is the sepulcher of a brave man, and Stu's story is not merely graven on this plaque, but lives on in our hearts as we think of him, and strive to follow his example. As we try to lead a life, or die a death, one half so noble as his."

Aaron closed his eyes, and placed both hands, folded together, above his heart. "Good-bye, Stu," he said quietly.

30

FAMILY TIES

Sun-girt city, thou hast been
Ocean's child, and then his queen;
Now is come a darker day,
And thou soon must be his prey.
—Percy Bysshe Shelly,
Lines Written Amongst the Euganean Hills

There were those who felt that the intent of Shangri-la was as stated in their formal manifesto: to explore and conquer the mainland. To others, the major intent was to create a world separate from their parents. To a few, the major intent was to party.

By agreement, anyone who didn't do his share, or compromised camp security, could be sent back to Camelot. Surf's Up was a more forgiving environment. There had been two such expulsions, both times at Aaron's insistence. There were no slackers at Shangri-la.

But children want the respect of their parents.

Despite everything that had been said and done, and all of the accusations and protestations of independence, it was noticeable that the streets were a little cleaner, that things moved with a little more sparkle and polish when the dirigible was due to come over from the island.

Much of the work stopped at least an hour before *Robor*'s imposing shadow fell across the land. The landing pad, surrounded by electrified fence and another trench, was cleared. The landing crews stood by. Everything and everyone was in place.

Aaron, Justin, Jessica, Chaka—the entire Board of the Star Born were there to meet *Robor*. Today there were special visitors inside.

The skeeters purred gently as they urged it toward its destination. Sudden music blared out: the Shangri-la Symphony Orchestra was now the town band, as Cassandra played a march composed by Derik and Gloria with theme suggestions from Jessica. The tune went from oompah to swing with odd transformations as the dirigible glided into the restraining web. The ground-crew volunteers hauled the mooring lines taut and cleated them down.

"Clear and secure!" Heather McKennie called. The pilot acknowledged, and let down the landing ramp.

Cadmann Weyland was the first out. He waved to Justin and Jessica as he strode down the gangplank. Sylvia followed, then the stooped figure of Big Chaka.

Cadmann and Jessica regarded each other. Justin watched carefully. This was the first time they had seen each other in eight weeks. The longest they had ever been separated. Their relationship had suffered a terrible blow: who knew what might happen?

Sylvia went to Justin, and embraced him. He wanted to lose himself in his mother's arms. He'd forgotten how much he missed her, how very good it felt to allow himself to be enfolded. She looked a little tired, a little more worn, but still wonderful.

But he kept a bit of peripheral vision on Jessica and her father, and he wasn't disappointed.

Jessica took the step forward, and held out her hand. Cadmann took it. He held it, and they looked at each other.

Justin could see Aaron's face over Sylvia's shoulder. As Chaka and Justin and Jessica embraced their parents, Aaron Tragon beamed like a proud schoolmaster . . . well, not quite.

"How is Mother?" Jessica asked finally.

"She's fine. Your brother Mickey is watching her. She wanted me to come over to check on you."

"I can believe that." Her eyes shone.

There was still so much in his face. She had looked up and into those eyes so many times, over so many years, and she had watched it slowly age like good leather. He was still the man that she knew, and she couldn't quite bring herself to say the things that she needed to say.

"Come on," she said. She took his hand, and led him away from the others. Aaron tried to stay in step with them at first, but she locked eyes with him. *This is about me and my father.* There really wasn't a place for him here. He nodded, and turned to something else.

Big Chaka embraced his son. "I saw the grendel brain scans," he said. "A month ago Tonya got bitten by a leechlike parasite, didn't she? While swimming upriver . . . ?"

Jessica led Cadmann though the streets. They rang with the smell of iron and singed plastic. There were a thousand different projects under way at the same moment. Everywhere, Star Born labored efficiently at a hundred vital tasks.

Little Carey Lou Davidson ran past lugging a bucket of plastic nails. He called "Hi, Cadmann!" and disappeared into a half-erected wood frame.

Cadmann waved back. "You've done well," he said.

"You must have been able to see most of this through Cassandra."

"Yes. That was nice, the virtual tour through the streets. But it's never quite real for me until I can feel the wind on my skin, and smell the trees."

They walked all the way through the town, back to the stone stairs cut into the mountainside. She took the stairs two at a time until they were above the rooftops, until they could see everything in the colony at one sweeping glance.

She sat him down, and took his arm, leaning her head against his shoulder.

"I wanted you to see this," she said. "I wanted you to really know that it wasn't just a pipe dream."

"I knew that it wasn't going to be that . . ." he said, and his voice trailed off. He was looking out over the mainland shantytown. From here, the individual human voices were as soft as wind chimes, and the sounds of industry dwindled to a burr. There was something of newness in the air, and it was easy to imagine that it was the beginning of a new world. Of course, in some ways it was. He could see more than the camp from here, too. From this altitude, he was looking out over a river plain, seeing the stretch of mountains gently wreathed in fog. There was a mystic quality to the scene. The land was waiting. The land was alive. Beyond the mists lay adventure, and romance.

The clouds on the horizon were a light haze shading slowly from blue to white, to blue again in the sky above. Tau Ceti burned a yellow-orange hole through the haze.

Cadmann inhaled deeply. Jessica watched as something within him tensed and then relaxed, but she didn't interrupt him.

What are you thinking, Father? She reached out to touch his arm, and felt him take her hand. There was a rough quality to his skin, a masculine smell to him, which was of infinite comfort. His face, so weathered by the elements here, so grooved by care and loss, seemed more angular to her. He didn't seem old to her now, as he often did. He seemed . . . historical. She almost laughed.

The silence stretched on, long and unnatural. Then Colonel Cadmann Weyland said to her, at last, "You may have done the right thing, but that can't make up for how it was done. Nothing can."

"Toshiro?"

"More than that."

"What could be—more than that?"

"We trusted you, then. When we found we couldn't, everything changed. Toshiro died because we no longer knew what we could expect from you. From any of you. From him."

"But he wouldn't—oh." She leaned her head against his shoulder.

"I'd have said that about you," the colonel said. "And did. Toshiro wouldn't kill Carlos. Jessica wouldn't—Jessica, I can stand being made to look a fool. Anyone who has to make decisions knows that will happen some day. But—you came into our home and took advantage of your status there. That can't happen again."

Her throat tightened.

"But there's another thing that you need to hear," he said, and his voice was surprisingly gentle. "I'm still your father, and I love you."

"Really?" she hated the sound of her own voice, the little-girl quality, the needing-Daddy's-approval quality. There was something there that she hadn't heard in her own voice for years, and she wasn't certain if she hadn't missed it.

"Really," he said. "I'll visit you here on the mainland. Both of your mothers will come over. But you're no longer welcome at the Bluff. Not now. Perhaps later, after we see what you do with your responsibilities here. Love you get just because you're my daughter. Trust has to be earned."

She reached up and kissed his cheek. Started to speak, and he said, "Shhh." She nodded, and looked.

"Is everything all right here?" he asked "Is there anything wrong?"

"What you see is what you get around here, Dad," she said.

He nodded again, and she wondered what it was that he had almost said, almost commented upon.

"Some of the First will never accept you," he said. "Will never be able to accept that you have a right to live the lives you want. To accept you as equal partners in this entire venture."

"What are they saying?" she asked.

"They suggest that you need to create your own society because you can't get along. That you have an adolescent need to beak free, regardless of consequences. It's not just the First who say it, you know. There are plenty at Surf's Up—what's left of Surf's Up—who'll say it too."

A pterodon flew past, close enough that a well-thrown rock would have clipped a wing. Cadmann watched it for a long time.

"The nest," Jessica said.

He nodded.

"But that was long ago."

A smile.

"Dad, I'd say the same thing old Hendrick did. I'd tell a child, 'Don't touch the eggs. We don't know what the pterodons will do, but you won't like it.'"

He nodded again and looked away from the pterodon to stare down across the dry rock areas to where the river lay beyond grendel range. It wound off out of sight, an old river running through a long-silted valley, a snakelike, misty ribbon.

"The wells are over there," Jessica said. "No connection with running water."

He nodded. "You've chosen a good site. I'd say Shangri-la is safe. Unless—"

"Yes?"

He shook his head. "In the military we called it 'taking counsel from your fears.' You can get so concerned about what might happen that you can't do anything."

"What's bothering you?"

"Suppose a grendel could control itself. Not go on *speed* until it got up here. I think one could make it."

"They don't, though," Jessica said. "They didn't back at the Grendel Scout camp, and that was a much better place for one to do that."

"I expect you're right."

"But we thought of that too," she said. "We have motion and IR detectors out there." She took a deep breath. "You said—we did it the wrong way, but it was the right thing. Did you mean that?"

He laughed. "I think that it's too damned easy to forget why we came. Lots of reasons, but all of us had a dream. We believed we could make a future."

"Dad—"

"Yeah, I know. You do too. And the ones we left behind thought we were crazy, just like some think that about you. Jess, what's done is done. You're here, you've got a dream. You have to follow it, just as we did."

"I don't think I ever heard you talk this way before."

"Sure you did, you just weren't ready to listen yet." He looked out at the distant, mist-shrouded peaks, and stretched elaborately.

"Want to climb them?"

"Reading my mind without permission again? We left a lot behind, you know. Not like you, here. We *really* left. We'd never go home, and there wasn't much chance anyone we'd ever known would join us."

"And no one has—"

"And no one has," Cadmann said. "And we wish we knew why, but we don't. Jess, some of the good-byes we had to say were pretty bitter, you know. But they were good-byes. Once *Geographic* boosted out, we were all there was and all there would be. We had to *trust* each other. Really trust, with our lives, later with our families. That trust was broken, once—"

"I know. Zack thought you might have killed your friend—"

"Not just Zack. Everyone." He paused to stare into the distance, and she knew that he was once again strapped to a table, drugged and helpless as the grendel toyed with him. It had happened many times before, but now Jessica felt as if he was someone she didn't know at all. He was angry, hurt, disappointed . . . and yet somehow, under and aside of all of that, there was still profound hope, and a level of trust that she wasn't certain she deserved. It hurt to look at him, and she opted to change the subject. "Are you ever sorry that you came?"

He shook his head slowly. "Not me. There weren't any wars. I have no political savvy. I wasn't going anywhere in the UN military bureaucracy."

"And what about your marriage?" she asked carefully.

Her father looked at her, smiled sadly, and lowered his eyes. "Sienna made her choice," he said. "I was the first to cheat. I was married to my job. It took me everywhere. I was never faithful to her. She knew it. I knew it. I thought that somehow . . . somehow we'd survive."

"Did you love her?"

"Very much."

"As much as you love Mom?"

For a moment she wasn't certain that he would answer; then he said, "Yes."

"As much as you love Sylvia?"

He looked at her sharply, and she didn't look away. He smiled, and the smile wavered and was gone. "No," he said. She nodded. He put his arm around her. "And not as much as I love you, either."

She leaned her head against him. Her voice dropped to a whisper. "Did I do wrong, Daddy?" Knowing that for her, the Stronghold was now on another planet.

"We all do, sometimes," he said. "But very few of us have the chance to do something great, to make up for it. You kids have that chance. I expect to watch you soar." She nodded silently. And together, they watched Tau Ceti dip toward the mountains, and darkness fall across the land.

✳

Old Grendel waited, and saw God return to the flat above the river. She wanted a closer look, but there were too many of the weirds, and they were alert. They had strung metal lace for barriers. She had seen animals touch those fences and recoil as if bitten or burned. She didn't understand such things, but was prepared to learn quickly.

She might be able to approach them from the rear. And dimly, she remembered a path.

She wriggled backward, retreating from her position. Careful. There wasn't enough water to cool her if her body went on *speed*. She had territory to cover.

31

FIRECRACKERS

Nature is but a name for an effect
Whose cause is God.
—WILLIAM COWPER, *The Task*

Cadmann woke before dawn. The rooms in the Visitors' Quarters were plain and bare, cots, sleeping bags and nightstand, bath facilities down the hall. When he came back from the toilet he wasn't sleepy. His backpack stood against one wall and for a moment he thought of getting out his mini-stove to make coffee, but decided against it. The stove's roar would wake Sylvia.

He dressed quietly and went to the mess hall to find coffee. The main room had an eastern view and he left the lights low, and scanned the horizon for the first sign of sunrise.

"Hello."

Cadmann turned to greet Big Chaka. "You have trouble sleeping too?"

"No, but I went to bed early," Chaka said.

"We all did. I've found coffee makings. Want some?"

"Please."

"Like old times. We don't go camping much now."

"Not since the children grew up," Chaka agreed.

An indifferent breeze blew down from the mountains behind them. Not warming, not cooling, just enough to ruffle the grass of the main compound, a slight ruffling of the grass in the glare of the safety floodlamps. There was a hint of light in the eastern sky. Cadmann and Chaka sat by the big window and waited for Tau Ceti to rise. There had been many times like this over the years, times to sit and think, to watch, to ruminate. Finally the first hint of light was golden blush above the mountains. Big Chaka sighed with pleasure.

"So," Cadmann said finally. "What do you think?"

"The children have done well," he said. "They have built a real community here."

"Yes. I'm impressed."

"And none too soon, I think. Avalon hasn't even begun to share her secrets," Chaka's voice was utterly content.

"This is what you came for, isn't it?"

"If you're an exobiologist, you go where the exobiology is," he said reasonably. "You know, we're probably the most interesting life-form on this planet."

"How so?"

"We should really study ourselves. Every single one of us came here because we had nothing—or not enough to hold us on Earth. I find that fairly telling, don't you?"

"You lost your family, didn't you?" Cadmann asked quietly.

"Yes." Chaka's toe drew a lazy circle on the wooden floor beneath him. "It was my fault. Food poisoning, in the middle Amazon. My family and I were there for the year conducting piranha research. There was a village celebration. They used some canned food they got from a trader."

His face tightened, but his voice was still steady. "Half the village died before we could get medical help. My wife and my daughter were among them."

"A good reason to get away."

Chaka took another deep sip. "I think that we had all just about used Earth up. I think that we all told ourselves different stories about it, but there were reasons. You were put out to pasture. Carlos is the remittance man of all time."

Cadmann grinned. "Isn't *that* the truth?" He was quiet for a moment. "How did you come to adopt Little Chaka?"

"You didn't know?"

"I never asked. One day we just noticed that he wasn't rotating out of your house."

"An accident, really." Chaka said. "We just gravitated toward each other. You know . . . it's odd, but Little Chaka might have been better suited to ectogynic birth than any of the other children."

"How so?"

"Well, he was New Guinea stock. I know that . . . I peeked. But he's huge at least partially because his parents received such fine nutrition. His father had a literary scholarship to Harvard. One of the cultural outreach programs. His mother was from Papua—a first-generation immigrant, and a national-caliber runner. Sprinted her way to a degree in poli sci. Both descended from people used to group parenting . . . as opposed to the nuclear family. Do you see where I'm heading?"

"I think so . . ." Cadmann mused.

"Most of the Bottle Babies are of northern European stock. A thousand generations of nuclear family. Which they were denied here on Avalon. And Little Chaka, who has the best resistance to that particular loneliness, had in some ways the most support."

"So you're saying he's not like the rest of them?"

"It's possible. He seems to have come out pretty well, don't you think?"

Cadmann thought of a question he had never asked. "What was your name before you changed it?"

"Denzel Washington." They both exploded with laughter. When they died down again, the first morning shadows streaked the ground outside. "When I was in college, it was quite fashionable to take African names. Who the hell knows about my real ancestry? It's all too mixed up. So I just latched on to a Zulu name, and ran with it. And I was young enough to choose the name of a warrior king."

Cadmann laughed with deep satisfaction. "A New Guinea Islander and a Chicago exobiologist both named after a Zulu war chief. That's rich."

The mess hall door opened, and Aaron and Little Chaka came in. Aaron paused in the doorway. The sky outside was just light enough to provide a background, and Aaron seemed huge, intimidatingly large. That was certainly an illusion, but . . .

Cadmann levered himself to his feet, consciously standing erect. Aaron was no taller than he, but was . . . larger. More full of life. Cadmann felt old. A baton was changing hands here, and it was impossible to mistake it, or mistake the implication.

Jessica came in behind Aaron. "Hi, Dad."

"Thanks for bringing us coffee," Aaron said. "Any left in the pot?"

"Sure," Cadmann said. "What's the schedule for the day?"

"We thought we'd show you around," Aaron said. "There's a grendel lake down at the river forks thirty klicks south of here. It looks like the grendels cooperate in maintaining dams. Like Earth beavers."

"I would certainly like to see that," Big Chaka said. "I want to give my report on the snow grendels—"

"Yeah, what did you find?" Aaron asked. "We paid high for that head."

"I believe my findings are significant," Big Chaka said. "Possibly even worth that price. But I would like to observe the beaver dam before I draw my final conclusions. Has anyone taken water samples from that 'beaver' lake?"

"No, that would be dangerous," Little Chaka said. "Is it important?"

"It may be."

"Well, we can try," Little Chaka said. "But first you should see them. They'll be most active just about lunch time. We'll go look, and you can give your lecture at dinner time."

"Good."

Cadmann said, "Sylvia complained about lack of exercise last night. She may not want to spend the day in a skeeter looking at grendels."

"That's all right," Aaron said. "There's lots around here to look at. But that dam is in grendel country, rules say to take two skeeters. Jess, how about you and Justin go as backup for the Chakas. Cadmann, if Sylvia doesn't want to go to the grendel dam, we can hike up to the lake this afternoon."

"Lake?" Cadmann asked. "How far is this lake?"

"About ten kilometers," Aaron said. "Don't worry, it's not a grendel lake."

"We thought that about half the lakes on Camelot Island," Big Chaka said. "But there was always a grendel. Always."

"Not here, though," Little Chaka said. "Guaranteed. No grendel, no samlon, and plenty of other wild life around the lake. Snouters. And some spider devils." He grinned. "We caught you some alive, but you killed them."

"They certainly died," Big Chaka said. "Something missing in the artificial ecology we set up for them. Possibly we didn't give them enough meat, or the wrong kind. We'll have to set up cameras to observe them in the wild."

"Sure," Little Chaka said. "One of these days."

"You don't sound very interested."

Little Chaka shrugged. "Dad, there's so much to learn here, and those are just bigger editions of the clothesline Joeys we have back at Eden Oasis. We've watched those for years."

Jessica came over. "The ones at Eden are interesting, though. Their mating rituals are a little odd—I wonder if these do the same things?"

"Carnivorous Joeys?" Cadmann asked. "I guess I haven't been following this."

"Well, they're related to Joeys," Big Chaka said. "Some structural differences, but yes, they're Joeys."

Jessica nodded. "The ones at Eden use those webs to catch the local equivalent of bees and insects. And birdles. I've seen them catch birdles."

"But these are larger and go after bigger prey," Aaron said. "Their bite is poisonous."

"Not quite," Big Chaka said. "That turned out to be a symbiotic bacterium that lives in their mouths."

"I wonder if they're related to the bear?" Little Chaka said.

"Bears? Son, you haven't told me about bears."

"We've never seen one, Dad. Not up close. Cassandra caught a film of a herd of chamels kicking a critter that was maybe a meter and half long, but it was in the forest and we didn't see the end of the fight. We think they killed it."

"It was about the size of an Earth black bear, so we called it a bear," Jessica said. "But they must be rare. We've never found one."

"They can't be all that rare," Aaron said. "They influenced the behavior patterns of the chamels. But we sure can't find one anywhere."

"Little herbivorous Joeys," Big Chaka mused. "On Camelot and on the mainland. Then at Eden there are larger clothesline Joeys that string out sticky ropes and catch bees and birdles to eat. Here there are even larger spider devil Joeys that can eat a small snouter. And now there's a bear? Is it related to the Joeys too?"

Little Chaka shrugged. "No data. Look, we've got a couple of hours before we go look at the beavers. Let us show you around here after breakfast."

✳

Old Grendel was as close as she could come to happiness. Contentment, perhaps. She had found the water she sought, a pool fed by water that flowed down from the mountains. Cold water. Water that came from the ground. She dove in, and swam against the water, down into a passageway just wide enough for her thickness.

As she wound through subterranean passages, through places she hadn't been since she was a swimmer, she had to conserve her energy. There was no light here, and little heat.

There was danger above, and the danger grew stronger daily. She could smell the changes, and if she didn't respond to them, she was lost. She had lived long enough to have a vague abstract sense of her own mortality. She did not want to die. In the back of her mind, she perceived how this might be prevented.

If only she could make contact.

She swam until there was no air left in her lungs. In agony, she continued. The pain in her lungs eased, became something else, a familiar sensation usually perceived as rage and terror.

There was another use for *speed*, one that the weirds had not dreamed of. It was an oxygenator, and her body could use *speed* where there was no air. It enabled her to stay underwater longer than the weirds would believe possible.

She glided. There was no light, but she could smell the currents, feel the water flow from above her, and move through the caverns toward her destination. There were times when rock squeezed her hard, but Old Grendel was a lean one, and she could contract her body into a compact missile.

Fire burned within her, a slow blaze of complete exhaustion. She had been underwater for almost twenty minutes now, crawling and swimming continuously, and moving steadily up and up. Moving. She knew that she might be crawling to her death, but she was driven to know more. The risks she took now might change everything. The weirds were intruders in a situation unchanged since the beginning of time. She had to know more about them. She had once thought of them as prey. They might still be that, but they were something more as well.

Her fear was fading now . . . and when her fear was quite gone, she would be dead. She understood that she was nearing the end of all limits, that only few seconds remained . . . and then . . .

Light above her. She moved more quickly now, holding on to the last fading traces of her fear. She plunged up into the light, up into the wavery oval, through the water, out into the air, great lungs like bellows, gulping and expanding. Life was hers once again, and she might yet cheat the great mother, death.

Time raved at her back, but she could do nothing now but breathe. There was no *speed* left in her. She couldn't fight a snouter, now.

✳

Not long after dawn, they walked northwest from Shangri-la.

A pufftree shook violently as they approached the strip of forest. Justin looked for what had done that, but there was nothing to be seen.

Shangri-la was built on a flat area. To the east the land fell away to the river and grendel country. North and west were mountains. A thin strip of forest ran along the base of the mountains. The trees grew like green puffballs of varying size, shells of branches and orange-veined leaves, hollow inside. They'd spaced themselves, leaving room for man-sized creatures to squeeze between.

"Every pufftree is a little ecology," Little Chaka said. "Each one a little different. It's better to have armor, but if you probe with a stick first you can avoid getting bitten. There's a vicious little Joey that likes to lurk in here, and where the Joeys didn't get to— Here, Dad—" He bent over one of the smaller trees and pulled the branches apart with his hands. Holding the hole open with his elbows, he poked his stick and flash inside, blocking the opening with his body.

"Nothing," he said.

Katya had a bigger tree open. She was ready to dodge away, but— "Nothing big. I can smell something ranker than Joeys. We scared them away."

Their nice little walk had turned into a mob scene. Aaron, Carlos, Big Chaka, Little Chaka, Jessica, Sylvia, Katya. . . . Justin met his stepfather's grimace with a helpless grin. Any living thing would flee the pounding of feet.

Little Chaka was investigating another pufftree. He said, "I was going to say, don't squeeze between two trees unless you've looked inside. We'd better do that anyway. It's a symbiosis. The way the trees space themselves, they can force big animals into range of the things that live inside. I've found a carnivore Joey and two kinds of nesting birdles, both vicious— Hey!" His stick poked and probed as if he were fencing, there in the dark inside the puffball. He retreated, and a big flying-saucer crab buzzed out after him; and another; three, four. Chaka was tapping them lightly, knocking each off balance as it came near, and the birdles were furious. Suddenly they all veered off and away, downhill.

Big Chaka was sitting against a puffball, laughing. It was clear he didn't have the strength for anything else. Sylvia and Katya were snerkling behind their hands, and Cadmann was suddenly into a rolling belly laugh, and what the hell. The others sat down to take a break.

Uphill from the fringe of pufftree forest was rock and low scrubby bush like things with thorns. This was serious climbing. Cadmann would have been slowing the rest if Big Chaka hadn't slowed them further. But Big Chaka was seeing things: wildflowers, an abandoned birdle nest, old and fading tracks of something bear-sized.

They'd gone less than two kilometers in the hour since they left the pufftrees.

Thirty meters away, Aaron said, "Ouch!"

"What's going on?"

"Something bit me." Aaron hopped to his feet, and slapped his chest. "Three of the darned things," he said. "Not a sting, a *bite*." Something that looked like a tiny crab or a big flea lay crushed on the ground. A second crawled away slowly.

Carlos picked the crushed life form up on the end of a foot-long twig. Enough of its insides bulged out that it adhered to the twig easily. It was thumb sized, with a sharp-looking pair of mandibles. Suddenly, its shell unfolded, and crumpled wings began to blur the air.

"Whoa!" Carlos said. The little wings beat so violently that the whole twig shook. The twig jerked and trembled, and then was quiet.

Cadmann peered at the thing more carefully. "Damn," he said, "but that was fast."

"Energetic, too," Dr. Mubutu said. "It looks a lot like *speed*, doesn't it?"

The others gathered around. "Where did you find this?" Cadmann asked. "Where were you sitting?"

They looked at a patch of ground near Aaron's feet, and found no more of the little creatures.

From a few feet away Carlos called, "Over here!"

He poked under a bush dotted with light purple, somewhat fleshy flowers that reminded him of orchids. Several of the insectlike creatures hovered around the blossoms like hummingbirds.

"Nectar?" Katya asked.

"Nope. Something stinks."

They brushed blossoms aside, and uncovered the decomposed body of a creature the size of a woodchuck. It seethed with little crabs.

"Jesus," Cadmann grunted. "Are these the local substitute for flies?"

"Bite like a bitch," Aaron said.

Sylvia took out her first-aid kit. "Let me see."

"It's just—"

"Let me see," she said.

"Yes, ma'am." Aaron unfastened his shirt.

Sylvia swabbed the wounds clean, then poured on peroxide. It foamed as if it would eat him alive. "There. It looks clean enough but—Dr. Mobutu, may I borrow your portable unit?"

Little Chaka was carrying for both Chakas. He shrugged off his backpack and unzipped it, pulling out a metallic boxy contraption as big as both his hands: a portable analyzer. Sylvia took the twig from Cadmann, teased the dead bug off the end, and dropped it into the box. She touched an oblong button on the side, and it began to hum. In a moment the bug would be flash burned, and the results relayed to the main camp and uplinked to Cassandra. With luck she would then report that there were no toxic substances—

Blam.

The miniature unit jarred in her hand. Seams popped.

They all jumped. Then Big Chaka quickly leaned forward and sniffed. Black smoke rose from the ruined analyzer.

"Dear God," Sylvia said shakily. "What was *that* all about?"

The device's shattered components barely clung together. Carlos said, "Pranksters?"

For a moment, the glade crackled with tension.

"Pranksters?" Sylvia demanded, still shaken. "What idiot would sabotage your analyzer?"

"Calm," Carlos said. "I'm sorry. I thought it was obvious. I see that Dr. Mubutu understands."

Big Chaka nodded. He turned to Cadmann and said, "Tell me . . . if you put a chunk . . . say a chunk the size of your fingernail . . . of *speed* into an analyzer, what would it do?"

"*Bang?*"

"We need to find another of these things. Don't disturb those on the corpses. We may not want to irritate them."

They had the crushed bug on the end of a stick. Justin and Katya had built a small, busy fire of sticks and bits of moss. Chaka Mubutu held the bug out over the fire. Its legs curled, its shell peeled up and—

Blam.

The sharp sound was as loud as a firecracker, and about as powerful. The tip of the stick flew into bits, and they jumped back a foot or two.

"Freeze me blind," Cadmann said.

Dr. Mubutu spoke gravely. "Excuse me, ladies and gentlemen, but I think that we can state, officially and for the record, that we have discovered a second life-form on this planet that uses *speed.*"

"What exactly does that mean?" Sylvia asked.

"I want to think on it before I say." Big Chaka looked thoughtful. "We have a lot to talk about tonight when I give my report," he said. "But now I want to see the beavers."

Carlos looked thoughtfully eastward. "I think I will follow those bees," he said. "Katya can show me the beavers another time."

32

THE BEAVERS

Bees accomplish nothing save as they
work together, and neither do men.
— ELBERT HUBBARD

"So," Carlos said, climbing steadily. *Dios mío*—he was glad for the regular fitness sessions with Cadmann. It felt as if his muscles would burst free of the bones. Torture! "How are things with young Weyland?"

Katya laughed, and held a branch aside for her father. She paused, stopping to search for the trace of a trail. She held her hand up, and whispered, "Stop. Listen."

He did, and heard the sounds of wind in the trees, and a far-off animal burr. And something else.

An insect sound. A slight buzzing.

"Look," she said. Another dead animal lay before them, this one picked to the bone. A couple of the weird bee-crabs picked over the bones. She whispered into her collar. "Cassandra, we have a visual bee sighting. Small carcass. Six or seven bugs."

"Acknowledged."

She wiped her forehead with her bandanna, and leaned back against a tree. "Well. I guess you were asking about my love life?"

"Prying," Carlos said distinctly. "I was prying."

"Yes. Well, I think that we're getting along fine. We've had some genuine moments here. I like what's happening." She smiled at her father shrewdly. "Why? Why are you so concerned about me? You've done quite well all these years, and you've never had a real relationship."

"None permanent, but some were very intense."

"But none permanent. Bobbie?" she asked.

He shrugged. "I just never got that close again. Parlor psychoanalysis might say that I don't think I'm worthy."

"And you think that I should? Isn't that a bit of a double standard?"

"You're worthy."

"Well, hey," Katya said, and blushed. She'd been watching the bees come and go from the carcass. Now she pointed. "The nest must be over there, beyond that ridge. Shall we go look?"

*

Cadmann felt most comfortable after he began to perspire. It felt as if the rust were working out of his muscles.

They had climbed high enough above the forest that he could see over it and down into Shangri-la, see and feel the pulse of life within. It reminded him of a time long before, when he had looked down on Camelot. That was in the colony's early days. He was a younger man. A stronger man. A man with far fewer doubts and aches. He was with his best friends, Ernst Cohen and Sylvia Faulkner.

She was pregnant then, pregnant with Justin. She had struggled to keep up. Not admitting her weakness, the . . .

Very real differences between men and women.

He and Ernst. How much he had loved Ernst. And how much of that love was the sort of love you feel for a faithful animal? One who never questions, never rebels, who follows you without question? Dr. Ernst with ice on his mind. Dr. Ernst, once one of the most brilliant humans alive, and now with the mind of a twelve-year-old. If that.

How much is our humanity measured in terms of our relationships? Every man feels more . . . human in the presence of a faithful animal. Or slave?

God. He hated these thoughts. And here was Aaron, so much like Ernst had been. Strong. And tall. And brilliant. But Aaron had his mind. *All* of his mind.

What he had never really had was a family.

If there were problems in that young head, well, for God's sake! The kid was only nineteen years old. What would he be doing if he were on Earth? In his second year of college? Perhaps a grad student. Or maybe he would have taken a year or two off and backpacked through Europe. Or spent a year on an engineering scholarship on one of the energy satellites?

Maybe he would have lucked out. The lunar colony. Or maybe he would have done what Cadmann himself did, and take a commission. At nineteen Cadmann was at West Point, preparing for his first command.

But no Terrestrial option would have placed Aaron in the kind of situation he faced on Avalon. He was making decisions that might well influence the whole future of humanity, here, a thousand billion miles from the cradle of mankind. Too much stress. Too much isolation. Too little support.

It was his job to reach out to Aaron. Perhaps it wasn't too late to be friends. He had to try.

✳

Just after local noon Justin and Jessica flew barely thirty meters above the river and followed it south toward the fork. It was an old river with many twists and turns, but it ran fairly straight here as it fell four hundred meters in less than twenty klicks. Tau Ceti burned brightly through thin high clouds, and Justin watched Skeeter I's shadow as it was overtaken by Little Chaka's craft. He resisted the urge to turn their trip into a race: Big Chaka was Skeeter IV's passenger, and Big Chaka hated *speed*.

Their radio crackled. "How close have you been?" Big Chaka asked.

"We've scouted by air many times," Jessica answered. "Haven't had time to organize a trip on foot. That's grendel country, and we try to stay out, because the only way we know to deal with a grendel is to flush it out and shoot it."

"And that tends to disrupt the ecology," Justin said. "Aaron doesn't like that."

"Nor should he," Chaka said.

"Yeah. Anyway, this is a genuine Avalon Surprise. We seem to find a new one every week."

They were approaching the fork where two rivers combined to become the big river that ran south past Deadwood and on to the sea. They turned to follow the northwest branch, and just beyond the fork Little Chaka slowed and hovered his skeeter. They were above a wide rough oval of blue water. At the far downstream end the hills on either side of the stream came together to form a narrows. A line of boulders stood in the water there, and behind the boulders a matted webbing of tree trunks and branches formed a dam. Broad, powerful dark shapes swam in the lake.

Justin held his breath. This was something that they hadn't even videoed for Cassandra. Little Chaka wanted it as a surprise for his father. There was a long pause. Skeeter IV hovered only twenty meters or so above the water. The water surface rippled in waves. A broad, powerful shape glared up at them. Its oddly flattened body reminded Justin of an aquatic ankylosaurus. Broad, powerful tail, triangular head. He wondered if it had feet, or flippers. One thing was certain: despite the surface differences, they were looking at a variety of grendel.

"Like a beaver dam," Big Chaka finally said, wonderingly. "It's beautiful."

Jessica and Justin exchanged smiles. "Have you ever actually *seen* one, Dr. Mubutu?" she asked.

"You bet. In Kalamazoo, Michigan, where I grew up."

"And there—" Little Chaka said. "Do you see?"

"I sure do, son." Big Chaka's voice held deep contentment, as if he were listening to a new music composition, or enjoying a good meal. "Two grendels are pushing that log into place, and another is watching us watch them. Take us closer to that spillway, please. The one on our right."

"Sure—"

"As I thought," Big Chaka said. "Note the branches placed at the spillway. They're straining the water there, but—now look at the other spillway area. A different structure."

Justin steered the skeeter to the downstream end of the lake and hovered above the dam. "I never noticed that," he said. "But look, they strain the water over there, here there's that series of pools. Reminds me of— Cassandra, what does that remind me of?"

"Searching—"

"Salmon ladders," Big Chaka said.

"Fish ladders," Cassandra said at almost the same time. "Structures to allow fish to swim upstream at dam sites. Used extensively on the North American continent on Earth."

"Cassandra. Enlarge those animals," Little Chaka said.

Jessica linked with Chaka, so that she could get the same visuals. A holographic window opened in the middle of their windscreen.

"Beautiful," Big Chaka repeated. "Just what I thought."

There was no doubt about it. There were at least six shapes in the water. A scale running at the lower edge of the screen said that they were about two meters in length. Two of them carried chunks of tree limb. Two were wedging mud into the cracks of their dam. A grendel's work is never done.

"Social cooperation," Big Chaka breathed. "We wouldn't have believed it back in the old days, but I knew that something like this might exist. Now take us upriver, and set us down about a klick or so above the dam."

The two skeeters wheeled northward. "Cassandra," Justin said. "Safety scan, please."

"I see nothing in your area. The lake grendels are concerned with their dam."

"Is this the only dam?" Big Chaka asked.

"Negative," Cassandra answered. "Prior to the recent flooding there were seven between here and the sea, and I can identify four more upstream. The nearest downstream from here is fifty-seven kilometers to the southwest."

"Thank you."

"Should we land?" Justin asked.

"I see no obvious danger," the computer answered. "I cannot answer the question as asked."

"Cancel," Justin said. "All right, it looks safe. Let's do it."

They landed on a mound of rock fifty meters from the river. Jessica was out first, grendel gun at the ready. Big Chaka had already shouldered his backpack. He darted toward the river. "I need water samples."

"Are you sure about that?" his son asked, anxiously.

"Absolutely. You don't think that these creatures would go through all the trouble to build a dam like this if they could hunt, do you?"

"I don't know. But if they can cooperate with each other, why can't they cooperate with hunters?" Justin demanded. "Oh, well." Justin swung down out of the pilot's seat and checked his rifle.

"Cassandra. What observation capability do you have?"

"Satellite Four will remain in observing range for twelve minutes, resolution one meter," the computer answered. "There are grendels in the water six hundred meters downstream. I detect no large land animals near you."

"Keep looking." The river looked peaceful. Maybe fifteen kilometers northwest, snowcapped mountain peaks stood out with startling clarity. There was another range visible to the northeast, and behind that range the Veldt stretched north and east for a thousand kilometers.

"Come on," Big Chaka called out. Little Chaka carried a handheld scanner, and a rifle slung over his right shoulder.

Justin caught up with Little Chaka. "He *lives* for this, doesn't he?" Justin scanned the river. His head swept slowly from left to right. He knew, without looking, that Jessica was doing the same.

The riverbed clay was yellowish, sun-blasted and cracked in rivulets. The warped and twisted trees along the banks suggested alternate periods of flood and drought.

"What are you looking for?" Little Chaka asked.

"Samples. The usual," his adopted father said, but there was something about his voice that said: *I'm not ready to talk about it yet.*

"Does this have anything to do with the grendel autopsy?" Jessica asked. "Or the deaths?"

"Everything on Avalon has to do with grendels." Big Chaka smiled faintly. "Maybe one day that won't be true. But for now . . ."

He knelt down and took a flask from his pocket. He scooped a small sample of mud into it. "Is this where Tonya was swimming when she picked up the fluke?"

"No, of course not," Little Chaka said. "We don't swim here. There are grendels out there!"

"Ah. Well, it will have to do," Big Chaka said.

Little Chaka looked at his scanner. "I really don't want to stay here any longer than we have to."

Big Chaka nodded regretfully. He looked down to the south. Eight hundred meters away, grendels were operating within a social contract. He would have to see that phenomenon, and study it at length.

"Maybe tomorrow, Dad," Little Chaka said softly. "Let's get out of here."

Big Chaka nodded. "Yes, I must prepare for my presentation this evening."

"Need us?" Justin asked.

"Thank you, but my son will be more than sufficient help."

✳

Justin and Jessica followed the Chakas back to Shangri-la and watched them land safely. Tau Ceti beat on them through the windshield. The air whipping through the vents seemed to have flowed over a blast furnace first. Jessica wiped her sleeve across her forehead. "Polite, wasn't he?" Jessica said. "My son will be more than sufficient—" she giggled.

"I noticed that," Justin said. "Imagine, he's embarrassed to say he wants some time alone with his son. So what do we do now?"

"We could go find Carlos and Katya," Jessica said with amiable malice.

"Dad and Sylvia. Aaron's taking them up to the lake." He banked and headed off northwest.

"I'm roasting," Jessica said. She uncorked a thermos and gulped water, then handed it over to Justin.

He drank gratefully. Even the water was warm. "Pretty fierce," he said.

She nodded, and looked back down at the terrain below them. It was broken by rock and trees, sloping up toward the mountains still to the west.

"You know what we could do?" she asked. Suddenly, her voice sparkled.

"What?"

"Let's go to the swimming hole for a dip."

"If we can find it." He thought for a moment. "Cassandra, did we tell you to label any place near Shangri-la as a swimming hole?"

"Yes. A meadow in the woods eleven kilometers northwest of your present position is designated 'The Old Swimming Hole.'" A red circle appeared on the skeeter's map display.

"That's it. Scan the area—"

"Done," Cassandra said. "No dangers detected. The area is designated safe from grendels. You are reminded to scan the meadow before landing."

"Yeah, yeah," Justin said.

The meadow was an oval a hundred meters by sixty. A sluggish stream ran through it, deep as a shoe top, and in the exact center was a circular pond ten meters in diameter.

They flew around the perimeter of the meadow. "Nothing there," Justin said. "Cassandra, you agree?"

"Affirmative."

He dropped the skeeter onto the thick grass about twenty meters from the pond that was all that remained of the lake from which the meadow formed. The meadow grass was about knee high, and not very thick.

"Race you!"

"Last one in is a rotten Scribe belch!"

Justin reached the hole only two steps ahead of Jessica, but his momentum belly-flopped him into the water.

He glared down at the dripping muck on his shirt.

"Yerch," he said. Jessica could hardly restrain herself, and finally collapsed to the shore, holding her sides and bellowing with laughter.

"You should . . . see yourself," she gasped, red-faced.

"Hah hah," he said.

He began to shuck himself out of the clothes. Wrung his shirt out and tossed it up onto the dry ground. Followed with his shorts. "This is great," he called out to her. "Come on in."

She hesitated for a moment, and then said a silent what-the-hell, and shucked herself out of her clothes and dove in.

Justin hurled a shoe, then another, then his balled-up underwear. Nice grouping.

Jessica swam with powerful strokes. The hole was only ten meters across, two meters deep at its deepest. The water was crystal clear, right down to the rocky floor. No nasty surprises lurked in the darkness.

With an uncomfortable bit of self-awareness Justin noted that Jessica's strokes were actually more masculine than his. He tended to be more fluid, almost elegant. Aaron had both qualities, and it was one of the things that let him swim rings around—

Dammit, he refused to let things get complicated. Right now life was good.

The sky was very blue, and the clouds were very white. The twisted trees framed the swimming hole beautifully. "Race you," she said. "Ten laps."

He sighed, but gritted his teeth. All right. He was faster on the land, but swimming was a toss-up.

Justin bore down, blanked his mind, and began to cleave the water. In the effort, in the struggle, both of them forgot everything but the effort, and it was a glorious day. Jessica slid up next to him in the water, and shoveled a wave into his face. He splashed back the race completely forgotten.

For the moment, both of them were completely content.

They swam twice more, and on the last attempt, he beat her. She gasped for one more race, and he declined. He was completely drained. His breath came in great sobbing gulps, but he dragged himself up onto a rock, and looked down at her.

She looked up at him, and laughed, and suddenly something in her eyes changed. "Justin," she said. "Look at your side."

Something nestled against his ribs that looked like a mass of plastic blood. It was pale, almost transparent, but was shot through with veiny structures. As he watched, the veins pulsed and engorged with blood.

"Jesus," he moaned. "More of these jellyfish things?"

She climbed out of the water. "Stop complaining. At least they're not toxic. They just want a little blood. You're being childish and inhospitable."

"Hah hah. Why don't you come up here and help me be even more inhospitable still?"

"At your service," she said, and climbed up.

The leech-things were fairly harmless, transparent, not much thicker than leaves. They only became visible when engorged with blood. Many of the rivers and lakes had them—in fact, the entire continent was generously supplied with parasites—but none had transmitted any amoeboids or other bacteria. They just stole blood.

Jessica went for her backpack, opened it, and took out a saltshaker. She sprinkled salt on the leech.

There was no pain, and Justin had time to look at her. Dammit, he wished his mind would stop that. Somehow, it just seemed as if her face had changed, or as if he hadn't ever really looked at her before.

She tucked her knees up, and wrapped her arms around them.

"Now we wait for a minute," she said.

They had been close like this many times before, ever since childhood. Nudity was nothing new or unusual for them. But now . . .

Now the curve of her back, the shape of her smile, even the dampness of her hair seemed so inviting, so . . .

Before he knew exactly what he was doing, he leaned over and kissed her. He held it for a moment. Her eyes went very wide, and then she drew back, startled.

Her eyes narrowed. "What was *that* for?"

"Just a passing thought."

"Uh-huh." He couldn't tell, but he thought that her mouth, that tanned, pouting mouth, had curled into the slightest of smiles.

The silence between them grew strained. Justin's body had several map-shaped red splotches where the parasites had fallen away. Antiseptic was swabbed on, and he felt fine now. But somehow, neither of them had remembered to put their clothes back on.

"You need to take better care of yourself," Jessica said. She ran her finger along the horseshoe ridge of muscle on his upper arm, and then, as if a sudden thought had interrupted the first, she leaned back, and turned away.

Justin leaned forward, and kissed her shoulder. Then softly, he rubbed his cheek against it. A day's stubble gave a sandpapery edge to the motion.

Then he kissed it again, and pulled back.

Their eyes met, and it was one of those moments where the rest of the world drops away into nothing, where the rest of the sights and sounds and smells of the universe simply vanish. There was nothing in the entire world but her eyes, and then her lips, and the fresh, salty taste of her mouth, and her hands whisper-soft upon his shoulders.

It was a vortex. Innocent, and light, but hypnotic. The kiss lasted for perhaps twenty seconds; then she pulled back, and there was something in her eyes that he had never seen in them before. Yearning, perhaps. And sadness. She leaned forward and kissed him back, softly, and then more urgently.

The heat was just beginning to grow when she placed her hands, her palms flat against his chest, and pushed him firmly away.

She laughed, and stood, tossed her hair, and ran into the woods.

It was a challenge as old as time, as old as the man-woman thing that drove all human life. It wasn't a race. It was *the* race. And the grand prize was . . .

He jumped off his seat and ran, laughing, into the woods, the tangled knotted, vine-hung woods that grew here on the far side of the mountains, and he saw that he could catch her. There were three reasons—one, he was a little faster, except over long distances. Second, she had to break the trail. All *he* had to do was follow.

Third, and most importantly—she wanted him to win.

He lost sight of her for a moment and—

There she was, just ahead of him. She turned her head around to see him, gave a little squeak, and . . .

Collided with a spider devil nest.

33

LOVE AND FEAR

Death, in itself, is nothing; but we fear
To be we know not what, we know not where.
—JOHN DRYDEN, *Aureng-Zebe*

They had crossed the ridge and were back in the forest. Sylvia stepped out to pass Cadmann, who was taking a little extra time to study the trees and the paths. She watched Aaron carefully. He was so tall, so well formed. His muscles slid smoothly under his tanned skin, and he moved with such confidence. Almost like some kind of machine, and her heart went out to him. She had never been a mother to him, had never offered him any of the comforts that might have made his life easier. And she yearned to do something . . . anything . . . to bridge the chasm between them.

"So . . . you come up here often?" she asked lamely, surprised that she was able to get that much out between labored breaths.

He smiled down at her. "I try to get up into the hills as often as possible," he said. "It gives me a chance to feel in synch with the land."

"This . . . is really what you wanted all along."

He nodded. A small, warm smile creased his lips. "Isn't it what you wanted? All of you?"

"I suppose so." She walked along with him for a time, wondering how to broach the one question that burned in her mind. "Aaron . . . you and I have never had much time to talk."

"A couple of wonderful dinners though," he laughed. "I can still remember the menu. Corn bread, turnip greens, prime rib."

She knew that she had invited him to the house, but for the life of her she couldn't remember what had been said, or eaten, or done. And that was a terrible pity. Her child, but she couldn't be completely certain of any single interaction. She was struck by a wave of remorse so powerful it shocked her.

"Did it . . . bother you?" she asked. "That you never had parents?"

He laughed. "What are you talking about? The whole colony was my family, remember?"

The next question was unspoken. *Did you ever wonder who your parents were? If either or both of them were here on Avalon? Did you ever look into the faces of the Earth Born, and wonder if one of us was The One? Did you ever look at me and wonder, Aaron? Did you ever cry at night because no one would take the final responsibility for you? No one would give the final damn?*

But she couldn't ask those questions. Not yet. Maybe later. Later, when she had the opportunity to get him by himself. Later, when maybe they could both get a little drunk. That might be the best choice after all. It might be the only choice.

There were more bees here.

Cadmann adjusted his binoculars, and watched as a cloud of Avalon insects fed on the corpse of some kind of marsupial. "What do you think?" he asked Aaron. "Did the bees attack it?"

"We've never seen attack behavior from Avalon bees," Aaron said irritably. "Scavenging, yes, a lot of that. I would bet you that poor critter fell out of the tree and broke its neck. The body began to decompose, and the scent attracted the bees. I don't think those are killers."

There was a steady line of bees arriving, eating, circling in a little lazy pattern abuzz with other bees (as if they were having a little community hoedown, Cadmann thought), then heading back off into the distance.

"Cassandra, note the direction of the bee travel."

"Noted. Combined with data supplied by Carlos it is now reasonable to conclude that the nest is some twelve kilometers to your northeast."

"Probability?" Cadmann asked automatically.

"Numerical estimate impossible."

"That's interesting," Cadmann said. "Your fuzzy-logic program used to give numerical estimates. What happened?"

"My exactness criteria were changed."

"Oh? By whom?"

"I do not know," Cassandra said.

"Edgar," Cadmann muttered. "One of these days I'll kill him, so help me— You said data supplied by Carlos. He's found bees too?"

"Affirmative."

"How far is this lake now?" Cadmann asked.

Aaron said, "Maybe another hour. Mostly level from here."

"And downhill coming back," Cadmann said. "Okay. I wouldn't want to miss Chaka's lecture. I—think it may be important."

"What about the bees?" Sylvia asked. "Chaka seemed very interested in them."

Cadmann nodded. "He sure did. But they'll keep until tomorrow. Here, need a hand over that rock?"

"Yes, thank you. It's strange," she said. "It's hard to believe he's the same boy you used to take on Grendel Scout overnighters. Eight years old? Nine?"

"When what?"

"The swimming competition. Remember that?"

"Where Justin nearly drowned?"

She nodded her head. "He always pushed himself so hard against Aaron."

"No need for him to do that," Cadmann said. "Justin is his own boy."

"But to be a man he had to be like his father. And you were the closest he could come."

Cadmann knew that she was getting at something but wasn't quite certain what it was. "So?"

"So . . . he watched the two of you together. You and Aaron. Just like I have. And he sees what I see."

"And what is that?"

"That you and Aaron are two of the same type. Justin wants you to love him. Aaron wants to *be you*. Which of them will really get your love? Which will get your respect? And which of those things would a boy rather have?"

Cadmann brushed a column of branches out of his woman's face. "Are you saying that I would rather have had Aaron as a son than Justin?"

"No. I wouldn't presume to say that. But maybe Justin *thinks* that you would rather have had Aaron than him. And sometimes, that's all it takes."

Was it true? Was there a place within Cadmann that preferred Aaron as an heir? Even now? More than Justin or . . .

Or Mickey? His own flesh and blood. God. He never spent time with the boy. And now Mickey spent most of his time up in the mining camp where Big Chaka did biology and Stevens was rebuilding the mining equipment. Before Linda's death, the last time Mickey had come down of his own accord was to watch Stevens get creamed by Aaron in the debate.

Great.

Cadmann Weyland, Father of the Year.

It was probably too late to do anything about that. How much of the competition between Justin and Aaron was his fault?

He didn't know. He really didn't. All that he could do was to try to heal the rift, if he could. While he could. And to that he pledged himself.

✳

Sylvia watched Aaron. He was so strong, so handsome, so very much a leader. There was so much in the way that he swung his arms, so much in the way he called back to them, that reminded her of Cadmann. Whoever this man Koskov, the one who contributed half of Aaron's genetic material, had been, she knew instinctively that she would have liked him.

She allowed herself a momentary fantasy. What might it have been like to accept the father's genetic material in the more conventional fashion. . . ?

But there was the very real possibility of damage, things wrong with Aaron that she couldn't see, sicknesses of the spirit beneath anything that she could reach. And if that was true, whose fault was that?

No one's.

So strong, so much a leader, so handsome, and possibly damaged. What kind of mother would she have been? A lot of pain bubbled up with that thought. Pain, and thoughts very different from the intellectual justifications they fed each other about the children. She should have nurtured him in her body. Let him feel her love, her fear, her longings. These are the rhythms of human life. The extreme mood swings of mothers—in a sense, didn't they train the children? Hormonal communications, saying: *This is life, my child. These emotions, the highs and the lows. Drink deeply of all of it but no matter what it is that you feel, in the midst of it . . . there is love, there is this total acceptance within my body.*

These experiences Aaron had been denied.

And this was something that she had to live with now. But perhaps, just perhaps, there was still time to do something about it. And if there was, she would.

✳

"It's the richness of it all," Cadmann said. "Everything depends on everything else. Big Chaka showed me twenty parasites and symbiotes living in just the spider devils."

"Samlon too." Aaron smiled. "Every samlon is a colony."

"And these horsemane trees are like a world unto themselves. Hel-lo!"

Those three trees stood like winter-naked beeches. Their manes lay broken, in three parallel lines. They must have fallen away in one piece and broken on impact. New manes were growing, not much more than green fur.

And Aaron was laughing. "Avalon Surprise! Funny, isn't it, how it always makes sense after you *know*. What happens is, this breed drops its entire mane every so often. It keeps down the parasites. Then it's got to survive while it grows a new mane, so it stores a lot of sugar. We've been thickening the sap by vacuum evaporation. You'll have to tell me, Cadmann, Sylvia; you've tasted maple syrup."

"It won't be the same. Not made that way," Sylvia said. "If you don't caramelize maple sugar, it tastes like sugar water. The flavor comes from half-charring it."

Cadmann had been looking about him with new eyes. "There are a lot of those. One out of four trees is growing a new mane. Why didn't I see it before? Why are they all doing it?"

"Chaka said higher insolation," Aaron said. "More sunlight means more sugar means more congress bugs and Joeys and everything else that lives in a horsemane. When the tree's supporting too many squatters, it just pushes the house over."

"We get to those rocks, I want to stop. I've got a pebble in my shoe," Sylvia said.

Cadmann looked at her a moment. "I'll just move on ahead. Aaron, I wouldn't do that in strange territory."

Aaron caught the implication. "We've been dumping *speed* in this lake once a week for the past six months. It doesn't drain, Cadmann. There aren't any grendels here. I was hoping we'd find you our bear, though."

"You mentioned that at breakfast."

"There was something like a bear here two years ago, when we did the pre-liminary. Three hundred kilos, it looked like. Possibly an overgrown Joey. We can't find hide nor hair of it now."

"Maybe it hibernates?"

"It isn't winter."

"Estivates, then."

Sylvia stopped to adjust her boot. Her eyes met Cadmann's briefly. He smiled and walked on ahead, leaving her with Aaron.

*

A dozen times, in two dozen different ways, Sylvia almost asked Aaron the crucial question. *Do you know that you are my son? Do you care?* Would it be good for him to know? Did it matter?

And because there was no answer to any of her questions, she wanted to engage his interest, his mind. She wanted to know who the young man was behind the perfect physique, the handsome face, the piercing eyes.

"What was it like for you?" he finally said, breaking the silence. "In the very early days?" He stopped, and then smiled almost shyly. "No. That's not really the question I wanted to ask."

"What is?"

"The question I really wanted to ask was why did you really come to another star?"

"I don't understand."

"I know the official answers: exploration, adventure . . . but why you? Why this particular adventure? All of you. All of the Earth Born have a conservative streak which would seem to be completely different from the high-ho adventurers that came out here originally. So . . . what's the real truth?"

She was a little startled by the question, but caught the meaning behind it almost immediately.

They told themselves that they came to capture and tame a new world. Settlers had always dealt with such emotions—and dealt with losses such as the Earth Born had sustained.

They told themselves that they grew more conservative, more fearful because they didn't know if anyone would ever come to join them from Earth. Or, indeed, if something had happened on Earth, something terrible, which precluded anyone else from following them to the stars.

But maybe . . .

"You're quiet," he said.

"I was just thinking. That was a good question. I guess if I was to answer for myself—and I certainly can't answer for anyone else—I'd have to say that I had my husband, and he had a dream. I shared the dream. Maybe not as much as he did."

"What did you lose coming out?" he asked.

"I had family. Friends."

"And career?"

"No! Avalon fits my career fine. But I think on some deep level I got pulled out of my academics by my husband."

"And then you met Cadmann?" Aaron smiled.

"Aboard ship. You know a lot about those early days," she said.

"There are a lot of diaries and journals on public record. Interesting blank spots in them, too. A lot of public video. It was easy to see that your attraction to Cadmann began while you were still married."

She sighed. "He was dashing. And I think that I'd never met anyone quite like him. And I . . . guess that it was a little overwhelming. A new world, with new sights and smells. I think that there is a part of a woman that wants to line up behind or beside the strongest, wildest male she can find, and have his children."

"But you didn't do anything about that?"

"Not until after Terry died, no."

"But you thought about it."

She had to grin. "Yes, I thought about it. Now that's enough questions, darn it." *Stop prying into Mother's business. . . .*

His smile was secretive but warm, and he broke the trail ahead of them step by step, her son making the way for the mother he didn't know.

✴

It was what mountaineers called a "hanging lake" tucked onto a ledge. The ground sloped up steeply on the south and west sides, so that long shadows fell on that side of the water well before it would be dusk anywhere else. Now those long shadows stretched across the lake, creating a false evening. Cadmann believed that he could hear the hum of nearby bees, but could no longer see them.

His war specs were on thermal mode.

The shadows went orange. The trees surrounding the lake floated in a ghostly haze. There was little there that could have been seen in broad daylight. The entire mood was quiet, calm.

A sudden movement behind the stand of trees captured his attention instantly. What the hell. . . ?

A small, bustling shape emerged from the brush. A snouter, one of the piglike things common in the lowlands and reasonably plentiful on the high plateaus. It saw Cadmann twenty meters away, squeaked, and started to turn.

In a sudden blur of motion something tore out of the woods and slammed into the snouter so fast that he didn't have time to think. He watched, fascinated, as the monster that had suddenly emerged raised its head, blew *flames* into the night air.

The back of Cadmann's neck went cold and clammy.

A grendel.

God. What was it doing *here?*

Well, in one way it was a stupid question. At the moment, it was feasting. Cadmann shouldered his rifle, and prepared to fire. The grendel stopped.

And looked up.

Directly at him. Cadmann's finger was on the trigger. He felt the tension of it, felt the trigger's breaking point, knew that another gram of pressure would send the bolt of electric death on its way.

The grendel's eyes. They *saw* him. And for the first, the very first time ever he didn't feel emptiness there. It wasn't death and destruction.

It was . . . something else. Something even more disturbing.

He waited for the grendel to attack. Why? Was he giving it a chance? Was that like some bullshit Western gunfighter credo, some small-town marshall in a bad B movie? *It's your move, Ringo. . . .*

He didn't know why, but he just couldn't bring himself to pull that damned trigger. There he stood, facing this thing with its teeth slimed with blood, its muzzle befouled with black, and the snouter's carcass still twitching in front of it. Cadmann just couldn't bring himself to move.

Cadmann heard motion behind him. Sylvia and Aaron. Aaron's rifle was off his back and into firing position—

Cadmann waved violently. NO! Aaron paused.

The grendel lashed its tail around and into the corpse. It dragged the body into the brush, and was gone.

Cadmann lowered the rifle.

"That was a grendel!" Sylvia said.

Cadmann nodded.

Sylvia looked at him strangely. "You didn't shoot. You didn't let Aaron shoot."

"We were in no danger," Cadmann said. "It wasn't going to attack us. It was just hungry."

"Yes, but—a grendel?" Sylvia said wonderingly. She turned on Aaron, blazing. "You said this lake was safe!"

"It was," Aaron said. "We were sure it was. There's no way a grendel could have got in here—"

"Except that one did," Cadmann said. "And I think that's enough excitement for the day. Let's call in the skeeters for a ride back."

Aaron nodded. "Right. And I want to ask Chaka a few questions. . . ."

✳

Old Grendel ran.

In an instant she was out of sight of the weirds. She didn't slow. She was into the blowholes before they could have seen where she disappeared. She was underwater and swimming hard before the *speed* could leave her blood. If the

Strongest One changed her mind, brought other weirds to kill her, they would not find Old Grendel.

Her life had hung by a ragged toenail. But she had learned! *That* one had not killed her. That *other* was about to kill her, and *that* one had waved her back. *That* one was the Strongest One, and she was willing to deal with Old Grendel!

They would meet again. But not here. She began to prepare for the long swim back to the river.

34

THE DEVILS SING

As lines so loves oblique may well
Themselves in every angle greet:
But ours so truly parallel
Though infinite, can never meet.

—Andrew Marvell,
The Definition of Love

Carlos paused on the far side of a glen. The bees had disappeared into the trees, and there was nothing to do until he spotted another one.

Katya offered him a drink from her canteen. They leaned against the tree together. "Let's rest here for a minute. We'll catch the next bee that comes along."

"You know," Carlos said carefully, "I really wasn't surprised that you wanted to come over here. Considering that Mr. Justin was here."

She laughed.

"Yes. That's what I thought." He paused for a moment, and Katya leapt into the breach.

"You know," she said, "Justin's great, but there's something missing."

"And what is that?"

She shrugged. "I'm not sure. But sometimes I think that all of the freedom we have has made us too blasé. I . . ." She shook her head. "I don't want to sound too retro."

Carlos's brown eyes softened. "You know, sometimes I forget that you are a woman."

"Well, thanks a lot."

"No. I mean that I forget that you're grown. It is impossible to ever forget that you are female."

She brushed a hand through her hair, shaking out a magnificently leonine mane. "Really?" She seemed cautiously pleased.

"Do you realize that this is the longest period of time that we've ever been apart?"

She nodded. "Have I changed much?"

"No. Not really. But when I think of you, I envision a little girl chasing after me, trying to get my attention. If I see you every day, it doesn't really hit me how wrong that image is. But after months . . . well, the contrast jars a little."

"I hope you like it."

"I love it. Love you. You're everything that I might have hoped for in a daughter."

She took his hand. "Is something bothering you?"

He sighed. "I don't know. Maybe I grow more conservative with age. I was always the camp rake. I had my pick of the women here—whether they were married or not."

"I'm shocked."

"Naturally. It's just one of those things that is true—women have never been difficult for me. Sex has always been natural and comfortable. There was never a lot of moral or spiritual baggage attached to it."

"Just a natural human function? That's what you always taught me."

"But understand—we came from a culture in which human beings have been limited in their sexual expression for thousands of years. The aftermath of a terrible sexual plague left Earth even more conservative. And when we finally came out of that time, there was a general celebration, a rejection of much of what had gone before."

"Sounds a lot like Avalon."

"No. It wasn't. Because remember that European culture's underpinnings were a guilt-ridden vision of sexuality. Perhaps the twenty-second century's hedonism was a healthy reaction to that conservatism—but the truth lies somewhere between the extremes."

"Meaning?"

"It may be something is lost when all of the restraints are thrown away."

"Are we moralizing here?" she teased. "Carlos? The great seducer himself?"

"I'm not talking about right and wrong. I'm asking *what works best?* People are lonely, sweetheart. And afraid. And will do anything to fill that loneliness—for a minute, an hour, a lifetime. Sex is probably the very best way to feel . . . how would you say . . . not alone."

"Sometimes," she admitted. "There are other times when it can make things worse."

He nodded his head. "I've had a long time to think about this. I think that each stage in a relationship has a different level of communication. In the beginning, both lovers are cautious, and learn about each other gradually. They share memories, take each other to favorite places, and slowly begin to touch. As they get more intimate, they communicate faster and more intensely."

"Sex is probably the ultimate," Katya said. "All the senses are engaged at the same time—"

"If you do it right."

"I'm your daughter. You expect something less?"

"Touché. What I'm saying is that two people eating dinner together can exchange virtually no information, and feel that their interaction was complete. Narrow-bandwidth communication. But sex is so intense that it seems that it just *has* to mean something. It feels as if you just learned profound and complex things about your lover."

She nodded. "We lie to ourselves about how well we know each other."

"Too often, we try desperately to believe that this other person is the missing part of ourselves—even if only for the night. Maybe it isn't love, but . . . how about . . . friendship? Caring? Compassion?"

"Let's say I agree with you," Katya said. "I'm still not sure where you're heading."

"I think I've always known that the ideal of sexual chastity was just absurd. It seemed to go against nature. Why give a young man his greatest sex drive at fifteen, and tell him he can't indulge it until he's twenty? Clearly, this wasn't nature—it was harnessing a stallion to a plow. On the other hand, you can't just rut at will, either. Back on Earth, it led to so much unwanted pregnancy and disease and disruption that it fit the image of a mortal sin."

"Women aren't men," Katya said. "We see—feel things differently. And we want more. Here on Avalon we've been free to do everything we wanted—"

"Was it enough?"

"I don't know. We thought so, but—"

He nodded. "Did you want more of a courtship ritual?"

"Something like that. Everyone knows what everyone else's body looks like. Everyone talks about what everyone else is like in bed. There might be anticipation, but there isn't much mystery."

"And you want that?"

"Part of me does. Just a part, I think, but that part feels hungry."

"What would you like with Justin?"

"You know, there *is* something, but I don't quite have words for it. We've known each other all our lives. Sometimes we've been lovers, and sometimes not. Sometimes we haven't even been friends. . . ."

"And now?"

"I don't know. Maybe it's just the discovery of a new land and all of that. But the only way to take this land is with children."

"That's the way we felt, a long time ago," Carlos said. "I think that we lost a little of that as soon as it became clear that the birth rate was going to be sufficient. But . . . on a place like this, so wide and broad, I'm not surprised."

"Something inside me just decided that Justin is the one."

Carlos let Katya take whatever time she needed to find the right words.

"Some little switch turned on by itself," she continued. "I thought that I had everything that I wanted, both freedom and security. But it turns out that I want something else. I want someone who belongs to me."

She looked up sheepishly. "Is that selfish? Is that petty?"

Carlos squeezed her hand. "No. It used to be what everybody wanted. Then we talked ourselves out of it. Maybe we're just rediscovering how much of that is in our basic natures. I've never been one to fight against my urges. Neither should you."

She grinned and squeezed his hand. Suddenly she jerked her head around, eyes darting as if tracking something invisible.

"What is it?" Carlos asked.

"Two bees," she said. "Moving like bullets."

Carlos adjusted his war specs until he saw two flashes. "They're going right across that valley," he said. "And over the next ridge." He estimated the distance. "Too far for today. Let's go back. We can start in the morning."

"I'll get Justin to pick us up," Katya said. She thumbed her comm card. "Justin—"

The computer answered. "Justin and Jessica have landed in a meadow and are temporarily out of communications," Cassandra said.

"Are they all right?"

"I have detected no cause for alarm," the computer said primly.

✳

Jessica lunged backward, trying to rip herself free of the entangling web.

The forest was all deep shadow, vines and webbing strung among horsemane trees. In the shadow above him Justin caught a face like a snarling monkey, then the compact torso and long, long limbs that went with it. The beast wasn't moving. It was singing.

And Justin had dropped his pack, and with it his tracer, his knife, and all weapons. It would take a minute to run back to get them, and in a minute the creatures would be on her.

Jessica's face was turned away from the web, she had managed to get enough leverage to turn her head. "Justin! I can see four of them. They're just big Joeys. . . ." Her voice died.

Little snarling faces. They sang with their mouths open . . . sang way back in their throats. Big Chaka had examined several spider devil bodies. Their song would have been perfect for slow dancing. Justin could make out hideous shadows moving into place around Jessica. One tapped along the web, crawling down toward Jessica.

Justin scooped up two rocks. His first missed entirely. His second struck one of the creatures, and it scuttled back up into the trees. But two others were crawling cautiously down, testing their footing every step of the way.

Damn, damn, damn. He and Jessica must be larger than anything the Joey-things ordinarily hunted, but would size alone keep them away?

Jessica screamed at them. They retreated for a moment, then started down the vine again. "Justin," she said, her voice deadly calm. "They're not scared of us. They're coming back down. Not a whole lot of doubt about that."

Justin pried at a nearby branch. Dammit, it was more vine than branch, and entirely too pliable. He tugged at it, and it just bent. It could have held his weight.

He was desperate. The loam underfoot was thick and soft; years of fallen leaves had decomposed to make the rich compost. No weapons there. He was naked, dammit.

Freezing hell! The first time in his life that he let lust overwhelm him and *this* happens?

He went to Jessica, who had managed to pry her face an inch or two away from the web. "I think," she said. "I think that maybe I can get out of this."

Justin tugged a rock out of the ground, and touched it to the web. He pulled. The mucilage was horribly strong. The spider devils were centimeters closer, and the lullaby was calming him against his will. If he had the radio, just the *radio*, he'd turn it on high and play them some old Riot Rap—

"Listen to me!" she said harshly, almost a whiplash. "You have to go back for the grendel guns. I can keep them away that long."

He had a sudden, horrific vision of the piglet, and the spidery things which injected it with venom, and then tore it to pieces.

"The hell I will."

"Justin ! "

"The instant I go, they'll be all over you," he said. "We can barely keep them away with the two of us." And the wordless music was pulling him down to fatalistic despair.

Her breath was heavier now. "Well—it's the only chance we have. I can't break the glue."

"Sing!" Justin commanded.

"Sing? Sing what?"

"Anything! *For the beauty of our land, for the beauty of the skies.*"

It was a children's song they'd learned in school. Jessica joined him. "*For the love which from our birth, Over and around us lies—*"

The lullaby wavered, warbled out of tune and faltered. Encroaching spider devils backed away. This was something new. "It works! I can keep them off," Jessica said. "Get the guns!"

"It won't hold them. *Source of all, to thee we raise, this our hymn of grateful praise—*" Justin's mind ran feverishly. "Wait a minute," he said. "Let's just wait a minute. Look at this stuff. Remember what Chaka said? This isn't made from their own bodies. It's a patchwork, and the foundation is leaves. Chewed leaves. They spread this mucilage on top of it. And everything that they catch in here must struggle, so they have to keep patching it."

"So what?"

"So Chaka said they're at the mercy of their building materials. The web is no stronger than the plant material underneath it."

"How does that help . . . never mind," she said. "If you've got an idea, you'd better use it fast. *For the beauty of each hour, of the day and of the night, Hill and vale and tree and flower, Sun and moon and stars of light—*"

The spider devils crawled toward them. Their humming changed. "They're keeping harmony with us!" Jessica shouted.

"Change the tune! *The knight came home from the quest! Muddied and sore he came. Battered of shield and crest, bannerless, bruised and lame!*"

"That's a cheerful one!"

"Sing, damn it! *Here is my lance to mend. Here is my horse to be shot! Aye they were strong, the battle was long but I paid as good as I got!*" Justin tugged at the vine.

"I don't remember the words!"

"*My wounds are noised abroad. Theirs my foemen cloak. You see my broken sword, but never the blades that she broke!*"

Justin returned to the vine he had been unable to break, and examined it soberly. "I hope to God that you're as strong as you look," he said. It was five times thicker than any of the vines used in the web itself. How old were the web's supporting fibers? How long had they been in place? What was the average size and weight of the animals these creatures fed upon?

He wrapped both arms around the vine, and set his weight, pulling it toward the web.

The spider devils changed their tune again.

"Hurry!" she screamed. She tossed her whole body violently, and for an instant the spider devil scampered back up into the shadows. "*Here is my lance to mend! Here is my horse to be shot! Aye, they were strong, the battle was long, but I paid as good as I got!*"

With an effort that racked her spine, she turned to see Justin pulling the branch after him, forcing it to bend a few inches at a time. The soil provided little traction, taxing Justin's knotted, wiry body to the breaking point. He grunted and pulled, lost ground, pulled again, and couldn't quite make it reach.

Jessica sobbed. "No use! Get the—"

And then insanity. Justin braced himself on one foot, and took his left foot and reached up, jammed it between the strands of the web.

"Are you crazy??!"

"Fuck, yes," he gasped. Using the left foot, the stuck foot, for a brace, he jumped up with the right and jammed it through likewise. He was now suspended almost parallel to the ground, holding on to the vines with his arms, his feet entwined in the web. "Think about it!" he gasped. "We've probably got five times more stress on this web than it was ever meant to hold. Fight, damn it! We can tear this thing apart!"

Jessica was certain he had lost his mind. There was nothing to do but match his insanity. "*Oh, I am a cook, and a captain bold, and the mate of the Nancy brig—*"

"*And a bo'sun tight, and a midshipmite, and the crew of the captain's gig!*" Justin continued.

Her leg. One leg was almost free of the web—it had never collided. She pulled herself back, and the whole jury-rigged mass shifted. She ignored the chittering sound from the trees. Something scampered down, darted at her with open jaws. She lurched violently and shivered the web. The spider devil retreated a foot. "*O elderly man, it's little I know of the duties of men of the sea, and I'll eat my hand if I understand how you can possibly be—*"

She stretched out desperately with her leg, but couldn't reach Justin's vine. Too late, she saw the second spider devil. It crawled down from Justin's side, and bit his thigh.

He screamed, cursed, convulsed so violently that for a moment she thought he would rip himself free. No such luck, but the monster scuttled back up to safety.

Justin groaned, and his eyes rolled up in his head. His face was dark with effort, and blood drooled from the leg wound.

"Justin!" Jessica screamed, but was distracted by a pain in her hand. A bite, and a spider devil vanishing into shadow. Flaming agony spreading up her arm.

Pain and mortal fear gave her what muscular strength could not. Or maybe Justin's struggles had finally pulled the branch close enough. Jessica contorted, and hooked her leg over the branch.

The two of them, together, pulled now. Justin's mad eyes met hers, and he swallowed. "Come on, Jessica. One, two three—pull! *Says he, dear James, to murder me, were a foolish thing to do, for don't you see that you can't cook me, and I can—and I will—cook you!*"

They heaved with every ounce of strength they possessed, screaming verses to send the spider devils scurrying back up into the trees—momentarily. But now the entire nest had awakened. Five more spider devils, curious, worried perhaps, crawled back out of the shadows. They descended delicately along the ropy, gummy vines. They'd already picked up the tune of "The Ballad of the Nancy Bell."

"*For the joy of human love! Brother, sister, parent, child, friends on earth and friends above, for all gentle thoughts and mild—*"

"*Source of all—*" Jessica stopped singing as the devils joined in harmony.

Justin screamed as another monster bit him, and she barely jerked her face aside as a pair of jaws clacked shut an inch from her cheek.

"Heave!" he screamed, and they did, both of them, and the vine creaked, and their spines creaked, and the web creaked—

The web ripped. They pulled on the vine and a big piece of web came down. Old bones tumbled out from somewhere above.

"*To thee we raise, this our hymn of grateful praise!*"

Riiiiip. The spider devils shrieked and clambered over one another to get back up into the trees. The web was coming apart rapidly now. More of the vines began to break. Now they were supported by the mucilage alone, and that wasn't strong enough. Justin hit the ground on the side of his head. Jessica ripped half free, and screamed with laughter as a big chunk of web came with her. Her arm and both legs were free, and she had the leverage to pull the other arm free of the main web. A huge patch of gummy vines still covered her. She turned and tugged at Justin's legs until she had them free, and dragged him back away from the vines. His legs were swelling, black and red. Her arm was swollen too, and numb.

"Justin," she said. "Are you all right?"

"I think I can walk."

He stumbled a couple of feet, and Jessica put her arms around him, helping him back to the water. She snatched up their comm cards. "Cassandra," she called. "We've been bitten by spider devils. Need medical attention fast."

Justin's hands shook as he pulled his shirt on. He tried to get his pants on. When his hands touched the bruised flesh of his thighs, he howled, and had to abandon the attempt.

She studied his eyes. No dilation. The swelling didn't seem to be any worse, but that told her little.

"We're about ten minutes away," Little Chaka's voice said. *"Was this the same type of spider we captured on the march?"*

"Appears to be," she said.

"Then it should be no problem. Use antibiotic paste. The bites aren't lethal. Even the paralytic effect isn't that strong. They need a whole colony to subdue something maybe twice their size. How many bites?"

"Justin took two, maybe three."

"All right. Keep him warm. We'll be there in two shakes."

Jessica unrolled a blanket from her backpack and wrapped Justin in it. His teeth chattered. "I'm not going to die, huh?"

"Only if you pull another stupid stunt like that," she said.

"You. How are you?"

She held his face with both of her hands. "Have I ever told you," she said, "that I love you?" And she kissed him, very softly. Then the venom hit and she started to shake. She let go of him before he could notice.

35

AUTOPSY

Deduction is, or ought to be, an exact science,
and should be treated in the same cold and
unemotional manner.
—SIR ARTHUR CONAN DOYLE, *The Sign of Four*

Justin limped into the recreation hall, and received a brief round of applause
and a kiss from Jessica. It was sisterly, not at all like the kiss they had shared not
three hours before, but a sparkle in her eyes that told him that she hadn't forgotten.

Katya took his arm and hugged him. "I hope that your backside is healing."

"You have plans for that?"

"Indeed." She did *not* look at Jessica.

"So just what did happen?" Cadmann demanded. "How did you get caught by
spider devils without communications?"

Justin shook his head. "Duh. We'd been swimming, got in a race, and weren't
looking where we were going. Just horseplay."

"It's not a grendel zone," Jessica said. "That's a safe area—"

"No longer," Aaron said. "Chaka, we saw a grendel in the north lake. A *grendel.*"

Little Chaka looked puzzled. "How did a grendel get there?"

"And well may you ask." Aaron's voice was icily correct. "As I recall, you were
the one who assured us a grendel could never get into that lake."

"I did," Chaka admitted. "And I still don't know how. What happened?"

Aaron started to tell him. Silence fell around him. As his hands waved and
his voice rose and fell, Justin found himself grinning. Cadmann Weyland, face-
to-face with a grendel . . . but the danger was as nothing next to Aaron's *massive* embarrassment.

Aaron broke off. "Well, however it got there, the whole area has to be reclas-
sified as grendel country. New rules for visiting it. In effect now. Everyone
agree?"

There was a murmur of approval.

"That may not be the only surprise today," Big Chaka said.

Cadmann turned to him with a frown. "Good news or bad news?"

"Listen and decide for yourself," Chaka said enigmatically.

"Yes, well, we should get started," Aaron said. "Hell of a thing about those
spider devils, Justin. Hell of a thing." His expression was unreadable.

Cadmann hugged Justin and Jessica, and they sat together, the five of them: Cadmann, Sylvia, Jessica . . . just like a family again . . . but Aaron sat on the other side of Jessica.

What would have happened if the web hadn't interrupted them? What did he *want* to happen?

"We're ready when you are, Dr. Chaka," Aaron said.

The room fell quiet. Justin grinned as he noted another table. Big Chaka, Little Chaka, Trish Chance, Edgar Sikes, Ruth Moskowitz. Interesting family grouping *there*—and Big Chaka climbed up to the holostage.

He said (his voice resonant and musical, in teacher mode), "There is much to cover, but let's begin with grendels. You have all seen that grendels on this continent, especially in this area, don't act the way grendels did on Camelot Island. There was the incident today, Aaron, a grendel that did not attack you on sight. There are the dam builders, who certainly cooperate. And the snow grendels, who seem to hunt as a pack. And your other reports. I have examined every mainland grendel observation Cassandra knows of, and I can only conclude that mainland grendels are not the mindless killers our experiences on Camelot suggested. Grendels here—some of them, at least—cooperate on dams, and hunt in groups. They show a rudimentary sense of planning. Possibly time-binding—that is, they pass on knowledge to the next generation.

"The obvious conclusion is that mainland grendels are considerably more intelligent than our island grendels were. If Camelot 'normal' grendels have the intelligence of an Earth tiger, think of those here as tigers with the intelligence of an orangutan."

Aaron nodded slowly. "Frightening, but no more than we here had concluded, right?" He looked around the room and got approving nods from many of the Second.

"Dragons," Sylvia Weyland muttered.

"Dragons," Cadmann repeated. "Chaka, an intelligent grendel is the worst thing I can think of."

"Maybe not," Big Chaka said. "First, though, a theory. Here is a Camelot grendel. Cassandra, my file, Grade Eight Test Twenty-four, please."

Laughter rippled among the Second. Grade Eight Test Twenty-four in Big Chaka's biology class was very familiar to them. The beast floated before them, a composite of many grendels the First had examined after they were torn, charred, and otherwise mangled. This was no holo of a dead beast, but a mere cartoon.

As Chaka's hands moved, so moved a white arrowhead floating in midair: the cursor. The Camelot grendel opened like a puzzle box. The view zoomed in on the grendel's big blunt head. The head opened.

The sinuses were large: a grendel's head was half hollow. The brain showed convolutions shallower than those of a human brain. There was no corpus callosum connecting left and right lobes, in fact, the grendel brain *had* no lobes. It was more of a doughnut, and the snorkel ran right through it, sliding freely in its own channel.

"Now for a mainland grendel. Cassandra, my dissection file, Composite One. This shows features common to the snow grendels we examined."

Cassandra had painted parts of the corpse with a lavender tinge.

"We had to guess at some features due to the damage done when the grendels were killed. But there's enough." The snow grendel was longer than the Camelot grendel and about as thick. Its claws were bigger, with two dewclaws that faced forward. Big Chaka pointed those out with the cursor. "Brakes." He indicated the tail and the downward-hooked barbs: "More brakes. If you're going to run two hundred klicks an hour on ice, you need that. Trivial stuff, but now note the ventral surface. There's almost no belly armor. What's left is these four head-to-tail ridges, more skis than protection."

Aaron interrupted: the student asserting his freedom. "I get it. The thing expects to squat in snow and lose heat through the belly."

"That's what we think, but notice that it can't rear up to fight. Got to charge like a tank, with its head lowered, and *butt*." The cursor outlined the misshapen head. "More armor. Like a ram. It'd work better if the head hadn't been distorted."

That head was no cartoon. This was the hologram of a dead grendel's head.

Cadmann again. "Chaka, were they all lopsided like that?"

"We're lucky to have any kind of answer, the way our kids tore through these things. My son was much embarrassed."

Little Chaka said, "I brought back some pieces of skull, but they aren't big enough to tell. Maybe they're distorted too—"

"But there was enough," his father said. "Quite enough." The skull opened: a bloody puzzle box.

The head was half hollow, as with the Camelot grendel. The right side of the brain was grossly swollen. On that side the sinuses were shrunken and the skull ballooned out. There were thin spots in the massive bone.

Near the root of the brain on the right side, the midst of the convoluted mass of gray tissue was a tangle of . . . worms.

Unmistakable.

"Parasites," Justin murmured. "Flukes."

"We've already found six kinds of parasites. Four are types that infest samlon too. Our Grendel Scouts are familiar with those," Little Chaka said. "Dad—"

"Yes. This is the interesting one. It has caused localized swelling, and some changes in brain chemistry. We're still working on those. We've already established that there are abnormal levels of the grendel analog of acetylcholines present. Now look here." The light pointer wavered on an area far from the fluke. "Notice the dendrite structure here. Very dense. Nothing like what you find in uninfected grendels. And here. Here's an uninfected grendel for comparison."

The contrast was dramatic. Where the first grendel brain had a complex web of tissue connecting different parts of the brain, the other was bare.

"Good Lord," Sylvia said. "I should have noticed—look at the bare one there. Doesn't it look as if that structure there was just made to have something wrap around it? Chaka, is that possible?"

"Is coevolution possible? Of course."

Katya giggled. "Could that fluke be, well, a *fluke?*"

"It could be, but I doubt that. We have examined three other parasitized grendels, and have found similar changes in them."

"And these are grendels which behaved abnormally?" Cadmann asked.

Chaka nodded. "We believe that the parasite might be interacting in a symbiotic manner, stimulating brain growth, promoting a higher order of intelligence. It's not an unmixed blessing though. One of those grendels must have been dying. The brain case was filled and the skull was being torn apart from internal pressure."

"So they have to be infected young?" Cadmann said.

"Just so, when the skull is still soft, still growing."

"Coevolution," Sylvia said. "Tens of thousands of years—"

"Or longer."

"Or longer. We never found any of those flukes in island grendels. Did we? Cassandra, grendel history. Gross anatomy. Abnormalities in brain structures of island grendels?"

"One with what appeared to be cancerous growth. Nothing else," the computer said.

"So, no flukes on Camelot," Sylvia said. "Are they common over here?"

Big Chaka waved again and the river fork appeared in relief. "Here," Big Chaka said, holding his voice steady against age, "the beaver grendels. They're not hunters. They're fisher folk. They're also cooperative, and a lot more intelligent than the grendels on Camelot were. That much is certain." He paused, and smiled thinly. "And this afternoon we found the same parasites in their waters." He displayed the image. The parasites were flattened ovals, something like a tapeworm. A ruler appeared beside one of the flukes: ten centimeters.

"The waters north of here swarm with them. We don't know what this means. Maybe something very bad. Maybe good. An intelligent grendel might learn that attacking humans means death. Such creatures can be taught. An intelligent grendel is also one which can travel further from its home waters without burning to death."

"Every silver lining has a cloud . . ." someone said.

"We will continue to look into this as we evaluate your new data."

"What about the bees?" Aaron called. "You said earlier today this might involve bees. I've been wondering how?"

"Patience," Chaka said. "I'm only now forming a theory. Note we have an abnormal grendel. We thought we understood grendels, and now it turns out we don't."

The cursor flicked, and the dissected grendel disappeared. Now they were looking at a delta-wing crab twice as large as a watermelon: a magnified "Avalon bee."

Big Chaka said, "Now, the bees are a problem of an entirely different order. They aren't really bees, of course. They're a flying version of the Avalon crab. They are highly organized. Some varieties are carnivorous."

Sylvia exclaimed, "Oh, don't tell us they're parasitized too!"

Chaka Senior smiled thinly. "No. I wouldn't do that. But they certainly have a level of organization that wouldn't embarrass any terrestrial bee colony. And that may be enough. Intelligence need not be the product of a single brain. A colony can behave intelligently."

He paused for a moment. "Indeed, in many ways you and I are colonies of dissimilar cells, and our—minds—may be the products of a number of independent actors. So may it be with infected grendels—and with bee colonies as well."

"Minsky," Little Chaka muttered. "A society of minds."

"You said a problem of a different order," Cadmann said. "What did you mean?"

"I think it is now clear that these are the creatures which killed Joe and Linda Sikes."

There was a general murmur, and Justin saw Edgar Sikes's head come up. Edgar's fingernails must have been digging holes in the wooden table.

"Please explain," Cadmann said.

"Look at this," Little Chaka said, and the cursor danced over the image. It didn't look like a terrestrial bee at all. "A tough shell that sprouts fixed wings for gliding. Motor wings aft. The forelimbs are modified as claws. The key was my son's recording of this activity." The cursor moved again, and now there were animated holograms of a swarm of the beelike creatures feeding on a dead grendel. With the grendel to give perspective they could now see that the "bees" were actually the size of Sylvia's palm, plum-sized, five to seven centimeters across: much bigger than the thumb-sized leaf cutters around Paradise. "They scavenge on grendels."

"So?"

"So . . . so if a grendel dies, burns itself up with *speed*, it isn't going to completely expend the oxidizer. The scavenger which eats grendels is going to have to develop a mechanism for metabolizing *speed*."

"Good Lord," Sylvia said.

Big Chaka slipped his glasses off, and polished them carefully. "What we think is that the bees . . . or whatever we decide to call them . . . are an order of necrophage flying pseudocrustacea. They like grendels for food, and either scavenge them, or trap and kill a grendel who can't get to water. Further, I believe that they've done it for millions of years, long enough to have either evolved a means either to produce *speed* themselves, or to store it. Store it and use it."

"Bees on *speed*," Cadmann said slowly. "*Carnivorous* bees on *speed*. Christ on a crutch."

"What in hell is a bee?" Hal Preston asked.

"Come on, you know," Katya said. "There are hives of them out by the berry farms. Bees, you know, they fly and if you get too close to the hive they sting? You need them to fertilize fruit trees—"

"Here!" Edgar Sikes cut in impatiently. Among the holograms around Big Chaka appeared another: a Terrestrial flying insect as big as a dog. "Dr. Mobutu, you had to have *some* reason for calling them *bees?* And it sure wasn't the way they're built."

"No, it was the way they *build*," Big Chaka said. "Earthly bees make elaborate nests. They collect nectar from local plants and use it to make stuff they can store. They're stratified into castes, with a queen to lay all the eggs and drones to fertilize her and myriads of workers. Well, we know that these Avalon bees are stratified, though we don't have details yet. We've only studied the leaf-eating bees, but their nests are like underground cities. Edgar, they even have the bee trick of using antibiotics. Do you remember that?"

Trish touched Edgar's elbow; he bit back a venomous answer. "'Fraid not, Doctor."

"Honey would rot if bees couldn't mix the nectar with an antibiotic. Some Terrestrial bees even make their honey from carrion. Most Avalon bees make their honey from leaves, but they have their own antibiotic, and again, they can use it to preserve meat."

Edgar sat down abruptly. He looked gray. He'd be seeing the same images that were running behind Justin's own eyes. *Linda Weyland and Joe Sikes thrashing within a dark fog; red-and-white bones falling to the ground; a fading buzz-saw sound as the black fog blows clear. Ten thousand flecks of human flesh flow into the ground to become dark incorruptible pools of viscous fluid. . . .*

Whispered conversations buzzed around him. Justin noticed Jessica staring at the holograms, frowning at what she had heard. Then, tentatively, she raised her hand. "Chaka. If we assume that the bees have been around for, say, a million years . . . mightn't that explain what happened to our mining apparatus?"

The room was dead silent.

Aaron was the first to speak. "Freeze me alive! You've hit it! Fossilized bees in the coal? The *speed* might act like flecks of dynamite under circumstances like that—"

Suddenly the entire room was vibrant with discussion. Aaron stood in the middle of it. "I think that this is cause for celebration," he said.

"Why is that? These bees—"

"Don't you see? I think that we are entitled to an apology. For months, one ugly question has hovered over the entire colony: Who sabotaged the mines?

"And there was a second question: Who or what killed Linda and Joe? Now we've answered both questions. The bees came through the pass— Cassandra, what were the weather conditions at Deadwood Pass when Joe and Linda were killed?"

"A hot dry sirocco wind blowing from the western high desert."

"Sure," Aaron said. "And that's what did it. The wind picked up a swarm, blew them across the desert and over the pass. Linda and Joe had the bad fortune to be in the way. They were stripped to the bone in minutes by starving, disoriented necrophage bees."

Sylvia looked devastated. "We were so careful."

"Careful to avoid the Avalon ecology rather than understand it," Cadmann said. "And that one falls right into my lap. I thought we could do it. I thought Deadwood Pass was safe. Oh, Lord!"

"What?"

"Eden Oasis. Just luck the wind didn't blow that way while it was full of Grendel Scouts! The worst of it is, I knew all along the only real safety was in understanding what we faced, and I didn't do anything about it."

"I didn't want you killed by the dragon," Sylvia whispered.

"We all thought the same thing, amigo," Carlos said. "We did." He gestured toward Aaron and the others. "They had a different view."

"But you do see the danger?" Big Chaka said carefully.

Aaron nodded. "It's a real danger, but being eaten by bees is no worse than being stung to death by a colony of them back on Earth. Individually, they are probably pretty harmless, and anyway they generally stay in the lowlands where we don't go. In some circumstance that we don't completely understand, they swarm and can reach highlands like Deadwood Pass. Fine. We will study them, and become aware of them. We can build shelters. And now, more than anything else we need to find out—why did Cadzie Weyland survive?"

There rose a buzz of speculation. Big Chaka cleared his throat. "We need to learn more about bees."

"So let's go on a bee hunt!" Carlos cried. "Katya and I know where to start in the morning."

"Not alone, though," Aaron said.

"We will not leave the safe area—"

"I'm afraid there is no safe area," Aaron said. "Not since we saw the grendel this afternoon. Chaka, just how could a grendel be there?"

Little Chaka shook his head. "I have no idea. I would have taken a mighty oath that there was, there could be, no grendel there."

"Avalon Surprise," Sylvia said.

36

BEE HUNT

Linnaeus, Carolus, 1707–78, Swedish botanist and taxonomist, considered the founder of the binomial system of nomenclature and the originator of modern scientific classification of plants and animals. In *Systema naturae* (1735) and *Genera plantarum* (1737) he presented his classification system, which remains the basis for modern taxonomy. His more than 180 works also include *Species plantarum* (1753), books on the flora of Lapland and Sweden, and the *Genera morborum* (1763), a classification of diseases.

–*The Concise Columbia Encyclopedia*

Cadmann watched the skeeters take off, then returned to the dining hall to rejoin Sylvia. "Bees," he said. "I can't get over it. We were so bloody careful! Divert the streams, build grendel-proof shelters. Satellite observations. Nothing could get to Deadwood Pass—how could we know a swarm of Avalon bees would blow over that pass?"

She reached across the table to take his hand. "It wasn't your fault, you know."

"The hell it wasn't. We had all the clues, explosions in the mines, and instead of coming over here to look for the real cause we wondered how the Pranksters could have done it."

"More my fault than yours, then," Sylvia said. "I'm the biologist. And I never guessed. Cadmann, stop blaming yourself."

"Sure."

The comm card chirped.

"Cadmann here."

"Amigo, we have it."

"The nest?"

"A nest, certainly."

"How big is it? How close are you?"

"I'm looking into a long valley," Carlos said. "I'd see more from a peak—Cassandra, *that* peak—Cad, the valley runs northeast from here, with a meadow down the center. The peak, call that Spyglass Hill for reference, is at the southeast end, forty-three kilometers distance bearing two-sixty-five degrees from Shangri-la. It's a long flat valley nestled in between ridges. There's a shallow

333

stream. No indication of grendels. Let me say that again, no indication of grendels."

"There wasn't any indication of grendels at the lake up there either," Cadmann muttered.

"I have not forgotten that. The nest is below the peak. It's the size of a hill, a lumpy hill with no sharp edges to it, ten meters at the tallest. It's big, I make it ninety meters by a hundred and eighty. I'll make my way to the top of Spyglass and get a better measure, but it's big. Cad, it might not be the only nest. We've all converged on this valley, six search parties following bees, and we all ended here."

"*Compadre*, that implies a lot of bees."

"You know it, Colonel."

"Okay, we'll come look." He glanced at Aaron . . . but Aaron didn't try to interrupt, and this wouldn't be Cadmann Weyland's first siege. "We need poison gas . . . wouldn't it be nice if they had a ton of cyanide sitting in a warehouse?"

"No cyanide, but we do have some good insecticides," Aaron said. "You insisted. Remember? Do you think we will need them?"

"Probably not. Carlos, don't get too damn close to that nest. Bees protect their hives, and Avalon bees have a similar lifestyle."

"It's very likely they will," Sylvia said. "There would be strong evolutionary pressure to do that. Carlos, he's right, be careful."

"You know it."

✳

"Here," Carlos called. "Follow the coffee smell."

Carlos had a full campfire going, with long sticks poking out of it, and a coffeepot braced on the sticks. Pouring, he said, "I thought I might want a torch right handy. Those bees are like little flying firecrackers, don't you think? Your people used to celebrate the Fourth of July that way, before the Green laws got so anal retentive."

Cadmann sipped, looking down through war specs.

The bees were big enough to see as individuals, even from here, from a hundred and twenty meters away and uphill. There were thousands. The nest . . . hard to tell where it ended; the edges faded out into low bushes and tall swamp grass.

Magnify. "There are several varieties," Cadmann said. "Most are under ten centimeters across, but there are larger ones too."

"Possibly soldiers," Sylvia said. "Terrestrial ants and termites develop lots of different forms. I never heard of bees doing that, but I don't suppose there's any reason they couldn't." She moved up beside him and adjusted her war specs. Then she shuddered. "They don't look dangerous."

"Even so, I would not care to go down there and dig up the nest," Carlos said.

Cadmann continued to study the valley. "There doesn't seem to be much that's moving down there," he said. "Except for the bees."

Aaron fished out his comm card. "Aaron here. Who's on duty?"

"Trish Chance."

"Trish, we need things to happen fast."

"Gotcha."

"There are a lot of these things here. They don't look dangerous, but how would we know? Look to the arsenal. Flamethrowers need to be charged up. Think about anything else we can use. And what skeeters do we have?" Aaron demanded.

"Three charged up. One out. It's been cloudy, and the batteries—"

"Right. Okay, hang on to one for equipment. Cassandra, what small mesh nets are available?"

"Four of the twenty-meter nets, one damaged. The others would not hold a creature of the size described."

"Thank you. Trish, get somebody to bring out those nets. Cassandra, please keep available a current display of nest locations as they are reported."

"Done. Ask for NETMAP."

"Netmap, please," Cadmann said.

His war specs dimmed, and when he looked out into space he could now see a projection of the valley. A blinking net of bright lines surrounded an irregular mass that looked vaguely like an African termite nest. Dimmer lines indicated areas where more nests were suspected.

"Thank you. Enough."

The image faded. Aaron still asked questions and gave orders. *Doing as well as I would, and he knows what's here. He'd have been a good officer back when we had wars.*

✳

Three skeeters rose from Shangri-la. A fourth, not yet in, would take off as soon as various factions could agree as to what should go aboard.

"I just want to be sure we learn everything we can from here," Cadmann said.

"We have to take it to the bees sometime," Aaron said.

"I know. Cassandra, is there any way we can get an ultrasound map of the inside of that thing? Before we open it up?"

Carlos said, "Cad, I'll go off down the ridge if you'll give me the war specs. Give Cassandra a view from some other directions."

Cadmann pulled the specs off his tired eyes and handed them over. "Have you got a flashlight?"

"I do," Katya said.

Sylvia said, "Want some company? Yes, Cad, I have a flashlight."

As the three receded, Aaron said, "They must find this stuff pretty dull."

They hate arguments, Cadmann thought. "I love it myself," he said. "Planning a siege. Aaron—"

"I'd go in now."

"I wouldn't even try to take out a *wasp's nest* at night."

"They'll be torpid," Aaron said.

"We'll wait," Cadmann said.

Unsettling shadows fell through the valley. To Cadmann's tired eyes, the bees were no longer visible as bees, only as swirls of motion. There were more now, streaming back into their nest.

Pterodons, much bigger, still wheeled in sunlight. "Those must stick to the heights," Aaron speculated.

Sylvia said, "And fall to the bees when they get old and sick." She shivered. Cadmann fished a windbreaker out of his pack and helped her into it.

Bigger pterodons yet were converging above. These pterodons had never seen skeeters, and the sight gave them fits. One skeeter wheeled off and began to circle the valley. Three more followed each other down to Beehive Peak.

They unloaded tents and safety domes and crates of electronic gear, as well as tanks of insecticide. He watched a grinning fifteen-year-old lugging a box of thermite grenades.

He was a little alarmed to see someone as young as Carey Lou this close to danger, but he kept his mouth shut. He'd just have to try to insure that danger was kept to a minimum.

"Everybody carries a safety sack!" he bawled, and there were no disagreements. If Carey Lou dropped his for even a second, he would tan his hide!

His comm card was talking: Trish. "Dammit, I say we attack it tonight. They won't be as active."

"You heard Colonel Weyland," Carlos said. "We can't see well, we don't know what we're up against. It's insane not to wait for daylight—"

"All right. Let's say we wait for daylight," Evan Castaneda said reasonably. "What then? We don't have enough poison to take out one of those things. I think we should postpone the whole thing, go back and cook up about a hundred gallons of nerve gas—"

"We need to study them—"

"We'll study their corpses! These things killed Linda! And Joe—"

"Ah, I think—" Aaron tried to say.

Carey Lou broke in, his thin, reedy voice excited. "Wait a minute. We learned it in school, we used Foo Foo gas on a grendel twenty years ago. Like napalm, right? We can hit 'em with that, like in the movie Them. Drive 'em down into the nest, pump more in the top, and just cook the sonsabitches!"

The group fell silent, awed by the purity of their youngest member's bloodlust. Aaron's face had darkened.

"We appreciate your sentiments," Cadmann said reasonably. "But try to watch the language."

"Oh, yeah," he said sheepishly. "Sorry."

The last skeeter settled near the others. Little Chaka eeled out, turned to help Big Chaka. "There is," said Big Chaka, "definitely another nest at the north end of this valley. Maybe three or four."

"Damn," Cadmann said. "Cassandra, get together with the Chakas and make some maps. We don't want to rile more than one nest at a time. Trish, you still on? How close are we to having those nets? I want to look them over."

"Listen," Big Chaka began. "About your assault. Have you considered—"

"Freeze it. Consider *this*," Aaron snarled. He had a thermite grenade in hand, and twisted it atop his grendel gun.

Cadmann said, "Hey, kid—"

Aaron fired downslope.

His war specs spoke to Carlos in Cadmann's voice. *"Carlos! Katya! Get back here fast! Get to the skeeters!"*

"We're nearly back. What—"

Katya gaped down at the mound, her jaw dropping.

"Aaron fired an incendiary into the nest!"

"What? Why?"

Answer came there none. It was the kind of question that can cause strokes.

The beehive's peak erupted like a volcano. Puffs of flame, first, and then swarming points. Thousands of points of fire streaked away like rapid-fire tracer bullets, and exploded in tiny flashes.

Other parts of the mound erupted too. (Katya was sprinting, but Carlos couldn't do that and watch too. Cassandra's record depended on his war specs.) The peak of the beehive was 120 meters distant, but the hive had more exits, more showing every second as fireballs followed by swarms of tracers. One source was only fifty meters downslope, and that next was closer yet.

The terror wasn't the flaming bees, Carlos realized. Those made a hell of a light show, dying in vengeance for Linda Weyland and Joe Sikes. Carlos shifted his war specs to infrared.

The firepuffs were almost blinding. But there they were, the bees that weren't burning, flying in all directions, tens of thousands of bits of red-hot shrapnel looking for any enemy at all. A thousand abruptly converged in the air like an explosion in reverse, and that poor bloody pterodon wouldn't reach the ground as anything but bones. Carlos broke into a run, watching his feet and to hell with Cassandra, there were cameras on the skeeters.

Aaron was grinning like a grendel. "It didn't take all that diddling around! All it takes is one incendiary round per beehive! Flying firecrackers, Carlos said—"

Cadmann boosted Sylvia into one of the skeeters and pulled himself after. "Start the motor on idle."

"Trish, no problems?" He laughed at his buzzing comm card, Trish attempting to chew him out. "Right. Cadmann, there's a time to just *do something*. There's another nest confirmed, right? So when we go after that one tomorrow, we'll know a lot more about beehives than we knew ten minutes ago. Here comes Katya."

With Katya were both Chakas, looking madder than hell. Aaron's buoyant mood began to deflate.

Big Chaka's voice was tight and angry. "What in the hell was that all about?"

Aaron explained. "I was getting revenge for Linda and Joe, and killing about ten thousand dangerous animals. And I'm going to kill fifty thousand more tomorrow, right, Cadmann?"

Cadmann was watching the Chakas. "I don't think they agree."

Little Chaka looked at Aaron with open irritation. "If this planet has taught us anything, it's the danger of mindlessly throwing an ecology out of balance. Under normal circumstances these things don't hurt human beings. But guess what? Two klicks from the north end of this valley is a river. For twenty klicks east and west, we have had unusually low grendel sightings. Doesn't that suggest something?"

Aaron looked as if he wanted to choke. "Suggest *what?*"

Little Chaka's voice was infuriatingly reasonable. "I think that the show is over for the evening. Let's go back to Shangri-la. We can go bee hunting again tomorrow, but this time, let's go to find things out. We can always kill them."

"They're the enemy," Aaron said.

"They may well be," Big Chaka said. "But they are also a largely unknown enemy."

"What my father is saying," Little Chaka continued, "is that we don't know enough, and until we do, *leave the bees alone.*"

Aaron met Little Chaka's gaze for a blistering ten seconds; then something shifted between them, and Aaron was the one to nod acquiescence. "All right," he said finally. "All right."

37

THUNDER

The best of men cannot suspend their fate:
The good die early, and the bad die late.
—DANIEL DEFOE

Edgar looked up from his computer screen to find Trish glowering at him. He said, "I take it you got my note."

"Note. Yeah, note, I got your fucking note."

"Gotcha! Hey, I didn't intend it to make you *that* angry. I have to go back to the island. They need me. Ruth needs me."

"Ruth Moskowitz is a *lame*. What has she got that can even hold your attention?"

"Trish, look up a name. Pygmalion."

Trish sipped past the white foam on her cup. Toshiro had taught her calm. "Who was Pygmalion?"

"Greek sculptor. Made a statue of a woman, then fell in love with her. The gods brought her to life to stop his whining. Trish, what did you see in a lame like me?"

"Power, dammit, Edgar! I saw you make a hurricane!"

"You were already in my pants."

"Yeah. Well. Aaron needed you. Not just the hurricane, he needed you to shut up about how bad the weather's getting. Otherwise the Star Born might wait it out before they came back here. So he told me to distract you."

"Distract," Edgar said.

"Well, I don't think he . . . hah. He'd dumped me for Jessica, but he never stops screwing any woman. I was ticked. *How* I distracted you was the *last* thing he expected. After Toshiro died, he kind of hinted that I could kind of let you alone."

Edgar grinned. "Do you mean to say we've been cheating on Aaron?"

"Yeah. Pygmalion, huh?"

"Yeah. You shaped me, Trish. Then you kind of lost interest because I didn't need you quite so much—"

"—And you'll drop Ruth!" Trish wrapped her hand around his wrist as he was about to speak. "When you've really put her back together, you'll know it. You'll lose interest. Then come brag to me, Soft One. I may have sculpted some Scouts by then, but I'm always open to a brag."

✳

Perhaps a dozen pairs of human feet had passed this way before them: not enough to actually create a path, but enough for the broken twigs and turned earth to mark the way easily. Aaron or Little Chaka led, Cadmann in the middle or taking the rear.

Again, this was disorienting. How many times had he broken trail for these boys, while they tromped loyally behind? Too many to count.

He watched Chaka. The big shoulders, the broad hips worked steadily as they climbed the path. He felt perfectly comfortable with Little Chaka. He had seen Chaka angry, sad, happy . . . in the full spectrum of human emotion.

He watched Aaron more carefully. More carefully now than ever. Aaron was getting everything he had wanted.

True, it had cost Toshiro his life, and almost torn the colony apart, but Aaron had what he wanted. There was something vastly self-satisfied and relaxed about him, similar to the attitude of a man who has just enjoyed really great sex. And for Aaron, perhaps that analogy wasn't wholly inappropriate.

Aaron whistled tunelessly as he led. There was something about him, something not quite . . . connected to the ground that he trod. *Above it all.* That was Aaron. *Above it all.*

And in that moment, for reasons that Cadmann couldn't be quite certain of, he knew that Aaron had indeed seen all sides of the *Robor* incident before it ever happened. Knew that Aaron realized that death was the probable outcome. There was no way to prove it, but Aaron had used them all, all of the stresses, all of the arguments, all of the efforts.

From the very beginning, it wouldn't have mattered how things turned out. No matter what happened, Aaron Tragon was going to win.

Eventually Aaron's will and most secret plans would control the colony. The foundation of Camelot was the group efforts of a hundred and seventy people, based on principles voted and designed before they ever left Earth. But here . . .

Like it or not, the entire colony would be the outgrowth of one man's personality. One increasingly disturbing man.

He watched Aaron. Step after step. As perfect as a machine. His body perfect. His mind as remote and inaccessible as the farthest misty peaks of Avalon.

By the time they stopped for lunch, Cadmann's mood—if that was what it was—had burned away with the early haze.

They sat on an overhang looking down on Shangri-la a thousand feet below and twenty kilometers distant. The domes and rectangles of the camp stretched out beneath him.

"Penny for your thoughts," Aaron said comfortably.

"I was thinking about the early days," Cadmann replied. "God, it seems so long ago now."

Off in the distance, a pterodon swooped down after a birdle. The birdles were known to invade pterodon territory. Birdles were herbivorous, and the pterodons carnivorous, but the birdles spoiled hunting, scared away prey. So mated pterodon pairs swooped and squawked, gained altitude and buzz-bombed the giant beetles, driving them away. The efforts were never effective beyond a day or so. Birdles were tenacious.

Aaron watched him, an indefinable sadness in his eyes. "What happened, Cadmann?" he said at last. "I remember you, back in the old days. You were full of fire. You're not old. But you're starting to think you are."

Cadmann laughed. "Older than you think, boy." Aaron was right. There was something different about his attitude. He was thinking of everything in the past. Looking back like . . . an old man. Christ. When had *that* happened?

"It was *Robor*," he said finally. "It was getting there too late. It was killing Toshiro."

Chaka tried to interrupt, but Cadmann shushed him. "I'm not interested in technicalities, Chaka. It shouldn't have happened. And it's also the physical pain. I hurt myself up there. I still feel it. I'm just not the man I used to be."

Aaron gazed at him, and for a moment . . . just a moment, for the first time in Aaron's adult life, Cadmann had the very distinct feeling that something had really registered in there. Something had been touched emotionally. There was no joy, no triumph in Aaron's face.

"I'm sorry about that," Aaron said. "I never intended that to happen."

I may have intended to rip the colony apart. I may have intended to steal an invaluable piece of property. I may have not given a damn if one of my friends died—or you died, Cadmann.

But I never intended to break you. That I would not have done.

It was utterly strange how clear that voice rang in Cadmann's head. Strange how certain he was that that message passed from Aaron's mind to his. Strange. It was an apology of some kind. And odder still, he found that he accepted it.

They studied each other for almost a minute, and then, hesitantly, almost shyly, Aaron smiled. Then he stood, and held his hand out to Cadmann. "Come on," he said. "Let's keep moving."

"If I don't, I'll stiffen up." He dusted his pants off. "Don't ever get old, Aaron. It's no fun at all."

"I'll keep that in mind," Aaron said, and again, they both laughed.

The conversation ceased as they toiled up a mountain crest. Cadmann was beginning to enjoy himself. These kids were stronger and fitter, but he knew how to use what he had. Knew how to relax between steps, husband his resources.

They stood up at the crest for a few minutes, sipping water, and breathing hard, looking down as if they were titans bestriding the world. All of Avalon seemed stretched out beneath them. They might have been balanced between worlds. To the east, grendel country, and the forests and savannahs that would eventually be crisscrossed by the roads and cities of an expanding human empire. To the west, desert and terra incognita.

Who knew what existed out there? Sandworms on *speed*, maybe.

Directly below them now, a branching curl of river, a ribbon of blue down at the base of the mountains. "We're going to a little valley we've spotted from *Geographic* and mapped by skeeter," Chaka said. "Nobody's done it on foot, and we need to look around. There's running water, but we won't get close to it."

"Grendels?"

"You bet. Lots of samlon. Last time through, it was fairly *working* with them. I think it's getting to be that time again."

"Damned glad your bloody base camp isn't near running water."

Aaron chuckled. "No. You wouldn't have let us do that, Cadmann. The First would let us get away with anything at all, as long as we carry those great stinking stacks of Cadzie-blue blankets; but not that. And even when the weather changes, and the rivers swell, we're not likely to get grendels. Too far from the water."

"Of course, if it's raining hard, that will cool them just as well."

"This is true," Chaka admitted, "but we've got our defenses, and our shelters. And there are no guarantees."

"No there aren't. I'm not even sure I wish there were."

They descended the ridge, making their way down toward flatlands. A small valley was visible now, a verdant crease. Chaka guided the conversation as they walked.

He pointed to the eastern horizon. "Storm clouds?"

Chaka and Aaron studied the cloud patterns. The clouds were moving south, and unlikely to bring rain or grief to Shangri-la. But there had been small storms, little atmospheric disturbances almost constantly for the past month. What was coming was coming faster, that much was sure.

"The weather's never been like this," Cadmann said.

Aaron said, "I finally did get to Surf's Up. Absolutely scoured by waves. They had to move all of the kids back to colony. Most of the beach houses are gone. Mine too. There's nothing but foundations left."

They talked broadly and companionably of weather and atmosphere, climate and crop conditions, blue skies and hailstorms, for almost an hour as they descended to a glade. Chaka pointed to an ancient, overgrown mound. "I saw this from my skeeter."

Cadmann approached it cautiously. "Bee hive?"

"Yes. I wasn't certain from the air, but it looked abandoned. Weathered. Maybe they migrate. Maybe they raid an area for everything it has, and then die out. I don't know."

Aaron nudged it with his toe, thoughtful. The mucilaged earth tower crumbled a little. He pushed against it some more and a chunk of it broke off. "It's brittle. Resistant to most weather, though."

"How long abandoned?" Cadmann asked.

"A year or two," Aaron said.

"Look! A cluster of Joey bones." Chaka was up in one of the trees, peering around.

Cadmann grunted and dropped his backpack, climbed three or four meters up the trunk, alarmed at how heavy and clumsy he felt.

A trio of little Joey skeletons greeted him. They were snugged between branch and bole, dead in their own nest.

"Definitely bee country," Cadmann said soberly.

They continued along, spotted several more abandoned bee nests and more caches of old skeletons. Often the bones lay as if carefully placed by some nit-picking archeologist. Bees didn't leave enough on the bones for it to be worth any scavenger's time to drag them away.

They reached a lower shelf, even thicker with trees and brush and grass. Then took another steep decline, and reached another shelf.

And more bones.

It was Cadmann who first mentioned that the animal sounds had died away.

"You noticed it too?" Chaka asked. "I was wondering if that was just my own morbid imagination."

"No, it's not." Cadmann looked back at Aaron, trailing slightly to their left, a thoughtful expression on his face. Whatever he thought, he was keeping to himself.

The terrain was looking more and more . . . well, picked over. No pterodons. No birdles. No Joeys. Nothing. The back of Cadmann's neck itched.

"Look," Chaka said soberly.

Chaka pointed at a skeleton the size of a small deer, with short forelegs. It poked out of the ground. Chaka knelt and dug carefully with his knife, and unearthed the rest. Cadmann turned his head away.

This creature had died digging into the ground. Its head still remained, and its shoulders, a sort of monkey-looking thing with sharp paws. The attempt to claw its way into the ground had failed. The mummy was hollowed out, its mouth still open, clotted with dirt. Its eyes were open. Staring into its own grave.

Chaka made a blowing sound and stood, wiping his hands on his pants. He walked in a widening spiral, and found two more skeletons, of similar creatures that hadn't been as successful at burrowing. "This is wrong," Chaka said. He walked to the ridge. Below them was another flattened area, and then a cliff. Distantly, they heard rushing water.

Cadmann said, "Lovecraftian, maybe. What are you thinking?"

"Wrong." Chaka ran down the slope, digging in his heels. He saw Aaron skid down after him. There was a tight, controlled expression on Aaron's face, one that Cadmann hadn't seen before. Some game was going on here, and he was one step behind the other players.

He scrambled down the next decline, using roots and rocks to steady and slow his descent. He watched, increasingly disturbed, as Chaka poked about. This was a lushly wooded area, girdled with bushes and trees and grass. There were signs that it had been lusher still, but some of the vegetation had been badly chewed.

Except for the distant mournful *skaw* of a pterodon, it was just too damned quiet.

They found bones. Bones of creatures mouse-sized, rabbit-sized, and one as big as a wolf.

Chaka pulled his belt knife and cut into the wolf-sized creature's rear leg bone. He poked around in the dark interior. "Until we've got a better word, we can call this stuff marrow. This is still moist. I think that all of this death happened within the last seventy-two hours."

Chaka pushed himself up and walked out to the edge of the cliff, looking out over the valley beneath. His face was deeply troubled.

"Weather's getting bad," he murmured, so low that Cadmann almost couldn't hear him.

Aaron had heard. "True enough."

"Ordinarily, the bees build nests, raze an area for maybe a decade, and then move on. Probably spawn a dozen queens each, or however they work it. But in times like this . . ."

"What?" Cadmann asked. He was afraid he wasn't going to like the answer.

Chaka looked back at Aaron, standing only a few feet behind him, and he shrugged. "The plains will flood. A lot of the nests will drown—no, they won't. The bees will have water traps built into them, for sure. And as soon as the first water recedes, the bees will migrate. Massively. Some of them are starting to expand westward now. See? The animals up here never evolved to deal with bees this way. A few Joeys are one thing—we're talking about the eradication of square kilometers of wildlife. It's been two hours since we've seen a single living animal, gentlemen. Those rain clouds? Those are the beginning. And the bees want the high ground. Probably this whole region belongs to them, every fifty years. Then the population pressure drives them back to the lowlands. But when the rains hit . . ."

Aaron's voice was very flat. "What?"

"The bees are spreading everywhere, breeding whole hordes of queens and seeding them on the wind. These are species that never evolved to deal with bees, because bees were never here. The grendels—I've figured that out. There are so many other animals breeding their hearts out that the grendels aren't eating *any* of their samlon, so they're *all* turning into grendels. Edgar's been raving about the weird weather. We've seen it. Those bees are getting ready for the winds to scatter them everywhere!"

Cadmann nodded. "Sounds right."

Little Chaka spoke very carefully. "I have to tell Father. Do you realize that we're going to have to evacuate the mainland? And I mean *right now*—"

Cadmann caught a motion out of the corner of his eye, and it was a fatal half a second before he realized what was happening. Aaron, incredibly, was unshouldering his rifle. Chaka's rifle was in his hands. He was raising it, even as Cadmann felt his mouth form the word: "No!"

Chaka was closest to Aaron, and Aaron shot him first. The biologist had only begun to react when the bullet snapped his head back. Chaka's entire body straightened. He tumbled back over the cliff, the entire left half of his head a wet red ruin.

Cadmann had already leveled his grendel gun as the sound of the first explosion hit his ears. Chaka had not yet fallen. As Cadmann fired, Aaron dropped to one knee. The grendel charge went over Aaron's head. Cadmann corrected his aim and fired again.

He had aimed for the center of mass, and the center of mass for Aaron Tragon was covered by the rifle. Aaron flew back, hands splaying, hair flying out with the electrical shock. His mouth spread in a wide O as the dart released its charge. Aaron landed on his butt, three feet away. He shook himself like a big, sick dog.

Cadmann thumbed another dart into the breech and realized that it would take five seconds for it to charge. Grendel guns were backup weapons, used as part of a team effort.

Five seconds would be too late.

Chaka's gun. Cadmann dove for it, but Aaron was closer. Aaron screamed, scrambled up, and dove, and both pairs of hands closed on it at the same time.

For a second they tugged at it, their faces only inches apart. Then Cadmann released it and swung his right fist, connecting with Aaron's jaw just below the ear. Aaron's head snapped back, and his grip on the gun loosened, but as he went back his right leg whipped around, and the foot connected with Cadmann's face. Cadmann lost control of the gun, and rolled back, screaming as his shoulder thumped against the ground. His *bad* shoulder. Shakily he got to his feet at the same time that Aaron did.

Aaron's hands were curled loosely, spread roughly shoulder distance apart. Ready to chop, or punch, or grasp. His right shoulder was leading, about thirty percent of his weight on the front foot.

Cadmann felt sad, and tired, and old. Christ. Of course. Aaron was one of Toshiro's karate students. Probably his prize student, excelling at hand-to-hand combat as he did at everything else. Aaron was probably stronger than him, faster than him, fresher than him. Aaron would be dead in about twenty seconds.

Cadmann reached to his belt sheath and drew the Gerber Australian Bowie knife. Nine and a half inches of steel. He had carried it since Africa, a present from one of the NCOs he had lost in Mozambique. It felt heavy in his hand.

"Come on, boy," Cadmann said. "Let's get it over with."

Aaron looked at the knife, looked at Cadmann's face, and back at the knife. He dropped his hands. "I . . . I can't fight you," he said.

"You don't have a lot of choice here," Cadmann hissed. He slid in a little closer. "Why'd you do it, Aaron?"

"They would have *listened* to you." He held his wrists up, hands together. This boy was surrendering! What the hell was he supposed to do?

"They would have returned to the island. Everything would have been over."

"That's no reason to kill." But in the back of his mind, a voice whispered: *For Aaron Tragon, maybe it is.*

"Kneel down," Cadmann said.

Aaron obeyed. His lower lip trembled. A single tear rolled down his cheek.

"Cross your ankles and sit on them." That was a satisfactory unready position. "Take off your belt."

Aaron's hands went to his belt, slid it out of its loops.

"Make a noose on the end, and put your wrists through it. Tighten it with your teeth." Aaron did, and then, unsolicited, wrapped the belt around again. Tears were streaming down his face. He looked up into Cadmann's face, and his face had softened. Damn it, he looked too much like the boy that Cadmann had taught to swim, had taken for hikes.

God. How had it all gone so wrong so fast? Cadmann switched the knife to his left hand, and reached down to pick up the rifle.

Aaron's palms flat on the ground. Aaron's body uncoiled, spun. Aaron's legs lashed out, caught Cadmann in the side. The knife spun out of his hand. Aaron moved in, a leg whipping out. Cadmann barely got his hands up in time, caught the shock of it on his shoulder and jaw. Pain. Blackness and the taste of blood in his mouth.

Cadmann charged in like a bull. He was mindless of the whipcrack kicks, or of Aaron's bound wrists chopping at his lowered neck. He smashed Aaron back, hammering with both hands. No karate. No judo. Just short, devastating hooks to the body, trying to break him in half one-two, one-two, one-two.

Grabbed belt. Wheeled, pivoted, threw Aaron by the bound wrists. Perfect leverage and timing. Aaron wheeled though the air, hit hard, rolled over groggily, and his hands—

Found Chaka's rifle. Braced butt against chest. Fingers found trigger. Cadmann froze in place.

Aaron's face twisted in anguish.

A single, tormented word:

"Father."

And then thunder.

38

THE GATHERING STORM

But evil is wrought by want of thought
As well as want of heart.
—THOMAS HOOD, *The Lady's Dream*

Edgar and Trish were alone in the communications shack. Because he had chosen this time to show her how to build weather models, they were the first to hear the choked and frantic words. "Mayday. . . . . Mayday . . ." Unmistakably, Aaron Tragon's voice. The voice of a man very near the edge.

Edgar was more curious than anything else. He leaned over Trish. "Wasn't Aaron out with Cadmann and Little Chaka?"

"As far as I know," she said. She stabbed at virtual buttons with a single forefinger. "Go ahead, Aaron. We read you."

"In Skeeter Twelve. Coming over the ridge now. My God. Grendels. Grendels everywhere."

Edgar sat bolt upright. *"What?"* He slammed the general alarm circuit, and across the entire camp, klaxons began to scream.

Justin heard the alarm and shot a look at Jessica, who narrowed her eyes. There was a paired series of electronic screams, not the dreaded single bleats that would have indicated visual sighting by guards at the periphery. Still, it was enough to raise the hair at the back of his neck

Grendel guns, never far away, were snatched up by eager hands. The entire population of Shangri-la emptied into the square. Eyes alert, heads swiveling, voices raised in alarm.

Trish appeared in the door of the communications shed, and searched the crowd until she found Jessica. She headed straight for her friend. Justin watched the two of them huddle. When Jessica turned around, the blood had drained from her face.

Justin scanned the crowd quickly. Sylvia Weyland was nowhere to be seen. He remembered that she was up at the mining site, supervising.

The faint burr of a skeeter worked its way into his consciousness. Before he could fully register it, Jessica turned toward him, took a halting step, and then froze. Her face tilted to the ground. It tilted back up. Her eyes streamed.

They met in the middle of the press, and she leaned sobbing into his arms.

Skeeter Twelve landed four minutes later. Four dozen anxious Star Born surrounded the skeeter pad, silent as Aaron Tragon emerged.

He was muddy, and bleeding, and bruised. His shirt was torn almost completely away. He looked like a man utterly lost.

Justin was the first to his side, and said, "Tell me."

Aaron looked at him. "I tried. I tried, Justin."

Justin grabbed Aaron's shoulder. "Tell me, goddamn it!"

The autogyro's rotors slowed, then stopped. Aaron leaned back against the cab.

"We were heading back along ridge twelve. The clouds were looking bad, and we wanted to make better time. There is a cliff there above the river. Chaka stopped, told us to look down. God." Aaron's shook as he wiped his brow. "The grendels were spawning. The samlon. They boiled in the river. It was . . . it was spectacular. They were so far down, I thought we were safe. Then the ledge gave way under our combined weight. Cadmann and I jumped back in time, but Chaka went over."

He paused, and during that pause, Big Chaka pushed his way through the crowd and came to stand before Aaron, looking up at him with an expression Justin found unreadable. Justin started to speak, but Big Chaka put a hand on his arm, imploring silence.

"He slid halfway down before he caught himself. He twisted something. He was too close to the river. Cadmann and I went after him. There were roots poking out. We used those.

"It had been raining up there. The bank was unstable. Cadmann got to Chaka, helped him up. They slid. Cadmann stopped their slide, and I got down closer. Then the grendels had us spotted."

"Grendels," Big Chaka said.

Aaron nodded with infinite regret. "They boiled up out of the water. Six, seven, eight of them. Little ones, but a *flood*, once they realized that there was food. Cadmann screamed at me to get back. I ignored him and tried to get to them. There wasn't enough to hang on to. I shot one with the grendel gun. Cadmann shot two more with his rifle, and then one with his pistol. They got to Chaka first . . ."

He buried his head in his hands. "They screamed. They screamed. Oh, God, I never want to hear anything like that again. They were screaming curses, and killing grendels. For every one they killed, two more appeared. And they both slid down into the water, and then there was nothing but blood.

"I don't know how long I hung there, watching the water. Then I climbed back up. I was numb." He held up his hands. They were torn and bloody. "I lost my grip a few times, but I made it back to the top. I'd . . . I'd torn my shirt. Lost my comm card. By the time I got back to the skeeter, the weather was turning bad. I called in a Mayday. I couldn't think straight anymore. I flew back."

He met Jessica's eyes. Then Justin's. Then Big Chaka's. Jessica moved up to hold him.

The group was silent. Justin was shaking.

Big Chaka looked up at the sky. It was massed high with dark, angry clouds. "How long before the storm?"

Almost in answer, drops began to fall.

He hung his head. "When it is over, we must go out, and see what we can recover of my son." He looked at Aaron again. Something—not anger, not grief—stole across his dark face, and then was gone.

✳

There was pain. Pain in his back, his head, a great tearing, burning ache that threatened to consume all of his thoughts, all of his life. It was just too large, bigger than anything he had ever experienced in his life. More than all of his previous pains combined.

There was cold. Wet. There was water around him. Near him. Flowing over him.

Little Chaka awoke.

Is my back broken? It was a natural question, one that he couldn't answer at the moment. In his entire universe, nothing existed but agony. Such questions would come later—if there *was* a later.

His eyes wouldn't focus. All he got were patterns of shadow and light.

What was there to remember? What had happened?

He remembered . . .

He remembered.

Aaron. Oh, God. Aaron had shot him. Was that memory correct? And if it was, why wasn't he dead?

He struggled to move. What could move? He remembered a flash of light, the struggle to get his own gun up to the aim, Aaron's rifle coming up. . . .

No, he was thinking backward, now. From the last thing he remembered to the beginning.

Calm. Try to remember. Aaron shot him. And then—? And then Cadmann would have shot Aaron. Chaka went quite calm on thinking this. He might be dead. (Was he already dead? Was this what death felt like? Just a slow sinking into the earth? Was there pain and wetness? Certainly he had been shot in the head. Certainly he was dead now.)

He had no hope of truly being alive . . . did he?

But he knew that he had been avenged. In fact, if Cadmann had killed Aaron, and if he, Chaka, was still alive (as he began to suspect that he might in fact be), then there was the chance that he would be rescued. Cadmann would burn in hell before he would allow one of his own to—

Chaka's eyes finally cleared.

He managed to catch the whimper in his throat before it escaped, but that didn't make his world a better a place to be.

There, in the water before him, was Cadmann.

He looked so like he always did, except his tanned face seemed pale. Cadmann's blue-green eyes stared at him, almost as if he were about to speak. Almost. The hole in his throat said that there would never be another word from him. Chaka squeezed his eyes shut. It took all of his strength, but he had to do it. He had no choice. He couldn't cope with *this*. It was worse than death.

He opened his eyes again, praying that it was a hallucination. It could be, couldn't it? It would change when he opened his eyes again, the way objects in a dream change if you look away and then look back again.

But Cadmann still floated there. Water flowed over the staring eyes. Cadmann's mouth was open just a little as if caught in midword. Trying to speak, to say one more thing, just one more before silence fell for all time.

Chaka wept.

Blackness came for him.

He didn't know how long he was unconscious. He woke to a nightmare. He felt *it* moving through the water. He couldn't bring himself to open his eyes.

It was there in the water with him.

A grendel. He felt the heat wash from its body, could hear its sinuous splashing. It looked as big as a house.

Coming to consciousness meant returning to the house of pain. Chaka yearned for death. This was the passage. This was crossing over into the other world, a world without pain. A world where Cadmann awaited him, watched him now. *Be brave, my friend. Don't fear the dark. . . .*

He heard the breathing, and then no breathing, just a hissing gurgle. He opened his eyes. No grendel . . .

At first his astonishment surprised even him. What in the hell was going on? Then he saw the snorkel. It barely crested the surface of the water, Cadzie blue. The grendel herself was a shadow beneath the surface. Just barely beneath the surface. Watching him.

Even in the midst of nightmare, the biologist in Little Chaka was intrigued. This was the first grendel snorkel anyone had seen on the mainland. The water was so damned shallow. So why did the bitch even bother? She couldn't have been stalking him. She couldn't have had any reason to *hide* from him, God knew. So what in the world . . . ?

A splash in the water near her, and suddenly something flapped in her teeth. God. A samlon. Her head came up out of the water just a little, and he could see that the samlon's legs were too well formed. It was almost *that* time. Now that he became aware of it, he realized that the water was filled with these shapes. Dozens . . . hundreds of samlon.

Why didn't she just eat him? Was she saving him for her progeny? Was she a fat, overstuffed old bitch who wanted a special treat for her darl—

Sudden pain ignited in the right leg. With the dregs of his strength Chaka craned his neck, watched the head of something black and clawed emerge from the water, watched it wriggling as it savaged his thigh.

He thought that no fear remained in him. He was wrong.

Chaka tried to scream. Somehow, being devoured by a pack of infants was infinitely more frightening than a single grendel's fangs. This . . . *nibbling* would go on and on and on.

His shriek sounded like the cry of a child's doll.

The water thrashed, and suddenly the half-samlon was up in the air, in the mouth of the grendel, bitten in half—and spit out.

She looked at him again. What in the hell *was* this?

✳

Three weirds. One dead, one fled, one dying.

The weird who had spared Old Grendel's life . . . what reward would Strongest One expect or accept? That one who would teach Old Grendel how to shape the magic that would hold the universe prisoner, to enslave God and God's daughters . . . that one lay dead in the water, its life's blood spreading through the lake, to summon Old Grendel's daughters.

The one who had killed Strongest One, *that* was Strongest One now. If Old Grendel could reach her as she fled . . . what would she do? Work out her rage on the weird who was the ruin of all her ambitions? Or force that one to serve her, teach her? It didn't matter. That one was beyond Old Grendel's reach.

The third lay helpless and wounded. In minutes it would be eaten by her own children. She had to make a decision, and quickly.

She looked up at the darkening sky. Felt the fat droplets splattering against her. The world was drowning, the Death Wind would have the land, and no time remained.

She turned her back to the man. She thrashed her tail, and carefully hooked it through the outer layer of skin, the loose, half-shed skin that all of the weirds seemed to like. The weird thrashed and fought and she thought for a moment: *What to do?*

Yes. She knew now.

She dove beneath the water, hauling the weird with her.

✳

Rachael Moskowitz didn't turn as her husband entered Camelot's main mess hall and wrapped his arms around her waist. None of the First spoke. The news from the mainland, the word of sudden savage death, had hit them hard.

And now this: on the communal vidscreen, *Geographic* beamed them an image of the storm descending on Shangri-la. Camelot had been lashed by rain for almost a week, but that was only the fringe of the storm that would cross Shangri-la.

"How did she take it?" Rachael said. "How is Mary Ann?"

"Mickey told her, personally," he said softly, pressing his lips against her ear.

Rachael nodded. "That was probably best."

"He said she's all right. Just all right. Wants her children around her."

"Ruth," Rachael murmured. "God. We need to get through to Ruth."

Zack stiffened a little. Ruth had betrayed them. But . . . but she was their only child, and it was time to forget such things. "We'll patch through. The important thing is *Robor*, and *Robor* is safe at the mine. We can be sure of that. Cadmann made sure of that."

They were quiet for a moment, watching the colored swirl that represented vast masses of warm and cold air fighting above the mainland.

Rachael shook her head slowly. "Cadmann. Somehow . . . I always thought he was immortal."

"*He* never did," Zack said. "That's one mistake he never made."

39

BEES

Let Justice be done, though the world perish.
—Emperor Ferdinand I

Little Chaka awoke from a dream of drowning, and found himself vomiting water. He felt only confusion, and pain, and the savage certainty that he had gone beyond agony into death, beyond death into hell.

When the sick ended, he rolled over onto his side, not opening his eyes. He couldn't bring himself to want to look at the surroundings. The ground beneath him was rock, not the mud and silt of a riverbank. Distantly, water trickled into water. More distant still was another sound, a steady, drumming vibration.

He opened his eyes. There was nothing to see. He wasn't certain his eyes had opened at all.

But he'd moved, he could move his left leg and left arm. He told himself very firmly *not* to reach up and touch his head. He got his elbow under him, his knee, then his other knee, which felt limp and dead. He slipped, and almost went over the edge of a rock shelf, into water.

Water again? Where the hell was he? His left hand touched something cold and scaly. His fingers felt it, and he knew immediately what it was. A dead samlon. He could feel the scales, the fins now fully developed into legs. The teeth. Tiny spikes budding on the tail. Something had bitten it, its flesh torn and . . .

Something.

He stopped, quite still, and listened again. Out in the water. Something was moving. There came a sound. Not water sounds dripping from the rocks. Not the beat of his heart, or the thunder of his breathing

The grendel. The beast that had brought him here, unharmed. Which had left a dead samlon for him.

Food?

What the hell?

He was so weak. So weak. Impossibly, the darkness spun. He couldn't think, couldn't move. Lights appeared in the darkness, and then he was gone, wondering only at the very last if he would ever wake up again.

The sky opened, gushing with rain and lightning as if it had saved it all up since Avalon was new. On Camelot the waves pounded the already drowned Surf's Up, demolished it, drove its pilings into splinters and changed the very shape of the land.

The storm moved across the continent like a malevolent amoeboid monster. It hit Shangri-la like a bomb. The Second draped tarps across the unfinished buildings that composed half the camp, protecting the naked wood from the savage downpour. Then they took to their shelters, huddled together, and listened to the rain. They thought of the swelling rivers. Grendels would be out tonight, but there would be no scent in rain such as this. And so they were safe.

But quiet. Their mourning penetrated to the very roots of the colony. They had never known a moment as black as this.

Aaron sat near the fireplace in the main hall, his long arms wrapped around his knees. He looked out at the rain and said very little, as if words would somehow cheapen his misery. His eyes were red-rimmed.

The rain had hammered at them for twenty hours already, as savage as a hail of ball bearings.

They came and they went, but Aaron stayed where he was. Jessica was usually by his side. She needed the touch as much as he did, but it was hours before he could let himself be comforted. When he finally leaned his great head against her chest, and held her, and at last slept, Jessica felt her own grief at last. Bleakly, she wondered how it would feel when its full impact finally struck her. For now there was the rain, and the watch for grendels in the rain. She left Aaron asleep and peered through the window at the mess hall. She knew that Justin was there, and she needed to talk to him more than she could say.

She jumped as a hand touched her shoulder, but it was only Trish. "Go on," she said quietly. "I'll watch things over here."

Jessica nodded her thanks, and hugged her friend. *Was* Trish her friend? God, what a thought. What *was* everything, what the hell did it all mean? Toshiro dead. Joe and Linda dead. Stu dead. Now Chaka and her father dead. Why? Because Aaron had wanted to . . .

No. She couldn't allow herself to stumble down that road. Aaron would have saved them, if he could. Aaron was sorriest of all about everything that had happened. Aaron would have died to save Cadmann, or Chaka. Hadn't he said so? Didn't she know it?

Then why did she want to die?

She covered her head and went out into the storm.

Upstream of the base camp, the beaver grendels were in a panic. The river had swelled to twice its ordinary flow, and it hammered at them, drove at their nests and dams with a ferocity they had never experienced . . . but which something deep within them recognized.

Some knowing beyond their dim consciousness.

This is the time . . . this is the time . . .

So they fought to repair, and failed. And when the dams burst some were swept away and dashed against rocks. Others climbed blindly out of the ponds that had swollen to angry, storm-tossed lakes, seeking refuge from the tree trunks and jagged chunks of detritus that dashed them. Chunks of dams from their cousins farther north, chunks of their own dams. Blindly, they fought, but it was no use. And as the rains intensified, as the storms grew greater through the night and into the next day, the work that they and their ancestors had labored over for decades would be swept away as well.

Jessica found Justin in the mess hall, looking out of the window. Katya was at his side. Jessica felt a twinge, but there was nothing to be done. She had made her choice, long ago.

Katya pulled at Justin's arm as Jessica entered. He got up and kissed Katya's hand, crossed to Jessica, and hugged her.

God, it felt good. That hug was like physical nourishment. She just wanted to stay in his arms, and feel his heart beat against her, and feel that her entire life wasn't falling apart, that the tears streaming down her face would stop one day. That there was enough love in all the world to make everything right.

"Have you talked to Mary Ann?" he asked.

She shook her head. "I can't. Not yet. I talked with Mickey—he's the one who broke the news. I just can't talk about it over holo, Justin. I can't."

He nodded understanding. "I know. It was awful telling Sylvia. Jesus."

"How did she take it?"

"Well. They're busy up at the mine. There's a thousand things to do to get *Robor* lashed up and into the lee. It's safe—Dad made sure of that. It would be safe even against worse storm than this. But it keeps her busy, and I guess that that is a good idea."

She nodded, and backed away from him. She smelled coffee. "That smells good," she said.

"My manners."

God, how was he holding up so well? She knew how close he and Cadmann were. In some ways, terrible ways, closer than she had been.

Her heart broke again. Carlos brought her a cup of coffee, thrust it into her hands. "Your mothers, both of them, are very strong. If they weren't, they couldn't have survived this place. None of us could have. The weak did not make the trip. Those unsure of their strength took refuge in the HI."

Jessica stared. "Carlos? What does *that* mean?"

He shrugged. "Let's just say that I think HI was a convenient out for those who couldn't cope. Just work the garden. Raise children."

"Make sculptures?"

He smiled. "We all have our little refuges."

They paused, listening to the rain hammer against the walls, the ceiling. A steady, arrhythmic thrumming. According to *Geographic*, the first wave of rain would die away by morning. There would be peace, followed by more rain, in waves, for at least a week. And beyond that week, another storm front, and then yet another. They could wait it out. It was what they were here for.

"When the sky clears," Carlos said, "I'll take a skeeter up in the mountains.

To the coordinates Aaron gave us. I will find your father's bones, I think." He sipped at his coffee. There was something in his eyes that she couldn't quite read. "His comm card was still broadcasting. I will find his bones. I believe that I owe your father that much."

Then he closed his eyes, and drank, and didn't say another word for the rest of the night.

The merciless torrent tore the beaver dams into splinters, and the rivers swelled, changed course, flooded across the plains. Flash floods and waterspouts raged, whirled, tore the sky ever more brutally, made it bleed.

The water roared across the plain, and sank down into the nests, the bee nests that the Star Born had seen, but not understood. There were thousands of them across the southern portion of the continent. Each was home to tens of thousands of bees.

There was chaos, and they responded by huddling, and then swarming up and out. The water beat them back. They collapsed their tunnel walls to seal them, and then retreated into their deepest tunnels.

And waited.

For months now, they had fed their special variety of *speed*-enhanced "royal jelly" to selected embryos within the nest. Now it began to pay off, and the first of the new queens were shaking the water from their motor wings.

Edgar sheltered his head against the rain, and walked out in the ankle-high mud, and sloshed across the encampment. The lights of the distant mess hall were dimmed by the intensity of the rain.

He caught sight of a small shape huddled in the downpour against the wall of one of the dorms. Without knowing entirely why, he headed in that direction.

It was Ruth, and when she saw him coming, she ran in the opposite direction, sloshing through the rain. It was probably impossible but he would have sworn he heard a sound through the downpour, a small, hopeless animal cry.

He caught up with her, happy for his newfound stamina—it was damned difficult to make headway through mud this deep.

He grabbed a shoulder and spun her around. The rain had streaked her hair across her face. Her eyes were wide and staring. She didn't seem to recognize him. He guided her into one of the storerooms.

She shivered. Her teeth clattered until he thought that she would crack the enamel.

"What's the matter with you?" he asked.

She looked at him, through him. And was silent.

She stopped shuddering. Her skin looked very fine to him. Almost porcelain. Almost translucent. She looked to so innocent. So lost.

"You're going to catch your death," he said.

"I don't care," she said. "I . . . just don't care." She sounded so lost, so helpless.

He sat her down on a barrel, peeled the cowl back from her head. "What's the matter? Why don't you care?"

"I don't know what I'm doing here," she said.

He started to speak, then realized how hard it was for her to say even that much, and kept silent.

"I came for Aaron. I thought that maybe there was a way to be . . . with Aaron."

She lowered her face into her hands. "What am I doing? Why am I here?"

Aaron didn't want Ruth. Or anyone. All Aaron wanted was this continent.

"What you did," Edgar said finally, surprised to hear the words escape his lips, "was follow your heart. You had to try."

She looked up at him, and focused on him, as if she were seeing him for the first time. And then lowered her face into her hands, and began to sob. And finally, after a long time, he pulled a barrel next to her, and put his arm around her. She let him.

After a while she leaned her head against his shoulder, and she cried, and he listened to rain, for a long, long time.

✳

Two days later, the rains ceased. The waters began to recede, and the plains began to drain. The earth absorbed the waters, and finally the sun touched the earth again. Dark clouds still fringed the sky.

The earth trembled. And then began to crumble. And from within the ground crawled first one, then ten, and then a hundred, and then a million bees.

Tens of millions. Swarming. Hungry.

The Death Wind had come.

✳

The second day after the rains ceased, Carlos was in Skeeter II, Evan Castaneda in Skeeter IV. They rose up over the mountain ridge, floating like insects on a breeze. Justin crouched next to him.

"Are you all right, amigo?" he asked. The question was one of those existential absurdities that friends were obliged to ask each other. Justin looked at him bleakly.

He didn't answer directly. "Look at the grendel dam," he said instead, pointing below them and to the east. "Utterly destroyed. They're pretty harmless most of the time, I guess—but who knows how they behave in a disaster like this?"

"Mmm." Carlos swung around. There was a part of him that didn't want to complete their stated mission, that would rather do anything in the world than find what they expected to find.

"How is Jessica?" Carlos asked. His voice had grown quieter. Much quieter. Justin could barely hear it above the hum of the rotors.

"She's made her choices," Justin said. "She thinks she's more use back at the camp."

There was something that he hadn't said, of course: *Caring for Aaron.*

Something had certainly happened to Aaron up there. There was some core of the man that was different. Exposed. Torn. Damaged. *Something.* Justin couldn't quite believe Aaron's account of what happened. Something was wrong. Had Aaron panicked and abandoned Cadmann and Chaka? What was Aaron hiding?

Or perhaps it was just seeing death, so stark and violent. Justin remembered watching Stu die in the snow. The image was locked away from him where the pain couldn't reach. Where he didn't feel it. That way, he didn't have to think about barbecues at Stu's house, or playing five-card stud, or skeeter racing with a friend and brother. It was just too painful to think about those things.

And maybe that was what was killing Aaron. No one can ever quite live up to his own self-image. Maybe Aaron just got a dose of reality.

Justin ground his palms against his eyes. *Father. Cadmann. God, I'll miss you.*

They were maybe twenty minutes from the coordinates when the nightmare began.

The wind had shifted. He looked out of the main window, and saw a huge dark cloud billowing across their path.

"Hey, Justin. Any idea what this is? Where in the world would a dust cloud *that* size come from, after a rain like this?"

The question was hardly out of his mouth before the radio clattered in a burst of static. Evan. His voice was taut with fear.

"It's not a dust cloud. Mayday, Mayday—"

Justin saw the edge of the dark cloud touch Skeeter IV. Above the skeeter was a sparkling; the skeeter lurched. The blades were sparkling, little bright flashes in the smoke . . . and in that moment, Justin knew the face of their enemy. He screamed to Carlos, "Get us the hell out of here! It's *bees!*"

Carlos's hands were lightning at the controls. The skeeter tilted far over, away from the approaching swarm.

"Bees in the rotor blades. They're exploding. Vicious little flying cherry bombs—"

Death was coming. Death was almost here.

✳

Jessica and Aaron crossed Shangri-la's main square. The buildings had all stood up under the assault of the elements. When the tarps were dragged down, the new timbers were unwarped and sun-dried. There was repair work to be done, but it would be completed within the week. They walked out to the horse pen, next to the chamel pen on the outskirts of the camp, near the double electrified fences.

The chamels were muddied and streaked; in fact, they rolled happily in the mud. She let it touch her heart, bleakly. There was death here, but wonders too in a world that could produce creatures as beautiful as these.

A crowd gathered around them to hear the speech Aaron had promised them. Carey Lou gaped worshipfully. Beside him, little Heather McKennie held his arm. Trish and Edgar were among the throng, but she noticed that they weren't bonded as they had been only a week before. Edgar was holding hands with Ruth. They had spent a lot of time together over the last few days. There was no sexual heat between them, just gentle touches and a lot of quiet conversation.

Just holding hands. Almost innocently. Here stood a pregnant girl, and this young man, newly awakening to the hungers of the flesh. And the two of them had forged a bond of . . . innocence. There was no other word for it. Aaron had tried to separate him from Trish, and it hadn't worked . . . Trish had performed some kind of miracle on Edgar, saving him after Toshiro's death . . . but then didn't want him for herself. But seemed to have infected him with the Pygmalion bug.

Jessica was confused. And not a little jealous, and wasn't entirely certain why. She had all the sex she wanted. Why the hell would she covet . . . holding hands with *Edgar?*

"We have to rebuild," Aaron said. The sun burned down between the clouds, as if trying to make up for the burst of rain. It was lying to them: *Geographic* promised another downburst within a day or two. "We have paid too high a price. We must claim this continent for our own." His voice quavered. She had never seen him like this, never seen him quite so honest, so close to the bone. This was a new Aaron. Her father was dead, and into that vacuum had stepped a new leader.

She scanned the faces of the gathered. Family. Friends. Lovers. Standing in the muddied streets, contemplating the work to be done before the camp could come to life again.

But in the end, there would be Aaron. Aaron, who had led them back to the mainland. Aaron, who had risked his life in vain, to save the one man he loved more than any other.

She could see it in their faces. This tragedy would finally knit the entire colony together.

Dogs barked anxiously at the periphery of the camp. Jessica peered out over the crowd to see . . .

The impossible.

Just beyond the double electrified fence, a torpedo shape crawled through the mud. Slowly. Gradually. Tentatively.

The entire camp was utterly silent. Out of the corner of her eye she saw Aaron's face, and it was *ashen.* Whatever he had been about to say had simply died on his lips.

A grendel. A *huge* grendel. It approached slowly. And it was . . . dragging something.

Unmistakably, its barbed tail was hooked through the pant leg of a . . . a man. A black man. Trish's rifle went up to her shoulder, and Big Chaka Mubutu, standing beside her, said, "No."

"Oh, my God," someone said. "It's little Chaka."

Little Chaka???

"He's alive," Big Chaka said. Jessica felt frozen in place, unable to move. *How . . . ?*

She looked back up at Aaron, and his eyes were wide. Too wide, and she felt as if she were falling into them.

Aaron had seen Little Chaka die! Had seen him torn to pieces by . . . by grendels. Her world spun, and her eyes locked again on the enormous shape that had paused just at the outer ring of buildings, and made a kind of cooing sound.

Oh, my God. It was trying to speak to them.

"The fuck you don't—"

That was Edgar's voice. A slapping sound. Jessica heard a gunshot, loud enough to stun her hearing, blasting right next to her ear. Mud kicked up a few feet in front of her.

The grendel's head cocked. It watched them.

Edgar's hand was on the barrel of the gun. Aaron tugged at it. He was in such shock that he couldn't harness his strength, couldn't pull it away from Edgar for a critical second.

"It killed Cadmann!" he huffed. "It killed Cadmann. Let me—"

Big Chaka spoke quietly. "I thought you said that it was a raft of small ones. It was *spawning* samlon killed Cadmann. Killed my boy."

Aaron was silent. Trish looked at Aaron, eyes murderously cold. It was a community of guns, and guns were turning toward Aaron.

"Jessica," Aaron whispered. "It isn't what it looks like."

And in that moment she knew. She couldn't make the part of her that *knew* talk to the part of her that could *act*. She couldn't. But she knew for an instant, she felt the shields slide back and looked into the core of herself and knew, and felt herself falling into the abyss, and sealed it back up, teetering. Heard her own voice quavering, heard the lie as she spoke it to herself. "Of course. I don't know what they're—"

Big Chaka took a step forward. The grendel shook its tail, detaching it from Little Chaka's leg, and then backed up a few feet.

"My God," someone said. "It's smart."

"It brought Chaka back." Big Chaka punched a code into his comm card, and the fence power died. He swung the gate open. The crowd moved forward, the grendel retreating as they did. It backed up a dozen feet, and watched them carefully.

Big Chaka's yelled. "No one touches that animal. NO ONE." It was the first time that she had ever heard him raise his voice. Jessica stood with Aaron. Edgar's hand was on the rifle. Somehow, Trish had moved over behind Aaron. Her hand was on Aaron's other arm. Tight.

Aaron was frozen. His tongue dipped pinkly out of his mouth, moistening his lips. His hair hung down to his shoulders stringily. There was no life in his face.

"No," Trish said quietly, and her eyes met his squarely. "If you raise that rifle, I swear to God I'll kill you. Or Edgar will."

Aaron looked to Jessica for support. She was numb. This was all happening too damned quickly. Her chest felt like a skeeter had landed on it.

"My boy . . . ?" Big Chaka wept. "My boy."

The small man cuddled his son's body in his arms. They stayed like that for a long time. There was a stillness to the world, something that penetrated deeply, and Jessica couldn't bring herself to move

Under Big Chaka's direction three of the crowd picked Little Chaka up and carried him back into the camp. They swung the gate closed behind them. Outside, the grendel watched them. Big Chaka's eyes were on fire. He walked toward them, one hesitant step at a time. Then she realized that he struggled to keep from running, as if something connected him to Aaron Tragon that wanted to pull him faster and faster, as if he were a man out of control.

Big Chaka whispered something. When he got closer she could hear what it was. "He was shot," Chaka was saying over and over again. "He was shot."

"I told . . . I told you," Aaron said, trying to find words, trying to find anything to fill the void of silence that had suddenly opened all around him. "I tried to help. I fired at the grendels. . . ." There was spittle on his chin.

"You had a *grendel gun*!" Chaka screamed. "My son was shot with a bullet!"

"I . . . I . . ."

"Do you want to know what my boy said?"

Aaron shook his head numbly. A vast buzzing filled Jessica's head.

"He said: 'Aaron shot us.' That's what he said."

Suddenly, without any warning, Trish's belt knife was at Aaron's throat. "You incredible *bastard*," she hissed.

The center of Jessica's world was falling away. Aaron was crumbling in front of her. She didn't know what she was doing. Trish pulled the rifle from his hands. Limp hands.

Trish on one side, Edgar on the other. Aaron too shocked to fight, still staring at the grendel as if looking into the face of Judgment.

"You will stand trial," Big Chaka said. "And my son will testify against you."

Aaron struggled to find an answer, but before he could voice it, they were interrupted by a scream:

"*Bees!*"

40

DEATH

In War, whichever side may call itself the
victor, there are no winners, but all are losers.
—Neville Chamberlain

It was all coming together, again. She had brought the weirds a gift, and they
had accepted it.

She had wondered if their strongest would challenge her; she had wondered
how. Even the dam builders did not cooperate like weirds, and no grendel was
so feeble. But their strongest, the killer, was being restrained and led away.

And now they gathered round her at a respectful distance, making the
sounds they always made. The injured one had spoken to her in such a fashion.
It was their way of passing their thoughts from one mind to another. Old Grendel knew she couldn't do that. She must find another way.

And now another sound was rising. For a moment she took it for the sound
of their flyers. Then . . . her heart's desire was snatched from her again.

Not for a moment did she pause to regret. Old Grendel had marked the nest's
water source when it came within her sight and scent. It was an elevated structure at the hub of a web of streets. She was in motion before any weird had
noticed the sound of the Death Wind. With *speed* raging through her blood, she
wove a path among the weirds, brushing one and another but hurting none. She
ran straight to the tower and up one of the legs.

The water was covered with something rigid.

The Death Wind was a darkness across half the sky. She would never mistake
that for storm clouds. A dark tendril was reaching down, in the fashion of a tor-
nado, toward where the puzzle beasts laired.

She smashed through the cover and was into Shangri-la's cistern. She settled
in, lifted her snorkel, and let the heat and *speed* seep from her blood. The water
was humming, bathing her in the sound of the Death Wind.

✳

Carlos swung Skeeter II around in a circle, calculating wind and the direction of
the bee mass, and swung around back south. The wind blew northwest. Unless
the bees were heading to a particular destination, they would drift with the
wind. So it made sense to figure that they wanted the mountains—and that was
north. They were heading away from the plains, away from the flooding. Fine.
Justin had the cowl locked down tight. A few bees spattered against it, but these

bees weren't on *speed*. They weren't in an emergency state. On *speed* they couldn't cover the distance to get their queens to safety. They could be counting on a few dry hours. The rhythm of this damned planet had to be as deeply ingrained as breathing.

He watched Skeeter IV emerge from the cloud for a minute. Justin said, "Evan's going to make it! He's—" Then the cloud closed around Skeeter Four, and the sparkling pinwheel of its rotor flared outward. Something—a cloud of bees *ignited*.

"Holy Mary mother of God—" Skeeter IV was the edge of a fireball. Bees exploded in a *pop-pop-popping* that they could hear even over the whip of their own rotors, a machine-gun crackle, their carapaced *speed* sacs igniting as if they were a swarm of flying firecrackers. Evan's skeeter juddered sideways as if slapped by a giant hand. Then it was entirely enshrouded in flame. All that rang through the radio was Evan's anguished scream as his doomed skeeter spiraled and plunged and smashed into the rock below.

Justin's hands gripped the rail in front of him, squeezed. He had cut his hand on something. The blood ran in a thin stream, drooling down his wrists.

Carlos swung clear of the cloud of bees, heading back to the camp.

In the instant the crowd's attention went to the approaching swarm, Aaron took sudden, violent action. He stamped Trish's instep, and wrenched himself free of her grip. He turned and drove his fist as hard as he could into Edgar's face, breaking his nose and sending blood squirting down his cheek. Trish threw herself on him, screaming, biting, striking.

Jessica still couldn't move, as if trapped in a slow-motion universe of overloaded emotions.

Trish had Aaron down, a long bloody furrow along his cheek. Her knee pounded into his groin over and over again. Blinded by the blood in his eyes, Edgar kicked wildly. Screaming, Aaron got his foot into Trish's chest and push-kicked her away. She flew five feet and slapped into the mud. Edgar got a kick in at Aaron's head, then screamed as the first of the bees reached him and bit, tearing a little wedge of flesh from his cheek.

He forgot about Aaron and ran toward the nearest dorm.

Trish fled toward the rec hall. Beneath it was a Kevlar-reinforced shelter. Grendel-proof. Bee-proof? A mesh metal curtain hung across the doorway. Trish slipped through its folds. "Jessica!" she screamed from safety. A bee spattered against it, crawled, searching for a way in. She held her side, her face. They bled, where bees had bitten.

Jessica ran for the shelter. Aaron screamed, "Help me—"

And Jessica turned for a fatal moment. Aaron staggered up, and their eyes met. His arms went out to her—

A dark wind blew across her and covered Jessica in bees. Hair to ankles, all of her right side was twinkling black. She screamed, thrashed, tried to brush them away, tried to spit them out, tried to run. Aaron took two steps toward her, but it was too late.

Trish couldn't watch any more. She closed the door. Bees were clawing through the curtain.

Aaron took a step toward Jessica, out of his mind with pain, but . . . but he felt something, something that he had never felt before. He just couldn't let her die. He just couldn't—she was down in a mass of crawling black shapes. Her arm stretched out to him, scintillating black. She screamed. Bees crawled into her mouth. One burrowed out of her cheek. They were at her eyes. Aaron lurched away.

There were a few human shapes on the ground. Lucky ones were in Kevlar safety sacks, or wrapped in blankets. A few bee-ridden Star Born crawled blindly, being eaten alive. He slapped at his face as a bee went for his eyes. It bit his hand instead, nearly tearing off a finger joint. He had only seconds to live—

He saw the chamels. They were burying themselves deep in the mud and dung that filled their pen. Their exposed haunches shone Cadzie blue.

He dove for the mud pit, burrowing through the filth until he came up next to one of the chamels. Rolling in the muck, covering himself. Gouged in a hundred places, Aaron shuddered as chamel shit oozed into his wounds. His arm snaked up, grabbed the creature around the neck, held it close. This wasn't perfect. But the bees had other targets, horses and pigs and human beings. They might not find him. They couldn't find him. Oh, God, he hurt so much.

Jessica.

Jessica.

Wrapped in a blue blanket, Katya hammered on the mess hall's shelter door. The sound of the swarm was overwhelmingly loud, loud enough to drive rational thought from her mind. She had only been bitten twice, but the fear almost paralyzed her.

No response. She ran to a sheltered nook—a toolshed next to one of the dorms. In the mess hall, she saw a torch waving. Some idiot was trying to use fire to keep the bees at bay.

There was a sudden crackle, and five thousand bees just *exploded*. Fire and a machine-gun flashing *pop-pop-pop* and shredded crustaceans showered flame everywhere. Half of the camp was rain-drenched, and invulnerable. But half was unfinished, naked wood protected by tarps and then sun-dried for two days. That burned.

The acrid smoke stench wound its way into her nostrils, and she shut the door as tightly as she could. She pressed her hands against the wood. It was still damp. Oh, God. She hoped that was enough.

The door shuddered as bees rapped against it. Wood splintered.

Katya wrapped herself more tightly in the blanket, staring into darkness.

Flaming bees slammed against the metal walls of the communications shed. Metal wouldn't burn, but it was still a terrifying din. "Where's Edgar?" Ruth screamed.

Carey Lou gaped at her. Shock? Remembered, and said, "I saw him outside. Just before we sealed the door."

Ruth screamed again, but then fought her way back to calm. The radio behind her crackled. *"Hello? Can anyone hear me?"*

Ruth twitched it on, and cried into it. "Edgar?"

"Ruth? Yeah, it's me. I don't know for how much longer. The bees are taking the building apart. They're eating the wood. I managed to get here, but I don't know if I can get out."

"What's wrong?"

"Ankle. Twisted it pretty bad. I think that maybe I broke it. I'm in dorm number four."

She looked around the room. Under them in the shelter, there were a dozen Second. Here there was only Carey Lou. Bees batted against windows, which so far remained secure. "You don't think that you can get over here? Do you have a blanket?"

"It isn't that. The door is jammed. I can't get it open. They're going to take the whole damned building apart. I can feel it."

Ruth bit her lip. She opened the hailing frequency. "Is there anyone who can help? We've got problems. Edgar is in trouble."

There was no answer for several long seconds, and then, *"We can't get out of the shelter, Ruth. I'm sorry. Maybe when the bees go away. They're bound to at dark. Or if it starts raining again. He'll be all right."*

Ruth spun. "Give me your blanket, Carey Lou," she said. "I need two of them."

Carey Lou said, "What?"

"Don't worry. You'll be safe right here. Keep trying to get through to the mine. We need them to bring down *Robor*. We have to get out of here."

"In the middle of the bees?"

"Don't you get it?" she said fiercely. "This could go on for *months*. Everyone will *die* unless we get out."

Carey Lou nodded, and handed her the blanket. She wrapped the first one around herself, and draped the second as a cowl. "Good-bye, Carey Lou," she whispered.

"Ruth, do you have to go?"

She nodded. She paused at the door, wedged it open a few inches, and then slipped out, into the storm.

"Mayday, Mayday, " Carey Lou bleated into the microphone. "We need *Robor*. We need to evacuate—"

✳

Hendrick Sills scanned the communal living room of Deadwood Pass's dormitory. His eyes passed the overstuffed chair twice before spotting Sylvia Weyland, sunken deep within. She was peering out of the slit window set in the reinforced concrete wall, warmed by the crackling fire at her side. She seemed utterly lost in thought.

She was staring out across the complex. The mine was still perking along smoothly, producing its quota of plastic briquettes. At this point, it barely needed human supervision anymore. Analyzing units built into the bore head sampled the strata as it dug. There would be no more fossilized bee surprises.

Sylvia looked up at him, face placid. "How is the loading?" she asked. "Any problems?" *Robor* was scheduled to make a half-loaded mercy run back to the island. "I need to get home." She stopped, and seemed to consider her next words carefully. "I need to be with Mary Ann."

"We have an urgent message from Shangri-la," Hendrick said. "It's bad."

The placidity vanished from her face.

"Emergency at Shangri-la. They've got a swarm of those damned carnivorous bees. Most of them made it to shelters, but they need to evacuate. *Now.*"

She was out of her chair in an instant. "Evacuate Deadwood. I want everyone on board *Robor* in five minutes. I want weather charts, and a route to Shangri-la mapped by the time I'm on board. We're gone in ten." She paused. "And get every goddamed blanket in the camp."

Carlos lost control of the skeeter only ten feet from the landing pad. "We're going down!" he screamed above the roar of exploding bees. The ground looming up at them told the rest of the story. They bounced, hard, too hard. The door buckled in its frame, leaving an inch gap. Justin used his feet to jam a Kevlar survival sack into it.

"Mayday, Mayday," Carlos said with calmness that he really didn't feel. "Is there anyone out there?"

The air was so thick with bees that it was hard to see. Then the swarm lifted, and Shangri-la appeared through the haze. Bodies lay strewn in the streets, dotted with black shapes. Bees.

Jesus. You could watch the bodies melting.

"Mayday—"

"D-daddy?" They heard it. Katya's voice.

"Baby? Where are you?"

"*I'm in the toolshed next to the rec room.*"

"Isn't there anyone in the rec room?"

"*No one that close,*" she said. "*I can't get out. I don't have a blanket. Daddy, the blankets work! They keep off the bees!*"

"I see. Shh. Stay put, darling," he said.

Justin looked at him. "How are we going to get her?"

"In this," Carlos said. He started his engine again. The skeeter screeched as it lifted from the ground, and listed sideways, counterrotating slowly. It weaved, barely in control. The tail swatted against another skeeter, and Carlos cursed as he worked them clear. They climbed to rooftop level, fighting for control every inch of the way. Fire blossomed below them, smoke and flaming bees filled the air. The drumming sound above him was bees exploding in the rotors.

"We're going down again," he muttered. He aimed the autogyro at the rec room. When they crashed through the wall Justin jolted forward, smacked his head against the Plexiglas window. He groaned, seeing stars brighter than burning bees. They spun and the sheet-metal rec-hall wall buckled. The tail of the autogyro sheared and the batterly ripped free. Wires from the rec-hall frame ripped across the battery, and sparks showered. Bees exploded in midair, and the swarm lifted for a moment as thousands of them caught fire, popped, showered sparks and flaming *speed* everywhere.

Carlos's door popped open. He grabbed a Cadzie-blue blanket and wrapped himself in it. Justin grabbed one of the Kevlar safety sacks, and smashed his way out of his side of the skeeter.

They had to cover their faces with blankets, but they groped their way around the rec hall—smoldering now, as flaming bees sped this way and that, zipping like meteorites.

And this was a blessing in disguise. The bees had dealt with fire before, and had evolved a tactic to deal with it. They spread out, made it more difficult for the flames to spread from one to the other. . . .

"Freeze it!" Justin cried. "Get Katya out. I'll be right behind you!"

They made it to the toolshed door. Carlos pried it open, and Katya shrank against the wall. She was sobbing, but seemed unhurt. Carlos threw a safety sack to her. "Hurry! Get into this."

She crawled into the sack, and as she did, Justin hurriedly inventoried the shed. And there it was—a weed burner. Its nozzle would spray liquid fuel in a thin blazing line. He sloshed the tank, and found it only half empty.

"Get her the hell out!" he screamed. "Communications should be secure!"

Carlos didn't argue, just slung his daughter over his shoulder. "We'll never make it!" The bees were thick over there.

"Yes, we will." Justin lit the pilot on the weed burner. He pumped fuel through it.

He spun, sweeping the air with fire. Bees exploded, setting their neighbors aflame. Carlos had to turn his head away from the shower of flaming pseudo-crustacea.

The bees thinned in instinctive response to flame.

"Come on!"

Robor had only been airborne for ten minutes when the first bees hit them. They batted against the metal struts, and chewed harmlessly at *Robor*'s external skin. Sylvia watched them slap against the main windows. Some bees cracked open, leaving a smear of green and red. Most just bounced away, spiraling stunned into the void.

Carey Lou's voice crackled over the intercom. *"Watch out for bees in the skeeter rotors. Evan blew up. Can you hear me?"* He sounded desperate.

The corner of Sylvia's eye caught lights flashing red in front of Hendrick, just before a muffled *whump* shuddered through the ship. *Too late?* Sylvia felt like an idiot. "Of course! We read you, Carey."

"What the hell do we do?" Hendrick watched a new rush of bees crash against the window leaving blood and slime behind.

"Kill the motors!"

"Done. Sylvia, I think Skeeter Three is a deader."

A shower of tiny comets was drifting past the windows, exploding as they fell. *Robor* lurched sideways, then began a slow, ugly spin. Sylvia fought to stay calm. "They're thicker near the ground," she said. "Kill the skeeters, pump more gas into the bags, and *climb*."

Two skeeters still lived. Their rotors slowed within rings of fire. Stopped. Flaming bees spiraled past the front window like dying stars.

Hendrick flinched back. "They can't get in," Sylvia said. "Another fifteen minutes, and we'll be above them. Then we can start the skeeters again."

"Gauges say we lost our tail engine," he said pessimistically. "I don't know . . ."

"We've got two left," she said. "And they'll just have to be enough. Three hours, maybe four . . . I just hope the kids can survive that long."

Ruth was covered in blankets from head to foot. She knew where she was going, and didn't need to lift her head. She had walked this path a thousand times.

The chamel pen.

Something was going on behind her. A sputtering of flame. She could hear it, but she didn't dare look. Her toe stubbed something. Bones. She couldn't look, couldn't let her fear overwhelm her. It would have been entirely too easy.

Her hands, swathed in blankets, touched the chamel pen. "Tarzan?" she called, and then raised her voice more, hoping that the blankets didn't muffle it too much. "Tarzan!"

She had seen the chamels changing color, and guessed that they would be alive and safe. When she heard a tentative pawing to her call, she knew that her favorite was alive. More to the point, even in the midst of this horror, Tarzan still responded to her.

Something was nuzzling her hand. She didn't dare look. She was terrified at the thought of what bees could do to her eyes. Behind her, fire flared like a lightning strike. Bits of flaming bee spattered her blankets. She groaned in terror, then recovered and climbed across the fence. Tarzan let her mount him, then moved toward the locked gate. She reached out and felt her way to the gate, undid the latch, and Tarzan nudged it open.

Instantly the chamel tried to gallop for open space. She turned him around by wrenching with all of her strength, and started him back into the camp.

She was disoriented, and had to risk a peek now, no matter how much she loathed the idea. With one blanket-swathed hand she peeled up a slit in the blanket, just barely enough to admit light. Good. There was the mess hall, and there the quad . . . and there was the shack where Edgar would be.

* * *

Tarzan, camouflaged in blue, made his way slowly across the encampment. Around him bees flew, panicked now. One of the buildings had finally managed to catch fire. When wind blew bees through the flames they exploded, carrying the destruction farther. The only thing that saved them was the dampness of the wood. Flaming bits of bee landed in the moist wooden slats and smoldered or sputtered to greater, more dangerous life.

When Ruth reached Edgar's storage shed, she turned Tarzan, and climbed carefully off his back. She pulled down on his reins, and jerked. The chamel bucked up in the air once, twice. His heels slammed back into the door, chipping and then splintering wood. The door ripped free from the jamb.

Ruth heard Edgar scream. She hurried to him with the second blanket. He wrapped himself in it, and she helped him to his feet. Then she helped him onto Tarzan, and climbed on after him. She risked a peek to orient herself. The radio shack. They *had* to make it that far. Something crawled into her makeshift cowl, and she struck at it, felt it bite her. She grabbed it with her fist and *squeezed* as hard as she could. It wriggled and popped.

Tarzan was running now, screaming in pain. She peered down. He was fading! Stress, fatigue and fear had combined to rob him of his protective coloration. There were bees all over him, and she watched with dismay as they tore at his flesh. They pitched headlong into the street, driving the breath from her lungs, tangling her up with Edgar. Bees swarmed in on the helpless Tarzan, now reverting to his native tan color. And then he was streaked with red.

Edgar helped her to her feet, still swathed in his blanket. Together, they limped through the street, and up the ramp to the radio room, and the two of them staggered through the door.

They slammed it behind them and collapsed to the floor, screaming.

Something was hitting her, striking her, swatting at her. And Edgar. When she dared to open her eyes, she saw Carey Lou and Heather McKennie dancing, dancing. The floor was littered with dead bees.

The two kids were shaking. She looked at her hands. Streaked and torn. Edgar looked worse, but it was mostly cosmetic, except for a runnel along his upper thigh that oozed blood steadily. But they were alive.

"*Robor* is coming," Carey Lou said. "I got Sylvia on the phone."

An hour later, the rain began. As swiftly as they appeared, the bees seemed to disappear, going to ground or taking to the trees.

Edgar was recovered enough to take control of the communications. He managed to reestablish a link with *Geographic*.

"*Robor*," he said. "It looks like the safest way for you to make it down is through the western defile, follow the ridge." He had collapsed into one of the command chairs. His face was swollen until only one eye was functional. They were running out of time. When this rain stopped, the bees would be back. And back. And back.

The door to the communications room opened, and Justin, Carlos, and Katya crowded in. They were followed by the others, survivors, looking utterly bedraggled.

"*Robor*, this is Shangri-la . . ."

Robor was almost two thousand feet above his normal cruising altitude. Here there was no fear of bees, and the skeeter engines roared once again.

They managed to lash down about half the cargo in the dirigible's holds before the first of the winds struck them. It grew almost unnoticeably, a slow swell of rhythm, an interruption of the steady burr of the skeeter engines.

Then the rain hit like a solid wall of air. The stabilizers groaned, and *Robor* lurched and wobbled as he moved north on his mercy mission. The engines cried out, the wind slamming against him so brutally that it seemed that their entire world was coming to pieces.

But a kilometer at a time, *Robor* fought his way down from Deadwood Pass. *Robor* was coming.

Justin walked out slowly into the rain, to examine the bodies. He counted a dozen Star Born who hadn't reached shelter in time. Who hadn't had Kevlar sacks or Cadzie-blue blankets. *What was it with those blankets?*

He kept searching until he found what he was looking for.

There wasn't much left, but he recognized the clothes. He would have known her even if there were less left.

Katya was somewhere behind him. Perhaps she thought of speaking, then thought better of it. Justin knelt in the rain, and took his coat off. Slowly, he draped it over what was left of his sister, his love.

Then he gathered the bundle of red bones gently into his arms, and carried it out of the rain.

The weather had died to a slight drizzle when *Robor* finally appeared. The camp—what was left of it—was almost silent. Sixty-three survivors waited, faces upturned in the rain.

Robor was moored, and the exodus began. They handed the bodies—what was left of them—hand over hand.

And when the last of them was aboard, the rain had almost ceased. They could hear the buzz as the bees awakened.

Sylvia stood beside him, holding his arm. Her son seemed almost like a stranger, so intense was his focus.

"He's out there," Justin said.

"Who?"

"Aaron. He's out there."

"He's dead," she said.

Justin shook his head. "He's not lucky enough to be dead. Yet." He screamed out of *Robor*'s door: "I'll be back, you bastard! I swear to God I'll be back, and I'll kill you!"

She pried him carefully away from the door, and closed it on the camp, the shattered shell of Avalon's dreams. And then they lifted away.

The rain started again, and the bees still huddled in the forest, awaiting their time. The chamels had been set free, and were returning to the plains. The horses and other livestock were all dead.

For a few moments there was no sound, no movement, and then the mud stirred.

Aaron Tragon rolled half free of the mud. His eyes were wild and staring, almost sightless. He wasn't certain where he was. The chamels had trampled him on their way out, and he was badly concussed. His eyes wouldn't focus. He had to move. Had to hide. The bees would come back.

Soon. They would.

But his eyes wouldn't focus.

He flopped over onto his stomach, and tried to crawl away. There was something coming. Death was coming. He couldn't think. He couldn't move. But it was there.

Cadmann. Jessica. Toshiro. More. More. So much death. He hadn't meant for this. *Chaka.* Wait, Chaka wasn't dead. Was he?

His mind wouldn't work. So much death. He stood, bent far over around broken ribs. He staggered through the streets of Shangri-la, the camp that he had schemed and stolen and killed to build. It was destroyed. Empty. *Robor* was retiring in the distance, grinning like some vast grendel, floating away.

He heard a noise behind him. He was too tired, too confused to turn.

It was the grendel. The grendel god. He felt a wave of fear, of freedom approaching. His judgment. His salvation. He spread his arms and exposed his throat.

And then the grendel came to him. And she said *Cadmann* . . .

And the grendel took him by the throat, and she said . . . *Chaka.*

And the grendel devoured him, saying . . . *Jessica.*

And in the grendel he saw her heart, and the heart beat, saying . . . *Toshiro.*

And he passed into darkness and into death, and the grendel spake unto him, and she said . . .

Aaron.

We are one. . . .

41

CHOICES

—But there's a tree, of many, one,
A single field which I have looked upon,
Both of them speak of something that is gone:
The pansy at my feet
Doth the same tale repeat:
Whither is fled the visionary gleam?
Where is it now, the glory and the dream?

—WILLIAM WORDSWORTH,
*Intimations of Immortality from
Recollections of Early Childhood*

It was a beautiful day for a memorial, Justin thought. Tau Ceti shone down on the bluff, on the land that Cadmann Weyland had cleared, planted, tilled by hand . . . on the house that he had built with the sweat of his back.

And if he turned around, Justin could gaze down on the colony itself. See the crosshatch of roads that Cadmann had burned into the ground. The maze of homes he had helped erect. It was a place of love and life, crowded with babies to whom Cadmann Weyland was godfather, or guardian, or honorary uncle.

The Bluff wasn't crowded. The public funeral had been held a week before. This was just family. Just the kids, and Cadmann's wives, Katya, and Carlos.

Just the ones who loved the old man—and Jessica.

Jessica.

"We're here today . . ." He steadied his voice as much as he could. ". . . to say good-bye to two people we love." He stopped, dug his hands into his pockets. A sad, crooked smile plucked at his lips. "Isn't that just the way it is? No matter how much we say to someone while they're alive, there's always more to say. That' s the tragedy of it . . . but that's the joy, too."

He looked out at the mourners. They were seated in two rows of folding chairs. Carlos sat next to Sylvia, holding Cadzie, the sleeping child wrapped in a bright blue blanket. Sylvia held Mary Ann's hand. Mary Ann was pasty-faced, and so grief-stricken that she hardly seemed able to breathe.

"Dad," Justin said, "I can still talk to you, when I need to. And I will. We all will. Jessica—"

And here his words faded for a minute. There were things that he wanted to say: *You made the wrong choice, Jessie. You chose the wrong side. And in the end, you didn't think fast enough. God. I'll miss your smile, your laugh. I'll never forget the one kiss we shared, not even when they put me in the ground next to you. I loved you, Jessie. Maybe it wouldn't have made a goddamned bit of difference, but I should have told you. Maybe if I had. Maybe if I'd found the right way to say it, you'd still be alive. . . .*

Katya was smiling at him. Katya, who loved him, and wanted to bear his children. Katya, who must never know what his heart had just revealed to him.

Justin realized he had stopped speaking. He felt as if his mouth was packed with cotton. He had to say something. Anything.

Why was life so goddamned *hard?*

"Jessica," he lied, his voice breaking, "you were my sister."

Sylvia found Mary Ann in the master bedroom. In Cadmann's bedroom. Mary Ann sat on the edge of the bed, staring at the wall. Her hair looked not blond, but white.

"Mary Ann?" she said quietly. "Are you all right?"

Mary Ann looked up slowly. She smiled, a sweet smile, and patted the bed next to her. Even that motion looked tired. Sylvia thought that this was the first time that Mary Ann actually looked *old.*

"He . . . loved you more, you know," Mary Ann said.

Sylvia started to speak, to say something reflexively, but Mary Ann shushed her. "No. He was too much of a gentleman to ever break his commitment to me. But he loved you more. If honor hadn't been the core of that man, he would have left me. But he felt . . . obliged."

She smiled again. Her cheeks looked waxen. "I let you into my marriage, dear, for *him.* To hold on to him. If you were here, he wouldn't have to go to you secretly. He would have done that eventually, you know. And people would have talked. And felt sorry for me. I don't think that I could have survived that. So I let you in. And he stayed. Because he had no reason to go, don't you see?"

Sylvia reached out and took her hand. Regretfully, but firmly, Mary Ann pulled it away. "You have a wonderful heart, and you never tried to hurt me." She paused, then said matter-of-factly, "I've never liked you, you know."

Sylvia waited until the silence grew too painful, then told the truth. "I know."

"I've thought about asking you to move out. But it wouldn't be right."

Sylvia stiffened a bit. "If you want me to go, I will."

Mary Ann smiled. "I don't like you, Sylvia. But you have been a sister to me, for years. And you never tried to hurt me. I don't like you. But I do love you."

The room was very quiet. Mary Ann leaned forward, and kissed Sylvia's cheek.

Then she lay back on the bed, in the middle of the bed that she had shared with Cadmann for so many years, in which she had borne him children, and curled up onto her side.

When she spoke, her voice was very, very soft. "I'd like to rest now, if you don't mind," she said. "I don't know why, but I get tired so easily these days."

Sylvia rose from the bed and walked to the door, pausing to look back. Mary Ann's eyes were closed. She might have been asleep already, except for the very soft gasping sound she made as she cried out her good-bye to the man she had loved.

Sylvia closed the door behind her, and sagged against it, exhausted. She wanted to cry, but the tears just hadn't come, as if fatigue were mourning enough. Somewhere within her there must have tears for Cadmann, and for Jessica, for Mary Ann, and for herself. But they eluded her. Now she fought to find the place within her that held tears for Aaron, the son she had never held.

She could not find them.

She had never told him, and now she never could. And almost no one knew the truth. Certainly Aaron had not. But Sylvia knew. And her mother's heart knew that her love might have gentled him, nurtured him, even as her rational mind begged her not to carry that weight into her life. It was too much for one woman to bear.

What would Cadmann want?

I want you to live, he said in a voice so clear he might have been standing beside her. *Death comes soon enough. Live, my love, and be a comfort to Mary Ann. Live, and know I loved you more than I could ever say. I only hope you knew.*

"I knew," she whispered. "I always knew."

✳

Edgar led them into the kitchen/computer room. He felt them stop in the doorway, and turned to watch their reaction.

They had walked into an Avalon beehive.

Cassandra and the Chakas had constructed it in one-to-one scale. The hologram space was much larger than the kitchen itself. They had set off their insecticide bombs, they had placed their cameras, set off their monotone sirens, and recorded the sonics passing through the nest, all before the final swarming. Between the computer imaging and the fiber-optic cameras, they had managed to map virtually the entire bee colony.

It was like a volcano, with branching side pockets and rooms for the infants, breeding grounds, and a huge queen chamber. The creatures lay dead in heaps of thousands.

For that instant they were stopped by the wonder of it. Then Edgar's family pushed in behind him.

Edgar moved to the keyboard.

Ruth was just behind him, chin on his shoulder. Her body was starting to swell in earnest. Her father was trying to peer between them without getting too friendly with Edgar himself. Her mother Rachael hung back a little: Zack must be feeling claustrophobic too. And Trish was on the other side of Edgar, in contact along his whole left flank, and damn, it was hard to concentrate.

He felt barely able to move. His home had seemed big enough, too big even, when it was Edgar alone.

But his fingers remembered. The bee nest faded. Then the holostage ran through a rapid sequence of scenes while Edgar played tour guide.

"Shangri-la is essentially dead," Edgar said. "The instruments we left there make it a test case for what's happening to the continent.

"Not a living plant anywhere. The crops are gone right down to the dirt. You don't see any bees now, but any time something living comes in range, the bees boil out and strip it.

"This is of interest, though. Something *big*—grendel-sized—pushed in the door to that storehouse. Inside—" Dammit, he'd forgotten the code.

Trish reached past him and tapped. The screen went dark, nearly. "The lights are burned out," she said.

"Yeah, but look around. Near the back, a lot of cans are missing, and soft drinks too. That's a hot plate over here, and whoever was using it kept the area clean. He's gone now, I think. Aaron."

Zack said, "It may be you've got Aaron on the brain, Edgar. All three of you."

Zack, Rachael, Ruth, Edgar, Trish. They had to be together, but it was awkward. They kept adjusting their positions. Edgar could talk to Trish, Ruth could talk to her lover and her mother, Zack could talk to Rachael, and if Zack wanted to know about mainland conditions he had to talk to his son-in-law.

"I was never sure," Edgar said. "I told myself he set me up to fall out of that tree, but I was never sure until he killed Colonel Weyland. Now I want his blood."

Ruth said nothing.

Trish asked, "Uncle Zack? Don't you want Aaron dead?"

Zack said, "What are things like elsewhere?"

Bracketed between Ruth and Trish . . . he'd had daydreams like this, *sandwiched*, but he'd never dreamed of parents-in-law present. Edgar wondered if Trish was enjoying this. He was just glad he'd cleaned the place up.

He tapped and the view jumped. "That was a chain of grendel lakes, dammed lakes, when we planted the camera." The lakes were a wide muddy river now. Edgar's cursor indicated a distant dust devil dancing through stripped trees. "Bees," he said. "There aren't any more grendels here. Some samlon, maybe, but as soon as they come on land, sszzz. Even the beaver grendels must be eating their young now. It's the only way a grendel can stay alive while these death winds are blowing. And that is how Avalon evolution set you up, Zack."

He tapped again. Now the view looked across sparse, tall grass, with water gleaming in the distance. "Any idea where you are?"

"The Scribeveldt," Zack said.

"Yup. On the back of a Scribe. Katya set a skeeter down on Asia's back and left a camera."

"Huh," said Zack. He watched for few seconds. "Is that a pterodon nest?"

"More like six, but I haven't seen a pterodon since I started monitoring this. Then again, Asia has been easing her way toward the river. As long as the Scribes don't all go down to the river at once, the pterodons can commute. Asia will get her pterodons back when she leaves."

"Edgar, is that guesswork?"

"Pretty much."

Trish asked, "How close do the Scribes get to water? You still get pictures from orbit—"

"The paths still avoid each other. I think they don't want to mate. There are bees everywhere. They don't bother the Scribes much—"

"You can't go back to Shangri-la," Zack said. "Tell you what, Edgar. Work up a scenario. Your next colony on the mainland is in the Scribeveldt."

Edgar turned to see if his lover's father was serious. From many objections he picked one at random. "It's out of *Robor*'s range. We'd have to set up staging points—"

"Fine. In a couple of years your first staging point can be the minehead, or Shangri-la. You left supplies in both places, and—"

Trish burst out laughing. Her hand closed hard on Edgar's shoulder and shook gently. "Soft One, how can you not love it? We'll put little tent-towns on the knolls. They're not big, but the Scribes go around them and the grendels can't reach them—"

Edgar was studying Zack. He'd never seen the old man smiling like that. A mad smile. "Zack, didn't you use to be *way* conservative?"

"Sure. A little stodgy, maybe? Just do the best plan you can, Edgar. If it looks crazy we won't do it."

Ice on his mind. But—Rachael and Ruth changed glances, a secret look Edgar knew he'd better learn to interpret.

Rachael Moskowitz didn't have ice on *her* mind. And she'd supported Zack in power since before Edgar Sikes was born. But Zack kept making mistakes . . . well, one mistake, one backbreaker of a mistake, and ever since then—

Ever since then, every time he was challenged, Zack backed down. *That* was the problem, *that* was why his brain seemed riddled with ice crystals. He'd withdrawn his objections to the mainland colony. Was he regretting that now?

"Hell, we can live on the Scribes' backs!" Trish crowed. Zack nodded, just listening as she babbled. Trish loved the Scribeveldt colony. When Trish fell in love with an idea, she fell hard. She'd do most of Edgar's work for him. But had he, had they all totally misunderstood the First?

Edgar burst out, "Zack! What *was* it with those freezing blankets?"

They all looked at him as if he were crazy. Zack told him, "We kind of don't like that word."

"I kind of don't like f-f-soggy mysteries. Zack, you, the First were always so *sure* it was Cadzie blue that saved the baby. Why? I mean it's a *neat* answer, it turns out to be the color-coding for poison—"

"*Elegant*," Zack said. "You learned that word from the math classes, didn't you? Any solution that *elegant* has to be right. Except when it isn't." The old man laughed.

"Zack, Cadzie blue is *darker* than the color coding for poison."

"Is it really?"

"You *saw* it. Everyone on Camelot got videotapes of Asia through the war specs. We sent you photos. Aaron cut a great swath of Asia's lip and laid it across all those blankets. It's too pale." And why was he devilling an old man with ice on his mind? Edgar saw Ruth and Rachael listening and was embarrassed.

But Zack said, "*Ah.*"

"*What?*"

"Edgar, when you get old enough, you get a feel for patterns. Being smart doesn't do it. Only experience works. That pattern-sense was all we had. What you just said, nobody had *said* that before, just that way, to *me*.

"Stretch a piece of Scribe's lip in sunlight, it's too pale. Take pictures with a flash camera, it's too pale. Watch a Scribe through war specs, and by the time Cassandra gets through with the pictures—"

"It's too pale. Ice me down *now*, Lord."

"See, Edgar, the Scribe's lip is always underneath that overhang of shell, always in shadow. The bees see it as darker. Aaron took it into daylight—"

"And the flash on the camera lights it up, and Cassandra thoughtfully corrected the color for us, but I can check *that* part *right now*, Zack. *Cassandra!*"

✳

The reconquest of the mainland was two years in the planning.

The Scribeveldt had been too wet for going on two years. Vast patches of grass had died. The Scribes were fewer, perhaps because they had stopped breeding; but some of those camouflaged trapezoids didn't move. The camera on Asia's back had rolled past one huge empty shell.

Now the Veldt was drying off, grass was spreading again, and the paths Cassandra could see from orbit were forming knots.

"Everything is breeding like mad," Edgar told the colonists in the assembly hall, and the greater number who were only in virtual attendance. "I can't see any reason not to begin the conquest of the mainland with the Scribeveldt. And I see no reason not to go *now*."

And the questions began.

"We'll establish dumps at Shangri-la and Eden both. They're close together, they can serve as alternate routes. We don't want any cities there the next time Tau Ceti goes into maximum, but they're safe now."

And continued.

"Sure, grendels. We'll want to stay clear of the river, but we can run pipes. . . .

"There's no trace of bees, anywhere we've got cameras. Nobody thinks they're extinct, but they must have died back. . . .

"Before we build anything permanent in the Scribeveldt, we've prepared some hardened cameras. I want to know what lives *under* the Scribes. . . .

"Aaron? Well, something raided the stores at Shangri-la until they were almost gone. That was a year ago. Your guess. . . .

"The blankets? Yeah, Uncle Zack figured that out two years ago, and he was right. Zack, you want to explain that? Remember to talk slow for these people."

EPILOGUE
THE SHAMAN

✴

TWO YEARS LATER

Chaka scanned the bluff, finding no evidence of a grendel presence.

"We're clear, " he said. With Trish and Carey Lou watching shotgun, he rappelled down the side of the cliff into the water. The samlon were young. There would only be one grendel in this area, and that one was . . . well, curious.

They searched much of the day, and it was Chaka who found it, and called Justin.

A human skull, cracked and chewed, but human.

Justin took it from Chaka gently. He folded it to his chest and sank to his knees in the water, eyes half-closing. No one spoke. After almost a minute he slipped it lovingly into a plastic bag. Before Tau Ceti slipped below the horizon, they found part of a pelvis, and a few more bones, and that was all. Justin looked around the river, and then said, "All right. Let's go."

Chaka nodded, and they rode the winch up the cliff face, and didn't say anything more until they reached the skeeter.

Sylvia met them back at the camp. She was grayer now, but just as tall, her face more stern. Since Mary Ann's death a year before, she was, more than any other woman in the camp, the Matriarch. She had slipped into that role unwillingly, but with authority.

Carlos stood behind her, his left hand resting lightly on her shoulder.

It was almost dark, and the evening wind plucked at the edges of her coat as she waited for them to disembark. Justin stopped two feet away from her, his hands filled with the remains of his father, her husband, a plastic bag wrapped in black cloth.

Sylvia took the bag as if it were made of spun glass. "We'll bury him on the Bluff," she said.

Carlos nodded. "Exactly what he would have wanted." He squeezed her shoulder. "I have an urn," he said quietly. "I have worked on it for a year. I would like to show it to you."

Suddenly, her eyes burned. Sylvia closed her eyes hard. Now was not the time. Later perhaps. Now she would be strong for Carlos, as he had been strong for her. They had almost lost equally. Not quite. But almost.

"There is only one more thing to do, then I can go home," Little Chaka said. Big Chaka was back on Camelot Island, too infirm for travel now. He spent most of the time at Surf's Up, puttering, writing his memoirs and training the two new dolphins. Little Chaka didn't really like being away from his father for extended periods.

Edgar and Ruth were beside them. Scully followed her with a tight fist on her skirt. Ruth's son, and Edgar's. The genetics might have been Aaron's but Edgar had been there to help deliver Scully. As far as he was concerned, he was the father.

"How do we go about this?" Edgar said.

"We are going to find a skeleton, or we are going to find Aaron," Justin said. "One or the other. But I want to know that he is dead. It ends."

Chaka cocked his rifle. "It ends."

They searched all that day, and into the night, and found no trace. They knew Aaron had survived the bees. The storehouse in Shangri-la had been raided regularly for canned goods. But though they scoured by skeeter and by foot, with Cassandra's eyes and with hunting dogs, over swamp, Veldt, mountain, and river, of Aaron himself there was no trace.

On the third day, just as the hunting parties were quitting for the day, dogs barked and guards yelled at the southern end of the camp.

Two figures approached a rebuilt section of fence. One was human. One definitely was not.

Justin was barely aware of Chaka and Trish at his side, Sylvia behind him, as he ran to the fence. With every step, the hated face and form of his enemy grew clearer. All the world seemed to focus down to this one man, his entire life to this single moment.

Aaron walked with the help of a crutch. His right leg looked as if it had been broken and badly set. His once beautiful face was scarred and puckered with pink weals. His left eye was glazed and sightless.

The grendel . . . God, the *grendel* . . . walked alongside him.

Without thinking, Justin raised his rifle. Chaka pushed it aside. "Wait," he said breathlessly. "Wait."

Aaron turned and spoke to the grendel in a clear, commanding voice: "Stay."

And it *did*. It squatted, waiting. A whisper ran through those assembled. There was just no believing this.

"Aaron Tragon. I arrest you for murder—"

Aaron laughed in his face.

"That is so like you, Justin," he said in his calmest, clearest voice. "Trying to arrest someone who isn't here."

Justin was dumbstruck. "*What?* What are you trying to pull now? Whatever it is—"

"Aaron is dead," Aaron said. "Dead. Aaron is eaten." He smiled, and looked out at them as if what he had said made sense. Just *exactly* as if it had made sense. Justin wanted to laugh. But couldn't. And didn't like that at all.

Aaron looked at them as if they were his dearest friends, long-lost kin with whom he longed to share a deep and precious secret. It was damned strange. "I can give to you what you have always wanted," he said confidently.

Trish finally spoke. "And what the hell is *that?*"

"Peace," he said. "Peace with the beasts." He turned. "Come," he said.

And the grendel came, and sat by him. It made that cooing sound.

"Yes," Aaron said to it. "They are afraid. You are afraid. It is a place of fear."

Justin's head spun. Hatred and confusion and a strange excitement so intense it felt like nausea welled up strongly enough to cause vertigo. He turned to Chaka. "He's crazy. Just plain nuts!"

Chaka said, "Are you sure? And what difference does it make? Can *you* talk to grendels?"

Trish's arm trembled. Her rifle went up, but Chaka's hand closed on the barrel. "No!" Chaka said. "You have no right. If anyone has the right, it is Justin." He paused, that confusion entering his voice as if it were an emotional virus. "Justin—what do *you* say?"

Justin could barely move, couldn't think. *An intelligent grendel.* And a human being who could *communicate* with it. What would his father have given for this? He could blow this insane bastard's head off right now—

And betray everything that Cadmann had lived for.

"Goddammit, *kill him!*" Trish screamed. "Don't you realize it's just another of his con games? If you let him live, he'll *own* this planet in ten years!"

Aaron's smile was fond, but remote, the thin smile of one who sees more than anyone else and knows he will never be understood. "Trish, no one owns this planet," he said. "Neither human nor grendel. And least of all the man who was Aaron Tragon. But together . . ."

Nightmare, Justin thought. What would Colonel Weyland have done? We think we know so much more than they do, but— "Keep him safe," Justin said. "We need to ask Zack."

Trish and Edgar took Aaron's arms and led him away. He halted them when he came to Sylvia, and they stood and waited for him as if he were still the master. "I am sorry for what Aaron did," he said. "You will want to know that Cadmann died well." He nodded to his guards and limped away.

Sylvia watched as the procession receded. Her shoulders slumped. Suddenly, unbidden and unstoppably, the tears she had not cried for two years streamed down her cheeks in a cleansing torrent. As if a dam within her had suddenly given way. As if in some manner she didn't understand, Aaron Tragon had given her the greatest gift of her life.

✳

Chaka gingerly approached the grendel and knelt by it. She watched him in return. Amazed at his own daring, he actually reached out and ran his fingers over her pebbled skin, felt the living fire within, and marveled. "It *is* you, isn't it, Old Girl? Name of God," he whispered. "What are we going to do with *you?*"

✳

Old Grendel felt peaceful. Working together, she and the Strongest Weird had survived the bad times. Now the dark one she had saved before would stand between her and the others. Would protect her as she had protected him.

This was strangeness. But these weirds worked together like dam builders. She knew things. Could show them, perhaps. And as she grew older, and not so able to hunt, perhaps they would help her in turn.

She wondered about the Strongest Weird. For two years they had lived together, and she had begun to understand some of the weird's sounds. The world of vocal communication was another explosion of strangeness. She wondered what they would do with that one. Strongest Weird was a God of some kind. Perhaps they were all Strongest Weird's children.

She didn't know. But the Death Wind was dwindling. More bad times would come, but they would find something new in the world.

Grendels. Weirds. Together.